THE RUNAWAY GIRL

A TITANIC LOVE STORY

JINA BACARR

Boldwood

First published in Great Britain in 2020 by Boldwood Books Ltd.

1

Cover Design by Debbie Clement Design

Cover Photography: Shutterstock

A CIP catalogue record for this book is available from the British Library.

Paperback ISBN: 978-1-80048-154-1

Ebook ISBN: 978-1-83889-373-6

Kindle ISBN: 978-1-83889-372-9

Audio CD ISBN: 978-1-83889-368-2

Digital audio download ISBN: 978-1-83889-370-5

Large Print ISBN: 978-1-83889-712-3

Boldwood Books Ltd.

23 Bowerdean Street, London, SW6 3TN

www.boldwoodbooks.com

1

Cameron Bally Manor House
Ireland
9 April 1912

'Ava O'Reilly, you're nothing but a common thief who brings shame upon this fine house,' spewed Lord Emsy, wagging his fat finger in her face. 'What have you to say for yourself, girl?'

'A thief, am I, milord?' Ava shot back, refusing to cower before a man so pompous and full of himself, even if he *was* her employer. With his wing tip collar and fancy silk ascot, he reminded her of a leg of lamb gussied up for Sunday dinner. 'Says who? Your daughter?' She narrowed her eyes, staring her accuser down. Lady Olivia greeted her angry look with a swift turning of the head, her nose in the air, but Ava wasn't finished. 'I'd rather dance with the devil than believe her.'

His lordship growled. 'Then you *deny* stealing the bracelet?'

'Aye, that I do.' Ava smoothed down her shiny, black cotton uniform with her hands, making fists and fighting to keep her composure. Him with the glow of damnation in his eyes, accusing her like he was the Almighty Himself. She refused to back down. With the afternoon sun spilling an arc as bright as a pot o' gold at her feet, she wondered how she, the daughter of a fine Irish mum and da, could be so unlucky. But here she was, accused of thievery because she was caught reading a book in a place where a housemaid had no right to be. The library. Now she was paying the price for her thirst for knowledge.

'Well, how do you plead?' asked his lordship.

'I plead guilty to nothing more than reading your fine books.'

Ignoring her, Lord Emsy bellowed, 'Then how do you explain this?'

He dangled a slender rope of sparkling diamonds in front of her nose, taking her breath away.

Ava swallowed hard. Each stone was a knot on the noose tightening around her neck.

'I *swear* on me sainted mother's grave, I never seen the likes of that till this morning.'

'She's lying, Papa,' Lady Olivia decried. 'She stole it from my jewel case and was trying to hide it when I caught her.'

Ava gritted her teeth. They both knew it was a lie.

Aye, what was a lass to do? His lordship's daughter had hated her since Ava had first crossed paths with her, when she'd used the grand main staircase instead of scuttling down the backstairs. The breach of protocol had not only embarrassed the family, Lady Olivia scolded her, but Ava had attracted the eye of the young gentleman at her side. Lord Holm made no secret of his interest in the servant girl with the glorious red hair spilling down her back. Mary Dolores had warned her about him when Ava joined her sister to work as a housemaid in the grand manor.

A dandy, she had said, always ready to pat the bum of any servant girl he could get into a dark corner.

Did Ava listen to her? No. She was obstinate and bull-headed. A family trait, Mary Dolores admitted, shaking her head. Going through life casting her spell on every man caught looking at her. Ava paid them no mind, going about her way and insisting she didn't need a man to better herself.

Unfortunately, Ava couldn't control the wily fates determined to get in her way.

Her relationship with Lady Olivia became even more strained when Lord Holm saw her wearing a discarded dress belonging to her ladyship. Silk with delicate appliqué around the collar and cap sleeves, the vibrant emerald green set off her red hair.

And what was the crime in that, Ava wanted to know, since it was customary for servant girls to lay claim to their mistress's tossed-away garments.

Her ears burned when she overheard her ladyship say to Lord Holm, 'You never noticed when I wore that dress,' to which he replied, 'You never looked like that.'

His comment sealed her fate.

Now she'd get sacked for a crime she didn't commit.

Ava felt a growing bitterness prickle her skin, making her shiver. She couldn't deny she presented a threat to the daughter of the house. It was no secret her ladyship wasn't popular with the servants with her snotty airs and precise manners, ordering everyone about. More than one prayer was lifted up to heaven in the servants' hall in the hopes her outrageous flirting with the gent from Dublin would have her running off with the handsome man with arched, dark brows and a dimple in his chin. Till then, every time the young lord's head turned in Ava's direction, she loomed as a danger to her ladyship's prospects for a secure married life.

A danger that must be eliminated.

Lady Olivia made it her duty to make Ava's life miserable. She left empty tea cups scattered about after Ava tidied a room, complained about her blatant insubordination to Mrs Briggs, the housekeeper, when Ava failed to make a proper curtsy, then smeared the damp tea leaves Ava set upon the carpets to remove dust under the heel of her pointy boot.

Ava spent two days digging the crushed leaves out of the rug fibers.

By the devil, she'd not be done in by the girl's lies. Hadn't she made every effort to be a good housemaid? Learned to lower her eyes and not stare when the family was about. Cleaned up her ladyship's slops with a wooden clothes peg pinching her nose and set the hot brick at the foot of her bed so the snobby girl would be toasty at night.

But she had no intention of getting sacked for nothing more than a man looking at her, even if her mother *had* warned her. Ava let the moment wash over her, the poignant memory stabbing her in the heart, missing her mum so.

'A man may be God's creature, Ava,' her late mother, Mary Elizabeth Sullivan O'Reilly had drummed into her head, her pale grey eyes turning a deep slate when she noticed her younger daughter's curves, soft and round. 'But he's also an instrument of the devil's handiwork. With a face like yours, child, temptation will surely follow.'

No matter, Ava decided. She'd show them gentlemen she had more to offer. *Much more.*

She would challenge their minds.

She set her plan to work, reading and studying from the books in his lordship's library, though borrowing books was forbidden to the servants. Only family members could sign the journal on the desk. A ledger containing the names of the borrowers. Lady Olivia's name rarely appeared.

Ava closed her eyes tight, remembering how Mum oft reminded her that her curiosity for knowledge would do her in someday, but she didn't see what was so wrong about trying to rise above her class and gain the freedom that came with it.

Plato, Shaw, Shakespeare and Mark Twain.

Stories of grand adventure that thrilled her and made her yearn for a life outside of service. Something her sister didn't understand. What Ava saw as a humiliating job, Mary Dolores embraced as a proper and decent life for the likes of them.

Two orphaned sisters without kin.

Ava bit her lip. Her sister *was* right about one thing. She wouldn't be standing here now accused of stealing the diamond bracelet if she hadn't lingered in the library after she finished her morning duties. Hidden behind a tall Oriental screen, she was reading *Romeo and Juliet* when Lady Olivia bounded into the room before anyone upstairs was awake. Tossing cushions about, mumbling, looking everywhere until she found her bracelet under the blue damask divan.

Most likely her ladyship lost it while carousing with the young lord and didn't want her father to find out. Their engagement hadn't been settled and whispers in the servants' hall confirmed the young gentleman had yet to approach Lord Emsy with a formal request. That didn't stop the loose-tongued cook from gossiping about how her ladyship sweetened the pie by treating him to a taste of her cherry-tipped buds.

Ava smirked. Lady Olivia wasn't taking any chances on losing a fine catch like Lord Holm. When she caught her hiding behind the screen, she saw the perfect opportunity to accuse her of theft and ruin her.

'I shall ask you for the last time, Ava,' Lord Emsy demanded, his double chins wiggling, 'did you steal the bracelet?'

Ava refused to stand down. 'No, milord, I did *not* steal the bracelet.'

'Then you leave me no choice,' his lordship said, exhaling loudly, 'but to turn you over to the proper authorities at Cork for grand larceny.'

'But, milord—' Ava pleaded, fear rising in her so quickly she felt numb.

'Quiet, girl. You're confined to your room until further notice.'

'That's not fair! I didn't do anything wrong.' Ava flinched when Warner, the butler, grabbed her. She yanked her arm away, the fiery glint in her eye directed toward Lady Olivia. 'You've not seen the end of Ava O'Reilly, your ladyship. Someday I shall be a grand lady—'

'*You*, a lady?' Lady Olivia said, disbelieving. 'Don't make me laugh. You're not fit to be a scullery maid.'

Then she turned on her heel and glided upstairs like a pretentious swan, taking her aristocratic airs with her. Ava nearly died with embarrassment. Not because she'd called her a scullery maid, but at how the guilty could walk away free while the innocent paid the price.

Because she was born poor.

'No more chatter, girl,' said the butler, moving her along, but Ava dragged her heels, her mind spinning. Somehow, *someway*, she'd get free. Her ladyship felt Ava's gaze upon her and turned around, grinning at her with victory in her eyes. In spite of her determination to fight back, Ava felt the sting of hot tears on her cheeks. The girl's elegant and effortless exit made an impression on her she'd never forget.

She swore then she'd *never* be a victim again. She'd do *anything* to get above herself and make her place in the world. *Anything.*

And the devil be damned.

* * *

'Have you taken leave of your senses, Ava Madeline O'Reilly?' Mary Dolores paced up and down the small room they shared in the attic. Dubbed the *virgins' wing,* it wasn't accessible to male servants. 'You'll never escape. Warner placed a guard at the backstairs.'

Ava smiled. 'Then I'll sneak down the grand main staircase while the family is still sleeping.'

''Tis a fool's plan,' Mary Dolores insisted, wringing her hands on her apron and making deep wrinkles in the cloth.

Ava grabbed her sister by the shoulders and looked her in the eye. Mary Dolores was a tall, plain girl with faint freckles on her cheeks that begged for sunshine to blossom. They never would, working as she did from dawn till night. She hurt just looking at her sister's long, pale face, worn and tired, the life drained out of her.

'It pains me to see you trapped inside this house fourteen hours a day,' she said. 'Cleaning and dusting and tiptoeing about all day so as not to disturb a family who barely knows you exist. Why do you put up with it? Da wanted so much more for you.'

'But Mum would be so pleased to see both her daughters living in so grand a house.' Mary Dolores paused, her heart heavy. 'Why did you have to ruin it? Reading books no God-fearing girl would dare look at is one thing, but why did you take the bracelet, Ava? *Why?*'

'I *didn't* take it.' Ava whirled around in a circle, banging her forehead in frustration. 'What fairy curse is upon me that not even my own sister believes me?'

'I *want* to, Ava, but Lady Olivia insisted...'

'There's your problem, always believing your betters over your own flesh and blood.' Ava grabbed her sister's hand and bade her to sit down. 'Times are changing, Mary Dolores, faster than a fox with the hounds nipping at its tail. This world of grand manners and extravagant ways won't last.'

'What fool's talk is this, Ava?'

'I know. Every morning before breakfast, I read the newspapers before I place them on the trays. About how electricity and telephones will make communication faster... how a motorcar can cover the distance from here to Dublin in a day.' Her eyes glowed. 'Did you see Lord Holm's touring car? As big as a ship it is. I'm telling you, Mary Dolores, we're no longer doomed to spend our lives in service. With all them new things making life better for the likes of us, who's to say we can't find jobs and get our own flat?'

'But if you can't prove you're innocent, Ava, you'll never have a chance to do *anything*. You'll be hauled off to prison like a common thief.'

Ava shook her head. 'I've saved all my wages. I'm getting a job in a big factory and going to school.'

'How can you?' Mary Dolores said, worried. 'Even if you escape, they'll track you down wherever you go.'

Ava set her mouth in a firm line. 'Have you no faith in me? There's one place they'll *never* find me.'

'I don't believe such a place exists.'

'Aye, but it does,' Ava insisted. 'A place where the streets are paved with gold.'

Hands on her hips, her sister asked, 'And where is that?'

Ava grinned widely. 'America.'

* * *

10 April 1912

Six a.m. the next morning found Ava with her small cloth traveling bag packed with her few belongings tiptoeing down the grand main staircase, her head swinging right then left and back again. She wore her brown tweed suit, which was faded from too many washings, her white blouse, the round collar of which was smudged with dirt, and a worn black hat sitting at a cocky angle on her head. A slender feather curved over her right eye, giving her a provocative look. She reached the landing without incident, exhaled, and counted the remaining steps.

Eight, nine, ten.

She'd avoided running into the staff and no one in the family was about at the early hour. Only her own quick breathing filled her ears. She'd be on her way before anyone knew she was gone, then she'd navigate her way through the pine woods surrounding the estate and climb over the hedge of wild fuchsia to the road. There she prayed she'd find a passing vegetable wagon and a friendly farmer to give her a lift to Queenstown where she could book passage on a ship leaving for America.

Eleven, twelve, thirteen...

Nothing could change her mind, not even Mary Dolores crying that she'd never see her again. Ava tried to console her by promising to send for her when she reached America.

Fourteen...

'Going somewhere?' a deep male voice startled her.

Ava spun around and came face to face with Lord Holm.

'Yes, milord, I mean, *no*, milord.'

'Good. I'm in need of female companionship.' He leaned closer. She could smell brandy and tobacco on his breath. By his disheveled appearance, she could tell he'd been out all night.

'Please, milord, I – I have an errand to run for Mrs Briggs—'

'Come, girl, you're running away before the town constable arrives to haul your pretty arse off to prison.'

'*Milord!*' She stepped back quickly.

'Be assured, I'm not ringing the butler to put you in chains. Everyone knows Olivia concocted that ridiculous story about the bracelet to get you sacked.' He turned serious. 'She never dreamed her father would bring the authorities down on you.'

Frowning, Ava said, 'Then why don't she stop him?'

'My dear, you *are* a provincial. Olivia admit she was wrong? Especially when it involves taking a servant girl's word over *hers*?' He shook his head. 'That would upset the order of things and *that* would never do.'

'But it's unfair, Lord Holm.'

'Come with me.' He grinned. 'What I have in mind will be far more amusing than sleeping off this hangover.'

Ava crossed herself. What was he about?

'Oh, Lord, preserve my beating heart...' she whispered when he led her outside and she saw the French, burgundy red town car with big, black fenders and white-walled tires parked on the gravel. His lordship gave an order to his chauffeur who cranked up the car and then opened the passenger door.

Smiling, Lord Holm said, 'Get in.'

Shaking her head, Ava pulled back. 'I can't, milord. I'll be in a heap more trouble if I do.'

'I assure you, no one will know about our little game.' He took her by the elbow and held her tight. 'Now get into the motorcar.'

'But, milord—'

'Don't spoil my fun. I can't wait to see Olivia's face when she discovers you've slipped out of her noose.'

* * *

'I'm going to America,' Ava said when his lordship asked her about her plans. They'd been driving for a while with Lord Holm trying to entice her to let him drive her to Dublin so she could sup with him at the Royal Hibernian Hotel. She ignored his stabs at flirting, digging her fingers into the tuft velvet interior as soft as goose feathers and inhaling the smell of swank leather as intoxicating as brandy. She smiled. Riding to freedom like a real lady, she stared out the window. She marveled at how the motorcar sped along the road at a good clip, the trees going by so fast they blurred into a swash of green as long as a leprechaun's tailcoat.

'Which liner have you in mind for your trip across the pond?' Lord Holm rested his hand upon her knee. She moved away, but his hand remained.

'I intend to purchase a ticket on the first ship leaving.' She lowered her head. 'If the authorities don't find me first.'

'They won't get a word out of me.' He leaned toward her to kiss her, but she backed away. By and by, she had her pride. 'Come now, not even a kiss for the gentleman who rescued you?'

'You belong to Lady Olivia.'

'Ah, the loyal servant to the end. You're a remarkable girl, Ava O'Reilly. So remarkable I'm sorry we didn't become better acquainted.' He exhaled. 'Perhaps I can be of service after all...'

Curious, Ava watched him pull a folded-up note out of his pocket.

A wireless message.

He skimmed it as he spoke, 'There's a fine new ship from the White Star Line stopping at Queenstown tomorrow morning to pick up passengers before heading to New York.'

'Are you certain, milord?' Ava prayed it was so. She had no choice but to leave Ireland before the authorities caught up to her.

'Yes. My dear aunt, Lady Scranton, is aboard. According to her telegram, she boarded the ship at Southampton and will be getting off to join me at Cameron Bally Manor House when Lord Emsy makes the formal announcement.' He leaned closer. 'Yes, it's true what they say below stairs. I shall marry dear Olivia *and* her generous settlement.'

Ava let go with a contended sigh. *Thank the heavens.*

'May I be the first to congratulate you, milord.'

'Thank you, Ava, but I'd rather be aboard ship with you.'

She remained silent, not answering him lest she say something brash and all her plans were dashed. For once she kept her mouth shut, though she did give him a disapproving look.

'I envy the men aboard the liner they're calling unsinkable with you to make their voyage a pleasant one,' he said quietly, resolved to his fate. 'My aunt insists it's the finest ship to ever sail the seas with the best service imaginable.' He looked at her as if he were about to tell her a secret. 'In first class, I hear you have your own bathroom.'

Ava's mouth dropped open. 'A bathroom aboard ship to your own sweet self? Is that legal?'

His lordship laughed.

'What is this grand ship called, milord?' Ava asked as the sloping terraces of Queenstown came into view. She couldn't believe she was here, more determined than ever to book passage on this new vessel. If it was fine enough for a titled lady, it was good enough for her.

A teasing look came into his lordship's eyes, as if debating whether or not to tell her.

Finally, he said, 'The *Titanic*.'

* * *

Ava squirmed in her seat when Lord Holm brushed her cheek with his cold lips, trying to convince her to forget sailing on the *Titanic* and go with him to Dublin. She was not having it. She stuck her tongue out at him, stomped her foot and announced in a steady voice if he didn't stop the motorcar, 'I'll scream like a wild banshee.'

Aye, she was tempting the fates with her threat, but it worked.

Pouting like a little boy who'd spilled his pudding, his lordship deposited her in front of the shipping office for the White Star Line, then with a grunt and a sneer he was off, back to Lady Olivia as if nothing had happened.

But it had and Ava would never be the same. She was no longer the young girl who held her da's hand tight when she came to Queenstown with its narrow streets winding up steep hills. She relished the memory of those days, seeing him off on his fishing boat until the day he never returned. The sea claimed him as it had so many others, his body washing up on shore while his soul roamed free.

It broke her dear mother's heart, kind lady she was, her fingers always entwined around the holy black beads her sister in the convent fastened for her. She'd buried three sons before they reached the age of five. Children lost to the ills of being poor, then her husband to the ravages of the sea.

Six months ago, her mum had died, but not before she'd made Ava promise to join her sister in service. Now Ava had broken that promise and she was running off to America. With a price on her head.

Leave Ireland? Her home?

Was she daft?

Her parents were buried here, but she didn't have even a handful of dirt from their final resting place to take with her.

Only her mother's black rosary beads.

Ava gripped her hands together and beat upon her breast, calling upon the angels to help her.

Oh, God, please, she prayed, *tell my dear mum I'm sorry, but I have to do this. And please, oh, please, make her forgive me.*

She would, wouldn't she?

There was a steep price to pay if she were caught, but the wild intoxication of being free was a heady stimulant that surpassed any grim thoughts she might have.

Heart racing madly, she entered the ticket office, her decision made. Less than an hour later, she was the proud owner of a third-class ticket to New York costing her seven pounds and fifteen shillings after having looked over the contract and terms of the voyage and marveled at the grandness of it all, including the bill of fare.

The menu promised oatmeal, milk, bread and butter for breakfast. Her stomach growled. Hunger filled her belly as she stood on the pier at the rear of the White Star Line building, her skirts blowing wildly against her legs. Nothing mattered but the ticket she clasped to her chest. She closed her eyes tight, not believing her luck had turned. A sudden chill rattled her bones and for an instant she feared the north wind would swoop down and take the ticket from her, but she couldn't bear the thought.

She held it tighter. Her soul took flight, her heart clenched.

Freedom was hers for the taking.

The *Titanic* set sail tomorrow... and by all the saints who stood watch over the sea, Ava O'Reilly would be on it.

2

The *Titanic*
10 April 1912

If there was one thing that made Captain Lord James 'Buck' Blackthorn smile more than holding a pretty woman in his arms, it was a winning hand at cards.

To his dismay, at the moment he had neither.

'I'll raise you, gentlemen,' Buck said, stretching his long legs under the green topped playing table. He didn't relish playing against *boatmen*, professional gamblers who followed the sea, but he was in desperate need of funds thanks to a voluptuous blonde in Mayfair.

Smoking a cigarette out of an amber holder, Lady Irene Pennington had sought his protection, appealing to his chivalrous nature, though he had no doubt her plea was an act. Still, the gilded lily with the seductive smile made a man believe he was a king.

And *not* the second son of a duke without home or hearth to offer her.

She'd made him feel loved until her husband, a prominent public servant, returned home unexpectedly from a mission abroad and found out about the affair. That set Buck packing his bags and off on another adventure, much to the disappointment of her ladyship. She hated losing him. He made love as fiercely as he led his men into battle. Such vigor was wildly exciting to the aristocratic set and Lady Pennington was no exception.

A generous offer from his old college roommate, Treyton Brady, to join him and his fiancée aboard the *Titanic* had provided him with the perfect escape.

Which was how Buck found himself sitting in the first-class smoking room on the ship of dreams busily engaged in four-handed poker after the ship stopped to pick up passengers and mail in Cherbourg. The liner was headed next to Queenstown in southern Ireland and was scheduled to arrive tomorrow morning, its final stop before heading out to sea across the North Atlantic.

'Too rich for my blood, Buck.' Trey threw down his cards, picked up his highball from the cup holder and with a quick swallow of vodka, he was gone.

Buck cocked an eyebrow. *Odd*. Trey could well afford to stay in the game. That half-smile of his often meant something else was on his mind.

Most likely, he was off to flirt with the pretty passenger Buck had seen him talking to earlier on the second-class deck. Meanwhile, Trey's fiancée settled into her stateroom. Alone. Not surprising. His friend's romantic exploits with the fair sex were at times indiscreet, though his betrothed had yet to find that out.

An American thing, Trey called it.

Buck found it difficult to keep his mind on the game. Why the man neglected his lovely fiancée puzzled the Brit. Doe-eyed and chestnut-haired, Fiona Winston-Hale, Countess of Marbury, seemingly sailed through life in an effortless fashion and would no doubt choose to ignore Trey's eye for the ladies.

In reality, she fretted over every detail lest anyone discover what dire straits she was in. Due to massive debt incurred by her late father, the countess was in danger of losing Dirksen Castle, her thousand-year-old family home in Scotland. A fire had destroyed the east wing and Fiona had no resources to fund the major repairs.

So Buck introduced her to his friend from his days at Cambridge since Trey was considered quite a catch among the ladies.

The American with the pencil-thin moustache and easy smile was not only dapper and handsome, but heir to a vast fortune made in steel by his late father, F.G. Brady, a multimillionaire industrialist from New York.

While Buck was a member of the British peerage by birth, he was a soldier and high-society gambler by choice.

'I'll see you and raise you another fifty,' said the man seated across from him with a handful of chips in his hand. Mr Charters was a rich manufacturer from Liverpool with a big belly and an even bigger laugh.

'I'll raise you another hundred and call,' said the third man still in the game, a stocky man whose face bore the scars of hard living. He puffed on a big cigar.

Buck listened with more than curiosity when the man announced he was Mr Watts, a cotton exporter from North Carolina. He seemed quite pleased to be aboard the *Millionaires' Special* – a dubious moniker given to the ship's maiden voyage because of the wealthy men aboard. Notices had been posted in the smoking room warning about 'Games of Chance' and the likelihood of professional gamblers aboard looking for easy pickings at high-stakes card games.

The warning had little effect on the players.

Buck shuffled his cards. If memory served him, the man with the cigar *wasn't* Mr Watts, but a card sharp traveling under an alias. Which made him suspect the man was guilty of dobbing, marking the deck in such a way to tell whether a card was a king, a queen or an ace.

His gut told him the man had substituted a marked deck by the worn edges on the green, gilt-edged cards inscribed with the White Star Line burgee in the center. These swindlers played dirty and had the survival instinct of cockroaches.

He watched the man carefully, his bulging knuckles, broken numerous times, clear evidence of his dubious background.

The gent snorted. 'Too much for you Brits, eh?'

Mr Charters wiped his face with his silk handkerchief, then threw down his money. 'I'm in.'

'How 'bout you, Captain Lord Blackthorn?' said Mr Watts, putting down his cigar.

Smoke from the cigar resting on the crystal glass tray drifted toward him. Buck ignored it.

'A pair of aces, gentlemen.' He laid his cards down on the table.

'Three of a kind,' said the man from Liverpool with a hearty laugh.

'Sorry to disappoint you gents,' said the card sharp, 'but a full house takes the pot.'

The man snickered. He knew Buck was on to him and expected him to act like a proper Englishman and say nothing.

Not his style.

Watts had another thing coming.

'If this were a game at Pratt's or White's in London, sir,' Buck said, choosing his words carefully, 'I'd call you a swindler. However, since we're at sea, I'll wait until we arrive in New York to settle the score.'

'I reckon we settle it *now*.' The phony millionaire drew a pistol from his coat and pointed it at Buck. Mr Charters gasped, and then ducked under the table.

Buck smiled and didn't move a muscle. Inside he was seething, but cautious. A man with a gun was as deadly as a cobra.

You never knew when they'd strike.

'Are you suggesting pistols at twenty paces on the Boat Deck at dawn?' Buck asked, deadly serious while calculating his next move. He could duke it out with the best of them, whether it was in the ring or playing cards. He had a quick eye and a sure sense of timing. 'That will prove interesting shipboard entertainment for early morning strollers.'

'Your lordship ain't going to make no fool out of me.' The card sharp cocked the hammer on his pistol.

'You're doing a fine job of that yourself,' Buck said. 'Brandishing that pistol about like a wild man in a freak show.'

'I'd keep your opinions to yourself if I was you.'

'Put that gun down before it goes off and you find yourself in a *bigger* mess than impersonating a certain millionaire from North Carolina.'

'Are you calling me a liar?'

'I am, sir. I played cards with Mr Watts aboard the *Mauretania*. I've never found a more honest gentleman.'

Before the impersonator could fire off a shot, Buck pushed his chair away from the table and knocked the gun out of his hand, then slammed him in the ribs so hard the man staggered backward and fell to the floor. His pistol slid over the dark red and blue linoleum tiles like they were made of ice, his eyes fluttering wildly as he lay on his back, unable to get up.

The other gentlemen, engrossed in their card games, barely acknowledged the entire incident.

'I suggest you disembark when the ship stops in Queenstown, Mr *Watts*,' Buck said, shoving the pistol into his jacket pocket. 'I shall be on deck to make certain you do.'

'You British aristocrats think you're so high and mighty,' said the man, holding his gut as he pulled himself to his feet. 'Unsinkable, like this ship.'

Buck smiled. 'No one is unsinkable, sir, they just *think* they are.'

Disgusted, the card sharp stomped off. Buck didn't take his eyes off him until he was through the revolving doors. Then he gathered up the winnings and handed them to the portly man from Liverpool, who'd stuck his head out from under the table in time to see the entire scene unfold.

'Good show, your lordship,' said Mr Charters, slapping him on the back.

'A story to tell your grandchildren, sir, about your crossing on the *Titanic*,' Buck said, grinning.

'Your lordship!'

Buck turned to see a steward in his white jacket and brass buttons racing toward him.

'Yes, man, what is it?'

'Come with me *quickly*, your lordship,' he said, out of breath. *'It's urgent.'*

'Urgent?' Buck questioned.

'Yes, the Countess of Marbury needs your help straightaway.'

'Where's Mr Brady?' Buck asked, concerned.

'I don't know, your lordship. I looked everywhere.' The steward paused. 'Her ladyship asked me to summon you.'

Buck remained silent. Trey was no doubt regaling the second-class lady in her cabin with stories of his adventures in the Orient. Indeed, he'd spent most of his time at the bar in the Raffles Hotel in Singapore. *Damn* him. He'd hoped embarking on married life would settle him down.

Obviously not.

Buck had no intention of marrying. The former Army captain never imagined himself settling down. He didn't believe in love or marriage. He saw what it had done to his mother, a frail but kind woman who had left this earth far too early. In the end, she had suffered more from the pain of loneliness only a woman without a loving companion could understand. Yes, she had her sons, and Buck did what he could for her, but it wasn't enough. He hated his father, the duke, for how he'd treated her. Women were exquisite creatures to be protected and adored, he believed, not treated as property.

Buck had yet to meet a woman who intrigued him enough to give her his heart. He doubted he ever would.

He wouldn't stand by and allow his friend to treat the countess with anything less than respect. Buck admired her subtlety and graciousness, traits he found lacking in most women. She was a true lady in dignity and manner. He often questioned why *he* hadn't fallen in love with her since they'd known each other for years, but she was bred in another era when women hid their feelings. He liked a woman with spirit, a woman who challenged him.

Fiona was delicate and proper. Exactly what Trey needed.

'Is the countess hurt?' Buck wanted to know, hurrying down the two sets of stairs to C Deck. If he had to, he'd track his old friend down and drag him by the neck back to his duty.

The steward tried to keep up with him, suggesting they take the electric lift.

'It's not the countess, your lordship,' said the steward, wiping the perspiration from his face, 'but her lady's maid. She's taken a terrible tumble. Sprained her ankle.'

'Fetch the ship's surgeon and have him come to her ladyship's stateroom immediately.'

'Yes, your lordship.'

The steward dashed off, leaving Buck with a troubled mind. He intended to get Trey alone and set him straight.

I'll skin your hide if you pull this trick again. This isn't Cambridge and a student prank. Grow up.

Buck prayed he wasn't wrong in trying to protect Fiona from knowing the truth about Trey. She wanted life to be smooth and orderly and sweet. Trey wasn't suited for that, but her entire future rested upon this marriage. She was running out of time to save her heritage and Trey provided the perfect solution.

Buck would explain to her later, but for now it was up to him to make the crossing as pleasant as possible.

Which was why he went to her stateroom and didn't mention a word about Trey.

3

Queenstown, Ireland
10 April 1912

'Will you be needing a place to stay, lass?'

Ava turned, surprised. An oddly dressed man stood behind her, grinning. Striped jacket and piped trousers with a small bowler hat plopped upon his head. A peddler. How long had he been watching her? She'd thought about waiting on the pier till morning but that was impractical, even for the likes of her. Queenstown wasn't much more than a village with clapboard houses built on steep terraces with rows of shops along the quays.

She had every right to be cautious.

She was on the run.

She didn't dare set her feet to walking on the streets lest the local constable spot her. No telling how far Lord Emsy's influence and threats to send her off to prison reached.

'I'm leaving in the morning on the *Titanic*,' Ava said slowly, wary his type was oft filled with blarney.

'Florie Sims runs a respectable place next to the bakery and grocery,' he said. 'If you don't mind beady eyes with long tails staring at you.'

'Is there no other rooming house?' she asked, curious.

'Aye, but you can't beat the tariff at Florie's. A bed and morning porridge for three shillings a night.'

Ava frowned. After paying for her fare, she had little money left.

'Florie Sims, you say?'

'Aye.' He tipped his bowler to her. 'Be sure to tell her Jeremiah Cobb sent you.'

He smiled and she tried not to stare at his broken, yellow teeth. Long and pointy.

* * *

'I run a decent house and I don't take to no spooning with the gents in my place.'

Florie Sims made no secret of her disapproval of the whistles Ava elicited from the men on the stairs as the woman showed her to her room on the second floor. With a baby on her hip and another tugging at her skirts, Ava imagined the outspoken landlady couldn't afford to be particular about her boarders.

'This is it?' Ava said, not hiding her surprise when the landlady opened the door. She swore she saw a man jump out the second-story window onto the roof as they came in. She sniffed and the smell of sweaty bodies filled the air. Seemed the landlady was better at making the rules than enforcing them.

That wasn't the worst of it. Tiny cots filled the small room lined up next to each other in two rows at least five deep. Peeling wallpaper, a cracked, watermarked ceiling and a large porcelain bowl rimmed with faded rosebuds sat in a corner behind a screen.

A young woman lay atop the narrow bed, pretending to be asleep. No doubt she'd found comfort in the man's arms and now dreamed of him.

Ava winced as a pang of loneliness hit her. The only time she'd felt a man's arms around her was when the blacksmith's son kissed her in the church cemetery. After confession one unforgettable Thursday, the priest caught them and boxed the boy's ears and made Ava say penance on her knees for hours.

Why is it wrong to want a man's love?

To want him to touch her, make her dizzy with desire? To yearn for a man who could raise her spirits as high as the heavens?

Such thoughts tormented her, though she prayed hard not to yield to them.

'What did you expect, lassie?' Florie said when she saw Ava's nose wiggle with distaste. 'A royal manor house?' She shifted the baby from one hip to the other. 'I imagine the likes of you have seen your share of fancy bedrooms.' She chuckled. 'Take it or leave it. Four shillings a night with hot porridge in the morn.'

'Jeremiah Cobb quoted me *three* shillings.' Ava folded her arms across her chest.

'So you're one of Cobb's girls. I should have known. Three shillings.' She held out her hand. '*In advance*.'

Ava turned around and unpinned the handkerchief containing her money from inside her chemise. 'A trusting soul, aren't you?'

She smirked. 'I've had too many of my boarders disappear out the window come the first breath of dawn.'

* * *

It wasn't the fear of mice or loud snoring that kept Ava awake, but the worrisome fear she'd be found out and sent to the local jail.

A fine mess she was in, hiding out in a dosshouse until morning. Curled up on a cot in the corner of the small room, Ava guessed the other female tenant must be asleep, though she couldn't see much through the murky darkness. What kind of devil's underworld went on here when the sun went down, she could only guess.

And the *smell*.

Slipping her steamship ticket under the hard pillow, she put her head down. The pungent scent from the bedding made her gag, the fibers still damp with the stain of human desire. Ava had no doubt mice were the *least* of her worries.

She was about to close her eyes when—

A cold hand slipped up her leg and stroked her bare skin.

'*You dirty vermin!*' Ava cried out, jumping up and kicking him. A loud groan assaulted her ears.

'Leave her alone, Ned,' she heard a raspy girl's voice say in the darkness. 'I got what you're after.'

'Why can't I have a turn with her?' asked the man, grumbling close by. *Too* close.

'Because you're *my* beau,' said the young woman, coming into view. Ava could see her face lit up by the golden glow from the gaslight. And by the unholy, she saw a man grab the girl around the waist and fumble with her petticoat. It must be the same ne'er do well who put his hand up *her* skirt.

Turn away, Ava my girl, she could hear her mum whispering in her ear, *and protect your innocence.*

Ava couldn't stop the fervid thoughts clattering about in her brain. She froze when the girl lit a candle and lifted up her skirts so the boy could see her slender thighs. She looked away. With those two spooning nearby, she'd not close her eyes all night. Morning couldn't come quick enough for her. Then she'd be off to America. She couldn't count on anyone but herself to buy her freedom. Anything else was a threat she'd deal with, with her fists if she had to. She held fast to that gratifying thought, sending up a holy prayer to the angels to keep her safe till she got on board the ship. Only then would she have a chance for a better life.

All day and half the night Ava had kept to the dark corners of the lodging house, munching on the scraps she found in the kitchen. Rinsing her mouth out with well water the color of last week's washing. Looking at her steamship ticket for passage to New York. Over and over again, praying it wouldn't crumble to dust between her fingers.

She lay her head down on the cot now and reached under the pillow—

'It's gone!' she cried out. *How could it disappear? Wait!* The girl had boasted about getting what the boy wanted when Ava kicked the sod – it made sense now. *She stole her ticket to America.* That ticket was all she had to hold onto. No, *no*! An intense heat filled her, stripping away any shred of civility she had left, spurring her into action when she heard—

Laughter.

So they think I'm weak. No one's sticking me with a knife to the heart this time.

'Give me my ticket, *now!*' Ava yelled, bolting off the cot and grabbing the lit candle. The arc of light showered the room in an unholy glow as she stood down, facing the girl.

'Is this what you're after?' The troublemaker spat on the floor, and then threw the white ticket into the air, its fluttery descent to earth caught in the candlelight.

Ned snatched it from under Ava's nose.

'A steamship ticket, just like the landlady said.' He sounded impressed. 'I bet McGinnis will give me two, maybe three pounds for it.'

No, no. They couldn't take her dream away from her. They couldn't.

Nearly every penny she'd saved from her wages had been spent for her passage.

'Give it back to me!' Ava demanded, setting down the candle and making a grab for the ticket.

She missed.

Smirking, Ned tripped her and down she went, the breath knocked out of her.

The devil he was, but he'd not get the best of her. She'd seen how the world worked and how you had to fight for what you wanted. Aye, *fight*. And that she'd do...

The saints be warned!' Ava banged her fist into her hand. 'I'll not be done in by the likes of you.' Breathing hard, she struggled to get to her feet when—

'Open up!' yelled a woman's voice outside the door. 'I know you've got a man in there.'

'It's the landlady,' whispered the girl, turning down the gaslight. 'Go, Ned, *now!*'

Ned raced toward the open window leading to the roof—

But not before Ava grabbed him by his shirt tail and pulled him backward, making him lose his balance. To her relief, he dropped her steamship ticket before making his escape. She snatched it up and hid it inside her blouse, then let out a deep sigh.

Hours yet until the sun came up. But *nothing* would stop her from having her chance at freedom.

She lay down on the hard cot and slept with one eye open the rest of the night.

4

The *Titanic*

10 April 1912

'Her ladyship's maid must leave the ship at Queenstown,' said the surgeon, a kindly Irishman settled in his years.

And in his opinion.

'There's no permanent damage, doctor?' Buck asked.

'No, milord, merely a bad sprain, but she'll not be able to perform her duties aboard ship.'

Buck nodded, watching the countess sitting at the girl's bedside, holding her hand and wiping her brow with a damp cloth. Kind and considerate, Fiona never deemed it beneath her to help the girl, though she barely knew her. She'd foregone having a lady's maid back home in Scotland to cut back expenses, so Buck had secured a replacement from a reputable source in London.

Closing up his black bag, the surgeon said, 'I'll send a deck steward round in the morning with a wheelchair before we dock.' He smiled. 'Don't worry, she'll be good as new by the first summer rain.'

The elderly physician bade the countess goodnight, then he was off to treat numerous bouts of seasickness before turning in for the night.

The countess pulled Buck over to the side, out of the maid's earshot.

'Poor girl was standing on a stool, trying to put my hatbox on top of the wardrobe, when she slipped,' she said, her voice as soft as a whisper in a dark room. 'I shall never forgive myself, Buck.'

'It wasn't your fault, Fiona.' He sat down with her on the velvet settee in the connecting stateroom used as a parlor. He closed the door, giving them privacy. 'Be assured, Trey will compensate her for wages lost before she leaves the ship.'

'Yes, Trey has a most charming manner when it comes to women.' She said no more, but her silence told him what he wanted to know.

She was aware of Trey's indiscretions.

Buck studied her pleasant features drawn into a tight smile. In her blissful, sophisticated innocence, she gave the air of a perfect upper-class engagement, whatever the cost to her own happiness.

'You can leave the ship at Queenstown, Fiona, if you need more time,' Buck said candidly. 'I'll explain the situation to Trey.'

'No. I need this marriage, Buck, as much as *he* needs my title. I would have drowned in debt if you hadn't acted as a go-between for me.' She looked down, embarrassed. 'Things haven't been the same at Dirksen Castle since Papa died... Trey stepped in and spoke to my creditors... let's say he's been *very* generous.'

'I'll pay it all back, Fiona, if you don't want this marriage.'

'Dear Buck, always looking out for me since we met on that lovely summer day.'

Buck smiled. How could he forget the first time he had set eyes on her? Racing through the thick forest on a black mare, her long chestnut hair flying behind her, she rode sidesaddle with an elegant grace as if she were one with the horse. She had such poise then and she was barely seventeen.

He'd been spending time in Scotland at the Blackthorn family lodge after the nasty business with his father, the duke. As a young man fresh from Cambridge, Buck was gazetted to the Coldstream

Guards as a second lieutenant and served at the front during the Boer War as an intelligence officer.

By the age of twenty-one, he was one of the youngest captains in his regiment and had a promising military career ahead of him until his father insisted he settle down to a desk job – and marry an American heiress to enrich the duke's coffers *and* settle his younger son's future. His Grace couldn't conceive his son had a mind of his own and wouldn't be dependent on a woman. *Any* woman.

Buck shocked his father by resigning his post, but he retained his honorary title of captain.

Then he went into a self-imposed exile in Scotland.

Riding and hunting, enjoying the solace of the countryside, Fiona was just what he had needed. There he talked over with her the idea of joining the French Foreign Legion, their free and dangerous lives appealing to him. There was something irresistible about soldiers who owed allegiance only to themselves, he had said.

The countess had talked him out of it, as only she could.

She made everything seem so easy, this girl who loved to write poetry and knew exactly what to say and how to say it. She kept Buck coming back to Scotland, a place he loved and where he found peace. Although his father reveled in owning a forest filled with deer, the duke rarely took up residence there, preferring instead to use its existence merely for boasting purposes.

It became a refuge for Buck between adventures – amorous and otherwise. It was a quiet time in his life and his friendship with Fiona grew. By the time the countess matured into a lovely woman, the two had become good friends. Her father, the earl, hoped for an alliance between the families when Fiona became of age. He had asked one thing of the young man. Buck wasn't going to let him down now.

'I promised your father I'd look out for you.'

'Is that the *only* reason?' Her eyes searched his, looking for something he couldn't give her. It would be unfair to let her believe so.

'You know what I am, Fiona, a rogue with the scruples of a masked highwayman, intent on giving my protection to lovely ladies, but never falling in love.'

She sighed without embarrassment. 'How I *do* envy Lady Pennington.'

Buck cleared his throat. 'Does Mayfair gossip reach as far as Scotland?'

She smiled. 'We're not as out of touch as people believe, though in recent years I prefer to avoid the London Season.'

The time of year when society ladies traveled to the city for fancy parties.

At twenty-three, Fiona no longer possessed the first bloom of a girl enjoying her debut. With a vast estate and lands to run, it provided the perfect excuse for her to avoid the rush and bother of trying to snag a husband. She was a peeress in her own right, but she'd had few offers until Trey made his move. She was grateful he was willing to take on the enormous task of restoring Dirksen Castle to its former glory.

'I shall lose *everything* if I don't marry Trey. It's not just for me, but the tenants on my lands are simple people, toiling their plots for years and depending on us to supplement them in bad times. I hate to think what would happen to them if the lands were divided up, sold off, and the tenants ousted to pay my debts.'

Her shoulders slumped and although she tried to hold back the tears, she couldn't. Buck felt drawn to her, this lonely woman with such a desperate need to help those less fortunate. In a way, they were alike. Since his mother died, he had no family he could call upon. His elder brother, the heir to the title, whiled away his time in France, spending the fortune he didn't have, while his father, the duke, turned a blind eye.

The countess was also alone and he was determined to help her.

'Dry your tears, Fiona,' he said, handing her his handkerchief. 'There's a whole new life waiting for you in New York.'

She wiped her eyes, then laid her head on his shoulder. 'Oh, Buck, if only you could stay in New York and be by my side, I wouldn't be so frightened.'

'I wish I could, Fiona, but there aren't many jobs in New York for impoverished lords,' he said, stroking her hair. The cabin parlor felt airless, stuffy. Or was it because he found himself in an uncomfortable situation? 'After the gossip about my liaison with Lady Pennington quiets down, I must return to London to get my affairs in order.'

'I shall miss you terribly, Buck,' she said, raising her face to his, her lips so close they nearly brushed his mouth. She caught him off guard, making his back stiffen, his urges rising suddenly in spite of the awkwardness of the moment. He would never touch her, never spoil the closeness they had with an impulsive kiss.

He resisted her invitation and she let out a deep sigh, making him feel worse. He didn't feel noble or heroic, but what else could he do? He must face up to the fact it wasn't going to be easy to navigate his friendship with her over the next few days at sea.

He was about to break their embrace when—

'My, my, isn't this a cozy situation,' Trey said, bursting into the stateroom in a dramatic entrance, his tone angry. He slammed the door and leaned against it, arms folded. 'My fiancée and my best friend caught in an amorous embrace.'

The countess pulled away, embarrassed. '*Please*, Trey, you're being silly,' she pleaded, smoothing down her dress, her cheeks flushed though she attempted to add a lightness to her tone. 'You don't know how difficult it is for a recluse like me to travel these days. I've been all in a tizzy since I came on board and Buck is such a gentleman, trying to make it easier for me.'

'Fiona is right, Trey. If a lady can't turn to an old friend, then who can she turn to?' Buck said, standing up and facing his friend. The smell of brandy on the American's breath filled his nostrils, but it was the fierceness in Trey's eyes that made him determined to set this conversation on a calming course. 'She's quite upset over the maid's accident and since you were unavailable, she turned to me for support.'

Buck made no excuse about his obvious undertone.

Trey smirked.

'Always in control, aren't you, Buck?' Trey poured himself a glass of scotch from the crystal decanter on the silver tray. His voice wavered, slurring his words. 'Then again, you always were, even when we were Cantabs,' he said, using the slang word for students at Cambridge. 'Whether you were heading up the debating club or rowing against Oxford. I haven't forgotten what good friends we were back then, Buck, though at times you make it difficult.' Trey swallowed his drink, then banged the glass down on the small round table, startling the countess.

'Since you've returned to take over your duties, I'll retire to my cabin.' Buck turned to the countess and kissed her hand. She held onto him, not wanting to let go. After assuring her with a smile he wasn't abandoning her, he pulled away. 'I'll send a stewardess to assist you, Fiona.'

'*I'll* take care of that, Buck,' Trey said, the tone of his voice clearly indicating he wasn't amused to find his friend in the company of his fiancée. 'In case you've forgotten, the countess's welfare is *my* responsibility.'

'My only hope is *you* don't forget it.' Then, with a slight bow to the countess, he left. He'd dispatched many a cad to the mat over their treatment of a woman, but Trey was his friend. In spite of his impoverished state of nobility, the millionaire was jealous of him.

Afterward, Buck walked up and down on the Boat Deck, his collar pulled up against the wind, his thoughts scrambling. The ship moved silently, though he could feel the rhythm of the engines as he strolled the deck. The sea was calm, the cold night warning him the chill he felt wouldn't be short-lived.

His thoughts pushed on, wondering what insanity he'd inflicted upon the two people he loved most in the world by coming up with this marriage scheme. His motive was to see them happy, or as happy as two people could be who found themselves in the damnable situation of needing what the other had to offer. Even if it *didn't* involve the intertwining of the human heart, especially for Fiona. He admired her allegiance to her father and the tenants on her lands.

What next? Trey knew Buck had a fondness for his fiancée. No doubt the American suspected their relationship went beyond a social friendship, more so on Fiona's side than his, but Trey saw only a man and a woman who shared a personal closeness he didn't understand. God knew, Buck talked often about the pretty young girl he rode horses with on his trips to Scotland in glowing terms.

He wasn't blind to her affections, though he never gave her cause to believe he could ever care for her in the manner she deserved. She kicked him in the gut with her warmth and generosity, giving more than she received. Yet her goodness also created a tension between them that made him forget he was a rogue. *That* unnerved him more than anything else.

He'd resigned himself to spending his life searching for a companion who burned his soul with a fire he couldn't put out, who made him want to never stop kissing her.

Not a dear soul like Fiona who never ventured from the mores of society. She was in love with him, but she would never say so.

But he *did* remember one night when the moonlight cast a lovely glow on her skin and her eyes blazed with such want for him, he wondered if he was wrong about her, that a fire burned within her she'd never shown to him or any man but wanted to... no, he wouldn't bring that up. Wouldn't embarrass her or himself.

Not now, not ever.

5

Queenstown, Ireland
11 April 1912
8.30 a.m.

The morning sounds hit Ava's ears. Dogs barking, doors and gates slamming, vendors selling fresh prawns, horse-drawn carts rolling up and down the cobbled streets.

Get up, girl! Today's your day to claim your freedom.

Ava jumped awake, eager to be on her way to the *Titanic*. As her heart raced, she heard—

'Who is in charge here?' a loud voice bellowed from downstairs, making the hairs stand up on the back of her neck. A bitter taste sat on her tongue, her mouth dry. No mistaking the bloodcurdling brashness of the man.

The law.

They couldn't know she was here, could they?

'Mind your horses, mister,' she heard Florie Sims call out. 'I'm coming.'

Ava leaned over the banister and saw two men waiting for the landlady. The one in charge wore dark gray, his hat pulled down to mask not only his face, but what she imagined were his soulless eyes. She'd seen such men in her village, men who proclaimed they were upholding the law.

'I'm looking for Ava O'Reilly,' the man said, poking around downstairs. 'She rooms here?'

Ava gasped. It hadn't taken them long to track her down. Mercy, they'd not put their filthy hands on her.

'And who's asking?' Florie said, indignant.

'Constable Mason-Jones. I have orders to bring her in.'

'Humph, that don't surprise me none. She's upstairs.' Florie shifted her baby to the other hip.

Ava panicked. Oh, dear Jesus, give her the strength to escape this wretched man. She couldn't go back, she *couldn't*. Not when she was so close to boarding the grand ship. Holy Mary, it was a miracle she needed.

And it was right under her nose.

A breath of warm air as fragrant as spring touched her. Ava turned around.

The open window.

She smiled, hope surging in her heart. As fine an escape as if it were the door to heaven.

She had minutes.

She grabbed her small bag and plopped her black felt hat upon her head. She was about to pin her ticket for passage aboard the *Titanic* to her chemise when—

The wooden floor vibrated under her feet. Dear Lord, they were coming for her, as if the constable threw all caution aside, pounding his boots on the stairs.

Ava didn't waste another precious second. Clenching her ticket between her teeth, she tossed her small bag out the window she'd seen the man bolt through yesterday and jumped onto the roof. She shivered and judged the temperature to be about ten degrees. A brisk wind blew her hat off. The landing stunned her, but she didn't stop.

She got to her feet and saw her skirt had caught on a nail. She tugged on it, but it wouldn't budge. She pulled on it, ripping the fabric... and with the wind at her back sending chills through her, she climbed slowly down the shaky trellis laden with braided ivy so she wouldn't fall.

She kept going – what choice did she have? Hanging on for her dear life, promising the Almighty anything if He kept her going... pushing the bothersome ivy out of her face, thankful for the calluses on her hands from scrubbing the carpet keeping her grip strong until—

Her boots hit the ground. Without taking a breath, she grabbed her bag.

'There she is!'

'Stop in the name of the law, Ava O'Reilly!' she heard the constable yell down from the open second-story window.

She looked up at him, disbelieving. *Stop?* Was the man daft?

With her ticket clutched in her fist, Ava took off running, up one winding street and down the next. The smell of cooked onions and cabbages filled her nostrils as she sidestepped piles of horse manure in the middle of the road.

She kept going, the morning dew on the air giving way to a fine salty mist, sweeping away her fear. She wasn't safe. Not yet.

If the landlady confirmed to the constable she had a ticket on the *Titanic*, he and his man would come looking for her and try to stop her from boarding the ship.

What to do?

She found herself along the Deepwater Quay near the railway station. She looked out into the harbor. The *Titanic* was too big to dock here. The passengers and mail would have to be ferried out to the liner by tender.

Mail.

Her eyes grew wide. Bags and bags of mail unloaded from the train and piled up here on the pier waited to be put on board the tenders going out to meet the great ship.

A hundred, maybe two hundred sacks.

Ava blessed herself and swept her eyes upward. Sweet Jesus, was there any better place to hide?

* * *

Two hours later, emerging cautiously from between two large sacks of mail, Ava popped her head up, looking around in a slow circle for the constable. She saw dockworkers carrying sacks of mail loaded on their shoulders and heading for the tender, *Ireland,* to set them aboard. Calling out orders, smoking, the men didn't see her cowering behind the big, burlap bags.

A few passengers arriving late on the train hustled toward the *Ireland* while steerage passengers huddled together on the pier, carrying on with endless chatter and a tune or two. No police in sight.

Ava exhaled. The coast was clear.

A fine nap she'd had, covered by an empty sack and lulled to sleep by the sounds of the sea until she heard the blast from the *Titanic*'s funnel, announcing she was dropping anchor at Roche's Point two miles away.

Her heart rang with joy. She found a strange contentment in hearing the ship's whistle, as if the great liner was out there waiting for *her*, Ava O'Reilly.

She had in her mind to get aboard the ship by hiding in an empty mail sack. Then she heard two dock workers discussing how they dropped the big sacks into the mail storage compartment through the hatchway leading to the coal bunker.

What a sorry ending *that* would be. No, she had no choice but to queue up with the third-class passengers waiting in the lower receiving area of the shipping office, then make her way up the gangway to the tender.

Looking over her shoulder constantly, Ava took her place among the more than one hundred steerage passengers. She watched as each passenger showed their ticket and signed White Star Line contract to the ship's officer before they were allowed to go to the pier.

To her surprise, they were also subjected to a look-over from the American physician examining their eyes for infectious diseases.

Ava shook her head. She had no time for that. The constable could be close by.

What was a girl to do?

The first tender, *Ireland*, was about to leave the dock, but only passengers waiting on the *second* tier of the James Scott & Company shipping office were allowed to board her.

First- and second-class passengers *only*. No steerage allowed.

Ava tapped her foot nervously on the wooden floor. She *had* to be on that boat to America.

If she wasn't...

She pushed on, ducking down and sneaking through the chattering and anxious crowd, trying to keep her wits about her when she heard—

'Who do you think you are, the Queen of Sheba?' said a girl with a long dark braid wrapped around her head. 'Pushing and shoving us.'

'Leave me be, lass, or the devil will take you!' Ava cried out, anxious about being seen. She was thankful for the sunny day, its warmth overcoming the chill, knowing what was in store for her if she were caught.

'Will you listen to her?' the girl said loud enough for everyone to hear. 'A harlot she is, with hair *that* red.'

'Mind your mouth, Hannah,' said a younger girl, poking her in the ribs and urging her to be quiet. 'It's not God's work to spew such talk.' The girl was not to be deterred.

'She's calling on the devil,' Hannah continued, 'with us going to sea without a priest to say a prayer over our poor heads.' She blessed herself.

Ava crouched down out of sight. What in the name of the holy saints had she done to rattle this girl? She'd best not cross paths with her aboard ship. She was the type to cause trouble. The younger lass was a better sort, kind and pious, though she'd be as happy as a Monday pig squealing in a pen if she never laid eyes on them again.

Her heart racing, her fingers tingling, she was aching so bad to get aboard the *Titanic.*

She tried to quiet her breathing, lest she give herself away to the immigration authorities checking each passenger, when she turned and recognized two men walking through the crowd.

The lawmen she'd seen earlier at the lodging house.

They hadn't given up the chase.

Ava pulled away from the crowd, then sneaked up to the second floor of the shipping office. She was but a few feet away from the gangway leading to the tender, *Ireland*. Only a handful of first- and second-class passengers were aboard along with a few journalists. No one was watching her.

She could make it. *She had to try.*

The tender blew a whistle blast, the warning shouted loud and clear.

Ava heard footsteps behind her. She didn't turn around. Through sheer determination and spitting against the wind, she made it to the gangway, her feet skimming over the pier, her breathing tearing at her chest.

Clutching her small traveling bag, she raced across the gangway as it was being raised and slid onto the deck of the tender with her skirts flying up around her.

She didn't care. She'd soon be aboard the *Titanic*.

Then she'd be on her way to America.

How wonderful that is. How bloody wonderful.

6

Buck leaned against the open railing on the Promenade Deck and watched the tender, *Ireland*, draw alongside the ship, rocking back and forth from the swell of the seas. A flock of seagulls circled overhead, their loud cawing grating on his nerves. The sea was calm and would remain so, according to Mr Lightoller, the ship's second officer. They were making excellent time, he said. Twenty knots an hour before they stopped here in Queenstown. If they continued at full speed, they'd arrive in New York earlier than expected.

Not what Buck had in mind.

He needed time to match wits with the sporting gentlemen aboard to make back what he'd lost to Mr Charters. *Without* a marked deck. Buck didn't cheat at cards. He didn't have to. His experience in intelligence work served him well when it came to reading a player's facial expressions and body gestures. He also relied on his quick mind and skilled memory regarding cards played.

'Captain Lord Blackthorn?'

Buck turned to find a deck steward at his elbow. 'Yes?'

'Message for you, milord.' The deck steward handed him a note. Buck opened it.

See you in New York. Signed—Watts.

Buck looked up and saw the phony Mr Watts waving at him as he crossed the White Star Line gangway to board the tender. The bogus millionaire had no choice but to disembark. Word had spread quickly among the first-class gentlemen passengers about his deception and no one would play cards with him.

'Friend of yours, Captain Lord Blackthorn?' said the deck steward.

Buck acknowledged the boatman with a slight nod. 'Mr Watts and I have sailed together before. Pity he was called back to London.'

'Yes, milord. He'll miss the grandest adventure of his life.'

Buck smiled. 'Yes, won't he.'

He was about to turn away when he caught sight of a hatless girl on the tender, *Ireland*. She looked upward at the ship with reverence, as if she couldn't believe what she was seeing. Their eyes met, then, embarrassed, she turned away.

But *he* couldn't stop looking at *her*.

She was the kind of woman men fought over.

A *real* woman, he thought, not a goddess who sprang from a man's imagination, but a living, breathing creature who set his blood on fire.

A woman men cherished more than life itself.

Her hair blowing in the wind like rich, scarlet silk. Slim figure in a wrinkled, brown tweed skirt with a fitted jacket that belied her aristocratic lift of the chin. A girl with a natural beauty that made him ache to hold her in his arms and run his hands through that gorgeous red hair.

He saw her risk her own safety to help the Jesuit novitiate disembarking the ship when he slipped on the wet wooden slats and dropped his bag. She returned it to him, then blessed herself.

So she was an Irish Catholic girl.

Buck smiled. The tendency of their nature was to show a man spirit and temper, like a fine thoroughbred. Such awareness ought to make him proceed with caution, but he was past that. His need to feel a woman in his arms was strong, frustrated as he was with the pomp and absurdities of several ladies in first class making it no secret their stateroom door was open to him.

Beautiful as she was, he was certain the girl was no first-class passenger. Not in that homespun tweed outfit. Steerage, mostly likely. Her long glorious hair, the color of a deep red sunset, whipped about her tight jacket and down to her small waist, blowing in the wind like a sea siren beckoning him.

Who was she? And why was she boarding with the first- and second-class passengers?

Wait. The purser was talking to her as she started up the gangway and she, with her hands on her hips, was trying to explain something to him. The man kept shaking his head. She showed him what appeared to be a ticket. A *white* ticket. Third class.

He was right. He'd have to admire her beauty from afar unless he dared to mingle among the steerage passengers. Something unheard of even by Trey, who wouldn't stoop to dirty his boots with anyone below second class.

Buck held no such view and disdained the social gospel that dictated this way of living. He wouldn't accept the rigid boundaries that shaped the upper-class world he moved in. He found such ideas old-fashioned and meritless when it came to judging the qualities that mattered most.

Honesty and courage.

A thought of a different nature crossed his mind.

It wouldn't take much maneuvering to find his way down to Scotland Road, what the crew called the long, wide passage that ran along the port side of E deck. Tempting thought and the lady was worth the risk. He prided himself on his honor as a gentleman lord, but he had no doubt he wouldn't be the only man on board to notice the girl's stunning beauty. He could remain in control, not lose his head, but what if others couldn't? She'd be at their mercy, though by the way she carried herself, she was no wilting lily flower. Yet she presented a problem that scratched away at the armor of his duty. He was bred to protect, a duty he relished, but it never involved a girl such as this.

He couldn't stop looking at her as she reached the top of the gangway at the same time as a bumboat pulled up alongside the ship, and a man stood up in the dingy and yelled—

'Stop that redheaded girl! She's wanted by the law.'

That piqued Buck's interest even more.

A damsel in distress, is she?

A girl as beautiful as that couldn't be guilty of anything more than making a man fall in love with her.

He couldn't stand by and not help her. The girl had assisted a man of the cloth, *dammit*. It had been a long time since a woman had touched his soul.

Moving with long strides, Buck raced to the stairs leading to B Deck, confronting danger head-on as he always did.

No doubt about it. This trip just became a hell of a lot more interesting.

7

'*Stop*, I say,' yelled the purser. '*Stop!*'

'Not by the sword of Saint Joan, I won't,' Ava yelled out, spinning around on the gangway and running through the shell door leading to the lower deck for second class. She brushed past curious passengers, who didn't stop her.

God help her, the purser was after her and, she imagined, the constable, too.

She heard fast footsteps moving closer behind her. She eluded them by ducking behind a portly gentleman in a tight suit and his wife wrapped up in numerous black furs, mumbling in a language she didn't understand.

Neither did the purser.

He ignored the man calling out to him and kept running down the hallway. He didn't see her. Oh, Mother of God, whatever blessed thing she did in the past to earn this favor, she'd do it again. A *hundred*-fold.

Ava took off in the opposite direction, holding her small bag to her chest, running wildly and scolding herself for her own foolishness. If she hadn't been staring at the handsome gentleman, the constable wouldn't have seen her.

That had done her in.

Her with her fancy thoughts about how grand it would be up there on deck with him, standing under a delicate ivory lace parasol and holding onto his arm. He had a bronzed, raw appeal that made her tremble inside.

A wise girl has no time for the likes of him, she could hear her mum say and right she was. Look at her, pulling at her wool collar and breaking into a cold sweat, breathing so fast she thought she'd die if she didn't stop to catch her breath.

Ava kept running down the hallway until she came to a pair of baize doors. She had no idea where they led to. Did it matter?

She bolted through them into a lighted hallway, racing up the stairway, then the next, the steel tread beneath her feet giving way to smooth flooring. Polished, off-white wood hugged the walls adorned with fancy cornice work. Overhead lighting from rounded bulbs guided her.

Taking two or three heavy breaths to calm the pounding in her chest, she took a moment to get her wits about her.

She was safe. For now.

Closing her eyes, she leaned against the staircase wall, wild thoughts racing through her mind. Where was she to go?

'I've been looking for you.'

She opened her eyes and let out a loud gasp. She was taken aback by the utterly amused expression on the man's face. Dear sweet Jesus, it was *him*. The gentleman she'd seen on deck, watching her. And here he was, the fine scent of him filling her nostrils with a heady perfume she couldn't resist. What swayed her not to run was his sheer masculinity, drawing her to him as she looked him straight in the eye. Like a burst of golden sunshine he was, shining down on her after she'd been drenched by a cold, drizzling rain in her dark, gray world.

What lass wouldn't fall for his blarney? And like it, too. He was a handsome man, with black hair and black eyes that held dark secrets that could make her blush. He had an aristocratic air about him that tamed his wildness just enough to keep him on balance.

And put her *off* balance.

And that voice. Smooth as glass but deep as the darkest night when a girl should be asleep, but instead dreaming of him whispering in her ear and slipping his hands around her waist before he stole a kiss.

Aye, he'd be the undoing of her. She had to find her way down to steerage since she'd never pass for anything else. Her with Paris frocks and evening gowns? The saints were laughing at her, more so because she wished she could linger with the gentleman, flirt with him. That was a danger to her heart no girl in her predicament could afford. The law had found her and she'd best be quick about escaping.

Where was she? The hallway with its ornate walls and rich flooring spoke of a grandness she'd seen only in the manor house where she worked.

Make your move.

Stepping away quickly, almost too quickly, she flinched when his strong hands grabbed her around the waist, then hoisted her up into the air. Oh, the grandness of a knight he had and the strength of a warrior. But he could be as dangerous as a dragon's fiery breath for the likes of her. The heat of his body stole the dampness from her wet clothes penetrating her bones, warming her. Making her want something from him that melted her like ice under his burning gaze.

By the Virgin Mary, what next?

Ava wrestled to get away from him.

Struggling, she cried out, 'Let me go!'

'Be quiet, you little hellion,' the man said, his voice ringing with authority. She shivered. Did he have to sound so wonderful that a girl wanted to hear more? 'I know you're in trouble—'

'*Me*, Ava O'Reilly, in trouble?' she said, chin up, his powerful and pleasing presence arousing her. 'What makes you think *that*, sir?'

He put her down but didn't release his hold on her. 'Steerage passengers don't belong up here in first class.'

First class? She blinked. That explained the ornately carved banisters and wide staircases. She'd heard the steerage passengers extolling about the luxury on board, from the swimming pool and Turkish baths to fresh strawberries served in first class.

'Now if you'll point me in the right direction to the third-class deck,' she said, showing him her ticket, 'I'll be on my way.'

'And right into the hands of the law.'

She took in a deep breath. So he *did* know.

He continued, 'You have no choice but to allow me to offer you my protection.'

'And who are you, sir?'

He bowed slightly. 'Captain Lord James Blackthorn, at your service.' He winked at her and her toes curled. 'My friends call me Buck.'

By the holy stones, he was offering her escape.

Ava shivered and not from the cold. She'd never be safe with the likes of him making her blush and her knees wobble. Aye, his good looks could steal a girl's soul away from her. He was tall, muscular and possessed an arrogance that intrigued her. Not to mention a heat building inside her that warmed her insides like melted honey. He seemed more alive to her than any man she'd ever seen. A man who knew his charm and savored it.

'And why would you help the likes of me?' Ava demanded with a proud air.

He smiled at that, continuing to stare at her, his eyes dark and searching. 'Come with me and find out.'

Ava laughed, disbelieving. After all she'd been through and now this. Why did God put such temptation in her path? The devil himself he was, mischievous, wickedly self-assured and alive with a vitality that set a girl's pulse racing.

'Escape with you where?' she asked, the words flying fast and quick between them.

'To my cabin in first class,' he said.

'*First class?*' she said. 'With all them rich swells?'

It was too much for her poor, tired mind to take in. Here were riches beyond those she'd ever dreamed. Here was the smell of grandness, that rich, seductive, cloying smell that grabbed her heart and singed her soul.

To run off with such a man was a sin, the priest reminded her each Thursday in the confessional box, but the law was after her. They'd take her back to Cork in chains with the shame of stealing marked upon her forehead.

Ava was at a loss. What was she to do? No time to escape on her own. She could hear the sound of voices and footsteps pounding on the stairs, coming closer and closer.

'We must go, *now!*' he said brusquely. 'Or I won't be able to help you.'

The steadiness in his dark eyes wavered for a moment, as if they were caught in a sudden storm. A rush of adrenaline raced through her at hearing his chilly tone. The handsome gent wasn't playing games. He knew the consequences if they caught her. Locked up, then sent back to Ireland.

''Tis true what you say but...' She hesitated, still unsure.

He leaned down and smiled at her in such a way she wanted to believe him. 'I want nothing but to see you continue your journey... I swear on my oath as a soldier in His Majesty's service no harm will come to you.'

His words brought her to tears, though she refused to let them fall and show weakness in front of him. She had to do what he wished and face the consequences later. He wasn't a bad sort like Lord Holm with his glib talk. He was dressed fancy, but he was a man who'd served his country. That settled it with her.

Ava nodded. 'Aye, I'll come with you, Captain Lord Blackthorn.'

'*Hurry*, they'll be upon us in a minute.' He grabbed her hand and pulled her close behind him. Why did that feel so right?

Holy Mary, Mother of God, she prayed in a somewhat uncertain state of mind, her feet flying over the smooth flooring down the long hallway. Did the holy saints have something more alarming in store for her?

She found out when he ordered her to take off her clothes.

She'd nearly wrenched his arm off when he pulled her into his cabin, letting go with words no lady would utter, alerting the nosy stewardess smoking a cigarette in the darkened hallway. What if she told the captain?

Aye, she'd take her chances with the handsome lord.

'I asked you to remove your wet and ripped clothes,' he said.

'And why should I?' She jutted out her hip, determined to hold her own against him.

He turned around with his back to her.

'There, I'm not looking at you,' he said firmly. '*Now* will you take off those wet clothes so I can get on with my plan to save you?'

'You mean so you can turn back around and get an eyeful?' She laughed.

'You're trying my patience, Ava,' he said, perturbed. 'If you don't cooperate, I will have no choice but to turn you over to the captain.'

'Will you?' she said, stalling. 'If it's only a kiss you want, I can kiss you with my clothes *on*.'

That made the gentleman laugh. 'I have a proposal for you on a grander scale and it *doesn't* involve kissing.'

'By the souls of the martyred saints, you waste no time, milord.' She hesitated, trying to catch her breath. 'If I agree to do what you want, what happens after?'

'I will hide you where no one will find you.'

'And for *that* you expect me to sin with the likes of you?'

He teased her with, 'You could do worse.'

'And who says I couldn't do better?' she shot back. 'I'll find me a nice gentleman, one who won't ask bawdy things of me.'

He turned around and came toward her. 'Shall we let the captain decide your fate?'

She stepped back.

'I swear upon my mum's rosary, I'm not guilty of any crime,' Ava insisted, 'but if you're like most gentlemen, you won't believe me.'

He didn't press her further and insisted he'd offered her his protection without any strings attached and he was honor bound to stand by that.

'I'm still waiting for you to remove your clothes,' he said, agitated.

Ava was more intrigued by the double sink and commode. The canopied bed and elegant furniture polished so shiny it glowed. As grand as any room in Cameron Manor. *What to do?* The price to be paid for such grand living was her freedom. The very thing she sought to find on the *Titanic*.

She muttered a prayer, then said, 'If you're a true gentleman, sir, you'll turn back around and keep your eyes to yourself.'

'As you wish.'

'Now your mind can *imagine* what your eyes wanted to see.'

'I'm sure I won't be disappointed.'

'Skip your fancy talk, Captain Lord Blackthorn. *If* I do your bidding, and I'm still discussing that with the Almighty, it will only be to save my arse.'

'You needn't worry, my dear, I have no intention of taking advantage of you,' he said honestly. 'I've never made love to any woman unless *she* was willing.'

'Then what *do* you want of me, sir?' Glory be, she didn't see that coming.

'I want you to meet someone.' He tossed her a blanket to wrap around herself, then faced her. 'I can't introduce you to a countess looking like a street beggar.'

A countess?

She didn't protest when he hustled her into the bed with the night curtains drawn, and then rang for the stewardess. He charmed the woman with a phony story about needing a female attendant's uniform so the girl he met in second class could come and go without curious passengers asking questions.

Who would believe such a tale? Then again, why not?

The man was irresistible to women. And *she*, Ava O'Reilly, was no different. He was strong and appealing with a dash of the devil in him.

His lordship threw open the curtains after the stewardess left, dangling a black uniform and ruffled white apron in front of her nose. 'For you, Ava.'

'You want me to put on a *maid's* uniform?' Ava blurted out. 'I'll not do it.'

'You *must* and you *will*,' he said, exasperated, tossing the uniform to her and then turning around so she could dress. 'It's the only way I can help you.'

'I don't understand.' Ava fussed with the buttons on the uniform.

'You will when you meet the countess. She needs a lady's maid and since you're in need of a place to hide, I can't think of a better solution to *both* your problems.'

'Why would she hire the likes of me?' Ava asked, curious but still cautious.

'Her maid had an unfortunate accident and the countess needs assistance during the voyage.'

Ava shook her head, not believing the fates wouldn't leave her alone. Making her work for an aristocratic lady who was presumably lamenting over losing her maid as if it were the worst thing that could happen to her. Another creature cut from the same dull cloth as Lady Olivia.

Yet she had no choice, did she?

'I'm waiting, Ava,' he said impatiently, tapping his feet. To her surprise, he didn't try to peek.

Well, what's stopping you? Your pride?

Her mum always said she was a natural rebel and defied all authority, whether God or manmade. Ava couldn't deny it. She abhorred the strict rules of class that kept her from getting an education, but the world was on the brink of change.

It wasn't changing fast enough for her.

'You must understand, your lordship. I'm leaving my homeland to be rid of such frippery and do fine and proper work.' Ava started putting her clothes back on. She wasn't going to America all blushes and roses only to be pushed back into service. 'No, milord, I'll take my chances with the captain.'

'Then you won't change your mind?'

'No.'

'Too bad,' he said with a smug attitude. 'The countess's stateroom has its own private bathroom.'

Her eyes bugged out. 'You wouldn't fool me?'

He shook his head. 'I hear there are only two tubs in steerage for seven hundred passengers.'

'*Two* tubs for all them people?'

'Rather cozy, if you ask me.'

'And you call yourself a gentleman?' Ava asked. A girl *might* be convinced to meet this countess for a *private* bathroom.

He smirked.

'Sure of yourself, aren't you?' Ava said, putting the uniform on right quick. She fastened the buttons down the front, adjusted the pert round white collar and cuffs, pulled the apron with the White Star Line red flag logo tight around her waist, and then plopped the small white cap on her head. 'There. It's done.'

The gentleman turned and nodded his approval, then helped her push her long hair under the cap. He fancied to impress this countess by showing up with a lady's maid so she wouldn't have to lift her little finger to fasten a hook or pour a cup of tea.

'I'm thinking she has two heads,' Ava blurted out, not sorry she had.

'You're wrong, Ava,' his lordship said with reverence. 'The countess is a poetic and gentle soul, a true lady.'

'Who is she?' she asked, envious of the titled lady he held in such high esteem.

'Fiona Winston-Hale,' he told her. 'Sixth Countess of Marbury.'

An arrogant, silly woman, this countess is, Ava decided, following the gentleman down the hallway to the electric lift, keeping a discreet distance behind him. She showed humility when they entered the first-class elevator, standing instead of sitting on the soft sofa as her station dictated and keeping her hands folded like a good servant.

Inside she was feeling scared. The beating of her heart was like the loud ticking of a clock, much like the ongoing repetition of her life.

Tick tock... tick tock... always searching, but never finding the freedom she craved.

And now believing his lordship was interested in her, only to find out he didn't want her at all.

She was merely a way for his lordship to impress this countess.

Holy Mary, Mother of God, Ava could well imagine what her mum would say.

That she was a bloomin' fool.

And right she was.

8

'Countess,' said Captain Lord Blackthorn, 'may I present Miss Ava O'Reilly of County Cork, Ireland.'

'I'm pleased you've agreed to assist me during the crossing,' said the countess, her eyes glimmering with obvious suspicion as she looked her up and down. Ava expected little respect from this young woman wearing a silk dress the color of a tart persimmon. In all her time as a housemaid, she'd never seen a titled lady treat her maid well.

God help her ladyship if she knew what Ava was thinking. It was shameful, even for the likes of her. She was thinking that the countess wasn't pretty enough to win the heart of his lordship with her square face and small mouth.

But she had an advantage Ava didn't have.

She was a lady.

'Thank you, your ladyship,' Ava said, lowering her eyes and making a curtsy, though it wasn't perfect. If she was going to be a lady's maid to keep herself out of prison, she'd do it proper. She had her pride and right now it was still stinging from the rebuff she'd received from the gentleman the countess addressed as 'Buck.'

The countess *did* have a lovely smile, Ava had to admit, but that didn't do much to warm her heart toward her. She was still the enemy, a rival for the attention of a man so far above her, Ava might as well be asking for a place in heaven next to St Michael himself.

Still, Ava was frustrated, fighting against the turmoil within her roiling about like avenging angels. She was filled with an urge to run and forget this nonsense, but a voice deep in her head warned her not to break the promise she made. If she had nothing else, she had given her word and that counted for something.

She'd promised his lordship she'd behave, and she would.

For now.

'I shall leave you two ladies alone to have a chat and get better acquainted,' Captain Lord Blackthorn said, smiling at them, the twinkle in his eye telling her he'd rather stay and watch the sparks fly.

Then off he went. Why did the room have a chill after he'd gone?

Ava lingered by the door for some time before she met the countess's gaze. She found herself embarrassed, unable to move. *This woman don't want me here. Why? Because his lordship brought me?*

The countess continued to glare at her, her clear gray eyes shining like polished glass, yet it wasn't hate she saw in them, but sadness. She'd seen that look before. On Lady Olivia's face when her beau had flirted with her. As if, in spite of her grand title and his lordship making nice with her, she was a lonely soul.

Ava began to tremble. Had she been wrong about the woman?

She made a sincere effort to regain her composure when the countess asked her to serve tea from the lovely service on a silver tray brought to her cabin by the stewardess. Porcelain cups and sugar sticks, lemon dainties and small cakes topped with gingerbread spices that made her nose wrinkle.

Or was it the awkward stares from the stewardess that made her uneasy?

Titanic's whistles gave a long blast, the signal for the tenders and small craft to stand clear. Ava's heart raced. They'd be dropping the gangways and casting off the lines and the ship would be underway again.

She was so happy about going to America, she began humming an old Irish melody. And in first class, too. She took in the beautiful décor of the stateroom. Carved wooden moldings edged the ceiling and doorway, there was a brass bed with fancy embroidered coverlets and chairs covered with red velvet upholstery.

'I'm curious,' said the countess, her upper lip twitching as she put the delicate demitasse cup to her mouth, 'how did Buck find you on this big ship?'

'I lost my way when I came on board.' Ava's mouth watered, her stomach growling.

'His lordship rescued you?' The countess smiled, a warm memory lighting up her eyes.

'Yes, milady.'

'I'm not surprised. Buck has a habit of rescuing damsels in distress.'

'From the look in your eye, your ladyship,' Ava said, watching everything the countess did with the interest of someone curious as well as envious, 'I'd say you're also in distress.'

'You *are* an impertinent girl,' the woman said, though not with anger, surprising Ava.

'I saw how you looked at Captain Lord Blackthorn...' Ava stopped. She knew herself well enough to know her outspokenness could get the better of her.

'Interesting. He never notices, but you did.' She sighed. 'I shall put that into a poem.'

'You write poetry?' Ava asked, again surprised.

'Yes, I draw comfort and peace from expressing my view of what I see and hear.' She put down her cup and pushed it away from her. 'It allows me to pour out my soul.'

What was she *really* saying? Ava wondered, this woman who seemed to have everything a girl like her yearned for and had no hope of ever having.

That she was lonely?

The countess lifted her eyes upward as if asking God for help, a move that touched Ava deeply.

'Recite to me a poem you've written,' Ava asked, interested in what a countess would write about.

'If you insist.' The countess cleared her throat. 'She walks with the grace of a butterfly... her feet ne'er touching the ground... each step as smooth as silk... her skin as polished as porcelain... she is surrounded by a perpetual mist... she is not a woman... but a ghost with wings.'

'That was beautiful, Countess,' Ava said, impressed with how the countess held her head and hands in delicate poses as she spoke. Like the ladies in the classic paintings she'd seen at Cameron Bally Manor House. '*You* are the ghost, am I right?'

'Is it so obvious?' the countess asked, disturbed.

'Only to me, your ladyship,' Ava said honestly. 'I feel that way too, as if I'm floating through life without experiencing it. That's why I'm on my way to America, to make a new life for myself.'

'Then we have something in common, Ava.'

'We *do*, your ladyship?'

'Yes, I'm going to America for a new life as well.' She stood up and looked out the porthole. Ava couldn't see the expression on her face, but she could hear the catch in her voice when she said, 'My fiancé is traveling with me aboard ship. I'm going to be married in New York.'

Ava didn't hold back her tongue quick enough before she blurted out, 'To his lordship?'

'No, not to Buck,' the countess said, turning, her face lighting up when she spoke his name. 'Don't think I haven't tried. But I don't have what you have.'

'*Me*, your ladyship?'

'Yes, Ava. You have that certain something that attracts a man even more than a pretty face.'

'I don't understand, your ladyship.'

'Don't try to understand it, just accept it.' The countess looked carefully at her, her brows narrowing. 'Be aware, it can also bring you heartache.'

'You sound like my mum,' Ava said, her eyes misting at the memory. 'She said I was trouble as soon as I could walk when I tipped over the bowl holding the holy water. I spilled it all over myself and the village priest.'

The countess laughed. 'Oh, Ava, you have a way about you that's hard for anyone to resist.'

'It does my heart good to see you laugh, your ladyship,' Ava said, meaning it. She was beginning to like her, then she caught herself.

Hold back, Ava, my girl. Don't like her too much.

She still didn't trust her. True, she wasn't like Lady Olivia with her snotty airs, but she was one of *them*. An aristocrat, and in her mind, they couldn't be trusted. That put her in a dilemma. Did that include his lordship, too? He *did* keep his word, and for that she *might* forgive him his noble birth.

She assumed her position as a servant and said in a respectful manner, 'What dress will you wear to dinner, milady?'

'I'm dining in my stateroom tonight.'

'With your fiancé?' Ava asked, knowing better than to meddle, but she couldn't help herself.

'I'm dining alone,' the countess said, then went on to explain her fiancé was Treyton Brady, a wealthy industrialist and what they called 'new money' in America.

Why was she marrying *him* instead of his lordship? Ava wondered.

'I'm certain Trey will find suitable female companionship for the evening.'

Ava was taken aback. So he was like most gentlemen of his class. No wonder the countess was in a dither.

'Why don't you get rid of him, your ladyship, and find yourself a good man?' Ava said, forgetting her place and not apologizing for it.

'If only it were that simple.' The countess waited for her to refill her cup, and when she didn't, she set it down. 'I have obligations that involve things you don't understand.'

'What about *your* wants, your ladyship?' Ava tapped her fingers on her apron, wondering why the countess didn't pour herself more tea.

Are you daft, girl?

The Lord save her, she'd already forgotten her duties. Without missing a beat, she refilled the countess's cup.

'Don't *you* have the right to be happy?' Ava continued.

'I gave up that right when I was born a countess.'

Ava shook her head in dismay. 'I thought being poor was the worst thing that could happen to a girl.'

'No, Ava,' the countess said in a clear voice. 'The worst thing is to be in love with one man and have to marry another.'

* * *

Tidying up the cabin, the countess's words reverberated in her head, telling her this fine lady was in love with a man who didn't love her.

Captain Lord Blackthorn. *Buck*.

A happy tingling ran up and down her spine. Ava couldn't stop thinking about him and *that*, she realized, was her sin.

And her just knowing him these few hours, why, that kind of interest in a man was unheard of for a lass like her. Upstanding and kind. He wasn't hard to look at either. Tall with black hair and eyes that radiated even darker against his white silk shirt so impeccably tailored with a perfect collar. Dark suit coat that fit snugly and emphasized his broad shoulders, charcoal flannel trousers.

Even at sea, he had the air of a gentleman at home in a country house. Captivating and magically appealing to her youthful fantasy. Ava paid no mind to the rigid rules of society. She forged ahead with the curiosity of a schoolgirl, believing the fairy tale could come true if she wished hard enough.

Stop your dreaming, girl, he's not for the likes of you. This Captain Lord Blackthorn has a mysterious way about him that speaks of high living and getting his own way.

A man who lives for the thrill of the chase. Didn't he track you down and find you hiding in first class?

Have you no shame, Ava O'Reilly?

Counting Hail Marys in her head, Ava admitted she didn't.

She went about her duties, hanging up the silk dress the countess had worn earlier, noting the ivory lace collar needed repair and a tea stain marked the sleeve. If only she had essence of lemon to remove it. She dared not ask the countess. She was resting in her bedroom and requested not to be disturbed.

Ava arranged her ladyship's toiletries, noting the countess had packed the necessities, including hairpins, a toothbrush, tooth powder, cold cream, face powder, safety pins, collar buttons and needles and thread.

Even a hot water bag.

She was setting out her ladyship's dressing gown and hairbrush with a pearl inlayed handle when a knock on the door startled her.

Her heart stopped. Captain Lord Blackthorn?

Ava opened the door, straining to appear composed and matter of fact when in reality she was eager to see him again.

The saints were in a playful mood and instead of his lordship, a beguiling young man dressed in a black dinner jacket, white shirt and tie stood smiling back at her.

The countess's fiancé, she guessed.

Treyton Brady.

'What happened to the stewardess I requested to take care of the countess?' Trey asked, leaning against the doorway. Grinning, he looked her up and down with a traveling eye she found most uncomfortable and which made her mouth go dry. 'Though I must say you *are* an improvement.'

An American by his arrogance *and* his accent.

He folded his arms across his chest, waiting. Ava studied him. Treyton Brady was good-looking in a boyish way, but his smiling eyes looked older than his years. Sad, somehow. As if he shielded his thoughts from anyone who got too close.

He must have sensed her perceptive skills, for he gave her a big wink to put her off.

'I'm not leaving,' he continued, 'until you tell me who you are.'

'Since you ask,' Ava said hotly, 'and I'm in the mood for telling, I'm the countess's new lady's maid.'

'Really?' Trey said. 'Who hired you for the position?'

'Captain Lord Blackthorn, sir.'

He laughed. 'So Buck's not the only one slumming.'

'Sir?'

'Never mind. I'm here to escort the countess to the dining saloon.'

'She's dining in her cabin tonight, sir.'

He breathed out a sigh of relief. 'Tell her I came by and I'll look in on her later.' He started to leave, then turned around and said in a flirty manner, 'Before I go, what is your name?'

'Ava, sir.'

'We'll be seeing a lot of each other over the next few days, Ava.' He paused but Ava remained silent. He was baiting her. 'Quite a lot.'

'Yes, sir,' she said, gritting her teeth and doing her best to smile at him.

'By the way, Ava, if you're free later, I'm in need of a shine on my boots,' he said, tongue-in-cheek.

'Is that so, Mr Brady?' she shot back. 'Isn't it a shame I'm too busy tending to her ladyship to shine *your* boots.'

'Did you tell that to Captain Lord Blackthorn also?' he asked smugly.

Her mouth dropped open and she found herself unable to say a word. An unnerving occurrence for Ava. She was always ready with the fancy talk.

Not this time.

Before she could sputter a syllable, Mr Brady was off, whistling a tune. She peeked around the door and watched him walk down the hallway in a jaunty manner. He must have sensed her watching him. He turned around and smiled at her.

Trying to charm her he was. The gall of the man. Polish his boots. What boldness. Acting as if he was an aristocrat and spoiled by nature when she knew he was new money, lacking in pedigree *and* manners.

Another thought gripped her, setting off a devil of a chill in her that made her shiver. Would he tell her ladyship about her outspokenness?

What's got into you, girl?

Ava shook her head, knowing there were times to keep her mouth shut.

She grabbed a needle and thread from the countess's toiletries and began repairing the fragile lace collar on her ladyship's silk dress with tiny, neat stitches as the good sisters had taught her. A sudden need to do something with her hands filled her, while her mind went off in so many different directions she didn't know *what* to think.

Everything had changed with the arrival of Treyton Brady. Did the man have no feelings at all for the countess? A fine lady she was and yet he was acting like that.

A man of his wealth had great responsibilities and social duties, but he seemed more interested in flirting with her. Needing attention and wanting to be liked for himself and not his fortune. Pampered, spoiled, yet lost somehow, as if a great emptiness lay behind his questioning eyes. As if he didn't know where he belonged.

Like her.

A fine lot they were.

The countess, Captain Lord Blackthorn and Mr Brady.

A ship of lost souls.

Why did she get the feeling her life was now intertwined with theirs? As if she didn't have enough of her own problems.

She was wise enough to recognize she'd best mind her own business and not meddle with things she didn't understand.

Like why the countess was marrying Mr Brady.

She couldn't forget that with one wrong move she'd be back in third class, locked up like a drunken sailor, and then handed over to the authorities in New York.

Whatever happened, she wasn't going to serve time for a crime she didn't commit. This she swore on her sainted mother's rosary, even if she had to jump overboard and swim to America, as foolish a thought as *that* may be.

Be careful, Ava, my girl, she could hear her da's words ringing in her ears. *The sea is a cold, unforgiving grave for them she claims.*

All this talk of unsinkable and folks in first class acting as if they were sainted martyrs with everything owed to them because they wore lacy French drawers instead of cotton ones.

They weren't her betters on this ship.

They were all travelers on the Almighty's ocean, steerage and first class alike, and God help anyone who didn't know that.

She couldn't shake the feeling of dread that had come over her.

9

'You're on a lucky streak tonight, Captain Lord Blackthorn,' said the man sitting across from him, his mood glum.

'It's the sea air,' Buck said, leaning over and gathering up his winnings. His four of a kind had taken the pot. 'It sets a man's blood on fire.'

'I know a lady who achieves that same goal,' said the man on his left. Mr Guggenheim.

The men around the table laughed.

Except Buck. His mood had changed. All he could think about was the Irish girl.

Ava. A wildcat. Fighting him every step of the way until she realized it was for her own good.

It took all his mental capabilities to keep his mind on the card game. It worked. Over five thousand pounds tonight to line his pockets. He grinned. The girl might turn out to be his lucky charm after all.

'Speaking of fiery females, sirs,' added Mr Guggenheim, 'did you hear about the beautiful thief who sneaked aboard at Queenstown?'

A second gentleman gulped down his highball, then asked, 'What did she steal? Gold? Jewels?'

'I heard she poisoned a man when he wouldn't marry her,' added the third gent, lighting up a cigar.

'If she's as good-looking as they say,' said Mr Guggenheim, 'I'll take my chances.'

'You may get your wish,' chimed in his fellow passenger. 'The ship's first officer believes she's hiding in an empty stateroom. Could be the one next to you.'

Buck nearly choked. *His* stateroom was next to the American millionaire's.

'God knows the ship is only filled to half capacity, gentlemen,' said Mr Guggenheim. He turned to Buck, who had been strangely silent throughout the conversation. 'Have you seen our mystery woman, Captain Lord Blackthorn?'

'No,' Buck said in a careful manner, then added with a smirk, 'If I had, you gentlemen wouldn't stand a chance.'

His mind reeled. Five hours of playing poker after meeting up with the most beautiful woman he'd ever seen, only to hear the search for her was still on, was enough to rattle a man's nerves.

'From what I've heard, Captain Lord Blackthorn is quite a ladies' man,' said the gent smoking a cigar and not hiding the tone of envy in his voice.

Buck eyed him suspiciously. 'On whose authority, sir?'

The man blew smoke his way. 'Lady Pennington mentioned it to my wife.'

'The lady is mistaken,' Buck said, maintaining his composure. Inside he was amused. Was his former lover boasting or complaining?

'Perhaps,' the man conceded with a sly look to the other gentlemen. 'Didn't I see you board at Southampton with the Countess of Marbury?'

'Along with her American fiancé,' Buck insisted. He rose from the table and patted his breast pocket holding his winnings. He had no desire to get into an argument with these gentlemen when he had five more days aboard the liner to skillfully relieve them of their ready cash. 'Time for me to turn in, gentlemen. Until tomorrow night.'

Wandering out of the smoking room with his thoughts preoccupied, Buck paid little attention to the fog rolling in on deck. He was worried. What if Ava left the cabin and was discovered?

Nothing he could say would keep her out of the hands of the law. Yet he wanted to, desperately. Ava touched a nerve in him buried too long. She was real. Through and through, like a beautiful gem smudged with the dust of time but underneath, she was pure and fine. A rare woman when most females he knew sparkled with a false glow that dimmed after a while.

Not her.

She was worthy of a man's protection for no other reason than her honesty and fervent joy in believing she *could* better herself even in a world that wouldn't allow it. For a brief minute, he wondered if his father, the duke, would intercede for her on his behalf. He tossed that idea out quickly. The Duke of Clarington lived by a strict set of rules that governed society and wouldn't stoop to fund a local charity, much less give assistance to an Irish servant girl.

Buck replayed the afternoon's events over and over again in his mind, trying to decide whether he was a knight in shining armor or a damn fool. He couldn't be both.

Was that what fascinated him about the Irish girl? That she was a work in progress?

And *he* was her mentor?

Not a feasible proposition for a man in his position with little funds to finance such an undertaking. And why should he? He firmly believed no tactics, gentlemanly or otherwise, would work with the girl. She was safe with the countess, so his obligation to her was finished. He wouldn't see her for the rest of the crossing.

Who was he fooling?

Himself.

He couldn't forget her easy laugh or her sparkling green eyes, or how beautiful she'd looked when he'd pulled open the curtains on his bed.

He'd nearly lost his mind.

Buck suspected she was playing games with him and believed she was fully dressed. But no, she'd gone and done it on her own. Undressed after telling him she wouldn't.

He wasn't used to being challenged and he didn't like it. He would never force the issue. He considered himself a man of moral high ground when it came to how he treated a lady.

He smiled. Then again, Ava O'Reilly was no lady and that intrigued him. Along with her spunk and ability to speak her mind in a world where nobody did. Or was it the fact he didn't *want* to know what crime she was accused of? That he wished to keep his image of her as an angel wronged for as long as possible. He also had to admit his recent affair with Lady Pennington had left him with a deflated ego when the woman went back to her husband when he had had a bad run in a card game and couldn't keep up with her extravagant lifestyle.

'You can't afford me, darling,' she'd whispered in his ear. 'And *I* can't afford to be poor. What would my friends say?'

Ava was a different sort. The girl was too stubborn for her own good and insisted on honesty above all. Yet she was shrewd and remained cool under pressure when she challenged him, but he'd bet a night's poker winnings she was still an innocent.

But he knew he was playing with fire if the girl were found out. There'd be hell to pay with the captain for sheltering a criminal, even if she *was* a beautiful woman.

It wouldn't add to his reputation as a gentleman, though such things had never bothered him before. He plunged into an adventure first and asked questions later. He'd rather forge ahead than simply wonder what *might* have been.

Buck rather enjoyed the idea of a woman needing the protection he could offer her as a gentleman and *not* what he could buy her. His gambler's instinct never steered him wrong, making him dead certain none of the talk about her was true. Still, he had every intention of asking the Irish girl what her crime was before they docked in New York. Until then, he intended to hide her by putting her in plain sight.

With thoughts of their secret escapade continuing to make him smile, Buck decided to abandon the Promenade Deck and go up on the Boat Deck before retiring. A brisk breeze blew along the deck, making him pull up his coat collar to keep out the chill. He felt no creaking or shuddering beneath his feet as he had on other ships. Slicing through the cold North Atlantic at record speed, the *Titanic* had a steadiness about her that amazed him.

No doubt the girl would leave him in New York with half her story untold. *That* disturbed him more than anything else. Why was he drawn to her with such intensity? If she were a burning flame, he'd still want to touch her, be with her, no matter what the price. His mind gave birth to numerous fantasies, seeing her again, holding her, kissing her.

He continued walking, when he saw a woman wearing an ankle-length black coat, the wide collar and cuffs trimmed with silken braid and a distinctive plaid inlay.

The countess.

The woman's hood slipped off and her long red hair billowed over her shoulders like rolls of silk. It caught the glow of light as the wind's breath curled it like fire before she disappeared into the dark shadows on deck.

Ava. Damn it all.

What fool notion was she up to now?

'Have you gone mad, Ava?' he said, racing over to her and taking her by the elbow. 'They're searching for you everywhere.'

She turned around and grinned at him, lightening up his mood. 'Evening, your lordship. It does my heart good to think you're worried about my safety.'

'You were told to stay in your cabin, but when do you ever do what you're told?' he said, exasperated. 'Don't answer that. I already know the answer. *Never*.'

'I couldn't sleep, milord,' she said, her words honest and sincere. 'The countess said I could borrow her coat, so here I am.'

She wasn't trying to vex him, but she was doing a good job of it. A woman alone on deck this time of night was certain to be observed by the ship's officers and questioned for her own safety.

'Don't you realize you're in danger?' he asked, guiding her along the Boat Deck past folded deck chairs, the evening air brisk and sharp.

'I wanted to see if the stars out tonight are the same stars you see in Ireland.'

'Are they?' Buck said, softening toward her as they leaned over the rail. The cloudy sky they'd experienced earlier had given way to starry sparkles he swore shone brighter than on his last crossing. The North Star, the Milky Way. The view of the stars and the calm ocean took his breath away, made more so by the lack of lifeboats cluttering up the first-class section of the deck so as not to spoil the view. He moved closer to her, his shoulder brushing up against the soft velvet wrapped around her like a night carpet. She shivered, shuffling her boots on the wooden deck. A sudden need to touch her swept over him.

If only he could.

'No,' she said, unaware of the urges overtaking him, her breath misty, her words catching on the sea spray. 'The stars are brighter here at sea.'

'Why is that?' he asked, curious.

'Because here they can wander about in the big, black sky anywhere they choose.'

'And in Ireland?' he asked, guiding her away from the entrance to the first-class staircase lest an officer spot them.

'There they have to obey the rules and stay in their own patch of dark sky,' she said, turning and looking at him square on. She sat down on an empty bench. Her eyes glistened with mist or tears, he couldn't tell which. 'There they can never be free.'

'If you were a star,' he asked, 'where would you be?'

'Here, your lordship,' she said without hesitation, 'where I can glow the brightest. Look, there, on the sea.' She pointed to the starlight glistening like glass. Buck followed her gaze, the sparkle so bright since it was the only open space on the ship. 'So still it is, as if someone threw an enchanted stone into the ocean and calmed the waters.'

'What if you lost your way?'

'It would be worth it... to be free.'

Her words took him aback, making him wonder more than ever who she was, where she came from and why in God's name the law was after her.

'You *are* a dreamer, Ava, but tonight is no time for wishing for what we can't have.' He took her arm in his and stopped. The way she looked at him with such sadness disturbed him.

They sat close together, their frosty breaths as one, their eyes meeting, yet she revealed nothing more. As if she chose to keep her secrets hidden from him for a while longer. He *should* let her go, but first he must tell her what he knew.

'They haven't given up looking for you, Ava. If you're caught, I won't be able to do anything to help you.'

His words hit her hard, sobering her up. She nodded. 'I understand, Captain Lord Blackthorn.'

He let out his breath, relieved she knew. He came very close to taking her in his arms and tilting her head back for a kiss.

He didn't.

That would be the ruination of them both.

* * *

Lying in bed in her cabin, Ava looked back on everything that had happened to her since she had run away from the great house in County Cork. She had escaped from a lie that would be the death of her and found her way aboard the *Titanic*.

Into the arms of Captain Lord Blackthorn.

They're searching for you everywhere, Ava.

If they caught her, she'd never see his lordship again. That saddened her more than she thought it would.

She shivered, still chilled from her walk on the open deck. In her thoughts, she was safe and warm, wrapped in his embrace. Holding her against his chest, his lips brushing her hair.

It hadn't happened, but she wanted it to, and she believed so did he.

That was enough for the likes of her. If every moment, every step had been to bring her closer to him, then she would change nothing. He was a powerful protector but he'd never be with her, not a fine gentleman like him. The son of a duke, her ladyship had told her, and her the daughter of a fisherman and a woman who took in washing. They were good, God-fearing people and she knew in her heart they would like Buck.

How easily his name tripped over her tongue. And her not even knowing him long enough to say a novena.

Embarrassed by her brazenness, Ava buried her head under the covers. She held onto her black rosary as if it were a lucky talisman, clutching it to her breasts.

How she wished she were back in the small cottage she shared with her mum. The kind woman would fix her a nice cup of tea, wrapping the blue-and-white checkered quilt around the teapot to keep the water hot.

Ava was half-asleep when a disturbing sound grated upon her ears. She popped her head up from under the heavy bedding. Someone was weeping.

Could it be...

She got up from the bed and very quietly put her ear to the connecting door to her stateroom. Yes, she could hear the countess crying. A gentle crying, her sobs born not of despair, but of longing.

It hurt her to hear such sounds.

A different emotion tapped her soul with something unexpected. She sensed a bond forming between the countess and her that had *nothing* to do with class.

Two women longing for what they couldn't have.

That didn't change anything. A great social barrier divided them, one Ava could never hope to cross.

She lay awake for a long time, thinking about the countess with her privileges and fine manners. A new, unsettling thought made her lose a bit of her confidence. A small bit, but it shook her nonetheless.

What can I expect from this life if a fine lady like the countess isn't bearing up so well? Is it wrong of me, God, to want more than what I was born with?

Ava could find no answer.

The blessed saints be praised she should find herself in the lady's company. The countess was like a string of pearls, polished, glowing and fastened in a fancy setting. In the end, Ava had to accept the fact that even the most beautiful pearl had a flaw in it no one could see.

Nothing was perfect. Not family, not love nor social position.

10

12 April 1912

'Why didn't you tell me you met up with Captain Lord Blackthorn, Ava?' said the countess, eyeing her with something Ava hadn't seen before.

Jealousy.

'I was minding my own business, your ladyship,' Ava said, trying to defend herself, 'when Buck, I mean, his lordship, happened by and escorted me back to the cabin.'

Look at you, girl, uttering the man's Christian name as if the two of you were on intimate terms. No wonder the countess has gone pale under her face powder. Fine lass you are, adding to her troubles.

'You're as glib as the rest of them with your lies, Ava.'

Ava shot her a questioning look. They had been getting along so well. Whatever her ladyship's reasons were for talking about his lordship, Ava would never know. Whether it was merely a lonely woman who wished to take advantage of female companionship, or an idea had taken root in her mind she should be forewarned about him.

'I should have known Buck would sniff you out like a hound after its prey,' she continued without taking a breath. 'Take my word, Ava, you'll never change him. He's a man who does what he wants with *whomever* he wants without recourse.'

'It's not like that between him and me, your ladyship.'

Isn't it, girl? Are you turning into the liar the countess thinks you are? Or have you been telling untruths, especially to yourself, where his lordship is concerned?

'I fear you're as blind as I, Ava, and will suffer as I have.' The countess sighed and her anger dissipated. 'Forget what I said. I spoke the distraught words of a woman too long denied her heart's desire.'

There the conversation started and ended.

Her attitude this morning had surprised her, yet Ava yearned to know more about this quiet woman with an elegant style but a sharp disposition. She never expected the countess to bring up the subject of Captain Lord Blackthorn *again* as the morning turned into afternoon.

'Did Buck tell you how we met, Ava?' she asked suddenly after lunch, changing her point of attack with finesse.

'No, your ladyship,' Ava said, covering the lunch tray with a linen cloth. She'd finished her own lunch in her cabin and had gulped down the last of her tea when her ladyship had called out to her. Ava avoided taking her meals in the lounge for maids and valets on C Deck lest someone ask too many questions.

'I was seventeen and filled with romantic stirrings, no doubt fueled by my cloistered life at Dirksen Castle,' the countess began, reliving those days as if they were a prelude to a grand opera. 'I had few gentleman callers, since I had not yet been presented to their majesties at court. You can imagine how the appearance of a man like Captain Lord Blackthorn upset my everyday existence. Anyone who looks at him can see how he embodies courage and adventure.'

The countess stared off into space, thought a moment, then continued.

'I was out riding my favorite mare when I saw him. I was never afraid of venturing into the forest alone with its dim light and deep shadows. It was my refuge. The wind blew cold that autumn, the hills topped with brown when I raced through the forest, thick with pine against a sky deepening with dark clouds. The rumble of a coming storm echoed in my ears.

'Buck emerged from the woods with an animal vitality and an intensity which made me wish *I* was his prey. He possessed a rugged manhood any woman could admire and fall in love with. I was no exception. I was young and foolish enough to believe his charm was meant only for me.'

Ava remained quiet, imagining the countess as a young girl, wrapped up in the illusions of what she wanted her life to be – love, marriage and running her country estate. Life had altered her plans and she hadn't yet accepted that.

Loving Buck was her penance.

The countess cleared her throat and continued, 'I once thought we shared a common destiny and I intended to make that happen no matter *what* I had to do. When Buck last came to pay me a visit at Dirksen Castle, I tricked him into being alone with me in my bedroom. I wanted so desperately for him to make love to me, I stripped off my silk dressing gown and stood there naked, offering myself to him. I believed that if I ruined myself with him, he would do the right thing and marry me.

'I was so caught up in my plan, telling him I imagined him as lord of the manor, I didn't realize he wanted no part of it until it was too late and I'd bared myself to him. Buck wrapped the silk gown around me, kissed me on the forehead and put me to bed.

Then he left. Without saying a word or making judgment on me. He never spoke of it again and neither have I.'

She took a deep breath, then said in a calm voice without regret, 'I've never told that story to anyone, Ava. I don't know why I did now. I've had the strangest feeling since I met you that I *had* to tell you.' She laughed. 'I owe you a debt of gratitude.'

'*Me*, your ladyship?' Ava whispered, trying to take it all in.

'Yes. If I hadn't been so jealous of you, I never would have entertained the idea that Buck *does* love me in his own way.'

'What do you mean, your ladyship?' Ava said, curious.

'He arranged my upcoming marriage with Mr Brady, then came on this voyage to give me courage. No one else could have convinced me to agree to this crazy scheme.' She smiled. 'Without a doubt, Buck is the most charming and magnetic man I've ever encountered. I loved him then for what he did. What breaks my heart is I still do.'

Ava looked at the countess. With a wavering light upon her face, the flickering shadows heightened her cheekbones and gave her the look of a Madonna. But the woman was no saint. Underneath her calm exterior, Ava knew, she was hot-blooded and filled with a fever for this man. No wonder she treated him with an air of possession and was jealous of any woman he cast his eye upon.

I'll have to watch my step and not give myself away. Oh, why don't I just admit I want to be with his lordship?

Ava turned away, her heart racing wildly. She said nothing. She couldn't. Her emotions were eating her up inside. The situation was getting beyond her. Now she knew why Father Murphy sneaked a bottle of wine from the chapel storeroom every Thursday after confession.

It's a heavy burden to carry the sins of others upon your back, lass, leaving no room in your soul for your own. A dead feeling it is, because you can do nothing to help the sinner but tell them God forgives them.

And that she did.

* * *

Having bared her soul, a great burden had lifted from her mind and the countess now expected Ava to act as a lady's maid should. To respect her mistress's private affairs and perform her duties as if the conversation had never taken place.

'Why don't you go up on the Boat Deck and get some fresh air, your ladyship?' Ava said to her later in the afternoon.

'I've nearly finished this letter to Benson,' the countess said, sitting at the small writing desk and dashing off a few more lines before signing the letter to her butler with a flourish, then sealing it. 'Post the letter for me with the purser, Ava.'

'Yes, your ladyship,' she said, taking the letter and hoping the countess didn't see her hand shaking. The last place Ava O'Reilly was going to drag herself was the purser's office. She'd be locked up faster than a hangman's prayer.

What to do?

She had an idea. As deftly as a magician hiding a rabbit in his top hat, Ava slipped the letter into the countess's coat pocket, determined to convince her to post it herself at the enquiry desk with the purser. It wouldn't matter *when* the letter left her hand since the outgoing mail wouldn't leave the ship, but would make the return voyage back to England and arrive at its destination within a fortnight.

'I'm ready for that walk now,' the countess said, turning around so Ava could help her on with her coat. For a moment, Ava thought she'd invite her to go with her, but protocol said otherwise.

'It'll do you good, your ladyship.' Standing tall, Ava held the long, heavy coat, and not once did she open her mouth with a snappy retort. By the saints' holy prayers, would you look at her? Mary Sullivan O'Reilly's girl doing a right good job as a lady's maid and not complaining about it.

'Course, that didn't mean because she'd warmed up to doing the job, she had any intention of giving up her dream once she got to New York.

'You're a good girl, Ava, putting up with my tirade earlier,' said the countess, remaining still as Ava buttoned up her black coat. 'I was wrong to accuse you of anything more than infatuation with Buck.'

'It's true Captain Lord Blackthorn is devilishly handsome, your ladyship,' Ava admitted, her fingers closing the top button. 'But he's not for the likes of me.'

'Be careful, Ava, or you'll end up like me. In love with the wrong man.' The countess put on her black velvet cloche hat and pulled a fashionable black veil down over her face, her retiring shyness adding to her charm. 'I'm going to change that,' she said, pulling on her finely stitched gray leather gloves with the pearl buttons. 'For *both* our sakes.'

'What are you going to do?' asked Ava before she could stop herself.

The countess smiled, taking no offense. 'You'll see. I'm off to the reading room to lose myself in a novel until the dinner hour. When Mr Brady calls, tell him I'd be honored to dine with him this evening.'

'Mr Brady?' Ava's eyes widened.

What is the countess up to now? Look at her, smiling like a fiddler playing a happy tune.

'Yes, if we're going to be married, we should become better acquainted. After all, it's my duty to be a good wife. I owe it to him.' She paused. 'And to Buck.' She squared her shoulders, then headed to the door. Before leaving, she turned. 'I've been such a bore today, Ava. Why don't you take the afternoon off? Go for a stroll up on deck.'

Ava bit down on her lower lip. She'd gotten into enough trouble up on deck, but there *was* one thing she was pining to do.

'Would your ladyship mind if I made use of your tub while you're gone?'

'You mean, take a bath?'

'Yes, I've never had my own bathtub before.'

'Of course,' she said, laughing. 'You'll find everything you need on the washstand.'

Ava's eyes glowed. 'Thank you, your ladyship.'

Oh, if only Mary Dolores could see her now, dancing around the stateroom after the countess was gone.

11

'Is it typical for a ship like the *Titanic*,' Trey asked, 'to cruise at twenty-five knots?'

'Yes and no,' Buck said evasively. He grinned at the worried look on the American's face. Should he tell him the truth? The sea was dead calm. There was no telling how fast she would go. 'If we keep up this speed, Trey,' he said, 'we'll arrive in New York late Tuesday night instead of Wednesday morning.'

'God help me if we dock early,' Trey said dryly. 'I'll never hear the end of it from Mother if she isn't there to greet her future daughter-in-law. I wouldn't be surprised if she's learned how to curtsy, even *with* her arthritis. She's obsessed with the royals.'

It was well known among the elite that Treyton Brady received an income from a half-million-dollar trust fund. *But* he would lose claim to a twenty-million-dollar inheritance if he didn't marry a peeress as per his mother's wishes. With his bride-hunting trip to Europe coming to an end and along with it his freedom, Buck reasoned his old friend was getting cold feet.

There was something else, too. A change in both of them. They'd lost the devil-may-care attitude that had ruled their lives up to this point.

Trey, he could understand, but why him?

'My mother is so obsessed with royalty,' Trey mocked, 'she sent me numerous telegrams before we left England requesting more information on the countess so she can have her watchdogs check up on her. She can't understand *why* I didn't bring home an English countess instead.'

'I pity Fiona trying to explain to your mother why *she* inherited a peerage title when Englishwomen cannot,' Buck said glibly.

'I don't understand you English and your inheritance laws. God knows it would have made my life easier.' Trey shook his head in dismay. 'Now you tell me this ship will arrive earlier than scheduled. I'd rather find myself thrashing about in the Atlantic on a raft than deal with my mother.'

Trey had been in high spirits when he'd encountered Buck in the first-class lounge on the Promenade Deck. Their earlier run-in in the countess's stateroom had been forgotten, as usually happened with Trey. He held no grudges, especially when it was in his own best interests. Keeping Buck as his confidante achieved that goal.

The former British Army captain had no doubt his old friend was worried about the countess changing her mind about the marriage and had sought him out to make amends in the only way Trey knew how.

By acting as if nothing had happened.

He looked rather peeved at the idea of the ship arriving early, though he appeared rested. Buck smirked. Most likely the object of his late-night rendezvous in second class had found out he was affianced to the countess and thrown him out.

Who would be his next conquest?

He wondered if Trey realized his fiancée was not as reserved as she seemed.

He'd never forgotten the night Fiona tried to seduce him. Any man would have been flattered. *He* was embarrassed. He could never feel that way about her and that pained him because she deserved better than that. He felt guilty about avoiding her, but it was best to keep his distance from her until they arrived in New York.

Or is there another reason?

A girl with green eyes, red hair and a lovely figure.

Ava.

'Don't try to fool me, Buck. You've been carousing with that pretty Irish girl you hired to work as a lady's maid for the countess.'

'Be careful what you say about her, Trey,' Buck said with authority. 'She's an innocent girl.'

'That *is* a revelation. A woman immune to your charms.' He looked at his old friend with an expression that made Buck wary when he asked, 'Where did you find such a gorgeous creature?'

'The assistant purser recommended her to me,' Buck lied. 'She was a lady's maid back in Ireland.'

'She's a beauty all right. I have to admit I didn't have any luck with her either. She wouldn't give me the time of day.' Trey shrugged. 'Not that I didn't try, but if you *are* right about the ship's run, I have five more days to convince her a Yankee can beat an Englishman at his own game.'

Buck observed his friend with a new worry. The gambling mood had possessed them both, but it wasn't the ship's fast run at stake here, it was Ava's virtue.

It was then he realized his duty as her protector was far from over.

'I'm warning you, Trey,' Buck said, clenching his fists at his sides and trying to remember they were in the first-class lounge of the *Titanic* and not a dosshouse in London's East End. 'The girl will bring you nothing but trouble. Keep your mind on Fiona, your future wife.'

'I've tried, Buck, but the countess won't even sup with me. God knows what a fiasco our marriage will be if she won't have anything to do with me.'

The two men sat down in the comfortable round chairs and Buck gazed out the large bay windows at the panoramic view of the sea. The room remained at an even temperature though the marble fireplace was merely for decoration.

'You're not intending to call off the marriage, are you?' Buck asked, concerned.

'Of course not. This is one chap, as you English say, who has no desire to forfeit his lavish style of living, *whatever* the cost to his personal life.'

Buck's eyes narrowed. 'What are you up to?'

'We have a saying in America, Buck. If you can't beat them, join them.' Trey waved the lounge steward over and whispered something to him. The steward nodded, then returned with a big bouquet of American Beauty red roses tied up with a trailing red satin ribbon. 'I had the ship's florist make this arrangement for the countess.' He grinned. 'Do you think it will please her?'

'Her ladyship will no doubt fall into your arms and vow undying love,' Buck said, intending to convince the countess Trey was sincere in his efforts to woo her.

If she was still speaking to him.

The vibrant roses nearly put him in a romantic mood. He couldn't deny the scent was intoxicating and made him think about confiscating a fresh flower for a certain Irish girl.

'I'm going to leave the roses in her cabin with a note,' Trey said, standing up. 'Then I'm off to send Mother a wireless, telling her we're arriving in New York early. She'll be thrilled and will probably have a band playing when the ship docks,' he said with confidence in his ability to diffuse his mother's anger and get what he wanted – control of his father's fortune – by his charming subterfuge.

'Do you wish to make a wager on that?' Buck asked, baiting him.

'Don't waste your money, old boy,' Trey said with the total assurance of a schemer who knew the only way to get on in this world was to use his boyish appeal. 'That's one bet I *can't* lose.'

* * *

Buck was worried. He wondered if he'd set Ava up for a fall by hiding her with the countess and making her vulnerable to Trey's advances.

He wasn't a bad sort, Buck thought. Trey could be quite likeable when he wasn't trying to live up to his wild reputation as a millionaire's son.

It was time to speak to Ava about what would happen if she believed anything Trey might say to convince her it was his aim in life to help a working-class girl overcome the social barriers. His American friend had used that same ploy to find his way into the boudoir of many a chambermaid.

No time like the present to perform his duty as grand protector, he decided. He pulled out his gold pocket watch and checked the hour. Ava would most likely be taking tea in her cabin.

He never imagined the countess would thwart his mission.

'You haven't been to see me, Buck,' Fiona said with a lightness in her voice he wouldn't have expected.

He hadn't heard her come up behind him and, when he turned around, he was surprised to see this lovely woman smiling at him through her black veil. The tiny pinpoints of lace added a flair of mystery any man would find appealing.

Buck kissed her gloved hand, guarding his feelings. There was something regal in the way she held her head and the sway of her body. Coy, but ladylike. Trey would find her a most delightful companion if he was wise enough not to see her as a deterrent to his wandering ways.

'Trey intends to make up for the misunderstanding between you two yesterday.'

'That should prove very timely.'

'What's going on in that female mind of yours, Fiona?'

'I intend to make this marriage work, Buck.' She paused, thinking. 'I've decided to give Trey every opportunity to make me fall in love with him.'

'I regret things didn't turn out the way you wanted, Fiona,' Buck said, doing his best to sound sincere. 'I'm not the marrying kind.'

'Does Ava know that?'

'Ava?' he asked, taken aback. 'What does she have to do with it?'

'She's fallen head over heels for you, Buck. Oh, it's not the same deep love I have for you, but it could be over time. She's got a big heart and an inquisitive mind and needs a man to guide her.' She placed her hand on his forearm. 'Don't hurt her, Buck. She's a good girl.'

'She's the reason I've stayed away.'

'Funny, isn't it?' she said, trying to explain. 'You live by your wits and your courage, yet you don't believe that's enough to offer a woman. You're wrong, Buck. Someday you'll find out, and when you do, I pray it won't be too late.'

'Fiona, you don't understand. I—'

'But I do, Buck. It's been drummed into your head since boyhood that because you're the second son of a duke, you're destined to walk a tightrope in this twilight world of upper-class values and rules. That you don't fit in anywhere. I thought I was the woman who could change that. I wasn't. Is it Ava? I don't know. She's wild, brash and filled with mischief. Which makes me wonder about her.'

Curious, Buck asked, 'What do you mean, Fiona?'

'She has a way about her that speaks more of a girl from the hinterlands than a great house. I will tell you this, Buck, if she's a lady's maid, I'm Lady Godiva,' she added with a secret smile all to herself.

'I shouldn't have tried to fool you,' Buck admitted.

She smiled at the compliment. 'I don't know her background and I don't care. Whatever your reasons for bringing her to me, be careful. *You* may be the one hurt this time.'

'I'm surprised at you, Fiona,' Buck said, not trying to be discreet, 'being jealous of a servant girl.'

'Who said I was jealous?' she said with not a hint of the demure demeanor he expected of her. 'I'm just being practical.'

'Would you rather I dismiss the girl?'

She threw her head back and laughed. 'You couldn't if I wanted you to. She's taken it upon herself to prove to me she's a lady's maid as if her life depended upon it. She's even taken over my bathroom and is enjoying a soaking in my tub.'

'Ava's taking a bath?' Buck asked carefully.

'Yes. Would you believe the child has never bathed in a private bathroom before?' she said. 'She looked so delighted when I told her to take the afternoon off and enjoy a hot bath.'

With her book under her arm, Fiona wandered over to the pantry, where afternoon tea had been set up with a tempting display of finger sandwiches. She didn't notice the worried look on Buck's face as he followed her.

He felt his gut tighten. *This can't be happening.*

Trey was headed to the countess's stateroom with a big bouquet of roses, hell bent on leaving the flowers in the cabin. If he got the key from the stewardess and opened the connecting door and saw Ava naked in the tub—

Good God, he couldn't let that happen.

Trey was a man with little willpower and Ava was a woman *no* man could resist.

He prayed he got there before Trey did.

12

Like the devil himself had come to claim her soul, Ava grabbed the countess's dressing gown hanging on the hook and wrapped it around herself when she heard the outer door to the stateroom open.

It was too late.

She stared at Treyton Brady standing there with a big bouquet of roses in his hand and an even bigger smile on his face.

'What are you gawking at, Mr Brady?' she demanded. 'Ain't you never seen a lady taking a bath before?'

'Not one as beautiful as you, Ava.'

'Don't you give me none of your fancy talk, Mr Brady, I'll not listen.'

'I wouldn't dream of it,' Trey said, treading lightly, the wariness in his eyes telling her he was about to make a grand speech. And right she was, for the next words tripping off his tongue faster than a leprechaun's dancing feet were the biggest lie she'd heard in a month of Sundays.

'I brought you a bouquet of roses,' he said, pulling off red silken petals and scattering them in the bath water. 'Now you can bathe like a queen.'

'Oh, is that so, Mr Brady?' Ava said, her hands on her hips. 'And what else do you want?'

He folded his arms, wrinkling his mouth in a boyish grin. 'I could scrub your back for you.'

'I'm sorry to disappoint you,' she said, taking a step back. 'But I've finished my bath. Now if you would be so genteel as to remove yourself from the countess's stateroom, I would like to dress without the likes of you staring at me.'

Her brashness startled him. What did he expect? That she'd squeal and feign false modesty at his unexpected arrival? Barging in as he did without so much as a 'good day.'

She tried to keep from laughing. He looked so funny standing there in his blue serge suit and tight white collar nearly choking him. Even his pencil-thin mustache wiggled above his upper lip, so unnerved he was at seeing her wearing nothing but a dressing gown with her bare, wet feet making puddles on the linoleum tiles.

Their eyes met, but it wasn't the same as when Captain Lord Blackthorn saw her in her chemise. *He* made her heart beat faster, her legs go wobbly. Mr Brady reminded her of a schoolboy peeking at the girls bathing in the river in their underwear.

'I shall go, Ava,' Trey said, his eyes moving downward to her bare legs peeking through her dressing gown. 'But only if you come to my cabin later and dine with me.' Ava ignored his invitation. After all, he was an American, forward and indiscreet.

'How did you get in here, sir?' she asked. She refused to let him take advantage of her.

'The stewardess was kind enough to let me in. When I heard the splashing coming from the bathroom—'

'Since the countess isn't here, I must *insist* you leave. *Now.*' She pulled the dressing gown around her tighter. 'Or I'll show you how the Irish make duck soup out of American blarney.'

Trey was not about to walk away when he had the advantage. 'I'm a man of wealth and affluence, Ava. I can secure a good position for you in America.' He paused to let his words sink in. '*If* you play the game by *my* rules.'

Watch yourself, Ava O'Reilly. Him and his fine promises will cut into your soul and make it bleed.

No, she'd be hurting the countess. And that, she wouldn't do.

'I may be a lady's maid, Mr Brady, but I'm my own woman. I'll not be needing the likes of you thinking you can buy me like a box of bonbons.'

'My mother, Mrs Benn-Brady, has connections with all the best families in New York.' He snuggled up close to her, his hand reaching around her waist, making her stiffen. 'A word from me and you'll find yourself settled in a ten-room brownstone on Manhattan's Park Avenue with a comfortable job as a governess or nanny.'

'Don't believe a word he says, Ava.'

She froze. Captain Lord Blackthorn.

Her mouth quivered. By the saints of all mercy preserve her, it was his lordship himself standing at the door. She'd never seen him so angry. His dark brows crossed as if a tempest whirled around in his black eyes, ready to explode into fiery lights.

'Why shouldn't I believe him?' she wanted to know.

'I know Trey better than you do,' Buck said.

'Perhaps you do, Captain Lord Blackthorn, but are *you* offering me a job in New York?' Ava said with the color on her cheeks raised and her head thrown back.

She waited for his answer, but he said nothing. Her heart sank. Then so be it. The gentleman gave her no choice but to take her chances when the ship docked in America. She wasn't giving up the idea of finding good, decent work on her own.

'If not, sir, then I can take care of myself, thank you.'

'Listen to the little lady, Buck,' Trey said, squeezing her waist. She winced. 'She's as smart as she is beautiful.'

'I was wrong about you, Ava,' Buck said and turned to leave. 'You don't need a protector after all.'

Ava's voice caught in her throat, wishing he would say something, *anything*, so she could undo her foolish words.

Her eyes misted when, before he left, Buck looked at her with a chilling glare that made her shiver. 'Be careful, Ava, there are rough seas ahead.'

'Buck has it all wrong, Ava,' Trey said, unabashedly in a good mood, believing he'd won the unspoken bet between them and got the girl. 'He told me himself this is going to be a smooth crossing.'

Ava couldn't move, her heart beating so fast in her chest she felt faint.

What a fool she was, saying those things to him.

And now he was gone.

'I never thought I'd see the day Buck would walk away from a beautiful woman,' Trey said, a tone of astonishment in his voice as if he couldn't believe it. Something changed in him then, but she wasn't sure what it was. Still, his words snapped her back to reality. No time to cry over her foolish deed, though it still hurt like she'd been run through with the stab of a hayfork.

Ava turned to him. '*Will* you help me find employment, Mr Brady?' she asked, looking for assurance. She wondered if the countess could help her find work, but she was also a stranger in America and would have to rely on her new husband for any help she could provide.

Once they landed in New York, she'd have an impossible time getting through immigration with no inspection card. As a servant of the Countess of Marbury, no one would ask questions.

'My dear, you'll never rue the day you put yourself in the hands of Treyton Brady.'

Won't you, girl? Look at him, smiling and humming and kissing your hand before bidding you good night.

But Ava couldn't shut out the voice in her head that came upon at her at the oddest times. The holy priest said it was her conscience when she brought it up at confession. And though at times, she shuffled the meddlesome voice into a corner of her mind, today she couldn't.

Promising you won't be sorry for choosing him over Captain Lord Blackthorn, giving you the blarney about how he'll act the perfect gentleman for the remainder of the crossing.

Clever he is, leaving you in peace without so much as another peek at the swell of your breasts or a glimpse of your bare legs.

I'm telling you, you're wrong... she fought back, but the voice wouldn't be stilled and so she had to take it all in, holding her hands to her head.

Don't be fooled. It's untying the ribbon on your camisole he'll want once he has you in his clutches. Did you see the look in his eye? Heated and wanting. A hunger for the flesh that would send any girl running from him.

You can't run, lassie.

You made your bargain with the devil. There's no way out. No way at all.

Only a miracle can save you now, girl, and the Almighty has run out of miracles for the likes of you.

13

'By the grim look on your face, Buck, I'd say you didn't get the answer you expected.'

Glittering dark eyes stared at him, filled with curiosity.

The countess.

Would the woman ever let him forget he'd admitted he stayed away from her cabin because of his attraction to Ava? Only to race over there like a fool?

'You don't seem surprised,' he said.

'I'm not.' She adjusted her black cloche hat, with wisps of damp hair curling around the nape of her neck.

She'd set a brisk pace to catch up to him when she saw him come out of the first-class lift. She had something on her mind and she intended to say it.

'Ava is a lovely girl, Buck, but I imagine any man would find her hard to handle.' She grinned. 'I knew she could take care of herself.'

'Testing me, Fiona? Or Ava?'

She smiled wide. '*Both*.'

Buck took her arm in his as they walked on the Promenade Deck toward the Verandah Café. Two first-class passengers enjoying a late afternoon stroll before dressing for dinner.

It was the furthest thing from the truth.

Besides keeping the countess amused, Buck was doing his best to keep her from returning to her stateroom until he was *sure* Trey had left and Ava was back in her role as a lady's maid.

And *not* in Trey's arms, he moaned inwardly, with her swooning and succumbing to his friend's lies.

Why did that disturb him so?

Damn the woman. Standing there half-naked, her long red hair wet and shiny like a mermaid's, her skin glistening like stardust. Being so close to her had driven him mad, especially when Trey had squeezed her waist and she had done *nothing* to stop him.

Other women relished playing one man against the other. Ava was different. She looked as frightened as a hare caught between two hungry foxes. He wanted to carry her off and make her *his* woman.

But no, he left her, his pride intact. He convinced himself it was the proper thing to do. What other choice did he have?

He didn't trust himself around her.

So engrossed was he in speculating everything he'd done wrong, Buck could hardly concentrate on what Fiona was saying.

He'd said nothing about Trey bringing the roses to her cabin. He kept mum because he didn't want to see her hurt.

And he wanted to keep Ava safe.

Try as she may to make his life insufferable, turning every thought he'd ever had about females into a one-upmanship like no *man* ever could, Buck couldn't abandon her. Yes, he'd spoken in haste like a madman, but what he'd said was true.

He couldn't guarantee her a job.

As a governess or nanny and especially as the countess's lady's maid. *If* she'd take a job in service. With Mrs Benn-Brady sticking her nose into Fiona's background, she would also have her maid investigated. When it came out Ava was a fugitive from the law, she'd not only turn her over to the local authorities but make certain the countess was sent packing back to Scotland.

Buck made his decision. He intended to set the Irish girl up in an apartment when they arrived in New York. No strings attached. *Anything* to keep her from ruining her life by falling for Trey's promises. God help her if his old friend found out who she was. He'd want nothing more to do with her.

Today was Friday. He had tonight's game, then Saturday to pile up his winnings. No gambling on Sunday, though several gentlemen had entreated the chief steward to relax the White Star Line rules for the maiden crossing.

'I'm the luckiest man on the *Titanic* today.'

Both Buck and Fiona turned around in surprise to see Trey.

Trey continued, 'I'm dining this evening with the most charming woman aboard ship.'

'What's your game, Trey?' Buck asked.

'No game, Buck.' He turned to the countess. 'I'd be honored if you'll dine with me tonight, Fiona. I've planned a special menu for us to be served in my cabin.' He winked at her. 'We have much to discuss about our upcoming marriage.'

'I'd be happy to, Trey,' said the countess, beaming.

'If you'll excuse me, Fiona,' Buck said, 'I hear a pair of aces calling me.'

Buck strode off, leaving them whispering and hovering like two young lovers. Was this the same couple who had hardly spoken to each other the past few days?

What pushed up his dander more was the smirk on Trey's face. If he laid a hand on Ava, he'd—

Do what? She wanted nothing to do with him. That wouldn't stop him from coming up with a plan to get her away from Trey. For that, he needed to replenish his bank account.

Buck pushed through the revolving doors of the smoking room and joined a card game already in play. Whatever the odds, he'd need a hell of a lot more than a pair of aces to win Ava back.

14

Ava wound the brush through the countess's long hair.

Guilt washed over her, knowing her ladyship would have a fit if she knew the stakes wagered and won by her own fiancé with her lady's maid as the prize. Her breath caught when she thought about the insanity of it all, her talk about finding employment, when what Ava *really* wanted was for Buck to take her in his arms.

There, she'd admitted it.

Now get on with it, girl.

Her knees felt unsteady as Ava counted the brushstrokes.

'Eighty-seven, eighty-eight...'

How long could she keep her alliance with Mr Brady a secret from the countess?

Or better yet, could she wiggle out of it when the ship docked in New York?

She'd run away before, why not again? So what if it wasn't practical? Neither was finding herself alone in a big city with no money, no friends. What other choice did she have?

As if Ava didn't know.

She'd end up a wealthy man's mistress.

Ava O'Reilly, you should be ashamed, she could hear her mum's voice bursting into her thoughts with such passion her head hurt, *using such an excuse to cover up your wantonness.*

Her ears burned as if she'd been slapped. Her mother was right. She'd have to find another way out of this mess. If only the countess could help her.

'Ninety-nine, a hundred,' Ava finished, then put down the brush. 'You have such beautiful hair, your ladyship.'

'Thank you, Ava,' said the countess, tilting her head forward and pinning up her hair with the bobby pins she took from the sterling silver box. A box engraved with her initials and family crest. 'It's lovely to have you brush my hair. I always do it myself.'

'You shouldn't hide your hair under a hat and veil, milady,' Ava said, trying to build the woman's confidence.

'It's too late for me to change,' the countess added with a note of sadness in her voice.

'I don't believe that, your ladyship,' Ava said. 'Everything is different in America.'

'Is it?' said the countess with a smirk. 'American, British, it doesn't matter. We're all chattel traded for the benefit of the family. We have little say over what we can hope to achieve with our lives.'

'If you don't mind me saying so, Countess, it makes me glad to be born poor Irish,' Ava said lightly, not understanding why this creature with the porcelain skin wasn't in control of her own life. 'The only thing for me to worry about is my next meal.'

'You and I should trade places for a day,' the countess said, laughing and getting into the spirit of Ava's game. 'I can tidy up a room very well, thank you, and I imagine you'd make a lovely countess.' She let out a wistful sigh that put Ava on guard.

Ava flushed scarlet and turned her face away so the countess couldn't see her guilt.

There'd be no saving her soul from the flames of hell if the countess found out her fiancé had promised to help her. *And* held her tight around the waist with her decked out in her ladyship's dressing gown.

The countess must never know or Ava would be sacked before they landed in New York.

'Which dress will you need tonight, milady?' Ava asked, changing the subject.

'My violet silk with the lace sleeves,' she said without hesitation. Then she turned to Ava, her eyes pleading. 'We're dining in Mr Brady's cabin. Would you mind serving, Ava? I'd feel uncomfortable with a ship's stewardess prattling about with the dishes and tea.'

'Is Captain Lord Blackthorn joining you?' Ava asked, knowing it was none of her business. A girl had a right to know if she was going to be under the scrutiny of a man who believed she'd pull down her garters for any gent who offered her a job.

She *had* to change his mind about her, but how?

'No, Trey was insistent we dine alone,' the countess said, opening her jewel case lined with blue velvet. She took out a pair of Burmese ruby and diamond drop earrings. 'He was in an especially good mood earlier. Laughing and making jokes...'

Why shouldn't he be? Ava thought, opening the tall wardrobe and pulling out the silk frock with long lace sleeves and six tiny buttons at each wrist. Treyton Brady had found himself the benefactor of *two* women – one who would warm his pockets, the other his bed.

The Irish girl held the violet silk dress up to her as she looked into the full-length, standing mirror. She could see herself and the countess in the glass.

Two women, both slender and fair. Both wearing upswept dos.

Were they really *that* different?

One born to the manor, the other to serve?

Something raged inside Ava, catching her by the throat and refusing to let go. She *could* be a lady, if she had been gentle born and given the chance to learn how to walk, speak and dress.

Was that what she wanted?

'Aren't the roses Trey sent beautiful?' The countess grabbed a flower and inhaled its exquisite scent.

'Like you, Countess,' Ava said, fastening the screw-back earrings in the countess's lobes. The effect was stunning.

'The earrings belonged to my mother,' she said, her softness and usual reticence taking on an emotional fervor that surprised Ava. 'Before he died, I promised my father, the earl, I would wear them at my wedding. Since that day will soon be upon me, I can't let him down.'

So elegant she looked with the jewels sparkling as the drop earrings swayed against her neck. Mr Brady would be a fool not to fall in love with her, while she, Ava O'Reilly, was nothing but a dalliance to him. A privilege granted to the gentlemen of his class.

Try as she might, Ava couldn't change that.

* * *

'I have no doubt my mother will adore you, Fiona.'

Ava watched the countess embrace Mr Brady's every word. The Irish girl rolled her eyes and nearly dropped the hot casserole dish.

'Are you certain you don't wish me to assist you, miss?' asked the stewardess, noticing her awkwardness.

'Thank you, but I can do my job,' Ava insisted. Was that her speaking with such confidence?

Mr Brady also noticed. He kissed her ladyship's hand, then pulled out the chair for the countess while casting an approving eye in Ava's direction. His eyes burned, telling her he wanted her.

Ava turned away, her heart pounding, her cheeks flushed.

She felt another pair of eyes watching her.

Ava had to deal with the woman's curious looks.

'Ring the call bell if you need help,' the stewardess said.

The woman is no fool. She's seen how Mr Brady looks at me.

'I pray you're right about your mother, Trey,' said the countess after the stewardess left. She sipped her warm tea from the fine bone china cup decorated with a pleasant brown and white pattern. 'I must admit

I'm a trifle nervous about making her acquaintance. Will she be meeting us at the dock?'

'Most likely, but don't worry, Fiona,' Trey said, reaching across the small, round table and taking her hand in his. Ava wanted to choke when he caressed her palm with gentle strokes. 'I have everything under control.'

Do you? Ava muttered under her breath.

He looked past the countess at her as she dished out the meal onto the china plates. What was he about? Teasing the countess, then gazing at *her?*

'This is my first crossing, Trey, and I *was* a bit miffed at first,' the countess admitted. 'Seeing how we weren't getting along.'

'I aim to change that, Fiona.' He released her hand, but he continued looking at Ava. 'I'm delighted to find you so enchanting.'

'You don't have to lie to me, Trey, we both know this is a *mariage de convenance*,' the countess said without regret. 'But if we act sensibly, we can achieve our goals without inconveniencing the lifestyle of the other.'

'What *are* you saying, Fiona?' Trey began, pulling at his white collar and loosening his white bow tie.

Ava had to laugh. She never imagined she'd see him sweat like a farmer hightailing it after his prize hog.

'Illicit affairs are nothing new in my world, Trey. I don't condone them, but I refuse to allow such a thing to break up a marriage.' She smiled, then finished her tea. 'Remember that *after* we're married.'

By God, your ladyship, Ava wanted to yell out. *That's giving him a taste of his own medicine.*

The countess wasn't finished.

'Until then,' she continued, 'you are free to spend your time aboard ship with whomever you choose.'

What trickery was this? Ava thought, dropping an empty teacup. Fortunately, it fell harmlessly onto the plush carpeting. She stooped to pick it up, her mind spinning with the news.

The countess was opening the door to *her* bedroom.

'I shall enjoy spending the remainder of the crossing in *your* company, my dear,' Trey lied, speaking to the countess. She smiled and lowered her eyes, giving him the opportunity to seek out Ava. He grinned at her. The intent in his eyes was obvious.

I shall see you later in your cabin, he was saying.

Oh, no, you won't, Ava shot back with a fearsome glance.

Won't I? his eyes said.

No, her stony gaze told him.

'Anything wrong, Ava?' asked the countess, taking a bite of her asparagus, swimming in a rich hollandaise.

'I saw a rat,' Ava said, glaring at Trey.

The countess laughed. 'In steerage maybe, but not here.'

Trey took advantage of the moment. 'The countess is right, Ava. No rats here. Only a lady with her fiancé and a very delicious meal.' He paused, tapping his fingers on the table, then went on. 'What else have we to tempt a gentleman's sweet tooth?' he teased.

'That does it,' Ava said, slamming down the ceramic dishes on the silver-plated serving tray.

'Ava, what's wrong?' asked the countess, clearly disturbed.

'Ask Mr Brady. It's *him* who can do the explaining.'

'What's going on here?' asked the countess, wary.

'I'm through with him romancing you when he's no better than the louts in the local pub who'd peek up your skirts if they had the chance.'

Trey laughed so hard, he couldn't contain himself, while the countess looked perplexed. Obviously, the millionaire was having fun at her expense to show her he was a man to be reckoned with and wouldn't be pushed aside.

Look at what you've done, girl, ruined everything. You'll be thrown off the ship and hauled off to the nearest prison because you can't control your temper.

Will you ever learn?

The countess got up from her seat, looked at Mr Brady first, and then drew Ava aside.

'I admit I don't understand why you acted like that, Ava, but I'm grateful for your concern.'

'I'm sorry I spoke out of turn, Countess,' Ava said. 'But it disturbs me to see this gentleman take advantage of a lady like you.'

The countess laid her hand on the girl's sleeve. 'You're no lady's maid, Ava. That's what I like about you.'

'How long have you known, milady?' she muttered under her breath. She couldn't keep the surprise out of her voice.

'It doesn't matter. Captain Lord Blackthorn must have his reasons for bringing you to me.'

At the mention of his lordship, Ava went pale. 'What did he tell you about me?'

'Nothing, and I didn't ask. For your sake *and* mine, I suggest you finish your duties so Mr Brady doesn't suspect anything is amiss.'

'I'll do as you say, your ladyship,' Ava said, blessing herself. 'I promise.'

'Thank you, Ava,' finished the countess, grateful the bizarre incident had come to an end. Then with a grand flourish, she said, 'Now, shall we have dessert?'

* * *

Ava couldn't sleep.

She tossed and turned for hours, the gentle motion of the ship doing nothing to calm her nerves. How *could* she sleep? For the past hour she'd been privy to whisperings and moans that made her clasp her hands over her ears, so intimate they were.

The countess and Mr Brady.

Lord knew *what* was going on in there after Ava cleaned up and left the empty trays outside the stateroom.

Oh, why didn't the countess say something to him instead of sitting there with that fixed smile on her face? It wasn't proper. Him saying such lovely things to her ladyship while he was giving *her* fancy looks.

Loneliness lay behind the countess's pleasant smile. It hurt Ava so much she wanted to shake her and tell her to open her eyes before she opened her heart to him.

It wouldn't have done any good.

Afterward, she heard the countess and Mr Brady sneak into her ladyship's bedroom, the door slightly open. She couldn't help but hear the kissing sounds and such. She pulled the bedding up to her chin and stuck her fingers in her ears until the sounds stopped. Then it was quiet, so quiet she could hear her heart beating.

Until the door opened—

'I know you're awake, Ava.'

By the martyred saints, it was Mr Brady himself standing there. Leering at her.

She dove under the covers.

'Let me be, Mr Brady,' she said, her voice muffled, her eyes shut.

'You can't hide from me, Ava,' she could hear him saying to her, nice and sweet like honey dripping off a sugar bun. 'You and I made a pact and I've come to collect.'

Here in my own bed? Next to the countess's room?

Ava panicked. She had nowhere to run. *No*, she was *not* going to betray the countess's trust in her.

'If you touch me, Mr Brady, I swear you'll regret it.'

'I thought that would get your attention,' he said laughing. He approached her, but to her surprise, not in a threatening manner.

'I left the door ajar during my visit to Fiona's room,' he continued, keeping his voice low so the countess couldn't hear him, 'because I wanted you to know the countess doesn't find me as unattractive as you do. In fact, she rather liked it when I—'

'If you hurt the countess, I'll skin the hide off your sorry back!'

Trey let out a low whistle. 'Your concern for her ladyship is most admirable, Ava, but I'd be more worried about your own welfare if I were you.'

'What devil's work are you about now, Mr Brady?' she wanted to know, a new fear racing through her.

Did Captain Lord Blackthorn tell him the law was after her?

'I'm talking about our little secret.' He sat on the edge of her bed and took her hand in his. She was too shocked to pull away. To her surprise, his hand was warm. 'The countess need not know anything about it.'

'You mean finding me a job?'

'That is *exactly* what I mean.' He got up to leave, then turned. 'If the ship keeps to this speed, we'll be in New York late Tuesday night. Do as I ask and say nothing to the countess about our little arrangement and you will see how grateful I can be. I saw a different side of you tonight that intrigues me more than a quick romp between the sheets. You've got spirit and wit, Ava O'Reilly, impressing even this tarnished gentleman.' He smiled. 'Sweet dreams.'

Then he was gone.

Ava was uneasy. The knowledge that Treyton Brady needed something from her other than stolen kisses added a wrinkle to her already confused feelings.

Don't you see, girl? He *needs the countess more than* she *needs him.*

Ava put her hand to her mouth to stifle her laughter. What a fine and grand thing *that* was. In that moment, her courage returned.

Someday, when this was over and she was living in a fine house in America, He would lead the right man to her to answer her inner urgings. Feelings she didn't understand, but wanted to. Oh, how she wanted to.

You wouldn't be thinking of Captain Lord Blackthorn, lass, would you?

Oh, wouldn't she?

Ava pulled the covers up over her head, but not before her mouth curled up in a secret smile and she fell into a deep sleep.

15

13 April 1912

'The *Titanic* is a floating palace on the high seas,' Buck said to Thomas Andrews, chief designer of the *Titanic*, as he pocketed the receipt the purser had handed him for his cash winnings secure in the ship's safe. He'd heard about a band of steerage ruffians roaming about on the Boat Deck late at night from Mr Lightoller. 'You've done a magnificent job.'

Mr Andrews acknowledged the compliment with a nod. 'Every ship has its growing pains. Someone took off with the binoculars in the crow's nest and we haven't a spare, not to mention Mr McElroy here can't find a stowaway on board.'

Buck stood rooted to the spot. Were they talking about Ava?

'She's a fugitive from the law, Mr Andrews,' stated the purser. 'The crew has looked from bow to stern and they've not found the girl. They even searched the lifeboats.'

Mr Andrews shrugged. 'Not *enough* lifeboats, if you ask me.' He paused. 'God help us if we ever need them.'

'Any iceberg warnings?' Buck asked, trying to change the topic of conversation. He couldn't figure out why the White Star Line was so interested in finding an Irish servant girl.

'A few ships have reported seeing ice since we left Southampton, Captain Lord Blackthorn, but I wouldn't worry, not with E.J. at the helm.' He referred to Captain Edward J. Smith, the Millionaire's Captain. 'Even if the unthinkable happened, this ship is designed to float with any three of her first five compartments flooded,' Mr Andrews said proudly. 'As for that stowaway,' he said, pointing to C Deck on the ship's plans, 'there are several empty cabins here. The girl *could* be hiding in first class.'

The purser rubbed his chin, thinking. 'We'd better find her right quick or I'll never hear the end of it.'

'What has the girl done?' asked Mr Andrews, curious.

The chief purser went on to explain that she'd stolen a diamond bracelet from a prominent Irish landowner with high connections in the British Parliament. The Chairman and Managing Director of the White Star Line, J. Bruce Ismay, had given the orders to find her. If the press got wind of the story, he said, it would overshadow the news of the ship's fast run, not to mention garner bad publicity for *Titanic*'s maiden voyage.

'When we *do* find her, sir,' Purser McElroy continued, 'she'll be placed under arrest and confined below.'

'What will happen to her when we dock?' Buck asked cautiously.

'She'll be sent back to Ireland to face justice there.'

Injustice was more like it, Buck thought, bidding them good afternoon, then leaving them with the assumption he was headed for the smoking room.

But he had a more pressing issue on his mind.

Ava.

Send her back to Ireland to face justice, would they?

The girl would catch her death of cold in an Irish prison, not to mention succumb to the desperate, ferocious struggle to survive in a filthy place like that. Doing what she must to live another day.

She would be stripped of her petticoats *and* her dignity. Her innocence gone within a fortnight and sold to the highest bidder.

What kind of justice is that?

He wouldn't accept it. No more would she steal a bracelet than he'd cheat at cards.

It wasn't in her blood.

He'd bet his life on it.

* * *

'Where is she?' Buck asked, keeping his surprise at bay when the door to the countess's stateroom opened and the young stewardess came out. She was smiling and holding a pile of dirty linen. It was the girl who had given him the uniform for Ava.

'You mean the countess?' she asked, tossing the soiled goods into the basket left by the door. 'Or the pretty lady's maid?'

The answer hung in the air, unspoken but understood by the two of them. Buck grinned. The girl was no fool, but he sensed she rather enjoyed the scenario being played out on her watch and would keep her opinions to herself.

'The countess,' he said.

She nodded demurely, locking the door behind her. '*Both* ladies are spending the morning at the Turkish baths.'

'Thank you, Miss Sinclair.'

Without another word, Buck hurried down the corridor to the lift, making a quick descent to F Deck. He made a mental note to add a generous tip for the stewardess at the end of the voyage.

He had another surprise when he tried to barge through the swinging doors with the fancy Moorish décor.

'Ladies only until one o'clock, sir,' said the Turkish bath stewardess, Annie Caton, a matronly woman whom Buck judged to be around fifty. 'Gentlemen are allowed in from 2 to 6 p.m.'

'I have urgent business with a lady inside,' he insisted.

'I don't care if you have an appointment with Queen Mary, no gents allowed.'

'Then I'll wait,' Buck said, determined to find a way to talk to Ava alone when the two women came out. He *had* to warn her. She would be heartbroken if they sent her back to Ireland. And, he had to admit, he wanted to hear for himself the story behind the stolen bracelet.

Without warning, the doors swung open and out came the countess in an obvious hurry. She didn't see him, making her way toward the electric lift with short, quick steps. Where was Ava? That struck him as odd until—

Her cloche hat slipped and long red hair swirled over her shoulders as she disappeared into the lift.

By God, it *was* Ava.

What in damnation was the girl up to now?

It wasn't the first time she had wandered around the ship on her own. This time she seemed dead set on her destination, as if she knew exactly where she was going.

He waited for the elevator to return, got on, and then asked the lift attendant where the lady got off.

'C Deck, sir,' the boy said, grinning wide when Buck tossed him a five-dollar gold coin. Then he moved quickly down the corridor, his stride long and filled with purpose. Every nerve in his body tensed until he caught up to her and the rustle of her skirts rattled in his ears. Only one place Ava could be headed.

Trey's stateroom.

Buck cringed. Not if *he* had anything to do with it.

* * *

'I have the right to go where I please, sir.' Ava took a step backward, clearly surprised to find him at her heels.

Buck took a hard stand, determined not to be disobeyed again by this obstinate young woman. 'On this ship, Ava, you'll do what *I* tell you.' His tone was harsh but full of concern. 'That means staying in your cabin until we dock in New York.'

'Then what?' Ava wanted to know. 'You'll help me find a job so I'll have a roof over my head?'

Ava was many things, but Buck knew she wasn't a petticoat female in search of an easy ride. She wanted security. 'You have my word on it,' he rushed in a clear voice, keeping his expression calm, while inside the urge to hold her in his arms came again, a fine sweat forming under his collar.

Ava blinked, then shook her head. 'Am I hearing right, Captain Lord Blackthorn, or are my ears stuffed with straw?'

He sensed a spike in the tension between them, a whiff of skepticism. He'd have to play this right or he'd lose her.

'I've been very lucky at cards on this crossing, Ava, and it will be my pleasure to assist you in settling into a new life.'

'I asked if you would help find me a *job*, sir?' she asked, her patience unraveling.

'Not what I had in mind,' Buck said, stalling, realizing she did not grasp the concept of him setting her up in a residence where he would pay the bills and she would be taken care of. True, he possessed a dark, roguish side, but he had no intention of forcing himself on her no matter how powerful his urges became. It was his duty to watch over her, no matter how difficult she made it for him.

He had to admit it wouldn't be easy to maintain a playful flirtation around her when inside he was consumed with an unyielding passion to possess her that wouldn't be tamed. In time, he hoped she would find him an honorable protector.

He had to smile at that. Wasn't that how this entire episode began?

'You will be my companion, Ava,' he continued in a matter of fact tone, though inside he was barely keeping his frustration from boiling over. 'I will assume responsibility for all your expenses.'

She sucked in air, her eyes disbelieving. 'Holy Mary, I will *not*. Not until the day the saints spit on my mother's holy grave will I do such a thing.'

He took no offense at her rebuff. He'd expected she wouldn't be won over easily, but this conversation stirred something powerful within him he'd never experienced. As if *he* was the one being interviewed. That was very mind-bending since no female ever had that effect on him before. 'Other women have found the arrangement quite satisfactory,' he said without a trace of ego.

'By the Almighty, this is a story for the confessional.' She blew out her breath, exasperated. '*You* are willing to set me up in fancy digs, but not give me a job, while Mr Brady offered me a position and my own room in a grand house. *That* will be the end of me for sure.'

'Mine is the better offer, Ava.'

'Oh, is it?' Her eyes opened even wider. 'But you're not willing to make an honest woman out of me, though marriage to Mr Brady would be like drinking cold tea.'

'I wouldn't put it that way.'

'I would.' Ava put her hands to her forehead in frustration. 'I'll not be a gentleman's fancy painted doll, waiting for him to visit me while I read ladies' magazines and eat sweetcakes.'

Her irritated but hopeful look told him she was waiting for him to promise her what he couldn't give her.

He wasn't the marrying kind, his eyes told her, and no woman could change that.

Why, he wouldn't say. He didn't want *any* woman prying into his soul, however debauched it might be. He was well aware his lifestyle was outrageous and at times dangerous and he had a weakness for pretty women. It added to his reputation as a rogue gambler.

Whatever he felt for Ava, he admitted, was real. The warmth in her beautiful green eyes caressing him, the vibrancy in every word she spoke titillating him. Her honesty and belief in God moved him deeply, even if he could never tell her that.

'I know Trey,' Buck insisted, careful with his words. He didn't wish to tarnish his friend's character, but he had a responsibility to protect her. 'He won't go out of his way to help you without wanting something in return.'

'I can handle the likes of Mr Brady,' Ava said with confidence, and then without another word she fixed her hat and veil back into place and disappeared down the long corridor.

Buck turned to go after her, then stopped. The ship's second officer was approaching him. Mr Lightoller. It wouldn't do for him to get too close a look at Ava.

'Was that the Countess of Marbury I saw you talking to, Captain Lord Blackthorn?' the man asked.

'The countess?' Buck said, not admitting to anything until he found out what was on the ship officer's mind.

'Yes, I recognized her by the unusual plaid trim on her coat, but this is the first time I've seen her without a veil covering her face.'

'Charming, isn't she?' Buck said, taking advantage of the second officer's mistake. He chuckled. What would Ava say if she knew she'd been taken for a lady?

'She's a looker all right.'

'Yes, isn't she?' As an afterthought, Buck said, 'Any news of the female fugitive on board?'

'So you've heard the story, too?' He laughed. 'Every gentleman thinks he's seen her, and after every sighting, she becomes more intriguing.' His brows lifted. 'Whoever she is, she can't be more beautiful than the Countess of Marbury. Good day, sir.'

Buck said nothing. How could he? The man had nearly found Ava out.

He started after her, then slowed down. What was he worried about? Ava was safe for the moment, even with Trey. His old friend liked to boast about his exploits, but he was more talk than anything else. No doubt he was more interested in making Buck jealous. He wouldn't *dare* risk taking Ava to his bed aboard ship and having the countess find out.

Buck clenched his teeth. It would be different when they arrived in New York. Then he would have to convince Ava to allow him to protect her. Until then, he wouldn't bring up the subject again. He couldn't take any chance of losing her for good.

He headed for the smoking room. It was then he realized in dealing with her female fury, she'd had him at his wit's end. He hadn't mentioned that they intended to send her back to Ireland.

* * *

Captain Lord Blackthorn was the most unpredictable man Ava had ever laid eyes upon.

And now this indecent proposal. She couldn't stop thinking about it as she made her way to C Deck.

What was he offering her? To be kept locked up and paid for with his gambling winnings. A shocking event with him delighting in saying it, then doing as he pleased. Of course, *he* was a gentleman and could get away with it.

Not with her, he couldn't.

She had her pride. She was on her way to America to make a good, clean life for herself. She wouldn't allow her heart to be broken before she arrived. No, whatever fancy she'd had for Captain Lord Blackthorn, it was finished. She must lock it away in a secret place in her heart lined with velvet dreams that would never see day.

Even the idea of him taking care of her didn't sway Ava. Her life had been so hard that having a full belly and a dry place to sleep was worth the price of any fortune to her. As long as she was free. Freedom was as important to her as saying her prayers to the Almighty.

But *should* she dip her toe into the sinner's trough of unholy water in a weak moment, how could she be certain his lordship wouldn't change his mind and toss her into the street like old furniture?

She knew what kind of man he was. Hiding in the shadows with her nose in a book, she'd heard the ladies chatting in the Turkish baths about the handsome Englishman with the title and his lucky streak with cards. How he had been involved with the most beautiful woman in London until her husband found out.

Ava scoffed at that. And he wanted *her* to take the woman's place? Hardly. She was no seductress with fancy red lip salve and primped curls. She was a romantic soul and, she had to admit, inexperienced with men. Curious and wanting.

Something else bothered her about his lordship's proposition. The strong teachings of the good sisters about marrying a man in the eyes of God before he took her innocence was a hard thing for Ava to put behind her.

And now she *had* to give herself to a man without the blessing of God because her dear, sweet life depended upon it. She convinced herself it wasn't as bad a sin because she didn't love Mr Brady.

Oh, why was everything so confusing? Why were her feelings tangled up like spools of colorful thread come undone and knotted together? Why couldn't she be like other girls with the common sense to accept her given lot in life and not complain about it?

Why was she so willful?

Before Ava could find an answer to her questions, the door to the luxurious cabin opened and Treyton Brady stood there with the biggest grin on his face, waiting.

She walked through the door and into his world.

There was no turning back.

Ava managed a nervous smile. For God's sake, all he did was look at her, inspecting her, leaving her in suspense, wondering if he would have his way with her while making her uneasy. She felt her color rise, her breathing quick and uneven.

'Why did you slip the note into my apron this morning saying you must see me or I would regret the consequences?'

'A bit dramatic, I must admit, but necessary. I have a proposal for you.' He nuzzled her ear, his lips so close to hers she could smell fine brandy on his breath.

'Oh, have you?' she said. 'You should know Captain Lord Blackthorn approached me with a similar notion.'

'I'm not surprised. Buck is a master at appealing to a woman's baser needs. I assure you, Ava, he *will* tire of you and then where will you be?' he asked. 'Working fourteen hours a day in a sweatshop and living in a crowded tenement. I'm offering you much more.'

'And what is that, if I may ask?'

'You and I shall be allies, Ava.'

'Allies?'

'Yes. I believe my mother will try to undo my marriage contract with the countess.'

'Why would she do that?' Ava was puzzled. 'The countess is a fine lady.'

'I agree with you, Ava, but my mother is having second thoughts about agreeing to a family alliance with a Scottish countess.' He didn't explain further and Ava didn't ask, but inside she was forming a very low opinion of anyone who would harm the countess. 'That's where I need your help.'

'*Me*, Mr Brady?'

'Yes, I shall have you installed at my mother's limestone mansion on upper Fifth Avenue where you'll work as a housemaid. Mother is engaging extra servants to prepare for the wedding and won't suspect you.'

Ava made a face. She wasn't happy about being a housemaid again, but it was either that or grub for food on the streets of New York.

Trey paid no attention to her sour look. 'I shall expect you to listen and report to me any scheme she concocts to derail my marriage to the countess.'

Ava's eyes grew wide. 'You want me to spy on her?'

'Yes. I have no doubt you must have experienced similar goings-on in your last place of employment.'

'I did learn a thing or two about the ways of a big house.' Ava frowned. Lady Olivia with her lying and scheming had taught her no one could be trusted.

'In return for your loyalty, Ava, once I am married to Fiona, I shall see to it you have a permanent position in my mother's household.'

She thought carefully. The bond she'd forged with the countess required she ask, 'Are you in love with the countess, Mr Brady?'

He thought a moment and regarded her with a strange look that quickly disappeared, then said, 'I'm too callous and spoiled to love any woman, my dear. Except...'

He paused, his dark eyes pulling her into their depths with words that didn't need to be said. Ava looked him straight on, challenging him with: 'Then why are you marrying her?'

'She's charming, intelligent and understands me better than I understand myself. She admitted to me I didn't fool her with the roses, but she's willing to make the best of the situation.' He paused. 'I'm also smart enough to know when a woman is in love with his best friend.'

'You mean the countess and Captain Lord Blackthorn.'

'Yes. Neither Fiona nor I will ever get what we want, but we'll have each other.'

'What *do* you want, Mr Brady?' she asked, a curious flutter in her stomach telling her she already knew the answer.

'*You*, my dear.' He sighed. 'Of course, such a thing would never be possible under any circumstance.'

'Because I'm not a lady?'

'Yes. Even in America we abide by a class structure, though it's a matter of money and not blue blood that determines where you fall.' He finished his brandy in one swallow. 'I admit at first I was enchanted with the idea of taking you away from Buck, but you and I both know there could never be anything more between us than a casual affair.'

His look was intense, alarming her.

'I thought that would be enough for me,' he continued. 'I was wrong. You've stolen my heart, Ava. You have charm, wit and a passion for life I find most appealing. No wonder Buck is in love with you.'

She took a step back. *That couldn't be*. He must be mistaken. If his lordship was in love with her, then why didn't he stop her from coming to Mr Brady's cabin?

Treyton Brady kissed her hand. His lips were warm against her skin. 'Now you must return to the Turkish baths before the countess discovers you're gone.'

Ava nodded. The countess was excited about dining with her fiancé in the exclusive À la Carte Restaurant later and had decided to take advantage of the beauty treatments offered. Embarrassed by the idea of indulging herself in such luxury, she had insisted they keep her presence there low-key and give out no information.

He continued, 'This meeting will be our little secret, agreed?'

'Yes, Mr Brady.'

'Then it's settled. I'm off to send a wireless to my mother to inform her Fiona's lady's maid is leaving her employ when we arrive in New York and request she engage one for her. The countess has expressed a desire to take up residence in a hotel until the wedding, so you needn't fear her seeing you at the Benn-Brady mansion. After we're married, Fiona and I will take up residence in our own home.'

'You've thought of everything, Mr Brady, haven't you?'

'Not everything, Ava.'

He flashed her a disarming smile and she felt herself blush. The gentleman had said his piece like a priest handing out penance, but he caught her off guard with his next words. Words she swore came straight from his heart.

'I'll always regret not marrying you instead.'

16

Ava was in a tither tidying up the cabin when Mr Brady came to fetch the countess for supper. The two of them whispered and laughed as Mr Brady insisted on helping her with her satin-lined velvet cape with the fur trim instead of the long black coat she usually wore.

A fancy wrap for a special occasion, her ladyship said, giggling like a schoolgirl walking out with the farmer's son.

Where was Captain Lord Blackthorn this evening? Ava wanted to know. 'Dining in the first-class saloon with wealthy society folks hanging onto his every word,' Mr Brady said, winking at her.

Which left Ava alone in her cabin with no one to sup with. Here she was crossing the Atlantic on the ship of dreams, spending her days in a first-class cabin with everything so grand even the desk lamp didn't tilt when the ship did.

She was lonely.

Don't feel sorry for yourself, girl. You've got a place to put your feet up, a tasty meal to eat and a warm bed.

Fine for anyone to say, but it didn't take away her pain. Back in Ireland, she had Mary Dolores to listen to her ranting and woes. Ava frowned. If her sister knew what trouble she was in, she'd drag her by the hair to confession, blessing herself as she did so.

As she took off her cap and apron, she found the perfect excuse to go up on deck to see the lights and hear the music. The countess had dropped her gray leather gloves onto the carpet. Finely stitched, gray leather with a row of polished pearl buttons.

Dropped in haste while her ladyship tilted her head back for a kiss from her fiancé?

Her ladyship needed those gloves, Ava convinced herself. The evening temperature was dropping every night to near freezing and it was biting cold on deck. Surely the countess wouldn't want her to freeze, she thought, grabbing her ladyship's long, black coat. What was the harm in that? Besides, she'd loaned it to her before.

Ava sighed. Why *shouldn't* she go up on deck and listen to the music? She was a paying passenger, wasn't she? Well... steerage, but if anyone asked she'd tell them she was employed by a first class passenger as a lady's maid.

Buttoning up the countess's long black coat to hide her stewardess uniform, Ava ran through the long corridor and raced up the stairs to B Deck as if the devil himself were after her and returned the gloves to the countess.

The evening was far from over.

* * *

Buck could see Ava coming from the restaurant wearing the countess's coat again.

As fate would have it, making his rounds and headed on a collision course with the Irish girl was the ship's second officer, Mr Lightoller.

Buck panicked. What was she up to now? He couldn't for the life of him understand the girl's boldness. If the ship's officer saw Ava and addressed her as the countess, there'd be hell to pay when he met the *real* countess.

Ava would be found out and it would be his fault.

Moments like this made him doubt his sanity for getting involved with the girl and made him wonder why he couldn't let her go and be done with her.

He couldn't. He was hopelessly involved with her and he had to see it through.

Only one thing to do.

'Don't say a word, Ava, just come with me.'

* * *

Ava had no time to protest. A gentleman was at her back, his voice hot and heavy in her ear. He forced her to keep walking, his body pressed against hers but not before she hissed at him in annoyance. She recognized that voice, the rich timbre with the commanding tone that sent shivers up and down her spine. Such arrogance made her blood boil.

Captain Lord Blackthorn.

'*Damnation*, Ava, do what I ask for once. Your life depends upon it.' That snapped her back to her senses.

She turned around to look at him, see if his dark eyes were teasing her with a laughing pleasure, tempting her to sin with him for the price of a kiss.

He wasn't. His mood was dark and somber, thoughtful.

Shivers of a different kind rattled her bones.

Ava tensed. Something was about, but what?

He kept to the dark shadows, his hand firmly at her elbow, drawing her away from the corridor leading to the first-class stairs and lifts and back toward the restaurant. Away from a matronly, well-dressed lady and a ship's officer chatting and staring at her with curiosity as if she were the prize village pig.

'Is this another one of your tricks, sir?' she asked with defiance.

'Tricks?' he said, surprised. 'If saving you is a trick, then I plead guilty.'

'I can take care of myself, sir. Once we land in New York, I'll be free—'

'Not if they find you first, Ava.'

She shivered again. There was nothing threatening about his behavior, but she sensed danger loomed. Ava stared at him hard. His eyes reflected a truth that said loud and clear she was not to argue with him.

She looked away, still refusing to accept his bold advances under the guise of him trying to help her.

'I don't believe you, sir,' she said flatly. 'The petty crime of an Irish servant girl, innocent though she may be, can't be that important to the likes of the grand officers of this ship.'

'From what I hear, it's a matter of a stolen diamond bracelet.'

She swallowed hard. How did he find out?

He leaned closer, his hands gripping her arms, then he whispered in her ear, 'Have you hidden it on your person?'

She pushed against him, wriggling out of his embrace.

'I have *not*,' she said. 'I never stole nothing in my life.'

'Not even a man's heart?'

'No.'

'You're a liar, Ava, but a beautiful one.'

'And *you*, sir, are a scoundrel. By the soul of my dear sweet mother, I'm telling you the truth. I was framed, hoodwinked by the daughter of an earl.' She explained quickly what happened when Lady Olivia wrongly accused her of stealing the bracelet and her bold plan of escape that brought her aboard ship.

He listened without interrupting her, then swept her into a dark corner on the landing, the beauty of the aft Grand Staircase shielding them from prying eyes. 'I'm sorry I had to be so hard on you, Ava, but I had to find out the truth. You're in great danger. The steamship company doesn't want any bad publicity. If they find you, they will make sure you won't have a chance to prove your innocence. They'll send you back to Ireland *and* prison.'

Ava lost control when she heard that, her throat tightening so it choked her, her senses reeling. Ugly, terrible thoughts swirled around in her mind in a chaos of utter terror. She'd *never* let them put her in prison. *Never*.

She owed his lordship an apology.

'Forgive me, sir, I was wrong to act like a scared chicken with its feathers plucked.'

'Is that what you think of me, Ava? That I'm a hungry fox?'

He looked so serious, waiting for her to say something. She was under no delusion about him or his notorious reputation with women, knowing that by her actions she was in a spot of trouble and now digging herself into a deeper hole. She took her time in answering him.

'Since I first saw you, Captain Lord Blackthorn, I've had the feeling you're not the roguish gentleman you make yourself out to be,' she said. 'That you're good and fine and noble, but you're set on proving to the world otherwise.'

'What would it take to prove to you my intentions are honorable, Ava O'Reilly?' he asked, daring to clasp her gently around the waist and draw her against him until she was firmly in his embrace. His face was so close to hers she could feel his hot breath on her cheeks. His presence surrounded her, his expression indecently confident.

Damn him.

Standing tall in his evening dress, his height accentuated by his military bearing, she perceived him as a man lacking in neither courage nor daring. The fit of his black cutaway coat did nothing to hide his athletic build and emphasized his broad shoulders. His pristine white bow tie and white shirt spoke of impeccable manners, but it was his overt maleness that made her thoughts turn to sin.

He drew his finger slowly across her lips, waiting for her answer.

She shuddered.

Ava knew in that moment something had changed between them, something magical that glowed golden, but would never come again. As if they stood not on the grand ship *Titanic*, but back in Ireland on the greenest of green plots while the setting sun cast a shower of glimmering dust on them.

The dreamlike scene flickered before her eyes and a gentle happiness took possession of her. She put behind her the fact Captain Lord Blackthorn – Buck – wanted her not as a wife, but as a mistress.

That it was a sin against God for her to love this man. On this night, this hour, they were two passengers on a mystical journey that would soon end.

Not before she had one glorious wish come true.

'Dance with me,' she said, letting go with a low whisper, her cheeks flushed with the pleasure she anticipated she'd find deep within her. With him. In his arms.

'It would be my pleasure, my lady.'

He called her a lady and her heart soared, making her feet lift off the ground.

How grand was that?

The strains of a lovely waltz surrounded them as Buck held her closer around the waist and took her hand in his. A soft curtain of velvet shadows hid them from view as she glimpsed the blue-jacketed trio of musicians playing in the reception area. The romantic melodies of a viola, cello and piano reached out to her like a lyrical fantasy as if they were playing just for them.

She looked at Buck and sensed a playfulness about him that intrigued her as they danced to the music, him daring to hold her close. Their cheeks touched when the music changed to a sensual, hot rhythm with earthy overtones of lust and passion. Though she had no idea what she was doing, he guided her though a series of provocative dance steps that made her tingle inside as he dipped her backward, his groin pressed into hers.

A delicious warmth surged through her.

He held her captive, seducing her with eyes simmering with raw desire. His slicked-back dark hair was cut at an angle, emphasizing his strong jawline. His dark eyes were smoldering, but questioning, his brows lifted. His look cut deep into her soul, capturing the essence of her feelings for him.

She gritted her teeth to keep from trembling, aware their bodies were still pressed together and she was lost in a world of her own responses.

Unspoken words hung in the air.

Heat shot through her when he pulled her closer to him as the melancholy strains of the music evoked an impassioned need in her to follow him through the graceful yet difficult twists and turns of the dance. Here, away from prying eyes under the grand sweep of the staircase, hiding their daring movements.

A dance deeply moving, mysterious.

Cold fire singed her skin every time he touched her.

A melting of her senses caused Ava to close her eyes when she felt his lips brush her neck, the warmth of his breath on her skin making her shiver.

He was a skillful dancer and a firm press on her back made her arch in response to his command, then he twirled her in a circle. He lifted her up before spinning her around until she was too dizzy to do anything but go limp in his arms. She nearly died with pleasure when his lips trailed over her burning cheek before he kissed her, covering her mouth with his own, ravishing her with his need and making her squirm.

Before she could catch her breath, he ended the kiss.

'I'm not fooling myself, Ava. I know you don't find the idea of becoming my mistress a favorable one,' he whispered in her ear, 'but I feel your need for pleasure is as hungry as mine.'

'You are most presumptuous, sir, to think I would allow you to bed me.' What was wrong with her? This was what she wanted, wasn't it?

She'd never have another chance to be in his arms. When the *Titanic* arrived in New York, she'd be a servant girl again and he'd be a titled gentleman.

She'd address him as 'your lordship' and he'd cast nary a glance in her direction.

But for tonight, this ship of dreams was hers for the taking.

'I will ask you just once, Ava, then I will never mention it again,' he murmured in her ear, then nibbled on it. 'Shall we finish the tango in my stateroom?'

'Yes,' she said, her voice barely a whisper.

* * *

Her dream was coming true, that winged belief she could rise above who she was for one enchanted night aboard the finest ship in the world.

Lying in his brass bed, in his arms.

Wrapped up in silk and sweat, Ava had run so far away from the teachings of the Church, yet she dared all the holy saints to catch up to her and tell her why such an act was wrong.

In her heart she believed it was as blessed as the first spring rain drenching the budding blooms with the spirit of faith.

And the devil be hanged.

Looking at him all grand and handsome in his elegant evening clothes, Ava had every reason to believe he would show no restraint and make love to her with the same intensity he'd displayed since the first time they met. Her racing from the law, her face flushed, her body racked with fatigue, the fear of God coursing through her veins. Him finding her, grabbing her, so protective and daring he was, then keeping her safe.

What a fine memory it was.

Her mind, filled with hope and passion, could see this was her one chance at happiness.

If only for tonight.

She let down her hair. When she saw the gleam in his eyes, she knew the effect was stunning, her long red tresses flowing over her shoulders.

'Like star fire,' Buck said, holding her tight around the waist, then wrapping her long hair around his fingers and drawing her face close to his.

Impatience made her cry out. She was so aware of her own breathing, fast and hard, her lips parting, when—

He kissed her. Hungrily. With an intimacy she'd never known before in her life, as if he could deny himself the taste of her no longer.

Her hands slipped over his broad shoulders, pulling off his

evening coat, then clutching at his gentleman's white shirt. No gentleman kissed like this. He claimed her mouth with force, yet he was also tender. His kisses were all she had dreamed of and so much more.

A lovely aura of oneness encompassed her, touching him, feeling his muscles, strong and powerful. Her womanly instincts sparked, every inch of her becoming alive as she had never been before.

'Ava, my love,' he said, cupping her face in his hands. His words captured her mind, but his movements mesmerized her with a wicked promise she prayed he would keep.

His gaze slid up and down her body, inspecting her, caressing her slender thighs, as they lay side by side on the bed atop the satin bedding.

Her heart seemed to stop.

He'd never seen anyone so beautiful, he had said, each word a whispered caress touching her heart. This was a man who had captured her wandering Irish soul with his strength and power. She dared not hint at the desperation seething inside her to surrender to him, believing he would cast her aside for her recklessness.

No, she'd not wait any longer.

She pushed aside the ranting of her mind. With all her heart she wanted him and she wondered how long she could wait for him to take her.

By God, she *couldn't* wait. A girl had to do what she had to do.

She pulled away from his embrace and slipped out of bed, then took off the countess's long black coat. She tossed it onto the horsehair sofa and stood there, grinning to see him fighting to keep his composure.

Before he could stop her, she pulled off her stewardess uniform and tossed it carelessly on the carpet. Amused, Buck folded his hands behind his head and watched her.

Standing in her flimsy chemise and camisole, Ava blushed. Thank God for the fan in the ceiling that blew a soft breeze to cool her cheeks. Now to finish what she'd started.

Licking her lips, she untied the thin white ribbon on her faded camisole with great care before pulling the string free.

Her eyes never leaving his.

'You amaze me, Ava,' Buck was saying, his eyes traveling up and down the length of her as she pulled the camisole over her head and wiggled out of the garment. 'You know how to tease like the smartest sophisticate, yet I'd swear you've never been with a man before.'

'Is that what you think?' she teased. 'I'll not tell you, sir, but show you instead.'

Without hesitation, she undid the plain, round top buttons on her chemise and made no move to cover herself as her breasts spilled out over her corset.

'You little vixen,' he said.

He reached for her, but she stepped back.

Such fun she was having. She was alive in a wild way as she'd never been before, all the anticipation building inside her. Her need so great, she didn't care if she acted in a bold manner, exposing her desire to him as easily as she'd bared her breasts.

Buck never took his eyes off her. Danger lurked in his gaze.

Her heart slammed in her chest when Buck jumped off the bed and tore off his shirt, baring his muscular chest.

She trembled. She'd never seen a man so naked. So tempting.

Ava could no more look away than let the devil take her soul. It was maddening. His skin glistened with a sheen of sweat. A warrior's body, the muscles in his arms rippling when he reached out to touch her, the tendons in his belly hard, a man sculpted like a god, yet he was all sinew and muscle, flesh and bone.

He pulled her into his arms and together, laughing, they rolled back onto the bed.

Close to calling out every blessed name she could think of, Ava met his gaze, her nails digging into his arms.

Buck touched her breasts with slow strokes, then unhooked her corset and tossed it aside. Next, he pulled off her chemise and kissed her stomach, her thighs, *everywhere*, as if he wished to familiarize himself with every mole, every freckle on her body.

She groaned, the anticipation building in her until she could stand it no longer.

She pushed her hips up to meet him, him kneeling over her, when—

A loud *knock* on the cabin door startled her.

She sat up. A cutting chill raced through her. A numbness struck her and she couldn't move.

Again, the knock. *Louder* this time.

'Stay here, Ava,' Buck said. 'Don't make a sound.'

She nodded, then crossed her arms over her bare breasts. He drew the bed drapes closed to hide her, leaving her alone in the darkened alcove. She could hear the door opening, then Buck trying to quiet down the intruder, his harsh whispers giving no quarter.

Whoever it was, they wouldn't go away.

Ava blessed herself. She swore by all that was holy she'd done no wrong. She was a good Catholic girl, save for her weakness of the flesh that did no one no harm.

So what then was all the commotion about?

Had St Michael himself come for her?

17

Buck groaned when he opened the cabin door and saw the hysterical look on the face of the woman ready to skin his hide.

And Ava's.

The countess.

Hellbent on catching him with his pants down.

He was hot and sweaty and naked above the waist, his upper body shiny with sweat. She gawked at him, cleared her throat, then regained her composure.

He wasn't prepared for what happened next.

Fiona pushed past him and ripped open the bed drapes concealing the girl. Ava screamed, pulled up the satin bedding to hide her nakedness. 'Come out of there, Ava, *now*.'

Ava, with her head held low, swung her feet over the edge of the bed.

Finally, she said, 'Turn around, your ladyship, so I can hide my shame.'

Fiona looked smug. 'Why should I? You didn't hide yourself from Buck.'

'Don't be so hard on the girl,' Buck said, coming between them. 'This is all my doing.'

Neither woman could take their eyes off his naked torso, staring at him with hungry looks. He would have found the entire incident amusing, but he was aware there was more at play here than a lady looking for her maid.

The countess smirked. 'Really, Buck, she doesn't appear to be your prisoner. Rather, I believe *you* are *hers*.' She lifted up the girl's chin. Ava turned her face away in defiance but Fiona wasn't about to be deterred. She forced the girl to meet her eyes. 'Look at me, Ava, and tell me you didn't use your wiles to seduce him, as all pretty women do.'

Buck softened. 'There's no need to be jealous, Fiona.'

'Me, jealous?' the countess said, laughing as she turned to stare him down, her eyes blazing. 'Come, Buck. You know me better than that.'

'Then why *are* you here?' he asked, raking his hand through his matted, damp hair in frustration.

'I came to save the girl from making the biggest mistake of her life.'

Thrusting out her chin, Ava opened her mouth to protest, but Buck's next words stopped her cold.

'You're a little late for that, Fiona,' he said in a slow drawl, baiting her. The shocked look on her face confirmed what he wanted to know.

She still loved him. Buck backed down. He hated himself for that. How could a man live with himself for hurting such a dear soul?

'You *compromised* this girl?' the countess demanded to know. 'How could you do such a thing, Buck?' Her angry tone indicated she wouldn't leave without an explanation.

Was she upset or jealous?

Or both?

'Ava took off her clothes of her own free will,' he said with a calm demeanor, trying to soften the blow.

'That's cruel, Buck,' she said, hurt. 'You don't have to remind me of my foolish behavior that night at Dirksen Castle.'

Ava exhaled loudly but said nothing. Her cheeks were tinted pink. Buck was taken aback she'd admit such a thing in front of the Irish girl. The countess was alive with a feverish, unfriendly behavior that unnerved him.

He had to tread carefully, or he would find himself in an unpleasant situation, caught between two very unpredictable women.

Both were special to him, he acknowledged, though for different reasons. He greatly admired the countess, her goodness and her elegance. She was fair-minded and viewed jealousy as humiliating to a woman and showing her insecurity. He couldn't help but feel empathy for her.

That was before he dragged Ava into her life. He'd be the first to say he had misjudged the chemistry between the two women and now he was paying for it.

And Ava... *damn it all to hell,* what he felt about her no man had a right to feel without putting a ring on her finger.

Something he wasn't ready to do.

The last thing he needed was *either* woman angry with him.

'I'm not trying to hurt you, Fiona,' Buck said gently, 'but what happened between Ava and me has nothing to do with our friendship.'

The countess picked up her long black velvet coat, which had slipped onto the floor, and dusted off the collar with its plaid trim. 'I believe it does, Buck. You brought the girl to me and I feel responsible for her.'

'Don't you think *I* do?' he countered, hurting inside. He tried not to show it.

She looked at him with an accusing glare. 'Once you're through with her, then what? The girl will have nothing to show for it but a smile on her face.'

'You've made your point, Fiona,' he said, his mind fixed on the matter of keeping Ava safe. 'What do you suggest I do?'

'Don't see her again.'

'What?' Like hell he wouldn't. But he wouldn't tell her that.

'She can stay in my employ until we arrive in New York, then I'll ask Trey to find her a position.'

'Does this mean our friendship is also at an end?' he asked carefully.

'Yes, Buck. It should have been done with years ago, but I was too blind to see what you really are.'

'And what is that, if I may ask?'

'A selfish opportunist who can never truly love *any* woman.' She grabbed the Irish girl by the arm. 'Come, Ava, it's late and Sunday church services are in the morning.'

Ava, who had been strangely silent throughout their heated exchange, pulled away from the countess then grabbed her clothes. She stepped into her chemise and lifted it up to cover herself. 'Don't I have a say in my own life, your ladyship?'

'No!' Buck and the countess blurted out together, louder than the shriek of the ship's whistles.

Ava stepped back, her hands flying up in the air. Her jaw dropped as a sense of astonishment sparked in her green eyes.

'In all my days, who would believe a poor Irish girl would come between a countess and the son of a duke,' she said in awe, dressing quickly.

Buck ached inside, watching her, wanting to hold her again, caress every inch of her. Never before had he felt such a bond to *any* woman, even with all the responsibilities that came with her. Never before had he been willing to accept those obligations, retreating as he always did at the first sign of commitment. A jealous husband was just an excuse for him to break off the affair.

This time a jealous woman made him see the light.

He let the countess's words sink in, whirl around in his brain like a dervish, but the answer was always the same and one he never expected. A savage determination gripped him to possess Ava, not as his mistress, but as his—

My God, had he actually formed the word in his mind?

'Ava, I... I...' he stammered, the words not coming, though he tried. Why was his confidence wavering? Only one reason. His desire was tinged by the fear she'd turn him down.

A new and unbelievable predicament for him, but possible nonetheless.

'You don't have to say your piece to me, your lordship,' Ava said, her eyes pleading with him. 'The countess is right. *I have to stay with her.*'

He understood. His wild, impetuous Ava was holding her tongue, though it killed her.

Why? The answer was obvious.

She'd never get off the ship if the countess sacked her.

Buck found himself struggling with doing what he wanted or what would keep her safe. In the end, he had no choice but to go along with this charade or lose her forever.

'Goodbye, Buck,' said the countess, hustling the girl along. 'Don't try to see Ava again.'

With a pained look on her face, Ava's eyes met his, her heart wounded, but her spirit still wanting to fight.

Don't give up, Ava, the pleading in his eyes said, but it was clear they both wondered if they'd ever see each other again.

Then the women were gone.

Buck sat on the edge of the bed for what seemed like a long time, the girl's sweet scent rising up from the soft satin bedding and overwhelming his senses. He became aware of the rapid beating of his heart in his chest. An empty feeling added to his misery. He went over the whole damn scene again and again, coming up with the same answer every time.

Once he explained to the countess he *had* changed and his intentions toward Ava were honorable, she'd understand.

He never intended to hurt Fiona. In the end, she'd have to accept the fact he was in love with another woman.

She would, wouldn't she?

Buck cursed under his breath, trying to cope with what was, for him, a new experience. He'd never asked to fall in love with this girl, and now that he had, his whole life was turned upside down.

Who would ever have dreamed this wandering gentleman gambler would try to make an honest woman out of her, as Ava had so aptly put it, and that it would be so difficult?

Worse yet, he'd let her go in a reckless moment without letting Ava know how he felt about her. Damnation, she must hate him after this. He prayed she understood his silence.

Hell be damned, was he a fool? What woman would understand her lover abandoning her?

With a heavy heart, he paced up and down the room. All the eloquent excuses in the world wouldn't do him any good. He felt a strange sense of betrayal to Ava. He'd let her down, allowing Fiona to take her away.

He jammed through the stateroom door, looking up and down the long corridor. He was determined to tell Ava how he felt about her, but the two women were nowhere to be seen.

He ventured out, threading his way through the long corridor. He was shirtless, wearing only his black trousers. It was late. Ava was gone. He prayed she was already back in the countess's stateroom for the night.

Safe.

But for how long? The shadows were closing around the girl and there was nothing he could do to stop them. The ship's officers had their orders and would continue their search. Buck couldn't bear the thought of them sending her back to Ireland in chains. He believed her innocent and would risk everything he had to help her.

A deep sadness claimed his heart. He had the strangest feeling she was already lost to him.

He retreated back to his cabin and laid out his clothes for Sunday church services. He would attempt to make amends with the countess, make her understand his feelings for Ava were *not* that of a rogue, but a gentleman eager to court his love.

He opened the porthole in his cabin to get a breath of fresh air and a cold breeze blew in, making him shiver. A strange, clammy odor assaulted his nostrils.

Ice.

18

'Someday you'll thank me, Ava, for saving you from Captain Lord Blackthorn and his false promises.'

The countess poured herself a cup of lukewarm cocoa from a silver pot, her abrupt gesture telling Ava she was displeased with her.

'Will I?' Ava raised her eyes.

'Of course you will,' said the countess, sipping her chocolate. She left the sweet biscuits the stewardess had brought untouched. 'It's for your own good.'

'*And* yours.'

She turned to find the countess glaring at her with an icy stare.

Startled, her ladyship slammed down her teacup and rattled her saucer. 'Why, you ungrateful girl.'

Ava lowered her eyes, a pink tint flooding her cheeks. Her guilt showed as clear as if she'd been caught with her hand in the Sunday collection basket. She'd spoken her piece without thinking, the truth flying out of her mouth like avenging angels and with that, everything changed.

She'd struck a nerve in the countess, impulsive words falling from her lips that made the woman edgy and suspicious.

Ava froze. What made her outburst so unforgiveable was they both knew it was true.

You couldn't hold your tongue, could you, girl? And such a fine performance you gave for Captain Lord Blackthorn, keeping your mouth shut and acting all grand and good.

You'll pay for this.

'Explain yourself, Ava,' the countess asked, her eyes narrowing. She tapped her teaspoon against her cup in a nervous manner.

'I'll not take it back, your ladyship, and give you the pretty words you want to hear,' Ava said, staying true to herself. 'If I did, I'd be lying and that's a sin against the Church.' She was in enough trouble already with the Almighty to add to her woes. 'The way I see it, your ladyship, if *you* can't have Buck, *no* woman can.'

'Don't be absurd,' the countess said, trying to calm herself. 'It's true Buck hurt me, but it was my fault. I never wanted to see him for what he is. A selfish man with no scruples or morals. Do you think you're the first woman to fall for his lies?'

Ava's curiosity was piqued and, if she dared admit it, she experienced a twinge of jealousy. 'Who do you mean, your ladyship?'

'Why, the infamous Lady Pennington of Mayfair,' the countess said with a smugness that surprised Ava. As if she enjoyed taunting her with the woman's name. 'She is of no consequence as far as I'm concerned.'

'Why would you bother with the likes of me over a highborn lady?'

'It's very simple, Ava,' her ladyship said rather sharply. 'Buck is in love with you.'

Shock ran through Ava with the same intensity as if the countess had told her she didn't believe in God. It was one thing for Mr Brady to say such a thing, but the countess? Her heart accelerated, partly because she didn't believe Buck loved her and partly because she did.

'You're not lying to me?' she said, her voice hushed and reverent.

'Why should I?' the countess said, smiling. That innocent, ladylike smile Ava envied. 'Even Trey noticed how Buck looks at you. He warned me you were trouble.'

'*Me*, trouble?' Ava said, her thoughts blurring. What did the countess know that she wasn't telling her?

'When you brought my gloves to me, I saw a hungry look on my fiancé's face, a longing I'd never seen when he looked at me.' She traced the brown and gold Spode pattern on her teacup with her fingertips. 'After you left, Trey couldn't stop chatting about you. How charming you were with your funny way of talking and how you weren't afraid to speak your mind, not to mention your glossy red hair and good looks.' Ava didn't speak. Mr Brady's opinion of her caught her off guard. Not the kind of talk from a man who only wanted to bed her. What was he about?

'I suspected he might have a romantic interest in you,' the countess continued. 'He assured me he was simply admiring the local scenery, but he *did* admit to me that given the chance, any man would fall in love with you.' Looking up from her teacup, she seemed to stare right through Ava. 'When I returned to my stateroom and found you missing, I guessed where you'd gone.'

'So you came looking for me.'

'Yes. I thought I was over my feelings for Buck, that it didn't matter any more, but when I saw the two of you together, I lost my temper. How could it be that you, a poor girl with no family, no background, could take the man I love away from me? While I, a peeress in my right, couldn't make him fall in love with me no matter *what* I did? I have a title and lands, but they mean nothing next to a beautiful face and figure.'

'You *are* a beautiful woman, Countess.'

'Don't try to humor me, Ava. It's not becoming on you. I know what I am. Educated but plain, with a gift for romantic poetry but *not* for romancing a man.' She paused, her frustration showing in the tiny lines appearing around her mouth. 'Oh, why did I ever agree to this marriage? I could have remained a reclusive spinster and happily so with Buck at my side between love affairs if he hadn't met you.'

Ava's green eyes regained their usual sparkle.

'This isn't about me, your ladyship, it's about *you* wanting to hurt Buck by denying him the one thing he wants. *Me.*'

The countess scoffed at that. 'That's ridiculous.'

'Is it?' Ava demanded.

'Yes. I love Buck—'

'So do I, your ladyship. I would rather die than see anyone hurt him.'

A low, guttural moan erupted from the countess's throat, as if Ava had ripped her soul to shreds. She had. She'd torn away the silken fabric that shielded Fiona from the vulgar in life and made her see the truth.

That her love for Buck was stronger than the countess's.

This time she'd gone *too* far. The countess rose to her feet and slapped her across the face. *Hard.*

'How *dare* you!' she said.

Ava didn't move. She stood there, bewildered. Her cheek stung from the blow, but she didn't touch her face. She refused to show weakness in front of the woman.

'You needn't worry about me any more, your ladyship,' Ava said, struggling to suppress a cold shiver that had come over her. 'I can keep my mouth shut. I'll do my job as I'm told and give you no more trouble. I promise.' She started for the wardrobe. 'I'll set out your dressing gown—'

'*No.*'

'What?' Ava turned, panicked.

'Put on your dirty, old clothes and leave me alone,' the countess moaned.

'But, your ladyship...' Ava looked at her, a sudden overwhelming fear stifling her movements.

'Get out of my sight.'

Ava forced herself to ask, 'Where will I go?'

'Back where you belong. In steerage.' The countess looked her up and down with a dismissive glance. 'You'll never be a lady's maid, Ava, *or* a lady.'

'I'm just as good as you and this Lady Pennington,' Ava blurted out, getting her courage back. She was suddenly jealous of this other woman she'd never met. A woman whom Buck had once held in his arms. A woman he'd kissed.

'Nonsense, Ava. You'll never amount to anything.'

Ava pushed aside her anger, though she was hurting inside at the woman's cruel words. She *had* to get the countess to change her mind.

Her life depended on it.

'I beg you to think it over, your ladyship,' she said. 'The *Titanic* docks in three days. You'll need me to help you unpack your bags.'

'That's already been taken care of,' the countess said with confidence. 'Trey wired his mother to find me a lady's maid in New York.'

Ava squeezed her eyes tight in frustration. Mr Brady and his fine plans to have her spy on his mother. Now it was her undoing.

She had been sacked. The damage was done.

The countess put her finger on the call bell embedded into the bulkhead. 'I'll ring for the bedroom steward to take you back to third class.'

'*No*, your ladyship,' Ava cried, grabbing the woman's arm so hard she ripped the shoulder seam open. 'You can't do that, *please!*' Her desperate plea made her voice crack, her eyes tear. A cold shiver sliced through her as panic made her whole body stiffen. She couldn't move.

'You insolent girl!'

In a moment of fury, the countess tore open Ava's stewardess uniform down the front, the black buttons popping off like tiny pieces of coal.

Ava stood dumbfounded. She couldn't say a word.

'Trey promised he'd find me a *real* lady's maid,' the countess said, not stopping to take a breath. 'Not an Irish tramp.'

She could see the hurt and envy in her ladyship's cold gray eyes. All her catty sarcasm and playfulness were gone now. Ava realized with a sense of dread the countess *wanted* her to strike back, to lower herself to the disgusting creature she had called her to assuage her own guilt.

She wouldn't do it.

Her feeling of anger suddenly turned into a deeper and more immediate need not to let the woman take from her the one thing she had left.

Her pride.

Ava threw on her old tweed suit and grabbed her cloth traveling bag and her mother's rosary, then raced out the cabin door and down the corridor with the countess's threats still echoing in her ears.

'You'll not get the better of Ava O'Reilly,' she whispered to herself through clenched teeth. 'Not as long as I'm free.'

* * *

Dreaming of Captain Lord Blackthorn, Ava wandered up and down the labyrinth of long corridors of the great liner, holding on to her cloth traveling bag, skirting up the first-class stairs to B Deck, finding herself again marveling at the gracefully curving Grand Staircase with its oak paneling, gilded balustrades, and wide, sweeping steps.

Empty.

No one was about. The memory of her dancing with Buck so vivid in her mind, she let out a deep sigh. His kisses exciting her. His touch electrifying her. Was it only a few hours ago she'd thrilled so to his touch?

Daydreaming like the sinner she was, wanting him to hold her again, the emotion building in her to such a degree she thought she'd die if she didn't find him. She knew she shouldn't dally like a schoolgirl tying a silk ribbon in her hair, but she couldn't refuse her heart the sweet poignancy of this moment.

She couldn't deny her love for him and the joy he'd given her.

In her confused state of mind, Ava found herself staring down a long corridor with its thick, deep red and gold carpeting and ornate white paneling. She felt as if she'd walked miles along the passageways, never passing the same way twice.

Nothing looked familiar to her. She *must* be headed the wrong way.

To clear her head and get her bearings, she raced up the stairway to the Boat Deck and sought the fresh sea air. She stared over the wooden railing on the first-class promenade, confused and heartsick.

Trying to decide what to do next when she heard—

'Grab her!' shouted a seaman, filling her with panic and sending her scurrying along the Boat Deck railing. Her hands slid over the wood wet with dewy spray. She nearly dropped her cloth traveling bag overboard when she lost her footing and slipped on the teak deck. She fell to one knee, her heart pounding and her legs heavy as she tried to get up. She couldn't.

She grabbed onto the lower railing, when another seaman seized her under the armpits and dragged her to her feet.

'A stowaway.'

'Let me go!' She could feel his heated breath against the back of her neck, but she defied him in spite of the cold night air nipping at her cheeks.

Oh, why had she dared to go up on the Boat Deck? Why, in the name of the Mother of God, had she been so foolish?

'Let's see what you look like, lass,' the seaman said, curious. He released his hold on her.

'No!' Ava cried out, taking to her heels, but she didn't get far. The man grabbed her by her long red hair flying loose around her shoulders. She fell backward, landing on the deck, the breath knocked out of her.

'A beauty, she is,' the man said, turning her face to the light.

Ava winced.

'Must be one of them Irishers from third class,' the first seaman said. 'What's she doing up here?'

'If you know what's good for you,' Ava shot back, 'you'd best leave me be.'

'The lass has got spirit,' the first seaman said, chuckling, then he grabbed her arm. 'But does she have a steamship ticket?'

'I'm a lady's maid.'

'And I'm Mr Guggenheim's valet,' he said, laughing.

'Blimey,' added his friend, 'what's a lady's maid doing on the Boat Deck at midnight?'

'I – I'm meeting someone.'

The seaman leaned closer and she could smell the garlic on his breath. 'Who is the lucky gent?'

Ava said nothing, her face cold with sweat.

'Get Mr Moody straightaway,' he ordered. 'He should be coming off his watch. He'll know what to do with her.'

The seaman dug his hands into her jacket pockets, his eyes widening in surprise when he found her white steamship ticket and contract. Holding her by the wrist, he scrutinized them under the small glassed-in light beside the stair.

'Well, I'll be. You're the Irish girl we've been looking for.' He smirked. 'You've given us quite a run, Miss O'Reilly. We never would have found you if me and Willie hadn't come up here for a smoke.'

'What's going on here?' called out a young man rushing toward them. Ava stiffened. A ship's officer. Now she was had.

'We found your fugitive, Mr Moody,' said the seaman, pinning her arms to her sides.

'Are you certain?' the young officer asked, surprised.

'Yes, sir, I found these papers on her.' He handed him her third-class ticket and the White Star contract signed by her own hand.

She moaned.

'You've got her all right. We'll keep her confined below until we get to New York.'

Ava cringed.

Oh, no, dear Jesus, it can't be.

She kicked and screamed and pleaded, but it did her no good. They forced her to stand still while they tied her hands behind her back with thick rope.

She was their prisoner.

They dragged her down the crew stairways so as not to draw attention from passengers. Down, *down*. Deep into the bowels of the *Titanic* where no one could find her. She heard Mr Moody tell the seamen not to breathe a word about her capture to anyone.

Her shoulders slumped.

She would always remember this night by its smells – the fine tobacco and smooth bouquet of wine in first class tempting her, the lingering perfume of the ladies as exquisite as a fresh pink rose. The crisp, clean scent of the gentlemen's white shirts and cuffs and the pure-smelling lemon soap making her feel grand.

Like a lady.

All that disappeared when she found herself in the close quarters of steerage, where the curious women staring at her wore clothes heavy with the earthy, grassy smell of Ireland still clinging to their petticoats along with a spicy blend of herbs and oranges.

And the smell of fear.

Her own.

'Look who's come to join us, dear sister. If it isn't the Queen of Sheba herself,' the girl with the braid cried out.

Curious, Ava turned her head and recognized the girl with the long braid wrapped around her head.

The same girl who'd taunted her at Queenstown.

'Her hands are tied behind her,' her sister said with dismay, pointing at her. 'Mercy, what's she done?'

'Stole the silver from the first-class dining saloon, I'd say.'

The girl with the braid broke into wild laughter. With coaxing from her sister, they went back to their cabin, whispering and gossiping among themselves.

Ava would get no help from them.

The seaman hustled her along Scotland Road, then down deeper into the bowels of the ship to a lower deck. They tossed her and her small traveling bag into an empty cabin at the forward end, away from the snippety women.

It was half past midnight on Sunday morning when the door slammed behind her. Panic raced through her when Ava heard the click of the key in the lock. She tried to open the door from the inside, but she couldn't.

A sole electric bulb burned overhead. She closed her eyes and prayed.

She was alone. Abandoned.

Doomed to spend the remainder of the crossing locked up in the cramped two-berth cabin like a common thief. The pine paneled walls closed in on her, threatening to suffocate her spirit.

She had to keep her wits about her. She wouldn't accept the fact her plight was futile.

The seaman had cut the rope from her wrists, but her hands were still numb with cold. She yearned to slump down into the hollows of the spring mattress and get some sleep to quell her fears. She'd get no special treatment and she was of the mind they'd feed her nothing but water and potato peelings for the rest of the voyage.

Her final stop, Ireland.

Then prison.

The frightening reality of it all shot through her like jagged lightning striking her heart. Her shaking hands grabbed and clawed at the red and white coverlet she'd pulled off the lower berth, wrapping it around her as if it would hide her shame. Ava pushed away the stray wisps of hair hanging in her eyes and her fingers felt a large bobby pin entangled in a knot in her hair.

A crazy notion hit her. Could it work? Why not?

She pulled it out, snagging stray hairs and making her wince.

She bent it with her fingers, changing its shape. Long, wiry. Perfect to pry open the lock. She'd seen the impetuous young footman in the grand house open the servants' entrance the same way when the staff came home late after attending the village fair.

She *had* to try. It could be her key to freedom.

Ava slipped the straightened bobby pin into the slender lock and fiddled with it. Pushing it this way and that, scraping it back and forth, pulling it in and out, the hollow grating sound echoing in her ears. She worked at it for several minutes, shaking the inner workings of the brass lock back and forth until she felt it almost give when—

'Get away from that door!' yelled a male voice, angry and terse.

Startled, Ava dropped the bobby pin and it rattled onto the cold floor. Even if she could make it work, she'd never get past the guard. Tears welled up in her eyes. Not even the most eccentric saint would help her now. Acting like a common thief she was, as if proving their accusations true by her foolish act.

All her efforts were useless. They had posted a guard outside her cabin.

Escape was impossible.

She plunged into a frightening darkness, then her emotions burst into a wild torrent of tears. In the long hours that followed, she sobbed her heart out.

Not even a prayer to help her.

Such was her heartbreak, the accusing voices rattling about in her head were strangely silent on this night.

As if they too knew her fate was sealed and only God Himself could save her.

19

14 April 1912

At Divine Service the following morning, Buck made his way down to D Deck in time to hear the first-class passengers singing ‘O God Our Help in Ages Past’. Captain Smith led the service from the ship’s own prayer book, while the *Titanic*’s musicians provided the accompaniment to the hymn.

In something of a surprise, Fiona was nowhere to be seen.

He had also expected to see Ava.

Buck tried to hide his disappointment, scouring the crowd, maneuvering his way through the rows of green velvet upholstered armchairs and wicker chairs set up as pews. He wanted to believe Ava would scurry in at the last minute, all wide-eyed, looking at everything in that crazy way of hers he adored.

He mumbled the words of the hymn, his eyes still searching, but she never showed.

He prayed she hadn’t tried to attend Catholic services in second or third class. He admired her deep faith, but the likelihood of the ship’s officers spotting her there was too big a risk for her to take.

That didn’t explain the absence of the countess.

What was behind her lack of appearance? The day had begun with a little rain, but not enough to keep her away.

Obvious, isn't it? Buck acknowledged. She was still angry with him for trying to take Ava to his bed.

Proper behavior or not, he was sorry he hadn't.

Damnation, it was bad enough for a man to have to worry about one woman, let along two.

Ava *and* the countess.

After a soul-searching walk on deck after the service, Buck headed for the first-class dining saloon, clenching and unclenching his fists. There, he found Captain Smith and Mr Ismay engaged in conversation about the record speed the ship was making, giving Mr Ismay the opportunity to tell all within earshot he had no doubt they would beat the record set by the *Titanic*'s sister ship, the *Olympic*, on her maiden voyage.

The conversation took a turn when the captain read the wireless handed to him by a ship's officer. He looked rather glum as he passed the note to Mr Ismay.

Another iceberg warning?

'The Baltic is warning us about floating fields of ice,' said Mr Ismay, showing the wireless to the two ladies hovering at his side.

'Are you going to slow the ship down?' asked Mrs Ryerson with concern.

'This is the *Titanic*, madam,' Mr Ismay boasted. 'We're going to run the ship faster to avoid the ice.'

His glib reply indicated no one should take the iceberg warnings seriously.

Buck did.

He'd smelled ice last night. Keen in the air. He had no doubt about it.

What surprised him more than Mr Ismay's casual reference to icebergs was the absence of a customary lifeboat drill after Sunday services.

That disturbed him but he gave it no further mind when Mrs

Cardeza and her son approached him, chatting about looking forward to luncheon and asking where the countess was today.

Buck made excuses for Fiona, saying she was busy filling out her baggage declaration sheet and assured the wealthy Philadelphia matron she'd make an appearance at the evening concert in the lounge.

God help him if Ava showed up, since he suspected Mr Lightoller may have pointed *her* out to Mrs Cardeza as the countess.

He'd deal with that scenario only if he had to.

Until then, he worried about Ava. Some men might consider a woman in her predicament fair game. Trey certainly did.

Not him. Ava had inspired greater things in him, a willingness to settle down.

God help him.

But how to attain his goal?

He could never be close to Ava and not want her.

She was bold, vibrant, yet with a humble look in her eyes as if she was in awe of everyone and everything around her. Alert, passionate eyes lit by her God-fearing soul.

In that moment, Buck made a decision. He didn't care *where* she came from. A wretched shack with dirt floors or a lodging house sleeping ten to a room. He wanted to capture her body, her heart. Her mind. Damn it, he wanted *her*.

And to hell with what society thought.

What about his promise to Fiona not to see her again?

A promise he intended to keep only until he arranged otherwise. He didn't wish to spoil the countess's chance for a good match and a means to save her estate.

All these thoughts tormented him when he joined Trey for lunch in the first-class dining saloon.

'Fiona kept to her cabin this morning,' Trey told him as he scanned the bill of fare.

Buck remained silent. He had no doubt Fiona was still in a bother over discovering Ava in his cabin.

'Then you didn't talk to her?' Buck asked him.

'I didn't see Ava either.' A wistful sigh followed that he didn't try to hide.

'I didn't ask you about the Irish girl.' Buck ignored Trey's amused expression and decided on the corned beef and vegetables, though he had little appetite.

'You didn't have to. That hungry look in your eyes told me what you *really* wanted to know.' Trey smiled at him with not the slightest hint of embarrassment. 'You needn't worry, Buck. I've given up my quest to take Ava away from you. She's too valuable to me.'

'Explain yourself, Trey.'

Buck didn't trust him. Ava could be easily duped by someone as smooth talking as Treyton Brady. Her eyes drinking in every new thing she saw.

Damn, she wasn't safe from anyone.

'I'll fill you in on the details, old man, when we arrive in New York.' Trey leaned closer, his thin mustache curving over his upper lip. 'I *shall* tell you this much. My interest in Ava has nothing to do with nocturnal activities. I've come to an understanding with her that won't tarnish her reputation.'

'For your sake, Trey,' Buck said, knitting his brows together, 'I hope this isn't another college prank.'

'Really, Buck, you look as jealous as Fiona.'

'Fiona? What do you mean?'

'We had an argument over the girl last evening when Ava brought the countess her gloves.' Trey flagged down the steward and added dumplings to his order.

'You saw Ava last night?' Buck asked, focusing on his friend with avid interest.

'Yes. All I said to Fiona was that her lady's maid was lovely to look at, which didn't go over well.' Trey fixed a look on him that clearly said he was surprised at her reaction.

'That was *all?*' Buck found it hard to believe Fiona would lose her temper over that. Or was there something else simmering in her brain that made her more jealous than he believed?

'It didn't help when I added that *any* man would fall in love with the girl, but she wasn't the type you marry, simply have an affair with.' Trey paused, thinking. 'I lied. I've come to regard Ava as a woman any man would be lucky to have on his arm whether he was rich or poor, but I'd never tell Fiona that. I thought my casual observation would amuse the countess. Was I wrong. She insisted I take her back to her stateroom immediately.'

Buck laughed. 'Women.'

Now he understood. Fiona believed *he* intended to have an affair with Ava, something he had flatly refused to do with *her*. No wonder Trey's words had gotten under her skin.

'Between you and me, Buck,' Trey said seriously, 'I intend to make certain my mother doesn't change her mind about my marriage to the countess. Fiona is a decent sort and I don't want to see her hurt.'

His words heartened Buck more than he let on.

'Fiona needs a good man, Trey.'

'True,' he said wryly. 'But she still loves you, Buck.'

'I know,' was all Buck said.

* * *

In a tiny two-berth cabin in steerage, Ava fetched the chamber pot and leaned over it. She shut her eyes tight and braced herself.

This was how she was going to spend the rest of the crossing to America?

Leaning over a slops bucket?

More was the pity, but she couldn't stop the rumblings in her gut from rushing upward.

She retched into the plain blue pot, then gagged.

Sweet Jesus.

She sat very still, opening her eyes and staring at her hands clasped around the rim of the chamber pot. There wasn't a sorrier sight than herself tossing up last night's fine dinner.

Never had Ava experienced such a sick feeling. The lap of luxury it was and now this. Instead of being located amidships where the sailing was smooth, she was holed up in the bow.

Rolling... rolling... *rolling*.

Ava swore the ship rose and fell on a heavy rolling swell as she lay down on the lower bunk, praying for a quick end to her misery.

When it didn't come, she grabbed her black beads from inside her skirt pocket and started mumbling a rosary. No sooner did she say, 'Hail Mary, full of grace,' the cabin door creaked open.

She sat up with a start, her head spinning round when she saw Mr Moody and a steward come in with a tray filled with vegetable soup, currant buns, tea and—

Boiled potatoes.

'Aargh...' she moaned at the sight of the cold, soggy potatoes, then turned over on the bunk.

'Get up, girl, and eat your supper,' Mr Moody ordered.

'I can't... I'm sick.'

The ship's officer took a sniff and nodded to the steward. The man held his nose as he covered the chamber pot with a linen towel and left the cabin to empty it. Then Mr Moody set about the business that had brought him here.

'The seaman found your third-class ticket and White Star contract when he apprehended you, Miss O'Reilly, but *not* your inspection card.'

A ring of perspiration beaded on his forehead where his cap ended. He was decidedly nervous. *Why?*

He held out his hand, waiting. 'Your card, please.'

Ava moaned again. 'It's all a mistake, sir,' she pleaded. 'I swear on my sainted mother's grave, I'm innocent of any crime.'

'You must understand, miss, I'm just doing my duty.' He was becoming agitated. 'I must have your card. *Now*.'

'I don't have no inspection card,' Ava said, holding her stomach and pushing away the tray of food. She opened the lid on the teapot and the hot steam warmed her cheeks.

Whatever she'd said, Mr Moody didn't like it, his face clouding.

'Blast it all, the captain isn't going to like this. The ship will be put into quarantine for forty days if anyone finds out you *didn't* go through the inspection process,' he said. 'No one will be able to get off the ship in New York. I can imagine what Mr Ismay will say, not to mention the bad publicity for the White Star Line.' His voice took on an accusing tone when he said, 'If you know what's good for you, miss, you'll not tell a soul about this.'

And with that he was gone.

The door slammed behind him, but instead of the click of the key, she heard the sound of a padlock being fixed into place on the outside of the door.

She was worse off than before.

Ava crawled back into the bunk and wrapped herself in the red and white coverlet, her mind scheming. She wasn't beaten yet. Sick as she was, she hadn't given up. Before the ship arrived in New York, she'd find a way out of here.

That she *swore* as she got on her knees and prayed to the Holy Mother.

Amen to that, Ava O'Reilly.

* * *

'I say, rumor is they found the Irish girl,' uttered the gentleman behind Buck, so loud it broke his concentration, pulling him right out of his poker game.

What the hell did the man say?

'Who?' asked a second man, inquisitive.

'The whole ship is talking about her, old man. The girl who sneaked on board at Queenstown.'

'Very well done,' was his cohort's reply and the gentlemen clinked their glasses together in mock victory.

Buck's heart stopped. Christ.

Ava had been found?

It couldn't be true.

She was safe with the countess in her stateroom, *wasn't she*?

Glancing down at his cards, he tapped his fingers on the green felt table, thinking. Hell, what if this outrageous talk *wasn't* a rumor? What if the girl had shown up at the Sunday evening concert and someone had spotted her?

That alarming thought shot through him and made him tense his shoulders. No, she wouldn't do such a foolish thing. Fiona would have sought him out, sent word to him in the smoke room.

What then was the answer?

His head throbbed. Pounded. Grabbing a stack of gaming chips from the pile in front of him, he made his bet.

And listened.

The inebriated gentlemen behind him continued their jovial conversation in lower tones, causing Buck to lean farther back in his chair to continue eavesdropping.

'I say, she's a clever piece of gossip to make a rather uneventful crossing more colorful,' said one man.

'Either way, I wager we never set eyes on her.'

'Shall we drink to the mysterious beauty aboard the *Titanic*?'

Who *were* these two upstarts?

He turned around to see them look at each other with amused expressions. No doubt they believed the Irish girl's existence was a White Star Line myth.

Bloody hell, he couldn't sit here another minute without exploding.

His face broke out in a cold sweat and his breathing became ragged, no doubt giving away his nervousness. His behavior was unforgiveable, going against the cardinal rule of a professional gambler.

Never show your emotions.

He couldn't help himself. He was about to jump out of his skin.

He downed his brandy, praying he'd heard wrong, at the same time gathering his courage if he hadn't. Warmth flowed through him like a lovely breeze on a summer's day, steadying his nerves.

At the same time, a wildness grew within him. Primal. Stirring. This was his last hand for the evening. A desperate urge to hold Ava again in his arms gripped him. Fiona or no Fiona, he couldn't wait any longer.

He *had* to make certain she was safe.

Which meant he must make a graceful exit. As a gentleman gambler, he had a reputation to uphold. It would be unseemly for him to dash out without finishing the hand.

He gave his cards a cursory glance. Two pair. It could be four aces for all he cared.

He folded, not giving a damn if he won or lost. A supreme urgency surged through him, dictating he throw caution to the wind. He collected his winnings quickly and bid his poker companions an early good night, much to their protests.

Then he sought out the gentlemen purveyors of this troublesome news. Good breeding required he ask a gentleman of his acquaintance for an introduction first before speaking to them.

To hell with that societal nonsense. Ava's life was at stake.

Buck approached them boldly.

'At the risk of being impertinent, gentlemen,' he said, not wanting to believe what he'd heard, 'where on the ship did they find the Irish girl?'

'Word is, your lordship,' said the first man, recognizing him, 'she was wandering the Boat Deck around midnight last night when a seaman spotted her.'

'Alone?' Buck asked, a queasy feeling knotting in his stomach. That was soon after he'd left Ava with the countess.

'Yes. Hearsay is the crew member who found her hiding in a lifeboat took liberties with her before alerting the captain,' he added, snickering.

That did it.

Like a commander surveying the dead after a bloody battle, Buck stared down at the man, disbelieving. He was stunned, unmoving, while the fury raging in him built to such a feverish pitch he exploded inside. He was so outraged he swore his eyes must be bulging out.

All he could think about was Ava being groped by an overly eager seaman.

It was too much for him to bear.

Buck groaned inwardly and barely held onto his temper. He felt strangely suspended, as if this couldn't be happening to him. He *must* remain calm, not strike out and knock the hell out of this imprudent messenger. His stance was both wary and defensive. He'd learned the art of subterfuge well. First as a soldier, then as a gentleman gambler. He'd spent years learning how to keep his composure while under fire.

Not tonight.

He was deep in his misery and couldn't stand here another minute and listen to them talking about Ava and act civil. It wasn't in him. He couldn't believe she was lost to him, *wouldn't*, damn it.

She meant more to him than life itself.

Without another word, Buck turned and raced through the revolving doors of the smoke room, then jammed down two flights of stairs.

The countess had a lot of explaining to do.

* * *

'*Damnation*, Fiona, are you telling me Ava isn't here?' Buck said, barely able to contain his anger. Only through intense control did he keep from raising his voice. God knew who could be passing by in the corridor and overhear them.

'She left rather suddenly last night.' Her voice was calm and disinterested. Or so he gathered she wanted him to believe.

'Then where the hell *is* she?'

'Isn't she with *you*, Buck?' Fiona said in a smug manner, though she avoided looking at him. She continued to put on a brave front in front of him, but her lower lip trembled.

'No.'

His answer was simple and to the point, startling her. She appeared genuinely shocked.

The countess picked up her teacup, then put it down again as if she didn't know what to do next, then turned sharply toward him. 'Oh, Buck, I'm worried. Where is she?'

'I don't damned well know. I checked my cabin on my way here. She wasn't there.'

Buck paced up and down. He had to keep moving or he'd go crazy. Thinking, *thinking* about Ava being held captive, her eyes wide with fear. On second thought, knowing Ava, when they apprehended her, she'd started kicking and screaming and spewing colorful expletives, threatening to bring the wrath of God down upon any man who touched her.

She'd be lost to him forever if he didn't act fast. He had to be prepared to do *anything* to get her back.

He felt for his pistol in his jacket pocket. An insane idea, but then again, he wasn't sane at the moment.

'Are you certain you two didn't have a lovers' row?' Fiona asked, digging for information.

Buck neither confirmed nor denied it, a brooding look in his eyes telling her that although he was a man of honor, he had something else on his mind and he wasn't leaving until he'd had his say.

'I haven't seen Ava since you burst into my cabin last night, hurling accusations around like a wronged goddess intent on destroying everything in her path.' Buck paused, frustrated. 'Damn it, Fiona, why didn't you mind your own business?'

'I thought it *was* my business, Buck, to protect that girl.' She stiffened. 'I know now it was merely jealousy on my part.'

The countess blushed, not surprising him. She *should* be embarrassed, haranguing him about his roguish and devilish ways and how any woman who loved him was squandering her life.

It was her sudden admission of jealousy, her lovely gray eyes warm and misty, her soft hair smelling of lavender, her words repentant and honest that finally calmed him down.

'Tell me what happened after you left my cabin, Fiona,' he said in a quiet voice. 'It may help me find her.'

The countess hesitated, then poured them both a cup of tea. She sipped hers slowly.

'We... we got into an argument and I said things to her I shouldn't have, Buck,' she said, her voice breaking, her tone repentant. '*Horrible* things.' She stopped, the degrading words not coming from her lips, but Buck could guess. How it must have hurt Ava, who, for all her impetuous and willful ways was a pious, feeling girl. A girl who would take to heart such an insult as God's truth and believe she was condemned to hell.

Especially coming from a woman like the countess.

He didn't blame Fiona. Her father had left her much to her own resources and she existed in her own little world within a world, where everything was done according to her whim. She was a creature who was neither woman nor child, but a storybook princess whose crown had toppled, and she had no idea how to get it back.

That didn't stop her from realizing what harm she'd done.

Fiona grabbed his arm, holding it tightly. 'Oh, Buck, I *swear* I thought she was safe with you.'

'Safe?' He shrugged. 'Far from it, Fiona. The girl is being held prisoner somewhere on this ship.'

'*Prisoner?*' she said, her hand going to her throat. 'In heaven's name, what for? Surely it's no crime for a steerage passenger to lose her way aboard ship.'

He attempted a smile, grim as it was. 'It's not as simple as that. Ava O'Reilly is wanted by the constable in County Cork, Ireland for stealing a diamond bracelet.'

'*What?*' she said, visibly shaken. She sat down on the settee, her face going pale. 'I don't believe it.'

'I don't either, Fiona. I'm certain she's innocent of the theft.'

Buck repeated what Ava had told him and that he believed her story. Fiona agreed, saying whatever Ava was, she wasn't a thief. She'd had every opportunity to steal from her, including taking her mother's priceless diamond and ruby earrings, and she hadn't. She'd even asked her if she could *borrow* two bobby pins, while some girls in service would have simply taken them when her back was turned.

Fiona heaved in a long breath then stood up. 'What are you going to do, Buck?'

'I've got to find out where they're keeping her and convince them to let her go. Then I intend to get her off this ship disguised as your lady's maid.'

'What if you can't find her?'

'I've won enough money at cards on this crossing to hire the best lawyer in New York.' He felt for the roll of British banknotes and American dollars in his pocket. Along with the money he had secured in the purser's safe, he calculated his winnings were more than enough to get the job done. 'Where's Trey?'

'We were going to do a turn on the Promenade Deck this evening, but it's so cold tonight he's coming here for an after-dinner drink.' Seeing he understood her feelings of remorse, she finished with, 'Ava's not the only one I owe an apology to. I misjudged Trey as well.'

Buck smiled and took her hand in his. 'Tell him I'm sending a wire to his solicitor in New York about taking Ava's case.'

She nodded. 'Bring her back, Buck,' Fiona said with an urgency in her voice that startled him. Were those tears in her eyes she was blinking away? 'And please, tell her I'm sorry. I didn't mean anything I said to her.'

'I know, Fiona.'

'One more thing, Buck,' she said in a clear voice as he headed for the door. He could see she had donned a winning smile and regained her composure. 'Tell her I said you two belong together.'

20

Ava sat on the lower berth under the harsh light overheard, sipping warm tea. She continued nursing her sick stomach and thinking about the whole bloody mess she was in. Locked up like a disbeliever, her unhappy soul on its way to perdition.

And her with no way of getting word to Buck or the countess. She was no closer to escape, her fingers moving along the black beads nonstop.

Nothing worked.

Not her banging on the door.

Then pleading with the guard to let her out. Not a peep out of him. She was doomed to wither away like a holy wafer left unblessed by the priest.

With that sad thought, the light overhead turned a dusky golden as if the light in her heart also dimmed.

If only she could break away from her captors.

How will you do that, girl? Fly like an angel? If it's wings you want, you should have thought of that before you let him kiss you.

Still, how lovely it had been, her living like a proper aristocrat in first class. Wait until she told her tale to Mary Dolores. She could see the two of them, munching on sweet biscuits in her tiny cell while she regaled her sister with stories about the countess and her beautiful clothes and the fancy chinaware. The mysterious Turkish baths, the lively ragtime tunes the orchestra played and the Grand Staircase more elegant than any she'd seen in a great house.

She missed Buck terribly.

Her unrest and impatient thoughts wouldn't stop, keeping her awake. A heady excitement raced through her when she thought about Buck pulling up her chemise and branding her with his searing touch.

Her breath quickened when she heard footsteps outside her cabin door.

She held her breath, listening.

Had the ship's officer come back to ask her more questions? No, what she heard was—

Women's voices.

Laughing, coughing and whispering.

She put her ear against the cabin door.

'Look, lassies, there's no guard,' she could hear a female voice say in a loud whisper. 'Do you think the girl is still in there?'

'Heavens, she is. Someone padlocked the door and left the key in it.'

The key. Ava nearly danced a jig. The seaman assigned to watch her must have forgotten to take it when he left his post.

'Help me,' Ava cried out, banging on the door. 'Unlock the door, *please.'*

'Oh, will you listen to the poor dear?' said a gruff female voice, its huskiness sending a familiar chill through her.

Ava cringed. Oh, no, not *her*. The girl from Queenstown.

'She wants out, does she?'

'Why don't we help her, Hannah? She's Irish, ain't she?'

'Peggy's right,' said another girl. 'What's the lass ever done to you?'

'Well, I don't know if we should...' stalled Hannah.

'Help me, please!' Ava yelled. 'Get me out of here.'

'And have the steamship company after me for helping the likes of you?' Hannah said, grunting. 'It's a wonder you don't ask me to pray to the Divine to save your arse.'

Ava was desperate, she had to do *something*, even if it seemed impossible.

'Get word to Captain Lord Blackthorn,' she said. 'Tell him I'm being kept a prisoner in here.'

'Listen to her!' Hannah said, her voice all flirty-like. 'His lordship, is it? Next you'll want him to send a fancy valet to fetch you so he don't have to muddy his boots with the likes of us.'

Ava could hear the girl leaning against the door, her wide girth no doubt warming the wood and her lack of personal daintiness smelling up the narrow passageway.

She couldn't be choosy. These women were her last hope.

'Captain Lord Blackthorn is a good man. He'll come for me if you can get a message to him.' Ava paused, then said, 'He's a generous man. He'll pay you—'

'Pay me, will he?'

Ava could hear her make a huffing sound.

'I'll not sin against the Lord by releasing you to a man who buys a woman for his own pleasure,' the girl continued with a grunt. 'And you so quick with the raising of your petticoats. I'll not forget how you acted like you was better than us.'

'*I'll* not forget the unholy name you called me,' Ava said, her ire up. 'Rolling off your tongue like melted butter.' She kicked her foot against the door.

'I'll say it again,' said Hannah. 'You *harlot!*'

Ava nearly ripped apart the rosary gripped in her hand, so angry she was. 'You – you *bitch!*'

Screeching and spewing words of damnation, the girl let her have it.

Ava sank to the floor, dropping her black beads. Now she'd done it. No amount of prayer would save her. They'd never help her, *never*. But she couldn't let the girl get away with her ugly talk. *She couldn't.*

'Enjoy the rest of the crossing, dearie. *Alone*,' she heard the girl say, crowing. 'I'll take the key with me as a souvenir of the grand ship *Titanic.*'

Ava heard her loud laughter and the other girls' unhappy protests, and then a male voice telling the girl *he* would take the key and for them to move along. The bedroom steward making his rounds, no doubt. She'd not get any help from him either.

The sounds died down soon after. Then quiet.

Except for the pulsating of the ship's engines.

Hot tears veiled her eyes and they burned something awful. In the whole of her life Ava had never felt more alone.

She wiped her face, picked up her black rosary, then huddled in the corner of the bunk with only her wounded pride and lost hope for company.

Clawing at the thin blanket, Ava tore it to shreds in a wild fury, but that did nothing to calm her heart. A greater fear ripped through her.

What grand plans did the Almighty have in store for her to make her pay for her sins?

21

Buck walked at a fast clip up to the wireless operating office on the Boat Deck. He pulled up the collar on his heavy overcoat. The wind had picked up, sending icy chills through him.

He paid no attention to his teeth chattering and his knuckles reddening from the crisp wind as he made his way through a tight passageway until he came to a cell-like room.

Quiet, except for the buzzing sound of the wireless machine. The Marconi operator tapped out messages that could travel as much as fifteen hundred miles at night. Other times the range was short and signals often hard to catch.

Buck *had* to get his message to New York.

Without delay, he handed the young man gaping at him a sheet of paper.

To E.F. Perkins, Perkins, Smith and Young, Attorneys at Law.

The Park Row Building, New York, New York.

Need to retain your services at once. Personal matter. Will explain when I arrive in New York. Signed – Captain Lord James 'Buck' Blackthorn.

'Send this wireless right away,' Buck demanded, then handed the operator a pound note.

'Passengers aren't supposed to be in here, sir,' said the young man, handing the message back to him. 'Leave it at the purser's enquiry desk.' He turned his back and picked up his headset.

'It's urgent, *please!*' Buck said, his voice cracking under the strain. My God, was that him? He slammed the paper down on the desk next to a tall pile of messages. 'A girl's life is at stake.'

The operator's face didn't soften, as if he'd heard that excuse before. The intense look on Buck's face told him he wouldn't take no for an answer.

'Hold on, Mr...' He picked up the message and looked at the signature. He snapped to attention. 'All right, *your lordship,* I'll get to it straightaway.'

'Please, and *hurry!*'

No more time to waste here. He intended to search every inch of this ship until he found Ava.

He was aware his message to Trey's solicitors wouldn't reach their business offices in New York for several hours.

'I never thought I'd see the day you hired a lawyer to keep a woman *in* your life, Buck,' Trey had said, then added in a serious tone, 'Ava is worth fighting for. She's a hell of a woman.'

He'd recognized the deep concern and humility in Trey's voice as that of a man not trying to hide his emotions. A reckoning of sorts that his friend wasn't as easygoing about his feelings towards the Irish girl as he pretended. That the caddish young man he knew had reformed. Because of Ava. That set his thinking on a different course, making Trey a rival for her affections. But he couldn't sort that out. Not now.

With those words ringing in his ears, Buck forged ahead, planning his next move. He prayed he'd have an answer to his wireless before they arrived in New York Tuesday night. He needed it as a bargaining chip with the captain if he didn't find Ava before then. Using legal maneuvers was the only way out for her. Perkins was a crafty, smooth-talking lawyer. He'd come up with some legal scheme to get her off this ship.

Buck saw a familiar ship's officer making his rounds. Mr Lightoller. He increased his pace and caught up with the ship's second officer.

'Bracing cold tonight, isn't it, Mr Lightoller?' Buck said casually. He pulled the collar on his overcoat tighter around his neck to emphasize his aversion to the chill.

Merely a ploy not to reveal what was *really* on his mind.

Ava.

And where in the hell she was being held on this liner.

'Yes, indeed, your lordship. The temperature's dropped to near freezing.' Mr Lightoller seemed in good spirits in spite of the drastic change in weather. He was a likeable chap with a keen interest in the seafaring life.

'Any icebergs about?' Buck asked, continuing the conversation.

'Mr Murdoch and I were just discussing that possibility,' Mr Lightoller said, referring to the ship's first officer. Then with good-natured humor, he added, 'We may encounter a small berg or two within the hour, but I wouldn't miss a good hand of poker waiting to see it.'

Buck laughed. 'Spoken like a true sailor, Mr Lightoller.' He paused. This was the opportunity he'd been waiting for. 'The smoke room was all abuzz this evening with the rumor they found the Irish girl,' he said, keeping his voice steady, his interest noncommittal. He was simply a curious gentleman making small talk. 'Is that true?'

Fortunately for Buck, the ship's second officer understood the importance of not letting ship gossip get out of hand.

'The official word from the captain, sir, is that it's just a rumor.' He hesitated. 'However...'

He gave Buck a quick glance, along with an honest but wary smile that said he shouldn't admit to anything.

Then, flicking on his flashlight, he walked toward the poop deck.

Buck followed.

'Then it *is* true?' Buck asked, looking out over the railing at the sea, still and shimmering like smooth glass. The night horizon was a wide stretch of ocean that seemed to have stopped with the *Titanic* gliding over it effortlessly.

The ship's second officer considered his options before he answered, 'Yes, we found her.'

Buck took a deep breath, then drumming his fingers along the wooden railing, he said, 'There's also talk the girl was taken advantage of by a seaman.'

Mr Lightoller cleared his throat and swung the light of his flashlight around in an arc as if to throw Buck off course.

'That is *not* true, Captain Lord Blackthorn. I can personally assure you the Irish girl has not been harmed.'

Buck let out his breath, relieved, then it hit him. Could he be talking about *another* girl? Mr Lightoller believed *Ava* was the Countess of Marbury.

'Then you've seen the girl?' Buck asked, digging for information. He *had* to know.

'No, Mr Moody is in charge of keeping her confined down in steerage. I value his word regarding the welfare of the girl.' He grinned. 'Though I heard he *did* have difficulty getting her to cooperate...'

In spite of his misery, Buck had to smile. That was Ava all right.

'But she's quite safe. No one but he and the crewmen have had contact with her. It must remain so for reasons which I am not at liberty to reveal.'

'Where is she, Mr Lightoller?' Buck said, pressing him.

'Why all this interest in a steerage passenger, your lordship?' Mr Lightoller asked, not understanding.

'Merely a sporting one,' Buck said with caution. 'I made a wager with another gentleman you'd find the girl before the end of the voyage.'

Mr Lightoller grinned wide. 'Go ahead and collect your winnings, your lordship. I assure you, the Irish girl is safe and sound down below.'

'Where are you holding her, Mr Lightoller?' Buck asked again, trying to contain himself, though he imagined a desperate fear showed on his face.

He shook his head. 'Sorry, your lordship, the captain would have me busted down to seaman if I revealed that information to *anyone*.'

With that, he bid Buck good night and walked toward the officers' quarters.

Buck stuffed his hands into his pockets. The night was perfect. Calm with stars in the sky, reminding him of that first night when he and Ava stood here and she told him she wanted to be free.

Now she wasn't.

She could be anywhere on the lower decks.

For the next hour he covered the area along Scotland Road on E Deck. Up and down he walked. Thinking, hoping. Looking for her.

His pulse quickened when he remembered how she'd looked at him. In her plain cotton chemise, she was beautiful to him. Her deep auburn hair shimmering an unbelievable red, her mischievous green eyes and oval-shaped face with a pretty, pink mouth.

He simmered inside at the thought of kissing her soft lips. She'd pressed up against him with a surprising hunger, almost a fierceness, such was her need, as if she couldn't wait to be loved by him. A move that touched him deeply.

Buck smiled. Ava was full of surprises, dashing about the ship in the countess's coat, undressing in front of him before he could undo a button on her chemise, standing up to the countess when such a thing wasn't done by a girl of her class. He imagined living with her would be like living with an impish but beautiful fairy who couldn't settle on whether she wanted to be a human or a nymph.

Such a thought tantalized him.

And pushed him forward in his quest.

He trekked the long distance to the steerage section in aft ship where the single women were quartered. As he poked around looking for a locked cabin, doors opened and electric lights went on as sleepy-eyed women peeked out to see what was going on. The entire incident caused a lot of murmurings and giggling as well as sneers and complaints from the women who mistook him for a drunken passenger looking for a bit of fun.

Some waved their arms about, shooing him away.

But not all.

Two young women invited him into their cabin for a spot of tea, but Buck politely declined, telling them he was looking for an Irish girl with red hair. The door slammed in his face with epithets spewed at him he'd rarely heard falling from female lips. He knocked on the next door and asked again. The door opened slightly, then closed shut when he heard someone snoring loudly.

Disappointed, Buck headed back down the corridor toward second class until the sound of footsteps came echoing down the linoleum-tiled floor behind him. A girl wearing a long nightdress with a frayed shawl wrapped around her appeared. He looked at her, curious. It wasn't her sweet Irish face that made him hesitate, but what she said that got his attention.

'Looking for an Irish girl with red hair, are you, sir?' she asked, glancing at him quickly to see if he was an honest sort.

'Have you seen her?' Buck asked, urging her toward the stairway where they could talk unobserved.

'Yes. They locked her up on the deck below us in the forward part of the ship.' She looked over her shoulder and, satisfied no one was about, she leaned over and whispered in his ear, 'The single men are berthed there.' She put her hand over her mouth to stifle a giggle.

He asked her name.

'Peggy, sir,' she said, lowering her eyes and rubbing her palms on her nightdress.

'Can you show me where she is?' Buck asked in a calm manner, but it still betrayed the desperation in his voice.

'No, sir.' She looked away quickly, but not quickly enough. Buck guessed she was familiar with that part of the ship.

'Why not, Peggy?' he asked, trying to cajole her.

Her eyes went wide. 'If Hannah finds out I'm missing, she'll box my ears something awful.'

'Hannah?' he asked.

'My older sister. She's jealous of the lass with the pretty face.'

'Please, Peggy,' Buck said, 'you *must* help me. This girl's life is at stake.'

'Oh...' Peggy said, blessing herself. 'Are you Captain Lord Blackthorn?'

Buck was astonished. 'You know me?'

She nodded. 'The girl you're looking for asked Hannah to get a message to you.' She lifted her nose in an uppity manner and danced around. 'But my sister is too devout for her own good, spouting holy verses and telling me not to talk to the handsome lads.'

'Where is your sister now?' he asked gently.

A big smile came over her face, her eyes lighting up. 'She's asleep, snoring like a bear *and* keeping me awake. I heard you asking about the girl, but I was afraid she'd wake up if I opened the door.' Peggy hesitated. 'Promise me you won't say a word to my sister, your lordship, and I'll show you where to find your pretty lassie.'

Buck nodded. 'I promise.'

Smiling, she grabbed his hand and showed him how she and her friends sneaked through the broad working alleyway from the aft part of the liner to second class, then down the stairs to the lower deck.

Within minutes, Buck found himself in the forward part of the ship near the linen room. Something tightened in his throat at the idea of Ava being kept here where the single men were berthed. His eyes burned and he swallowed hard. If anyone had touched her, he *swore* he'd toss the bloody bastard overboard.

'Where is she, Peggy?' he asked, not doing a good job of holding back his impatience. His words sounded harsher than he intended.

Peggy looked back at him, curious-like. She was smaller than he'd originally thought, leaning against the steel-walled corridor. She was shivering. Was she afraid of him?

He couldn't be certain. There was a cold clamminess in the passageway in spite of the close quarters.

Carefully, he put an arm around the girl's shoulders to lend not only reassurance, but to bring down the rising fear he saw on her young face.

Finally, she said, 'She's locked in a small cabin with a padlock on the door.' She pointed to the starboard side of the ship. 'Over there, your lordship, near the observation deck for them ball courts.'

Without waiting for the girl to follow him, he broke into a run, skirting down the narrow hallway past closed cabins where he could hear men talking, snoring, someone playing an Irish pipe. His heart pumped madly as he checked each cabin. No padlock on that door. He tried the next one… then the *next*…

Keep going. Don't stop. The girl had no reason to lie. Ava is here somewhere, I know she is.

Clenching his teeth, struggling to push back an overwhelming sense of alarm, Buck turned down a narrow passageway, his chest tightening with anxiety when—

A sudden lurch threw him off balance, a heavy *grinding* jar and creaking crash that slammed him into the steel-walled bulkhead.

Heart pumping, Buck got to his knees, every sense in his body on alert. It was almost as if the ship seemed to shiver, the vibration passing under his feet, then stop.

Wait, was he crazy? Or had the ship keeled over to the port side?

What was it? He'd heard a long, ripping sound like the ship had grazed something along its starboard side.

Had the *Titanic* thrown a propeller?

Or—

No. He *refused* to believe it. They couldn't have struck an…

Iceberg.

Could they?

The painful brunt of the blow had crunched his bones together with such force he swore he must have broken something.

Shocked, dizzy, Buck got to his feet, steadied himself, then kept searching for Ava. Nothing mattered to him as much as finding her. He had to keep going, an urgency about him that pushed aside any thought of danger.

Then he realized the ship's engines had stopped.

22

Ava couldn't stop shivering with fright. *What in heaven's name just happened?*

She had been thrown out of her bunk with a wrenching force and knocked her on her back. *Hard*. Pain shot through her, but she had no time to check for bruises.

The air in her cabin was damp and cold. So was her heart.

A feeling of dread haunted her that something awful had happened. It made her afraid to think about it, but she *must* cling to hope.

Ava pulled herself up, then looked down. She gasped. A steady stream of water along the floor lapped around her feet.

Seeping in from under her cabin door.

She froze.

Blessed Virgin, is the ship sinking?

She tried to convince herself nothing was wrong.

A loo overflowed, she decided, or the swimming bath. Something, *anything*.

It wasn't seawater lapping around her feet.

Was it?

Her mind reeled as she realized the water was coming in faster and showed no signs of stopping. Frantically she pulled her skirts tight around her legs then banged on the door.

Calling out for help.

She stopped, listened. Nothing. What was to become of her? It was late, no one outside to hear her or come to her aid.

She forced herself not to panic, hoping the water would stop flowing in from under her door. Instead it came closer and closer, stealing the warmth from her cabin and making her chilled.

She clenched her jaw at the rising sensation of helplessness overtaking her, then she heard—

Footsteps splashing through the water in the narrow corridor.

Ava swallowed and tried to keep her legs from shaking. Who was it? The ship's officer? A seaman come to rescue her?

They wouldn't let her drown, would they?

Use your brain, girl, why would they come to save you?

To them she was a petty thief and a nuisance. The whole ship would be quarantined if anyone found out she had no inspection card.

Let her drown like a rat, they would. And be done with her.

Who would know? Who would care?

No one.

No... no... *no*. Ava exploded into a scream, pounding on the door with her fists.

'Help me, *please!* Someone help me!'

'Ava, are you in there...? *Ava!*'

She put her hand to her mouth, not believing it was him she heard.

'Buck...?'

'Ava, oh, thank God I found you,' she heard him say.

'*Please...* get me out of here!' she cried out.

'I can't. There's a padlock on the door. No key.'

Ava leaned against the door, her spirits sinking. She'd forgotten the steward had taken the key and her freedom with it.

'Stand back, Ava—'

'What are you going to do?' she asked, her ear to the door, her heart racing.

'I'll shoot the lock off,' Buck said with urgency. She heard the sound of a hammer being cocked. 'Get as far away from the door as you can.'

Ava waded through the rising water to the back of the cabin and hunched down low in the berth, her fingers in her ears.

'*Ready!*' she called out.

'Hold steady, Ava.'

She jumped back when the shot rang out, then another, and the door burst open.

Her heart pounded. She couldn't believe her eyes. He looked like a wild avenger in black, breathing heavily and holding a pistol, his eyes blazing. Doing *anything* to free her and damn the consequences.

Buck.

Lord, she never thought she'd see his handsome face again.

She looked at him boldly. He returned her look. Never had she seen anyone look at her like that. The dark pools of his eyes brought to Ava's mind St Michael himself. He, too, carried a weapon and kept the heavens safe for all who tread there.

He was here now, strong and passionate. A man, not an angel, the very image of hope eternal lighting up her soul.

If the saints pierced her heart with a blessed arrow, she'd not fall. *Nothing* could stop her from racing toward him, words of joy falling from her lips. Tears running down her cheeks. Strong hands grabbed her, holding her close. She threw her arms around his neck, sobbing with relief so grand she'd never forget this moment.

Never.

'Ava, *Ava*...' Buck whispered over and over again, his lips close to her ear. His warm breath made her shiver again. This time with a feeling of completeness.

'How did you find me?' Ava blurted out, not understanding, only knowing that he was here with her now. She tried to forget the icy cold water splashing around their feet. She rested her cheek against his broad shoulder, his heavy overcoat rough, scratching her skin. She didn't care about *anything* but his hands steady on her shoulders, him explaining how a girl named Peggy had told him where to find her.

'We've got to get you out of here,' he said, 'though the ship can withstand several of her watertight compartments being flooded.' His face wore a look of deep concern. Only a man who loved her would look at her like that.

No more dallying, girl. Your lives are at stake. Find courage knowing he cares for you like a lad for his gentle lady love.

'This way, Ava,' Buck ordered, pulling her along behind him.

Without another word, Ava followed him down the narrow corridor, stepping carefully through the water. She smiled. This was the first time she'd obeyed him without putting up a fuss. Silly girl. The steady sound of his breathing reassured her in the loveliest manner everything would be all right.

She let go with a long sigh.

Nothing to fear any more.

* * *

They made their way up to the working alleyway on E Deck, where a scene of confusion came into focus before Ava's eyes.

Passengers, curious and upset. Crowding around them, some holding their bags with all their belongings.

An urgency about them.

The stale air blew hot against her skin in spite of the cold seawater lapping around her feet. She kept close behind Buck, holding onto his hand tight. She was unable to see much amid the low ceiling and naked light bulbs glaring overhead.

The feeling of confusion all around her worried her. She took it to mean the ship was damaged more seriously than anyone believed. Especially when she saw seamen scurrying about, passing the word on that seawater had flooded the mail room below.

Buck told her not to worry. Ava wasn't so certain. People pushed by them, heading all the way aft on E Deck, emotions running high. A noisy, restless crowd babbled in various languages, all jammed together. Children crying, women fretting, men blustering about, trying to find out what was going on. The deck stewards kept repeating, '*There is no danger.*'

No one listened to them.

Ava pulled on Buck's coat sleeve, her eyes questioning. He said nothing.

'Is it true there's no danger?' she asked, wondering how the stewards could say such a thing when water had flowed into her cabin faster than a holy baptism.

'We're not taking any chances,' Buck said. 'Follow me.'

They hurried down the corridor, hugging the plain white walls that seemed to go on forever. He explained to her how they could get to C Deck by crossing the open well deck, then jumping over the rope to the first-class quarters. After that it was a short distance to the countess's stateroom.

'I pray Trey is there with her,' he said, his tone solemn.

'So do I, Buck,' Ava said, then added what was in her heart. 'She's a fine and grand lady.'

Buck turned and studied her. Stopped dead in his tracks. Did her thoughts surprise him? It was true she and her ladyship had had words over him, but that hadn't changed her opinion of her. Ava bore her ladyship no grievance. It was her own foolishness that had gotten her into this mess and sent belowdecks.

Would you look at Buck?

He'd been in such a hurry to get them away from the confusion and now he seemed in a bit of confusion himself. As if he couldn't believe his ears. Was that a tender smile she saw lighting up his handsome face?

A warm flush spread over her cheeks. She had the feeling his lordship had something on his mind and he had to say it.

'Fiona didn't mean what she said to you, Ava,' he said, not giving the ugly words either woman had sputtered in frustration any credence.

She nodded. The wall between them tumbled down with her hearing so grand a thing as this.

As if he read her thoughts, he said. 'She begs your forgiveness.'

'She *told* you what happened?' Ava's heart thumped in her chest, surprise making her lower her eyes in embarrassment.

'Yes. She also asked me to tell you—'

Before he could finish his thought, a steward blasted orders in their ears, reminding her she could be spotted by the crew any moment. She turned her face away as the steward pushed them back and told them to clear the corridor while he threw open cabin doors and yelled, 'Tie on your lifebelts. Captain's orders.'

'Lifebelts?' Ava said, her feeling of security leaving her. 'What's happening, Buck?'

'Merely a precaution, Ava,' Buck said, avoiding her eyes.

No, there was more to it, Ava knew. She put her fingers to her lips. They were nearly numb. She glanced down at her feet. Her boots were water-soaked. A slow awakening slithered up her spine. Holy Mary, the ship *was* sinking.

'I want the truth, Buck.'

'Nothing is going to happen to this ship,' he said as if he read her mind. 'She's built to withstand practically anything.'

She shook her head. 'Something in my bones don't feel right. Like the day my da didn't come home. A fine day it was, filled with blue sky and a calm sea when I went down to the dock to wait for his tug to pull into the harbor. I knew something was wrong then and I know it now.'

'I'm telling you, Ava, this ship is *unsinkable*.'

'Is it?' she said, feistily. 'Taking on God's work it is, saying such a thing.'

Buck grabbed her by the shoulders and studied her face in the yellow light overhead. 'I believe we struck an iceberg.'

'An *iceberg*?' She shuddered.

'Yes,' he said, trying to keep his voice even. 'I'm certain another ship will come to our rescue if it comes to that.'

Ava felt a heaviness settling in the pit of her stomach. It didn't seem real. The jarring sensation. The water in her cabin. The idea the *Titanic* could actually *sink* was unbelievable.

An unholy chill shot through her and goose bumps pimpled the flesh on her arms at the thought of what would have happened if Buck hadn't found her.

Mother of Mercy, it was too horrible to think about.

'They'll be looking for me,' Ava said simply.

'Yes,' he said in a low voice, as if mulling over their options. 'They'll send a ship's officer to free you—'

'I'll *not* be free, Buck. They'll send me back to Ireland. *I know they will.*' She tried to ignore the intense emotions racing through her, not just the fear of being sent to prison, but the fear of losing his lordship.

Ever since he'd rescued her, she'd had a lovely feeling of lightness as though nothing could ever harm her again. His arms wrapped around her in that certain way that warmed her inside. A deep and hungry need to touch him, be with him, causing her to say reckless things. 'I couldn't bear to leave you, Buck. I – I want to go to America with you.'

'I'll take you back to the countess's stateroom.' He avoided her eyes so she couldn't see what he was thinking. 'They'll never look for you there.'

Her face colored again. He said nothing about keeping her with him. With the countess, yes, but not with *him*.

Doing his duty, he was.

She waited, her face still flushed from her rash words. A draft seemed to come out of nowhere and stirred the air.

She shivered in her wet boots.

'You're cold,' was all he said.

He took off his heavy black overcoat, his arm encircling her as he wrapped it around her shoulders and held her close. Ava tucked her chin to her chest so he couldn't see the tears welling up in her eyes. She'd never felt so protected before, wrapped up in more than his coat.

Could a girl like her have his love, too?

'I suspect the damage is more serious than they're telling us, Ava, but I won't let anything happen to you. *I promise*,' Buck said softly, pushing through the steerage passengers forming at the stairs.

Ava trailed behind him, a deep concern racing through her when she saw a steward attempting to keep the people back.

'Buck, *look*.'

'I'll see what's going on,' he said. 'Wait here.'

She nodded, but the bad feeling creeping over her wouldn't go away. That dark premonition came to visit her again. The sea taking her to a watery grave like a demon hellbent on claiming her unholy soul.

Ava would fight it. She wasn't lost yet. Not with Buck at her side. She was smart enough to know his comforting words and strong arms around her shoulders were all she had to cling on to. She was surrounded by passengers carrying traveling bags, straw cases, rugs and even small trunks, barring her way.

Buck, where was he?

She saw him up ahead on the stairs looking for her, when someone behind her yelled out, frightening the crowd gathered behind her.

Whatever he said made them panic.

They began rushing up the stairs like a human wave, propelled by fear. A big, burly man pushed by her, his thick arm blocking her way and shoving her back.

'Buck, *help me!*' Ava cried out, trying to get to him, but she slipped and banged her knee. Ignoring the sharp pain, she saw his lordship turn around, twisting his head left, then right, but he couldn't see her. How could he? She crouched close to the wall, trying to catch her breath. Then, her eyes widening with disbelief, she watched him disappear up the broad stairs amid the throng of people. And out of her life.

The sight of him leaving her startled her blood something awful.

She *had* to catch up to him.

Ava staggered, then regained her balance and lurched forward, trying to grab onto something, *anything*, when someone stepped on the hem of her skirt.

She turned around to see Hannah sneering at her. Did the girl have no mercy?

'Stay down here where you belong,' said Hannah, but Ava could see fear in her eyes and her lips trembling. 'You're no better than the likes of us.'

'You're a cold, hard creature,' Ava said, refusing to show weakness in front of the girl. 'You should be swept with shame knowing it. You'll not take me down with you. This I swear on my mother's holy grave.'

'Mind who you're talking to,' Hannah said with smugness, rolling spit in her mouth. 'Or I'll—'

A slender lass wearing only a long nightdress and frayed shawl pulled hard on the girl's long braid, making her yelp loudly.

'You're wrong about my sister,' the girl said, then blessed herself, her eyes shooting upward.

Ava recognized her voice. *Peggy*.

This was the girl who helped Buck find her belowdecks.

'Hannah lost her baby three weeks ago.' Peggy bit down on her lower lip. 'She's not stopped blaming God and the whole world ever since.'

'Is that true?' Ava asked the girl, searching her face.

'So, what if it is? I don't want your pity. God abandoned me because I...' She hesitated, her silence confirming what Ava guessed. In spite of the girl's sanctimonious talk, the child was born from a night of passion. 'Then He took my baby.' Hannah pushed back strands escaping from her long braid. Harsh words, but the way her hand shook, her eyes misting over, told Ava there still beat a heart under that arrogance. 'I never knew anything could hurt so bad.'

'And you think the way to get rid of that pain is to hurt *me*?' Ava asked, her voice firm. How well she understood the pain of loss, but that didn't excuse Hannah's lashing out at her. 'God hasn't abandoned you, Hannah. You have Peggy and you'll lose her, too, if you don't listen to Him and lead with your heart instead of your anger.'

'You think God will ever forgive me?' Hannah fought back tears as Peggy held onto her sister's hand, her eyes begging Ava for understanding.

Ava nodded. She owed this girl Peggy her life. She had no doubt what He wanted her to do.

'Follow me,' she said. '*Both* of you. His lordship will help us.'

'Glory be, God must have sent you to us.' Peggy grabbed her hand and squeezed it.

Ava squeezed back and smiled at her, then nodded at Hannah. Her ruddy face was drawn and her eyes downcast. It would take time for her to let go of her anger... but for now, she seemed somewhat repentant and that was good enough for her.

Next, Ava set about saving them from whatever insanity was about to befall them.

She rushed forward, Peggy and her sister close behind her. She clawed her way up the stairs with the Irish girls only to have the steward lock the gate and refuse to let them through.

Sweet Jesus, *no*.

'*Please*, let us through!' Ava begged, with Peggy and Hannah adding their voices to her plea.

The steward shook his head and turned his back to them. He refused to even look at them.

'We'll find another way up on deck, miss,' said Peggy, dragging her sister back down the long corridor, but Ava wasn't listening.

'Buck, *Buck!*' she cried out frantically, rattling the gate so hard her hands hurt, the metal digging into her moist palms. She wanted to tear down the floor-to-ceiling barrier, kick it apart, *anything* to get to Buck. Her restlessness had given way to a passionate fever that burned deep within her.

Never before, not even locked up in the cabin, had she felt such heart-crushing despair.

23

15 April 1912

Buck was frantic. One minute Ava was in his arms and the next she'd disappeared.

His efforts to get information had been for naught. No one knew anything. Even the steward believed the ship's engines would start up again and they'd be on their way.

Worse yet, Ava was gone. Not even a wisp of her long red hair anywhere in sight.

He felt as if he were living a dream and any minute he'd see her pretty face, her lovely green eyes teasing him with questions he wanted to answer and desires he hungered to fulfill.

Where did she go?

He swore she was right behind him… then she wasn't.

She was gone.

Buck looked up and down the corridor on D Deck. She was nowhere to be seen. Not finding her was driving him crazy. Was she looking for him? Searching every face, penetrating a man's soul with her wonder of it all?

Did she believe he had abandoned her?

His mouth tightened. He'd never abandon her, *never*.

And now he'd lost her.

Buck sighed inwardly. He *swore* he'd heard her call out to him, but he didn't see her in the crowd of steerage passengers surging up the stairs.

How could he? Chaos reigned everywhere. People running from one cabin to another, looking for lifebelts.

Lifebelts be damned, it was *lifeboats* this ship needed. He was one of the few on board who knew there weren't enough boats to save everyone.

Women and children first.

It was his duty to get Ava and the countess into a lifeboat. Surely the *Titanic* had sent out a distress call to other liners in the area. Another ship, maybe two were on their way and would arrive presently.

He shuddered. What if they didn't? No man would last long in that freezing cold water.

Buck raced back toward the stairs leading to E Deck. Every reasonable argument told him getting out of this alive wasn't in the cards.

This was one hand he would lose.

'Best not go that way, guv'nor,' he heard a seaman say as the bare-armed stoker pushed by him, his face and upper body smudged with black soot and a lifebelt under his arm. 'Them foreigners is all riled up. Poor bastards.'

'What happened?' Buck asked, his heart pounding. All he could think about was Ava caught up in the melee.

'Bloody steward locked the gate leading up to D Deck. No telling what them blighters will do now.'

Buck panicked, mind-numbing thoughts racing through his brain. Every instinct told him Ava was down there, waiting for him.

He jammed back down the broad stairs like a madman, never breaking his stride.

He wouldn't rest until he found her.

* * *

'Hurry up and open that gate,' Buck ordered the steward trying desperately to get out of his grasp. He'd grabbed the man, nearly crushing his arm when he saw him rattling a ring of keys.

'Unhand me, sir, if you don't wish any unpleasantness,' the steward said. 'Or I shall report you to the steamship company.'

Buck smirked. No doubt he was accustomed to dealing with the ruffians in third class. The man kept his official demeanor in spite of his obvious discomfort.

Not Buck. His whole body was tense, his pulse racing. Steerage passengers hovered behind the gate, clinging to their steamer trunks, their suitcases, mulling about, mumbling in a variety of languages and not understanding what was going on. Once the gate was locked, most had scattered, looking for other ways to get up on deck. He heard one man shout about a passageway leading to the top in the other direction, his enthusiasm spurring several passengers to scramble after him.

Only a few stragglers lagged.

Then he saw Ava, banging on the iron-latticed gate, waving at him and calling out his name. Relief filled him.

He let the man go.

'*Unlock that gate*,' he repeated, louder now. He kept glancing toward Ava, making sure she didn't disappear again.

'I most certainly will not,' came the insistent reply from the steward, a bespectacled man with droopy brows and a persnickety attitude.

'If you don't open that gate and let that girl with the red hair through, I'll blast a hole through that pretty white uniform of yours,' Buck said in a hoarse whisper loud enough for only the steward to hear.

'And who the bloody hell are you, sir?' He spun around on his heel, his manner indignant.

'It doesn't matter *who* I am,' Buck said carefully, then eased the pistol out of his pocket and poked the steward in the gut with the barrel of his gun. 'Just do what I say.'

His eyes popped out. 'Yes, *sir.*'

Rattling his big ring of keys, the steward opened the gate just wide enough so Ava could squeeze through and then slammed it shut. She rushed into his arms.

'Buck, oh, *Buck!*' she cried out, holding on to him.

Then the steward closed it again.

'What about other steerage passengers?' Buck couldn't believe the man wouldn't let anyone else through.

'Just her. No one else. I have my orders,' he insisted. 'We can't have them overrunning the ship. Immigration laws, you know.'

'*Damn* your bloody laws!' Buck yelled. 'This ship is sinking, you fool. Open that gate!'

The steward weighed his options. He didn't believe the *Titanic* was in any danger and folded his hands over his chest. 'No. It's against regulations.'

'We can't leave those people down there, Buck,' Ava cried out. '*We can't!* Peggy and her sister will drown if we don't help them. These women don't have a gentleman's protection like your first cabin ladies,' she said. 'They're on their own. I won't leave them down there to die, *I won't!*'

She ran away before he could stop her. The two Irish girls were nowhere to be seen as Buck went after her and pulled her back, picking her up in his arms. Most likely they were looking for another way up on deck. Ava beat her fists against his chest, but he paid her no mind, carrying her easily.

'Put me down, Buck!' she pleaded.

'Sorry, my love. You leave me no choice but to kidnap you.' A sadder note sat on the edge of his mind. She was right about the two Irish girls. They had no one to fight for them.

He wouldn't let Ava down. He promised her as soon as he got her and the countess into a lifeboat, he'd come back for the two Irish girls.

He never broke a promise.

He kissed her.

Holding her tight against his chest, he took in the salty smell of seawater on her and for a moment it reminded him of the danger they were in. Obsessed as he was over getting her into a lifeboat, she was so lovely, he didn't want to end the kiss.

He couldn't get enough of her.

She clung to him, her hands tight around his neck, returning his kiss with a hunger, almost a desperation, as if she knew it could be their last.

* * *

Ava still felt the danger rattling her bones as she held onto Buck's hand. They moved quickly down the corridor on C Deck, but to her surprise, he called out to an elegant gentleman heading off in the opposite direction.

'Have you assessed the damage to the ship, Mr Andrews?' Buck asked, never letting go of her hand.

Ava's eyes widened. *The ship's designer*. She'd heard Buck mention him a few times.

Mr Andrews pulled on his collar, his mood pensive, but even before he spoke, she saw the truth in his eyes. Ava had a moment of paralyzing fear that choked the breath out of her. The firm grip of Buck's hand holding hers gave her strength.

'The *Titanic* has another hour, maybe two,' Mr Andrews told them, 'before the end comes. Six compartments have already been flooded.'

God help us all, she prayed silently.

He straightened his jacket, pulled on his cuffs. 'I'm headed to the bridge to do what I can. Get the lady to a lifeboat quickly, then save yourself. Good luck.'

Then with a half-smile and a nod, he was off.

Ava knew he suspected she wasn't a first-class passenger, but he'd given her that respect and she'd always cherish that. But she couldn't forget Mr Andrews' chilling warning, making their mission all the more urgent to get to the countess.

* * *

The jealousy engraved on the countess's soul gave way to a warm welcome when she saw Ava, making the girl weep at the joy of it. She'd been sick at heart at the news that Ava languished in a cabin on the lower decks and would be sent back to Ireland.

Ava's heart beat rapidly. The countess was worried about *her?*

It was true. Long, dark lashes brushed back misty tears. The countess blamed herself for the girl's ordeal.

Ava begged her ladyship to shed her guilt and felt a powerful pull toward the woman and wanted things to be right between them again.

'It was my own fault for not trusting you with the truth,' Ava continued, feeling a bittersweet tug at her heart.

Her ladyship brightened at her words. 'Thank you, Ava. I could never forgive myself if anything had happened to you because of my selfishness.'

'Your eyes speak more than words ever could, your ladyship.'

'Call me Fiona... please.'

Ava grinned wide.

'No more time for dawdling, ladies,' Buck said, interrupting them as he grabbed two lifebelts from the top of the wardrobe. 'Put on your lifebelts.' The countess made a face. 'It's only a precaution, Fiona,' he said, helping her put the lifebelt on over her head. 'You'll be back in your stateroom in no time.'

Ava glared at him, keeping her emotions under control so the countess didn't see her hard stare. Would they? With the lower decks filling with seawater?

She looked from Buck to the countess then back again with a gaze both curious and disturbing. Why was he being so stubborn about telling her ladyship the truth?

She shook her head in dismay when she saw the countess give him an adoring smile, believing his further untruth about the ship being safe.

Ava thought about challenging him. How could she?

He kept up a running conversation about how the *Titanic* was as steady as a rock, while Fiona jostled about trying to decide what color scarf to wear. He avoided looking at Ava, instead devoting his attention to the countess and securely fastening the ties so her lifebelt fit snug on her.

When Buck was finished, she looked at her boxy shape rather dourly in the mirror. He assured her she looked charming, then asked her to retrieve her black cloche hat and veil to conceal Ava's identity.

Why is he treating the woman like a child? Ava wondered. She had a right to know the truth.

The ship was sinking.

Ava turned her eyes to the porthole, but all she could see was darkness. They had so little time left to escape. It was a chilling and horrifying thought and it made her all the more fearful about the safety of Peggy and her sister Hannah. Buck had promised her he'd not let them drown.

First, they must get the countess into a lifeboat.

'You're going, too, Ava,' Buck insisted.

'No, I want to stay with you.'

She didn't want to stir up an argument by being obstinate, but she had to try. Though the sea was dead calm, they both knew the ship was doomed.

'Fiona needs you, Ava.'

He knew exactly how to manipulate her.

'By the blessed saints,' Ava said, 'I'll not leave the countess's side until she's safe in a lifeboat and lowered away from this sinking ship.' She paused, then said in a low voice, 'I'll not go myself without you.'

Buck looked perturbed. 'You try a man's soul, Ava, with your wild ways and total disregard for authority.' He strapped the lifebelt on her in spite of her protests. 'I must *insist* you obey my orders. It's for your own good.'

'Don't ask that of me, Buck,' she said. 'I'm not afraid. A sinner I am, but I'm no coward.' She heaved a deep sigh. 'Never before in my born days did I believe I would find a good, kind gentleman like you.'

'Ava, you're such an innocent. I'm not as noble as you think I am,' he admitted.

'I don't care. I – I love you, Captain Lord Blackthorn.'

There, she'd said what was in her heart and she wasn't ashamed of it.

He seemed perplexed by her rash admission.

The air sizzled between them with words unsaid, desires so fervent Ava could barely stop from reaching out and pulling him to her.

'You and the countess must hurry to the lifeboats, Ava. I'll follow you later. You *must* go with Fiona,' he said, grabbing her arms and holding her so tightly it hurt. Not a whimper came out of her. 'We both know this ship doesn't have much time left before she sinks.'

You've met your match, Ava O'Reilly. His lordship isn't fooled by your scandalous games and saintly remarks.

'What about Mr Brady?' she wanted to know.

'Trey will help load the women and children while I go belowdecks and bring up the Irish girls and put them into a lifeboat.'

Ava knew she must let him go or risk the lives of Peggy and her sister.

A swish of silk and the scent of lavender caught her attention. The countess cleared her throat. 'I've brought the hat and veil for Ava, Buck.'

How long she'd been standing there, ready to go up on deck in her long black coat, red lace shawl over her arm and a pale ivory silk scarf covering her hair, Ava didn't know. A new seriousness had settled upon her features.

Fiona had heard every word.

She was very much aware of the danger.

Ava stared at her, then Buck, knowing once they joined the other passengers up on top, the world as they knew it would never be the same again.

24

Up on deck, Ava marveled at the evening mist hovering like a veil over the stars thick in the black sky. Hiding the truth with no shame. Others might believe the *Titanic* was unsinkable.

Not her. She knew the end was near.

She let out her breath and blew the mist away.

Would getting off this ship be as easy?

By the blessed heavens, she thought not. She'd never seen such confusion.

Ship's officers shouted shrill orders but were drowned out by the deafening sound of steam from the boilers blowing off overhead. Seamen turned the cranks so the davits swung outward until the lifeboats hung clear of the deck.

Ice lay scattered about on the starboard well deck.

A numbness filled her as though she were witness to some horrible dream and she couldn't wake up. She glimpsed movement out of the corner of her eye and saw a woman crying, while a gentleman tried to comfort her. Her heart went out to her when a ship's officer separated her from her husband and tossed the lady over the rail and into a lifeboat. The woman started shrieking.

Would she find herself dealing with such melancholy before this night was over?

There's something else troubling your mind, lass. You know what's got your blood fired up. The idea of losing him.

Love him while you can.

'You and the countess must get to the lifeboats,' Buck said. 'Nothing else matters.'

What about you, Buck? And Mr Brady? she wanted to scream.

The fierce look in his eyes told her to hold her tongue. He was wrong if he thought she was going to fold up like a church lily left to wither on the altar.

She shot him back an accusing stare. *You know as well as I do the Titanic will sink in an hour, no more than two.*

He squeezed her hand.

Being with him, she felt as grand as a countess herself. She prayed for a miracle. Who would have believed her own soul could know such affection from two such people?

If they were martyred saints, she couldn't love them more.

But there was another side to her story.

Nothing changed the fact Ava O'Reilly was wanted by the law.

To conceal her identity, Buck insisted she hide her red hair under the countess's black cloche hat and arrange the veil over her face. Then he pulled up the collar on the heavy overcoat he'd given her. If anyone spoke to her, she was not to answer. Her Irish brogue would give her away.

She was to keep her head down and—

'We must go to A Deck *now* to the lifeboat loading,' Buck said brusquely.

An all-possessing fear of being found out made her step quicker, her breath faster until they reached the forward loading area for the lifeboats on the Promenade Deck.

'Two ladies for the boat,' Buck called out to a seaman, his tone insistent.

'Right you are, sir,' he said. 'Stand back. We have to open the windows first before we can load here.'

'How long will that take?' Buck wanted to know, his dark eyes narrowing while he waited for an answer.

'Don't know, sir. Don't you worry, we'll get the ladies on board the lifeboat.'

'What about his lordship and Mr Brady?' asked the countess, clearly disturbed.

The seaman shook his head. 'Sorry, miss, orders are women and children first.'

'Buck—' she said, grabbing his forearm.

Was that panic Ava saw on her face?

'It's merely a matter of form, Fiona,' Buck said, keeping his voice steady, though from what she'd observed, no men were allowed in the boats on the port side. 'Trey and I will get into another lifeboat.' He turned to Ava. 'You and Fiona wait here until the windows are opened, then get into the boat straightaway. I'm going belowdecks for Peggy and her sister.'

'Here, Buck, take back your coat,' Ava said, untying her lifebelt straps, then slipping the overcoat off her shoulders but not feeling the chill. How could she? She was already numb inside, praying her worst fears weren't true.

'No, Ava, you'll need it.' She could see the deep concern for her in his eyes. 'It will be cold in the lifeboat.'

She shook her head. 'Peggy was wearing only a dressing gown when last I saw her. She'll freeze in the boat without it.'

'But, Ava—' Buck began.

'Ava can have my shawl, Buck,' the countess said, throwing the beautiful red wrap embroidered with her initials and family crest over Ava's shoulders while Buck refastened her lifebelt.

'Countess... I mean, Fiona,' Ava said. 'I don't know what to say.'

'Don't say anything. It's yours.' She grinned. 'I'll buy another wrap when we get to New York.' She turned to Buck and held his hands. 'We'll all be together then.'

'Yes, Fiona,' Buck said, smiling wide. 'We'll all be together then.'

Will we?

Ava knew that heavy thought lay on all their minds.

After several minutes of anxious waiting Trey appeared, two lifebelts in hand.

'Lucky I found these in my cabin, Buck,' Trey said, handing him a lifebelt. 'Or we'd be out of luck.'

'Yes, wouldn't we.'

Buck put on the lifebelt, but Ava could see the awkward glance he gave Trey when he thought she wasn't watching.

He wasn't telling her something, but what?

'Buck, you *will* get into another lifeboat once the women and children are loaded into the boats, won't you?' Ava asked him again.

'Yes, I'll meet up with you later when another ship picks us up.' He cupped her chin and turned her face up, then lifted her veil and said the words she longed to hear, 'Whatever happens, Ava, you will always be my lady.'

He bent down and brushed his lips against hers in a gentle kiss, a loving gesture that further pained her already aching heart. His words evoked a tenderness in her that made her forget where they were.

She had become strangely detached from the fact she was surrounded by passengers scrambling to get up on the Boat Deck and into the lifeboats being swung out.

'Yes, Buck, *always*.'

Her words were barely a whisper, but Ava knew he heard her by the smile on his face.

She pulled the red shawl close around her and arched her back. An unexpected stream of pleasure wiggled through her. The joy and pain were almost too much as he pulled away and left her wanting.

And alone.

He was gone on an errand of mercy.

She watched him until he became lost in the melee of passengers, stewards and ship's officers. Loud, bright distress rockets soared upward while the band played a ragtime tune to inspire reassurance.

Ava paid them no mind. She wanted to keep this moment in her heart forever.

It was the one thing no one could ever take from her.

A new fear gripped her when she realized the slant in the deck was steeper. Were her eyes lying to her or did the ship angle noticeably toward the bow?

Fiona noticed it, too.

'The ship's tilting, Ava. When is that lifeboat coming down?'

Ava slipped her arm through hers. Lord, the poor woman was shaking. She huddled closer to the countess and tried to remain calm as they waited on deck.

'Don't you worry none, Fiona, we'll be doing a jig in the boat before you know it.' Ava struggled to lend a humorous lilt in her voice, anything to alleviate the tense atmosphere.

'Are you afraid, Ava?' Fiona asked, hopeful she'd give her a feeling of comfort.

'Me, afraid?' she said with odd sensations cursing through her that even the angels watching them feared the worst on this cold night. 'Aye. 'Tis only a fool who shuts his eyes to the storm coming, as my mum used to say.'

Fiona smiled. 'Thank you. I feel better now.'

Ava hummed along with the tune the band was playing to keep up her own courage as much as the countess's. A loud noise interrupted her troubled thoughts. The ship's foghorn sounded, its solemn bass notes vibrating down to her soul. A horror that wasn't there before crept into her bones. If Buck didn't bring the Irish girls up quickly, they'd be drowned when the sea surged in below.

Ava continued to ponder the danger waiting for him belowdecks as she pulled down her veil and then blessed herself, knowing there was nothing else she could do but wait.

As if her life was suspended.

A strange silence settled in her then, the bright fire glowing within her from his lordship's kiss ebbing to barely a glow.

Oh, no, she couldn't lose that lovely feeling, *she couldn't*.

She wanted to run after him and feel his arms around her again lest her heart languish like a lonely wildflower growing atop a pauper's grave. Instead she held her place on the deck waiting for the lifeboat, her arm linked with Fiona's, knowing it was the right thing to do.

Ava looked up at the sky. It was getting on toward the darkest part of the night. The stars blazed overhead, but nothing could overcome the blackness settling in her soul.

Would she see Buck again?

She had to, but she couldn't shake the foreboding.

She felt as lost as a sinner with no faith.

25

Buck scurried back down to steerage along the maze of empty corridors and passages, a heated urgency surging through him in spite of the bitter chill.

A frantic race against time.

He held onto that truth when he saw several men on bent knee praying. A fervent aura held them in its grasp, holy and impenetrable, until each man secured his place in the hereafter.

Buck murmured his own prayer for salvation as he passed by them, then went about the business at hand.

Saving the two Irish girls from a cruel fate.

Slinging his heavy overcoat over his shoulder, he headed quickly to the aft women's quarters. The vision of Ava looking at him with such sadness branded her in his mind with amazing clarity. Her eyes aching for him to hold her, her face pale behind the black net veil, pink lips parted.

He'd never forget it.

Buck snapped back to his duty. Devotion to the task at hand took hold of him. With water sloshing around his ankles, he started banging on doors and calling out the girl's name.

'Peggy, *Peggy!*'

Damnation, why didn't she answer him?

Or was she already up on deck? Safe in a lifeboat?

He grimaced. He doubted that. Stark scenes of steerage passengers roaming around the third-class section of the Boat Deck, looking for boats that didn't exist, played over and over again in his mind.

At the same time, his ears buzzed nonstop, as if he could hear the girls' voices calling out for help. They were still down here. He'd bet on it. It was a losing hand, but he'd made a promise to play it.

'Peggy, where are you?' he called out. He was soaked up to his knees, his trousers wet and heavy. 'It's Captain Lord Blackthorn.'

'In here, sir!' a girl's frightened voice cried out to him. '*Help us, please!*'

He swung his head around, his eyes searching the narrow corridor. Where did the voice come from?

Rushing seawater slowed his progress, each stride slow going, but he plunged ahead, desperation to find them pounding in his ears. Pushing his shoulder into the wood, he shoved open the first cabin door.

Empty. Then the next and the next. *All empty*.

He came to the last one.

He grabbed the door handle. It wouldn't turn. What the devil. He'd *break* it down.

He pounded on the door hard with his fists. 'Peggy, are you in there?'

'Yes, your lordship,' he heard a girl call out, her voice hopeful. 'Hurry, *please*, the water's rising!'

Buck ripped off his cuff links and rolled up his shirt sleeves. Using his heavy coat as a buffer and all his strength, he leaned into the door and, with a loud grunt, banged against the panels until he felt it give. One more shove and he pushed the door open, the handle falling off and floating away on the fast-moving seawater.

Standing in the doorway, Buck took a deep breath and blew it out. He couldn't hide the alarm on his face. He was nearly too late. The seawater was filling their cabin fast, its sickly green color turning his stomach.

A dim light flickered overhead, but he could see Peggy and her sister sitting on their bunks, looking small and cramped in the four-berth cabin, their feet curled underneath them, their hushed voices saying the rosary in unison.

Compassion for these two girls overwhelmed him. A rush to keep them from harm took hold of him.

The girl named Peggy must be freezing, he thought, huddled on the edge of the bunk wearing only a dressing gown. There was enough of a chill in the cabin to raise goose bumps on his bare forearms. With a groan, Buck squinted to make out her sister squeezed into the corner.

She stared at him, her eyes glassy and wide.

From what he could see, their faces wore looks of sheer terror. After they'd wandered away from the locked gate, they had returned to their cabin. Alone.

'Christ,' he said.

What insane madness was about on this ship that no one tried to help these girls?

Leaving them to die.

The cowards.

Anger seethed within him. A deep shame for a class system that condemned these innocents to death came over him. Shook him until he lost all sense of trust in his fellow man to do the right thing.

An even deeper shame hit him, thinking only of his own plight and not those he hurt.

It wasn't too late to make amends.

Buck was determined to save these girls or die trying.

'Why aren't you up on deck?' he asked. 'Surely a steward came down to lead you up on top.'

'I couldn't leave her here, milord,' Hannah said, her loyalty to her sister steadfast. 'She's all I've got.'

'You're both coming with me,' he said firmly.

'I can't walk, sir.' Peggy showed him her swollen bare foot.

He hadn't planned on this. 'What happened?'

'I hurt my ankle when I slipped and fell in the wet corridor.'

Sweat trickled down his forehead. He'd seen similar injuries on the battlefield. A bad sprain and very painful. She'd never make it up top on her own.

He tore the flimsy bunk sheet into long strips and bandaged up her bare foot.

'This ship is going down,' Buck said. 'And by damnation, you two are getting into a lifeboat if I have to carry you both.'

Before the girl could protest, he picked her up in his arms. Her slender body cradled into his shoulder as she leaned into his chest. Her body was cold like marble.

He covered the shivering girl with his heavy overcoat and carried her toward the stairs, starting down the long corridor with Peggy in his arms and Hannah trailing behind them.

'The girl with the red hair sent you to fetch us, didn't she, sir?' Peggy asked, raising her head from his shoulder.

'Yes.'

A welcoming warmth replaced the chill in him thinking of Ava.

'I knew she wouldn't forget us,' Peggy said. 'She's a fine lass, your lordship. You're a lucky gentleman.'

An immediate kick to his gut sent him into agony.

The odds of ever holding her again were stacked against him.

Buck knew when his time came, he'd still count himself lucky. With Ava, he had something he'd never had before.

The love of a good woman.

Buck breathed in deeply.

He had to keep going. They were nearly at the companionway leading up to the emergency ladder. Then it wasn't far to the first-class stairway and up to the lifeboats.

With the girl in his arms, he moved slowly but steadily down the long, narrow corridor, the water rising up around his thighs. The naked bulbs overhead hissing and crackling in his ears.

Peggy rested her head against his shoulder, her sister tagging along behind him when suddenly the girl grabbed his jacket. Pulled on it hard.

'Look, sir!' Hannah cried out, pointing behind them.

It happened so fast Buck barely had time to twist his head around. His eyes opened wide, his concentration divided between keeping the girls safe and looking for another way out.

The bulkhead barrier behind them separating them from the flooded compartment was giving way.

What should have been a simple ascent up to the top had suddenly became a trap.

Unforgiving, deadly.

He wouldn't accept defeat. He'd not allow these girls to die.

He shot his head back around, looking for somewhere, *anywhere* they could escape.

An empty cabin? *No*. A trap with no way out.

Storage room? *No*. Filling with water fast.

Then he saw—

Lady Luck hadn't given up on him yet. Up ahead someone had left the door open that led to the second-class staircase.

He had to move out. *Now*.

In an instant, he slung Peggy over his shoulder, then turned around. Hannah stared up at him, panic slashed across her face.

'Take my hand, Hannah, *quickly!*'

She reached for him, her eyes fixed with a look of utter terror.

It was too late.

Buck braced himself as the bulkhead broke. Hannah screamed as he reached out and pulled her to him by her long braid. At the same time, her sister grabbed him around the neck so tight she nearly choked him.

Still, he held onto the girl's hair as the freezing cold seawater rushed around them like a river wild and furious, the torrent of water coming at them with full force. The green tide hit the three of them hard, washing over them and sweeping them away.

It was maddening. Horrifying. His inner turmoil rising up in him to a feverish pitch. His eyes, ears, mouth all filled with water, gagging him. He'd not let go of the two girls no matter what. He'd made a promise to *her*.

One Buck intended to keep.

He held his breath and thought of Ava O'Reilly.

26

Ava paced up and down the Boat Deck, twisting the red fringe on her shawl around her fingers, her mind reeling with doubt. Something was wrong belowdecks. Buck should have fetched the Irish girls up on top by now.

Do you have no faith in the man, girl? A brave one he is and honorable, too. Don't set him aside like leftover wine gone sour after Holy Mass. He'll not fail you.

Then where was he? Why wasn't he here? With her. And the countess and Mr Brady, both at her side and as nervous as hound dogs before a hunt.

They knew the ship was taking on more and more water by the minute and they hadn't much time before she foundered.

Fretting and sniveling, Ava pulled the shawl tighter around her. The agony of waiting intensified as the crisp night air shot up her nostrils, sending a fierce pain to her head that wouldn't stop. Down below she imagined seawater swirling through the narrow corridors like an eerie green dervish, reaching out to drown everything in its path.

Everything looked blurry to her from behind the black veil

covering her face, sticking to her cheeks and pricking her skin. Was her veil wet from the sea spray or her tears?

Where in the name of heavens is Buck?

'Why can't they make up their minds what they want us to do?' said the countess, breaking into her thoughts. Frustration and worry were both apparent in her terse words.

'Because they don't know themselves, Fiona,' Trey said, trying to explain. 'From what I heard, the crew had only a short lifeboat drill before sailing and no training in lowering the boats.'

'It's outrageous. Sending us up here on top,' the countess rattled on, 'and now they say go back down again to the Promenade Deck. Thank God it's not yet flooded, but it's too much to bear.'

Though the countess was born to privilege, Ava wasn't surprised when the countess abandoned her proper manners for the most human of traits. *Fear*. Fiona was holding up well, but Ava knew she, too, was worried about Buck.

She put her gloved hand on Ava's arm and drew her to the side, her lips tight together, her eyes wide. 'What if Buck came back and didn't see us?'

Ava shook her head. 'Don't worry, Countess. I imagine Buck is settling the two girls in a lifeboat with warm steamer rugs wrapped around their legs.' Her words sounded confident, but what did she know anyway?

The only thing Ava *did* know was that she didn't believe a word of what she was saying. Then again, the countess didn't know that.

'I pray you're right, Ava.' The countess muttered she was cold and Mr Brady suggested she take shelter in the gymnasium on the starboard side. He waited for Ava to follow her. She didn't. Instead she looked down the narrow companionway leading belowdecks.

What if he was trapped down there?

Trey must have read her mind. 'If anyone can survive this, Ava, it's Buck,' he whispered in her ear.

Ava grabbed his arm. 'What about you, Mr Brady?'

'Me?' Trey answered glibly. 'I'll go down with the ship with the rest of the millionaires.'

'Are you saying there aren't enough lifeboats?' Ava looked at him straight on, her heart accelerating. Unlike Buck, he didn't try to mask his thoughts. The serious look he gave her chilled her, but didn't surprise her.

'Yes. And I'm prepared to do my duty.' He caught his breath. Was that a spirit of resignation she detected in his voice? 'I want the countess to remember me as a gentleman, Ava. I haven't done a very good job pretending to be one during the crossing.'

'You're a fine gentleman, Mr Brady.' Ava stared into his eyes rimmed with guilt. She leaned so close to him she smelled whiskey on his breath. 'The countess and I both know it.'

He kissed her hand, his lips brushing her skin. 'Pity I won't have the opportunity to chase after you in New York,' he said, trying to keep his voice light. They both knew his obvious flirtation of whispers and bold promises would soon end. But there was something else in his eyes that stirred her heart in a way she never imagined. As if he truly cared for her. Was it there all the time and she'd been too naïve to see it? 'It would have been grand fun.'

In a daring move, Ava said, 'You never would have caught me.'

'That's what would have made it so amusing.' He made no apology for his remark.

Embarrassed by his forwardness, Ava turned around to make certain her ladyship wasn't within earshot. No, she could see her in the gymnasium.

'What will the countess do without you, Mr Brady?' Ava said, twirling around and speaking frankly, each word becoming a puff of cold air as the temperature continued to drop.

Her words took him aback. He swallowed. As if he'd just realized the finality of the situation. That their chance of survival was as unlikely as a Sunday sinner finding his way to heaven.

'I'm depending on you, Ava,' Trey said, making no excuses. He didn't try to keep his emotions under control. 'You must see to it my mother does right by Fiona,' he insisted, sucking in a harsh breath. There was an edge to his voice that wasn't there before. He sounded frustrated, his mouth set in a grim line. 'Don't trust her, and above all, *don't* let her bully you.'

Ava stared at him. Standing there so serious and reverent, like a priest preaching the evils of the devil. This was a burden she never expected. A vulnerable awareness that *she* alone was responsible for the welfare of the countess.

Her tone was steady when she said, 'I won't let you down, Mr Brady.'

So quick you are, girl, with the fancy speech. Are you sure you can handle what he's asking of you?

Ava *wasn't* sure. Her insides turned numb and she was so scared her hand couldn't find its way to make the sign of the cross. Trey didn't notice her discomfort.

Looking up at him, she met his eyes, eyes she often thought hid so much. Not tonight. She saw him fighting the hunger inside him to claim what he wanted, but couldn't have.

Her.

An awkward feeling bloomed in the pit of her stomach. Her heart belonged to his lordship. He slipped an arm casually around her shoulders and together they stood there at the wooden rail, talking.

The sea was as still as a millpond.

'My mother is a tough old bird, Ava,' Trey said, keeping his voice even. 'It won't be easy for you.'

'I'll do my best, Mr Brady.' Her heart pained for him, trying to keep his composure. She wasn't sorry she didn't yield to him.

Down below, chunks of ice floated by.

She shuddered.

'You're shivering, Ava,' Trey said, but he made no move to hold her closer, though she was sure he wanted to. His eyes narrowed, his nose twitched. Something had changed in him. When they first met, he'd flirted, sweet-talked, challenged her. Now he kept his distance, as if he, too, was surprised at this change in his feelings and he didn't know what to do about it. Whatever he was feeling inside, he kept to himself and remained a gentleman.

She studied his expression. His eyes blatantly said he would never stop wanting her, a silent warning if he stayed any longer he *would* do something they'd both regret.

She said, 'His lordship is fortunate to have a friend like you—'

'There's Mr Lightoller,' he said, cutting her off. 'Wait here, Ava. I'll see what the delay is in getting the windows open down on A deck.'

Then he was off, moving with the ease of a gentleman on a mission, catching up to the ship's officer and grabbing his attention. Mr Brady *was* a good man.

Ava needn't have worried about the countess seeing them. She had a more pressing issue on her mind. She came running out of the gymnasium, her face shiny and pale, lips parted. She was wildly agitated about something.

But what?

'My mother's earrings,' Fiona said, breathless from the exertion of pushing through the passengers huddled in the gymnasium, some women wearing only nightdresses and wrappers under their lifebelts. 'I promised my father I would wear them on my wedding day. I *must* go back to my cabin and get them'

'But, Fiona,' Ava pleaded, 'Mr Brady will be back to fetch us for the lifeboat—'

'There's plenty of time, Ava. I heard Colonel Astor telling his wife we'll all be laughing about this later when they have to row the lifeboats back to the ship.' Ava had the feeling the countess didn't believe that.

'I'm coming with you,' she said.

'No, Ava, I insist you stay—'

'Sorry, your ladyship,' she pushed on, 'I promised Buck and Mr Brady I'd get you into a lifeboat, and by the saints, I will.'

The countess's expression changed to a grateful smile. 'Oh, Ava, what would I do without you?'

Ava held her gaze, determined to show her ladyship only strength. Inside, her stomach churned, her back muscles so tight she found it difficult to move. Some force she didn't understand took hold of her soul as she followed the countess down three decks to her stateroom.

Why? They had plenty of time to get into a lifeboat.

It was unearthly quiet along the corridor. No one moving about. In spite of her anxiousness, Ava found a certain solace in the familiarity of things.

She wanted to place the experience in her memory forever, like pressing a fragile daisy between the pages of a book. Its brightness might fade, but not the hold it had on her heart.

Forcing her tense muscles to relax, Ava waited patiently while the countess tore through her wardrobe closet, looking for her earrings.

'Fiona, *we must go!*' Ava called out. She could hear what sounded like voices nearby. Most likely frantic passengers trying to make their way up to the Boat Deck from down below.

'Coming, Ava.' The countess appeared out of breath and listless. 'I forgot I'd hidden my earrings in a silk stocking.' She held them up, their ruby and diamond sparkle emitting a glow like a soft rainbow flame. Then she wrapped the earrings in a gray silk scarf and put them into her coat pocket. 'I couldn't let them go down to the bottom of the sea.'

'Hurry, Fiona.'

Without looking back, Ava rushed quickly along the corridor and up the wide stairs leading to B Deck. She could hear Fiona's soft footsteps behind her, then they trailed off. Her heart stopped. Where did she go? She prayed it wasn't the lifts. If the generator stopped working, she'd be stuck in the elevator.

'Fiona, where are you?'

'Down here, Ava!' the countess called out, her voice echoing from somewhere below.

Ava turned her neck to look over the railing.

She drew in her breath and a stinging made her lungs hurt. What she saw shocked her.

Four decks below at the bottom of the Grand Staircase, a swirling pool of seawater snatched up everything in its path. Dishes, chairs, lamp stands, metal ornaments with greedy intensity.

Fiona was nowhere in sight.

A painful ache shot through her hot as a fever.

'Where are you, your ladyship?' Ava cried out, her voice bouncing back at her. She stood under the large glass dome overhead dark with night and pricked with pinpoints of light.

Stars.

'I'm down here, Ava! I took a wrong turn,' she heard from the deck below.

Ava saw the countess poke her head around the bend of the landing, her face looking straight up at her. 'I'll be right up... oh, *wait*... I see someone floating in the water below.'

'There's no one down there!' Ava yelled back. Debris swirled around in the water, nothing else... then again, a poor soul *could* be trapped down there.

'It's *Buck*, Ava... I *know* it is.' She started down the staircase.

'Holy Mother of God, can it be him?' Ava whispered in an anguished voice, fear sending her into a different place where she didn't want to go.

'He's calling to me!'

Ava listened. She heard nothing but the rushing water.

'Hold on, Countess, I'm coming to see!' she shouted, then she stopped when she saw Fiona gaze up into Ava's eyes with the pain she'd kept hidden for so long.

The pain of loving Buck.

Ava winced, experiencing a moment of realization that rocked her being. That pain altered Fiona's reality, her eyes taking on a dreamy look that whispered of deepening shadows where light should have been.

As if the countess were in a trance.

Ava lived a lifetime running down the steps. She had to reach her. *Fast*. She looked again and again at the swirling water, nothing but debris. His lordship wasn't there, no matter what the countess saw in her mind.

'Don't look down, Fiona! *Buck isn't there.*'

The countess didn't hear her or didn't want to. She raced down to the next deck. The Irish girl peered down, *down* into the circular maze of steps leading to the flooded bottom.

Round and round the water swirled.

Dear Jesus, what was she about?

Pull yourself together, girl. Go after her.

Ava took two steps at a time, the stairs creaking under her feet, the ship leaning heavily to the port side. Fire pumped through her veins.

She was almost there.

Fiona stood up on her toes and held onto the banister, craning her neck. As if she *couldn't* give up looking for Buck. Her every move screamed her desperation.

'Buck... *Buck!*' she called out, frantic. Like an animal caught in a hunter's trap.

'He's not there, Fiona.'

May the Lord have mercy on her, so passionate was the countess's plea, it pierced Ava's soul. She eased toward her on tiptoe, careful not to startle her. A wee bit more and she could grab her hand and bring Fiona back up to safety. She felt her back muscles tightening again. 'We must hurry. Buck's waiting for us up on deck.'

'*No, Buck's... dead,*' whispered the countess.

Ava hesitated. She wasn't at all sure what to do about her outburst. She always appeared so genteel and in control.

But Fiona *couldn't* let Buck go. Couldn't release him from her heart, no matter how reckless her actions became.

Ava wouldn't allow her to suffer so.

'Don't tempt the devil, Countess. Him with his greedy hands wanting to take as many souls as he can on this darkest of nights.'

'What does it matter?' Fiona said, not looking up. 'Everything I care about has been taken from me.'

A sharp cry emitted from Fiona's lips.

As she reached out to grab Ava's hand, the heel on her boot caught on her skirt and she slipped, falling to her knees and sliding down the stairs.

'Fiona!' Ava screamed.

'Ava… *help me!'* she cried out, looking down, a desperate edge to her voice, a rush of disbelief attacking her mind.

Ava had seconds, *seconds* to reach her before she slid down four flights of stairs and into the freezing cold, swirling water.

'Hold on, Fiona, *I'm coming!'*

'I – I *can't.*' The countess tried to grab Ava's hand, but she couldn't reach her. The wooden stair underneath her feet shifted. Frantically, she reached for the banister, thrusting her gloved fingers through the ornamental railing, slick and wet.

She couldn't hold on.

'Oh, sweet Jesus, *no!'* Ava cried out, racing toward her. She watched in horror as the countess tried to regain her balance, her arms outstretched.

'*Ava…*' the countess forced out her name in a harsh whisper. Her eyes widened and a bone-chilling groan escaped from her lips.

'No, Countess, *no!'*

Before Ava could grab her, the countess lost her balance and fell backward down the stairs, her body rolling over and over and—

She landed at the bottom in a heap, the water creeping up toward her from the deck below.

She lay still. *Very* still.

Ava heard a scream like she never heard before.

It was her own voice.

She'd flood hell with her tears if any harm came to this grand lady because of her.

Ava hold tight onto the banister, praying to St Michael himself she wouldn't lose her grip as she walked sideways so as not to slip on the wet stairs, dragging the red shawl behind her, tripping over its long fringe. She ignored the howling sounds of the rushing water down below. Agony tore through her. Horrible, sad feelings she dared not let take hold of her.

Nothing was wrong with the countess, she told herself, *nothing*. A bump, bruise.

Nothing more.

Ava couldn't accept such a vile punishment as to lose the countess along with Buck and Mr Brady. She prayed, promising the Almighty that every day of her life from now on would be sacred and pure if the countess was unhurt.

It was all for naught.

The countess lay sprawled on the bottom step. Not moving. Her eyes wide open, her lips parted. Her cheekbones drawn taut. She thanked the angels the water hadn't yet reached this high on the staircase.

Ava froze. An edge of fear sliced through her, razor sharp and deadly.

What godless trick was this?

What?

The countess isn't dead. She can't be. It's not right to take so gentle a soul.

Ava lifted the countess's head and felt a moistness caress her fingers like silk.

Blood.

She must have hit the back of her head hard. Ava swallowed the cutting pain of disbelief. Her senses reeled at the sight before her.

This can't be happening.

Panic overtook her, a violent emotion slicing through her brain and making her cheeks hot. She pulled off the countess's glove, then began rubbing her hand back and forth, trying to bring her back.

She couldn't.

Finally, Ava leaned back on her heels, closed her eyes, and felt a sudden, fierce despair. So strong were her feelings for the countess, it was as if her own dear sweet mum had been dragged away by the devil himself. The pain so raw, she beat upon her chest to quell the agony. She heard the rustle of skirts rushing up behind her. A sharp intake of breath, then a groan.

Ava ignored it. She wouldn't let go of her ladyship's hand, her fingers stiff and cold, not even when she heard a woman's voice utter the words she didn't want to hear.

'The countess is dead, miss.'

* * *

Buck held onto the two Irish girls though excruciating pain shot through every muscle in his body, his shoulders bearing the brunt of it, as if ripping from their sockets. He wouldn't let them go. He'd promised Ava, the power of that promise fueling his strength to keep going. He didn't resist the rushing wall of water. Instead, he used it to his advantage.

To save the girls.

Survival was something you didn't think about, Buck knew, you just did it and thought about it afterward. He rode the wave back to the stairwell and dragged the two girls, soaking wet, up the narrow steps topside. Buck didn't think, just moved forward, his military survival skills coming to his aid.

He was well aware for him there *was* no afterward, but he wouldn't stop until these girls were safe in a lifeboat. He had to admit they never whimpered, never faltered, though Peggy was in terrible pain from her sprained ankle. They were a tough lot, these Irish girls, and admiration for their relentless spirit rose up in him. Their pride as well as their determination and loyalty was something he'd seen too little of in his upper crust world.

He *hated* himself for not admitting it sooner. If only he'd told Ava before he left her with the countess. He wasn't ashamed to admit how wrong he'd been about a lot of things. About honesty and truth and integrity, and how they weren't the exclusive property of the posh classes. If anything, he'd learned a lady wasn't defined by birth, but by actions.

And heart.

Ava would always be *his* lady.

His sharp intake of breath caught him unaware and he knew he *had* to find her. See her again.

Survive, *somehow*.

Scanning the faces on the port side, he didn't see Ava. Or the countess. Were they safe in a lifeboat on the glassy sea?

He wouldn't rest until he knew for certain they had escaped the sinking ship.

God help them, he thought. The water was below freezing. A rescue ship was on the way, according to a ship's officer. The *Carpathia*. Even at top speed, the steamer wouldn't arrive in time.

Until then, he had his duty as a soldier and a gentleman.

He carried Peggy, with her sister following them, over to the starboard side where the boats were loading faster. The canvas covers were off the lifeboats and the masts cleared. Seamen stood at the davits and uncoiled the lines after fitting in cranks.

Finally, he had the two Irish girls in a boat, wrapped up in steamer rugs, holding onto each other tight, their young faces streaked with dried tears.

'We owe our lives to you, Captain Lord Blackthorn,' Peggy called out, waving to him. 'Thank you.' Hannah nodded, shaking her head up and down. Their eyes were filled with such deep gratitude for saving them, that Buck found their adoring looks uncomfortable.

He felt guilty because it had taken him so damn long to realize a man of his station owed allegiance not just to women of his class, but to *all* women.

He watched the lifeboat being lowered down to the next deck to take in more women and children, the pulleys squealing as the boat was swung out and began its slow descent. There was an excited murmur from the passengers when the lifeboat nearly landed on top of the boat below. A quick-thinking stoker in the other boat cut the rope with his knife and the lifeboat was safely lowered to the water.

Buck stood at the rail on the Boat Deck, the wind coming up, the ship listing to the port side. He slapped his arms to keep the blood flowing, then took off for A Deck.

His job was done here.

Now to find his lady.

27

All the tears Ava couldn't shed before came now in a torrent of hopelessness.

Knowing the countess was dead struck her like she'd been slapped. Then in the next moment, a different pain made her clench her fists in anger.

Looking at the pale, still face of the countess. Her chestnut brown hair escaping from the silk scarf framing her face. The dead woman's doe-shaped gray eyes remained transfixed on her, but she couldn't read her last thoughts.

Somehow Ava knew they were of his lordship.

From somewhere deep in her soul, she let go with an agonizing groan. The countess was gone. If the hearts of the angels were as cold and dark as the black sea, she would lose Buck, too, before this night was over.

Sweet mercy, was this to be her fate? To lose the two people who meant so much to her?

'*Fiona*,' Ava whispered her name aloud and felt a sisterhood with her that went beyond their love of the same man. Crying like a babe she was, for this woman had been kind to her and she held no grudge against her.

'You must save yourself, miss.'

Ava shook her head. She raged against such a thing, wouldn't listen. She stiffened when she felt soft fingers pressing on her shoulder, urging her to look away. Finally, she turned and looked up. The woman's eyes centered on her.

It was the stewardess, Marta Sinclair. She'd seen her earlier locking the cabins to keep out looters.

'She wouldn't want you to grieve.'

'I loved her like she was my own kin,' Ava began, not ashamed to admit her powerful feelings for the countess. 'Her character, her strength. Her willingness to fight for what she wanted, though she was held back by what she was. A lady with elegant ways, so fine and proper. *That* she couldn't fight.' She paused, saddened by the hurt of it. 'I admired and respected her. She was a lady, yet she spoke to me as an equal.'

'Why don't you let the countess help you now?' the stewardess said, stepping back so as not to intrude further on her emotions. 'Take her coat.'

'What are you saying, lass?' Ava asked quietly. She could see the stewardess was bundled up in a gray sweater and long coat.

'She won't need it, but you will in the lifeboat. It's freezing cold.'

'I can't take it... it's unholy.'

'You *must*. I knew her ladyship but a few days, but I, too, fell under her spell. She'd want you to have it.'

'But I already took so much from her.' Ava bowed her head. 'Even the man she loved.'

'Did you, child?'

She raised her eyes. 'What do you mean?'

'Only a fool would be blind to the way his lordship looked at you,' the stewardess said with certainty. 'I noticed it that day we left Queenstown when he saw me watching the two of you. He had his eye on you then. No woman could hope to have that kind of fascination from a man, but you did. The countess saw it, too.'

Ava couldn't help staring at her. She felt unsettled with the woman saying such things about a man who had yet to tell her he cared for her in such a manner. Mercy, it was unseemly, but oh... how she wanted to believe it.

'Take the coat,' the stewardess urged her.

'*Jesus Mary,* I... I can't...'

Even in her grief, Ava was aware of a feeling that begged her to do what the woman asked.

'You *must.*' The stewardess knelt beside the countess and picked up her glove, then closed her ladyship's eyes.

Ava watched her with such reverence, she was afraid to move.

Look at her, removing her ladyship's lifebelt then unbuttoning her coat with her nimble fingers as only a woman used to dressing and undressing a society lady could do.

Not clumsy like her.

Within seconds, the stewardess removed the long coat from the countess's still body then her other glove, her ladyship's head lolling to one side like a lifeless doll. Then she smoothed out the brushed black velvet coat with her flat palms and held it out to Ava. 'Take her coat and gloves and *go.* You'll not have another chance to save yourself.'

'No... *I can't,*' Ava protested.

'*Here!*' She tossed the coat and gloves to Ava. She caught them in spite of her misgivings. Her mind whirled around in a circle, thinking it was against all that was good and holy, yet practical if she wanted to survive.

She let go with a long shiver as she unfastened her lifebelt and put the coat on over her tweed suit, as if hands belonging to the devil himself wrapped it around her.

She left it unbuttoned as the stewardess helped her tighten the lifebelt straps.

'How much time have we left before the end comes?' Ava wanted to know, tossing the red lace shawl over her shoulder, then pulling on the countess's soft gray leather gloves. A strange feeling, as if she also took on her fine manners.

'Not long,' said the stewardess. 'Now *hurry!*'

'I can't leave her here... *like this.*' Ava tossed her head back and forth, still not convinced. 'It ain't right.'

It did her soul in to see the countess abandoned and lost. She'd not leave her to be swept away by the wretched sea when the ship went down.

Again, she made her plea.

'We can lay her down in an empty stateroom, miss,' the stewardess said. 'Help me carry her.'

Ava nodded, lifting her ladyship up by her ankles while the stewardess pulled her up from under the armpits. She was grateful for the respect she gave the countess, a slender woman. It was no easy task to carry her, keeping her silk dress down over her legs and holding onto her ankles with a firm grip. Even so she grunted under the strain.

Taking small steps, together the two women carried the countess's lifeless body up the stairs, then down the corridor and into a cabin unoccupied during the crossing, then put her down on the bed.

'She'll be at rest here,' the stewardess said, blowing out her breath. She covered the countess with rose silk bedding up to her chin.

She lay in peace.

Ava blessed herself and said a prayer, then shook off the chill invading the room. When she dug her gloved hands into her pockets, she found the letter she'd never posted for the countess, a folded-up dinner menu, and—

'Holy Mary... I'd almost forgotten.' She pulled out a small silken bundle.

The earrings.

She bit her lower lip, and then unwrapped them. Hurt spilled through her heart with such a sharp poignancy her chest tightened and stifled her breathing. Ava closed her eyes tightly and heard the countess's words in her head.

I promised my father I would wear my mother's earrings on my wedding day.

When Ava opened her eyes, her gaze was fixed on the ruby and diamond earrings. They barely sparkled. How could they? The countess's vibrancy and love of life was what had made them glow with such beauty.

No gentle breeze nor brilliant sunlight would ever stir her ladyship's poetic soul again. Somehow Ava knew wearing the earrings on her way to heaven would heal her spirit.

Without a word, she fastened the earrings in the countess's ears. The drop earrings lay on the soft pillow, as if protecting her on her journey.

The stewardess ushered Ava out of the cabin then locked the door behind them. 'You must get to the lifeboats without delay.'

'Not until I find his lordship,' Ava said in a firm voice. 'I can't leave him.'

'You *must*. He's a gentleman and he knows what his chances are. He'd want you to save yourself. Now *hurry*.'

Ava turned to the stewardess. 'What about you?'

'Don't worry about me.' She managed a smile, but she was wiping the sweat from her face with her apron as though her heart fluttered with uncertainty. The knowing look in her eye made her uneasy when she said, 'Good luck to you, Ava O'Reilly.'

Then she was gone.

Ava owed the stewardess more than she could ever repay her and she would if it came to that. She had the feeling the story was not finished. For now, she must take it one step at a time.

She raced up the stairs to the Boat Deck and out into the cold night. Suddenly everything around her seemed different. Frantic, unsettled. As if she was coming undone. She didn't know which way to turn, here... no, *there*.

Tears blurred her vision. Losing the countess had disturbed her more than she thought possible. Left a gaping hole in her no holy thought nor prayer could mend.

Blessed Virgin, tell me, please, what was He about? It was cruel to take her and leave me. You'll get no more tears from me. I'll not leave this ship until I find Buck.

I owe it to her.

The countess.

* * *

1.45 a.m.

With the Irish girls taken care of, Buck headed toward the boats near the bow of the ship where he'd left Ava and the countess. He was so intent on his purpose he almost didn't see a woman waving frantically to him from a lifeboat being lowered on the starboard side. Calling out to him, moving her arms to and fro in wild gestures.

He sensed her desperation. Mr Murdoch yelled at her to sit down.

The woman sat down, and then popped up again. Calling out to him.

Was it the countess? No. It wasn't her demeanor. Then it had to be Ava. He'd left her with the countess waiting to be loaded into a boat on the *port* side. What the hell happened? If it *was* her, why was she still on board?

What is the fool girl up to now?

Worrying about her had become more important to him than anything else. If he didn't survive, who would watch out for her? That bothered him more than he cared to admit. With Ava, every damn thing she *did* affected him.

His eyes narrowed. By God, he couldn't make out what the woman was saying. The ship was settling rapidly in the bow, causing panic to spread among the passengers left on deck. Then he saw a flash when a ship's officer fired his gun as a warning, startling the crowd when men from steerage tried to jump into the lifeboat. That quieted them.

Not for long. Their high-pitched cries again filled the air.

Wiping sweat from his face with his jacket sleeve, Buck reached deep into his pocket and his fingers wrapped around his pistol. It was water damaged, but it would frighten off any lout who blocked his way. As a gambler who'd most likely played his last hand, he recognized the smell of human fear. It was more prevalent than the smell of ice.

He fought through the crowd to where they were lowering the boat and leaned over the rail. It was impossible to see into the boat, but it *had* to be Ava yelling at him. The crew had no experience lowering the boats and they went down over the side in uneven, jerky movements.

Seawater splashed against the hull and onto the decks below. He estimated the Boat Deck was about twenty feet above the waterline instead of seventy. He could see the woman yelling at him, standing up in the lifeboat bouncing back and forth as it was lowered down.

Then she lost her balance. She screamed as she pitched forward but a quick-thinking steward reached out and pulled her back into the boat. She collapsed in his arms.

Damnation, *was* it Ava?

If she'd fallen overboard, he'd dive in after her. He'd rather go down to the bottom of the sea *with* her than live without her.

And where was the countess? And Trey?

He didn't see his old friend anywhere. He was never sure about Trey's loyalty to any woman, but he possessed an unbending sense of fraternity toward Buck. He could depend on him to act in a gentlemanly manner.

And take care of the two women.

He *prayed* Trey was in that lifeboat with them.

His eyes burned from staring at her so hard. He had to make certain it *was* her before the seamen rowed away from the ship. If they were lucky, the ship would last long enough between the time of the collision and the sinking to avoid dragging the lifeboats down with it.

If they were lucky.

Never before had Buck had the urge to cheat death as skillfully as he won at cards.

'What the devil was that crazed woman doing?' he heard a gentleman say nearby, shaking his head.

'She's not the only female forced to leave her husband,' added another man.

'I heard that boat was filled with cabin crew members.'

Buck froze. The words set off a bell in his head. He squinted, but he could barely see the passengers huddled together in one dark silhouette. No moon overhead, but the lights were still burning on the lower decks. When the lifeboat passed by the open portholes, he could see the woman's face.

He let out his breath, surprised.

It *wasn't* Ava, but Marta Sinclair. The stewardess.

Why did she risk her life to call out to him?

'Buck!' he heard a voice behind him cry out. He spun around. It was Trey.

'Damn it all, Trey, where the hell have you been?'

Trey wasn't interested in answering his question when he had his own on his mind. 'Where is the countess?' he blurted out. 'And Ava?'

'Aren't they in a lifeboat?' he asked.

'No,' Trey said.

Buck gritted his teeth and fought against the unexpected kick to his gut. He felt a stab of guilt for not making certain they'd gotten into a boat, but he'd made Ava a promise to save the Irish girls and he'd kept it.

'Where did you leave them?' he wanted to know.

'In the gymnasium. When I returned, they were gone.'

'Bloody hell...'

Had the stewardess seen them? Was *that* what the woman was trying to tell him? Buck took charge. 'When was that?'

'Half an hour ago.'

'Did you check the countess's stateroom?'

'Yes. It was empty.'

He looked at Trey. He was doing his best to act calm, but he wasn't hiding his apprehension well. Neither was Buck. He clenched his fists, digging his fingers into his palms until they hurt.

'I'm worried, Buck,' Trey continued. 'I can't find *anyone* who saw the countess and her lady's maid get into a lifeboat.'

'Dear God,' he said under his breath.

* * *

1.50 a.m.

Ava strode up the open deck past the empty davits, the lifeboats now gone. She paid no attention to the gentlemen standing idly around borrowing matches from each other and smoking. She ignored their curious stares. She had one thing on her mind.

Find Buck.

There was no time to wish things could have been different. No words to express the scattered images and warm memories that fed her soul.

Ava stood at the rail and stared down at the ice-covered water below. She could feel the chill of death in the air. More than two hours had passed since the ship hit the iceberg. Where was Buck... and Mr Brady? Surely she had time to find his lordship. She'd say nothing to him about the countess, instead allowing him to believe she was safe in a lifeboat.

Why bring such sorrow upon him when she had not yet found the courage to accept it?

If they survived, he'd have to know.

If they didn't...

'Here's another woman for the lifeboat,' someone called out behind her, then grabbed her roughly around the waist, lifting her up like she was a sack of mail. Fear gripped her. Who was this madman who'd made up his mind she was ripe for saving?

She twisted her neck and saw a seaman. His cold breath hung in the air, his eyes tinged with blue shadows, his patience worn thin by women refusing to get into the boats.

'Holy Mary, you'll not put your hands on me,' Ava yelled.

'For God's sake, madam, we've got to get this boat away.'

'Take your bloody mitts off me. *I'll not go.*'

Spouting off like a wild banshee, are you, Ava O'Reilly? No doubt you're no first cabin lady with a mouth on you like that.

'Don't give me no trouble, madam,' said the seaman.

Ava struggled in his arms, her heart pounding, then sweet Jesus, the unbelievable shot before her eyes.

Mr Moody was headed her way.

A brave young officer he was and devoted to duty. He'd send her back down below to wait her turn.

She'd never see Buck again.

'Put me down,' she hissed at the seaman. Then with a swift kick to his knee, she broke free from the man's hold with determination more than strength.

Ava took off, racing down the wooden deck and pushing through the passengers. She could see Mr Moody looking on, then he shook his head and joined the men trying to launch the two collapsible boats.

He didn't recognize her wearing the countess's coat.

Blessing herself, Ava scurried down the narrow iron stairs leading to the Promenade Deck, praying her courage hadn't deserted her. *Someone* must have seen Buck.

She skidded to a stop, her chest heaving. *There*, that ship's officer loading the lifeboat. One foot in the boat he had, the other on the open square window ledge. Deck chairs laid against the rail became steps to the sill. Then into the dark the women went and the waiting boat hanging alongside the deck.

Not an easy task. The ship was listing heavily.

She had a vivid memory of seeing him before. Yes, with Buck after she left the Turkish baths.

Ask him, will you?

She stood still, her heart pounding, then pushed herself forward, suddenly possessed by a daring that surprised her.

'Have you seen Captain Lord Blackthorn?' she breathed in a low voice.

Ava looked at him, waiting.

'No, your ladyship,' the ship's officer said politely, then ordered a boy of about thirteen out of the boat until his father convinced him to let him stay.

Were her ears tricking her? What did he call her?

She turned to the gentleman assisting him. 'Who is that officer?' she forced out the words, her voice barely a whisper.

'Mr Lightoller,' said the man, an American by his accent.

She shook her head. The name meant nothing to her.

Before she could say anything, the ship's officer turned his attention back to her.

'Please, your ladyship, you *must* get into a lifeboat.'

Ava was stunned. *This time there was no mistake. Twice* he'd addressed her as *your ladyship.*

She asked, 'What did you call me?'

'Why, you're the Countess of Marbury,' he said, his words catching the interest of a lady waiting to get into a lifeboat. 'His lordship told me who you were when I saw you with him on C Deck.'

I was wearing the countess's coat that day.

'He spoke very highly of you, Countess. *Hurry*, this boat must be lowered away *immediately*.'

'I'm not... I mean...'

Would you shut your mouth, girl? The ship's officer believes you're the countess. His lordship was keeping you safe when the man saw you racing down the corridor like a crazy fool. He believed no one would be the wiser once you reached New York. Sticking his neck out for you, he was.

This is how you repay him?

Crying like a spoilt child?

Get into the boat before the devil himself tosses you into the cold, black sea. Then you'll be cast off like a shiny pearl sinking to the sandy bottom. Lost forever.

Or you can live.

If you pretend to be the countess.

Ava let the idea flow over her like a perfumed oil, appealing and seductive. Her mum used to say that hidden somewhere in her was the essence of a fine pearl.

That someday Ava would find it and it would bedevil her.

She scoffed at that. She'd once thought of her ladyship as a perfect pearl. A gentle lady taken by fate. She'd never get away with pretending to be the countess.

You have to, girl.

You owe it to the countess and his lordship to get into that lifeboat.

The tension around the boats quickened when a seaman shouted to Mr Lightoller that several men had rushed another lifeboat. In a flash, the ship's officer jumped aside and threatened to shoot them if they didn't let the women and children into the boat.

Ava didn't wait to see what happened next. She pulled up the velvet collar on the countess's coat and looked for a way out. She'd never be able to look Buck full in the face if she didn't keep searching for him and Mr Brady.

'His lordship will have my job,' Mr Lightoller said, grabbing her arm, 'if I don't get you into this boat, Countess.'

'*No*—'

'In you go.' Mr Lightoller was in no mood to listen to Ava's protests. He shoved her through the open window and dropped her into the last wooden lifeboat on the ship.

Only the collapsible boats remained, she heard him say.

Her heart jumped into her throat as they lowered the boat past the other decks all lit up, every porthole blazing with light. Bumping up and down, foot by foot, the sea on one side, the black hull of the ship on the other. It was so close to her nose she could run her fingers over its wet sheen.

An eerie fascination took hold of her, the liner tilting downward toward the bow.

The sea was barely fifteen feet below A Deck.

When the lifeboat hit the water, the slosh of the sea crashing against the sides of the boat grated on her nerves.

She didn't want to leave Buck. She wouldn't give up hoping she'd see him on deck.

Ava jumped up, scanning the frantic passengers leaning over the rail. She heard the ship's officer order the quartermaster to take charge, telling him to stand by while the other boats rowed away.

'*Sit down*, Countess,' ordered the quartermaster, 'or you may lose your balance.'

Embarrassed, Ava sat down, but the damage had been done. She could feel the curious stares on her from the women in the boat.

First cabin ladies, she guessed by their upturned noses and fancy manners.

Immediately she heard them whispering to each other.

It must be her.

Who?

The Countess of Marbury.

Are you sure?

Yes, I heard the ship's officer say so.

Ava lowered her head. Was there no getting away from it? The voices had warned her and now it had come to pass.

The devil had found her.

Ava O'Reilly was no more.

This was to be her private hell. To have what she'd always dreamed.

To be a lady.

But lose the only man she'd ever love.

28

Finding Ava proved to be more difficult and exhausting than Buck had imagined. He fought to make his way along the Boat Deck, seawater sloshing over the decks, passengers running like scared rats toward the stern. All this while the *Titanic*'s musicians played a lively waltz to prevent panic and keep the mood upbeat.

He shivered, but not from his wet clothes. Stiff with cold, soaked to the skin, he knew the end was near.

He looked down over the rail and estimated the water was less than ten feet from the deck below. How much time did he have left? Word was the engine room was filled up to the boilers and she was going down fast.

And *still* no sign of Ava.

He slammed his fist so hard into the railing it cracked the wood. He couldn't bear the result of his search. Wanting so *desperately* to find this woman, yet he was at his wit's end where to look next.

A cover of semi-darkness hovering over the deck did nothing to help him in his search, not to mention the damn number of ventilators and staterooms limiting his ability to see more than several feet in front of him.

Where the hell was she?

Somehow, he didn't believe Ava would risk the countess's life by not getting her into a lifeboat. Still, no one had seen the two women get away and for that reason he couldn't give up looking for them.

Or was it something else?

A gut-wrenching gnawing that kept eating at him. He couldn't shake the feeling *something* was wrong.

He stared at the black sea filled with ice chunks, all too aware his desire to save the woman he loved was no different than every other man on the ship. He respected that, but he wouldn't give up until he knew for certain Ava was safe in a lifeboat.

And then... he didn't want to think about what would happen when the end came. He was afraid, no sane man wouldn't be, but he would have to rely on his survival instinct being strong enough to pull him through.

Whatever he had to do.

Dive into the bloody sea if he had to. To *hell* with all these rigid rules of how he *should* act, he decided once and for all. She'd changed him. Made him see things differently. He didn't want to spend the rest of his life in boudoirs covered in silk damask and ripe with the smell of heady perfume.

He wanted *her*.

He was taken aback by this sudden rush of emotion he felt for Ava. It wasn't just that she was stubborn and pigheaded.

And beautiful.

God damn it, *she loved him*. She'd said so. Her sheer determination to tell him took him by surprise. He couldn't say it back, though God knew he wanted to. Years of flirting with pretty women and the words came easy to him.

Except with Ava.

He was saddled with doubt that because of his reputation, he didn't know if she'd believe him. And that hurt more than anything.

Buck swallowed hard. Everything she did came rushing back to him. She was part of his soul and he refused to believe he'd lost her forever.

A cold wind sliced through him, sending a sharp pain to his heart that made him groan. If anything happened to her because of him, he'd be doomed to hell and deservedly so. He *could* change, he told himself. Mistakes could be undone. All he had to do was survive. That kept him going.

Hope.

And faith.

He snapped to attention when he heard a ship's officer shout out they needed hands to clear the collapsible boats from on top of the officers' quarters.

Mr Lightoller.

Damn, were the emergency boats all that were left?

They were less than *half* the length of the wooden ones.

Buck could see the seamen fitting the collapsible into the davits while his ears rang when the crew detonated the last distress rockets. His head throbbed. God help the poor souls still trapped down below. He'd tried to help more passengers find their way up, but the rushing water made it impossible. A deepening guilt washed over him when the lifeboat was ready for loading and the ship's officer called for women and children. No telling how many steerage passengers hadn't found their way up on top.

Were Ava and the countess still on board?

Waiting for the boat?

Buck shook his head. Knowing Ava, if she was looking for him, she wouldn't respond to the call. She didn't listen to *him*, did she?

Still, he couldn't take that chance.

He pushed through the crowd, only to be stopped by a seaman. 'Sorry, sir, women and children first.'

'I'm looking for two ladies—' Buck began.

'I said, *women and children first*.'

Buck wouldn't be dissuaded. 'I demand you let me speak to Mr Lightoller.'

It was a risky move on his part since the second officer believed *Ava* was the countess. Buck depended on the frenetic atmosphere on deck to confuse the man's memory. Along with the fact Ava wore a veil over her face and the countess wore her distinctive black coat. Putting the two women into a boat would have been a blur to the ship's officer.

He hoped.

He needn't have worried. He couldn't even get near him. The officer ordered his crew to form a ring around the lifeboat to prevent a repeat of the stampede Buck had seen earlier when men with daggers and clubs rushed the boat.

'Sorry, sir,' repeated the seaman, his tone firm but polite. 'I must ask you to back away. We're lowering the boat.'

'I'm looking for the Countess of Marbury and her lady's maid.' Buck craned his neck to see who was in the lifeboat as it was lowered very slowly over the side, but the deepening darkness made it impossible. 'I left them on the Promenade Deck.'

The seaman didn't answer him. Buck refused to panic in spite of the red glow of the lights behind him casting an eerie spell over the scene. Instead a fiery anger swelled up inside him at the thought that he couldn't save her. God help him if *both* women were still on the ship. Only minutes left before the *Titanic* foundered and they'd all be tossed into the freezing, cold sea.

'Did I hear you ask about the countess?'

Buck spun around so quickly his wet shoes squeaked on the teak deck. To his surprise, he recognized American businessman, Colonel Archibald Gracie. A gentleman he'd seen in the smoking room, though they hadn't been introduced.

'Yes, the Countess of Marbury,' he said.

'You needn't worry, sir,' said the colonel with certainty. 'I saw the countess get into lifeboat number four.'

'What about her maid?' Buck rushed his words, not giving a damn about their implication.

His apparent interest in a servant caused a slight lifting of the colonel's brow. 'Sorry, your lordship,' he said, trying to be discreet, but Buck could see he watched his every move, puzzled. 'The countess was alone.'

'Was the boat filled to capacity?' Buck had to ask.

'No... about forty passengers.'

Buck couldn't believe it. *Where was Ava?* Each wooden lifeboat held sixty-five passengers. *Why the hell don't they fill the boats?*

The countess was *safe*, but he had no doubt Ava was still on board looking for him.

That wonderful, crazy Irish girl.

She's risking her life to find you. What other woman would do such a fool thing?

Taking a deep breath to get his pulse started again and nodding his thanks to a bemused colonel, Buck raced down the narrow companionway to A Deck. He walked with a brisk pace up and down on the port side, half expecting to see Ava waiting there for him.

He was disappointed. The deck was empty.

Not giving up, he started down to the next deck when—

'*Buck!*'

He raced back up the stairs. *Trey*. The American was out of breath, his face dripping with sweat, his features drawn. They'd split up to look for Ava and the countess with Trey searching the starboard side of the ship. He must have seen him topside and chased him down.

Buck studied him for a long moment. 'Did you find Ava?' he asked. He became uncomfortably aware Trey was watching him with the same intensity.

Trey shook his head. 'No sign of her *or* Fiona. They *must* have gotten off the ship in a boat.'

'Fiona's safe,' Buck said, patting his old friend on the back. 'Colonel Gracie told me the countess got away in a lifeboat.'

But not Ava.

'Thank God,' Trey breathed out, relieved. Then in the next breath he asked with an urgency that surprised Buck, 'Where's Ava?'

'No one has seen her, Trey,' Buck said in a low voice. 'She must still be on board the ship.'

Looking for me.

'No time to waste, Buck.' Trey swiveled his head from side to side, frantic. 'You go down to B Deck while I keep searching for her topside. We've got to find her.'

He started to run off. Buck grabbed his arm and pulled him back.

'You *must* save yourself, Trey,' he said with an edge to his voice that was more of a command above everything else.

'We've got to find Ava first.' Pacing up and down, Trey acted like he didn't hear him. What was wrong with him?

Swallowing hard, Buck pushed aside his own conflicting emotions. He couldn't forget another woman's happiness was also at stake. Gentle as a gray dove, but strong as granite, Fiona would need a protector if he didn't make it.

'Aren't you forgetting something?' Buck said, gritting his teeth.

'I don't know what you mean.' Trey looked puzzled, his jaw set.

'There's Fiona to consider,' he said.

'What about Ava?' Trey asked, his hard stare telling Buck something else was at play here. His composure slipped and Trey realized he'd exposed his deep feelings for the Irish girl. It wasn't a mad flirtation that kept his friend from saving himself, but something he'd been too blind to see.

His eyes burned with something Buck had never seen there before. Intense emotion that said his friend had not given up the chase after all.

He's also in love with Ava.

It was high time Trey grew up.

Buck heard the loud, creaking sound of a lifeboat being lowered near the open window frame where they stood. An idea formed in his mind.

'Fiona is depending on you, Trey,' he said firmly.

'But, Buck—'

'You wouldn't let down the countess.' The lifeboat was coming closer.

Trey straightened his shoulders, nodded. 'No, of course not.'

Out of the corner of his eye, Buck could see the boat inch down slowly by them. He was annoyed with Trey, but he didn't let on. He raced through an open door beyond the glass windows and leaned over the top edge of the port side of the ship.

The lifeboat making its descent hung not more than several feet from where he stood on the gunwale.

'Any more women up there?' a seaman called out to him.

'*No*,' Buck shouted back.

'Come on then, *jump!* We've room for one more.'

Trey was at his side in an instant. 'You go, Buck.'

'No, the countess needs you.' He gave him a half-smile. 'Besides, I'm a better swimmer.'

Trey shrugged. 'You always did win the bet, Buck.' As he stood on the gunwale, he stiffened, then turned slowly back toward him. 'See you in New York, old man.'

Then, after taking a moment to balance himself, he leaped into the air and jumped.

Buck's heart thudded. The stark realization that he'd never see his friend again ripped through him with the jagged pain of a knife. He waited until he saw him land square in the lifeboat *hard*, but uninjured.

Trey looked up at him. In the dim light he could see his friend toss him a wave. He was full of himself by nature, Buck knew, and was the first to admit it. Whatever their differences regarding women, he'd miss that about him the most. He wouldn't give up hope he'd see him in New York.

Trey grabbed an oar and begin rowing to get the boat clear from the ship.

Buck wasted no time starting back up to the Boat Deck. Seawater poured in through the door and the ship settled forward to a greater degree. The water came at him so fast, it nearly pinned him between the deck and its ceiling. He had to fight his way up, using long, hard strokes to get to the top.

Praying his luck would last, he made it up the narrow stairway and hit the open deck running. The mist still hung over the semi-darkness, floating around everything like a gossamer dream. He felt the panic and tension everywhere, the hard, hot pulse of the situation driving him forward. Water flooded the bridge and passengers climbed over the rail and jumped into the sea.

The moment held such horror, but Buck didn't let it deter him from his purpose. He wouldn't stop looking for Ava.

The *Carpathia,* the rescue ship, was still *hours* away.

If Ava was on this ship, he had to get her off *now*.

When he found her, he'd never let her go.

Hell, yes, he *would* survive.

Buck edged his way slowly over to the port side through the freezing cold seawater pouring over the Boat Deck. There he helped Second Officer Lightoller cut the lashings holding the collapsible lifeboat on top of the officers' quarters. No time to get it loaded in the davits. The two men floated it off the top, but they couldn't hold onto it and it crashed into the sea unmanned.

'It's every man for himself now, your lordship,' said the ship's officer.

'Right you are, sir,' Buck said, clasping his hand in a firm handshake. 'I'll never forget what you did getting the countess away in a lifeboat.'

'I must say, Captain Lord Blackthorn, she's quite a handful.'

Buck stepped back in his mind, knowing he couldn't have heard right. *Fiona a handful?*

'What did you say?' he asked carefully.

'I said that she's—'

His next words were lost.

Down, *down* dipped the bow and a great wave washed over the bridge on the Boat Deck below them, sending the ship's officer jumping over the low rail to assist helpless passengers thrashing about on the deck. Buck followed him. He could see steamer chairs sliding down the wet deck, the sea dragging along everything in its path.

Icy water slapped his thighs.

Buck held onto the rail as a reverberating rumble shattered his senses, as loud as an artillery barrage. Shattering his brain and making him shake. His head was jerked back so violently he swore his neck had snapped.

In shock, his ears went deaf and the screaming ceased in his head.

A man grabbed onto him, panicked. Buck strained to hold onto him, but the man toppled forward and down into the sea curling dangerously closer to where he was standing.

Buck continued to hold onto the railing, his fingers white, his knuckles bulging. Christ, the ship wouldn't last much longer. He was determined not to be dumped into the cold, black sea and he dared not lose his head.

There had to be another way.

But how? Fear energized the crowd of hundreds hanging on when the ship reached its tipping point. What struck Buck to the nerve was the realization the band had stopped playing. For the past hour the brave musicians had played one tune after another on the Boat Deck, alleviating panic among the passengers.

Now no one could hear anything but the rising, horrific sounds of the ship giving in to the ravages of the sea filling its decks.

The ship took a definite plunge, causing Buck to lose his grip on the slippery, wet rail. He slid down the deck toward the bow, every step he'd taken undone as he flew backward in a dark instant. He caught his breath, turned, and as he worked his way up toward the stern where the deck was still out of the water, a woman banged into him. Her scream came so close to his ear, his hearing shot back in a flash.

He tried to grab her. Too late. She flew by him and was carried away by the wave washing over the deck.

Buck moved fast, and if he dared admit it, he raced with fear clawing at his insides when the ship's bow lunged deeper into the water.

She was going down in a nosedive. Only one thing he could do.

Damn well better get it over with.

Buck stood on the top deck, his heart pounding, his whole being not letting go of this determination to survive. A filling up of his spirit gave him strength. A holy awakening he'd never felt before. Like he was in God's hands.

Ava would understand.

Amazing that at this moment, he embraced the beliefs of the Irish girl who had touched his soul with her own, believing he wasn't alone in his moment of need. Because of her. He made his decision as a great rush of water filled his ears. If he waited too long, he'd be dragged under when the ship sank.

The time was now.

Buck dove into the sea.

When he hit the deadly cold water, the sensation of being skinned alive struck him, every nerve in his body burning as the freezing water closed over him, shutting out the world above he wanted so desperately to find.

Using all his strength, he moved his arms and kicked hard until he rose to the surface. Shouts filled his ears. Screams. Deafening sounds.

The crash of metal. Two violent explosions.

He began swimming through the shadows dancing around him. Bodies bobbed up and down in the water, lit up only by the ghostly white of their lifebelts. Everywhere he looked, he saw scores of men and women fighting the sea, grappling with its pull and the icy water.

Their high-pitched cries rang through the air, accompanied by agonizing moans and ear-splitting sounds, while everything on the ship not tied down smashed together like wayward dominoes.

Waterford glasses shattering like ice crystals.

Thousands of china dishes crashing through their cabinets.

Tables and chairs flying everywhere, even through the tall glass windows and onto the deck.

A chilling numbness took hold of him as he stroked hard against the current. The familiar pattern of arm over arm, feet kicking, took over and he cut through the sea like he belonged in it. He swam clear and spied the collapsible he and Mr Lightoller had launched floating not more than ten feet away. He estimated a dozen or more poor souls standing on the upturned boat.

Seawater ran off him as he tried to climb aboard the upside-down lifeboat, the weight of the water pulling him back. For a moment he thought he wouldn't make it, then a powerful urge to live socked him in the gut. Something fierce inside him gave him the strength to grab the rope hanging over the side of the boat and pull himself aboard. Men bickering, shouting, no one in charge. Buck counted himself lucky, but for how long? A damning cold penetrated his wet clothes as he shuffled his feet on the upturned boat to balance himself. Water sloshing over his ankles, he didn't give up though his body felt numb, his eyebrows, his hair frosty from the cold.

Buck turned and saw a man struggling and kicking in the water.

His poker companion, Mr Charters.

'Boat ahoy, Mr Charters!' Buck yelled.

'*Good God*, it's you, your lordship,' the man sputtered, spitting up water and heaving deep breaths. He wasn't wearing a lifebelt.

Mr Charters flapped his arms about, getting closer to the boat, but not close enough.

Buck leaned over and reached out to grab the man's hand, trying to pull him aboard. He slipped out of his grip time and time again.

'*Stay with me,* Mr Charters!' he screamed, urging the portly gent to climb aboard the collapsible as if sensing his raw terror and trying to reassure him.

'He'll sink us!' someone on board cried out.

Buck paid him no mind. The man deserved a chance. They all did.

'Take my hand, Charters, *now!*'

'I can't.'

Knowing the poor man couldn't climb aboard, Buck ripped off the fastenings on his lifebelt, pulled it over his head and tossed it to Mr Charters. The Liverpool man caught it, then vanished back into the shadows of the sea.

Buck prayed he'd make it.

No guarantee he would either. The upside boat could barely hold the men standing shoulder to shoulder, trying to balance and prevent the raft from overturning, when a swell arose.

Horrified shouts, screams slammed into his head. Then an unbelievable shock went through him, seizing him in the chest when the boat tipped and into the sea he went, the below-freezing water sucking him down... *down*. He fought his way up to the surface again and again, knowing if he panicked that would be the end of him.

Floundering in the seawater, a terrified cry came from this throat. Without a life jacket, he faced the near certainty of drowning if the deathly cold water didn't get him first. His body heat dropped so fast he knew he didn't have long. Fifteen... maybe thirty minutes before his body shut down completely. He had a hard time staying afloat, his swimming skills keeping his strokes strong, but he couldn't keep his head above water.

Buck knew why. Without his lifebelt, the damn pistol was pulling him down. He yanked it out of his pocket and tossed it away.

Whatever else he had in his pocket went with it.

Buck struggled to reach the upside-down lifeboat when—

The wires on the forward funnel on the ship snapped and it crashed into the sea. Bright sparks and thick white plumes of steam poured out of it, crushing the helpless passengers caught below it.

Buck shuddered. He *wanted* to go back, help the poor devils, his nerves drawn taut and ready to break, but he realized he could do nothing to help them.

He swam hard and fast to reach the collapsible flung well clear from the sinking ship, then clambered back aboard the craft. He balanced his weight on the flat-bottomed lifeboat with the other men who'd managed to swim to the craft, including Second Officer Lightoller. He took charge of the motley crew.

Blowing his officer's whistle, his words came firm and fast.

'Hold steady, men... more to the left... now the right... keep your wits about you.'

'She's going!' Buck heard someone yell out.

Then he heard a guttural scream, followed by another and another. *What the bloody hell—*

He yanked his head around in time to see the ship plunge forward, its stern lifting out of the water at a low angle. The lights on the ship were still burning, but the forward part of the ship up to the second funnel was submerged.

His chest swelled with a violent pain when he saw the lights go out, deck by deck, then flash on again and finally go out forever.

The horror of what happened next would never leave him.

The ship of dreams was silhouetted against the bright sky as it cracked in two between the third and fourth funnel, the sound splitting his eardrums before plunging downward with a great booming, rumbling sound. The ship roared like a giant behemoth in the throes of a death rattle, the forward part diving down deep, *deep* into the sea—

Then the stern coming back to an almost even keel in the calm sea before it filled with water and went down, lost forever.

Miles below.

Never to be seen again.

A deadly chill stabbed him in the back and his heart continued to pound in his throat. He couldn't believe it. All he could see was a pale gray vapor hanging like smoke over the spot where the *Titanic* had disappeared.

The sea was so calm, so smooth, that the piercing screams and pitiful pleas for help sounded sharp and clear in his ears. Ghastly sounds no man should ever hear. He thought he'd go mad. He wanted to clamp his hands over his ears, to shut out the bloody screams. He didn't.

He could do nothing more. The sea would soon be swollen with floating dead bodies burdened with lifebelts that would keep them from sinking. No one could last more than thirty minutes in this freezing water before they went into shock and died, their hearts giving out.

He prayed for *all* their souls. Including his own.

Something he never would have had the courage to do before he met Ava.

Buck thought of her now, the lilt of her words ringing in his ears telling him—

Telling him what? Wait... he could hear her voice. Yes, it was *her*. He *swore* it. She was out there, swimming in the sea, alone.

'Ava... *Ava!*' he called out.

He leaned over the edge of the lifeboat, searching for her in the darkness, straining his eyes until they hurt. All he could see was the flickering of a green light coming toward them. Like her eyes, a lovely, sheer green.

In his mind, he *knew* it was a lantern in another lifeboat. But in his heart he wanted to believe it was her. Her arms outstretched and calling to him.

Buck smiled and reached out to her. There was a peace in him. He wanted to hold her, kiss her. This beautiful red-haired angel smiling at him.

He *must* save her. Or die trying.

His chest was sore and his arms ached so fierce from swimming they'd gone numb, but he couldn't leave her to drown.

He wanted so badly to believe it was Ava he heard that Buck dove into the dark, lonely sea before anyone could stop him.

And disappeared.

29

Ava held her head in her gloved hands. It wasn't that the fear of death was all around her, but that *she* was here in the lifeboat and not the grand gentlemen married to these ladies.

First cabin ladies.

Wearing fur coats and teardrop diamond earrings and big, feathered hats with silver hatpins. Smelling of lavender. Not the salty sweat of steerage.

Dressed in the pink of fashion, they looked as out of place in the lifeboat as perfect plump prawns tossed into a fisherman's dirty pail. Bickering among themselves about keeping their part of the boat *for their kind only.* Making comments about the sailor at the tiller smoking. And generally being what they were.

First cabin ladies.

Ava couldn't stop peering at them through the dark. Such a curious eye she had, she missed nothing. Like a fine new broom she was, its hay bristles sharp and pointy and with a passion for sweeping.

Brace yourself, girl, these ladies will want to know about you. Ask you questions.

Curious and probing, expecting you to fit into their world of fine manners and grand speech.

They believe you're a titled lady. If they find out you're not after they've accepted you as one of their own, oh, mercy, you'll be on the first steamer back to Ireland. They'll forgive you for ignoring them, but only on one condition.

That you are *the Countess of Marbury.*

That set Ava's heart racing. She felt as if she'd been turned inside out, exposed. What if they knew their husbands had been denied a seat in the lifeboat so a poor Irish girl wanted by the law might live? They'd feed on her like leeches until they destroyed her.

Ava had been foolish to believe the grand divide wielded by centuries of manners and class could be broken down by her love for Buck. She ached anew for him, to feel his arms holding her, his lips against hers.

He was so bloody handsome, strong and his eyes gleamed black pools she could get lost in. His mere touch made her spill over with a wildness that tempted her to sink into his arms. Inhale the breath of him into her lungs for the pure joy of being part of him.

Flesh against flesh, his great need matching hers.

Why did he send her away? *Why?*

It took her a moment to work it out. She remembered Buck's stoic expression and his fierce insistence that she and the countess get into a lifeboat.

He knew all the time there weren't enough boats for the men.

Ava had to do *something*, not just sit here, pretending she was invisible as if she were covered with black soot. What if passengers swimming in the sea needed their help? What if one of them was Buck?

They *would* go back to the ship to pick up survivors, wouldn't they?

The freezing cold bit at her cheeks like sharp icicles, making her shiver. The sea was calm and no moon. She leaned forward, squinting, her eyes trying to see as the lifeboat picked up more survivors. Seamen, but the poor devils were in a sorry state and were barely alive. Gasping for breath, their faces contorted with agonizing pain.

She'd never forget it.

Ava was jumpier than before, fretting with worry about Buck. She couldn't just sit here. She had to *do* something.

'I can row,' she said, keeping her voice low and doing her best not to speak any more than she had to, her with her peppery talk and country accent. In no time they'd guess her secret. *Then* where would she be? Settled in a locked room in a rescue ship when they were found.

Rumor was the *Carpathia* was on its way.

The quartermaster in charge of the lifeboat seemed surprised at her request, but grateful. Lord knew he had his hands full with an inexperienced crew. They had already lost two oars because of their clumsy efforts to pull together.

Ava took over from an exhausted seaman, his hands too cold to hold onto the oar any longer. She put her back into it, thankful for the countess's gray leather gloves to keep her hands warm as she bent to her oar in the snapping cold.

She put her shoulder to it and began to row harder on the calm sea, keeping the boat steady and pulling for her life. They had to get away from being dragged down into a swell when the ship went down. She saw the *Titanic* lit up, deck by deck, each porthole shining a beacon to the heavens, signaling the loss of so many souls on this wretched night.

Rockets lit up the sky.

The sea glowed with an iridescent shimmer of green light from other lifeboats. Already debris floated around them. Barrels and steamer chairs drifted by and banged into the lifeboat, while the crew's mumblings blowing loud in her ears gave her little comfort.

No compass or bread or water. No lantern. No one knows how to navigate by the stars.

Blimey, we're done for.

Farther and farther away from the ship Ava rowed, her heart heavy, her soul burdened down with such pain even a sinner like her couldn't bear it. They must have rowed over a hundred feet away from the ship when excited, horrified murmurs from the women caused her to lift her head.

What she saw made her gasp loudly.

The *Titanic* was sinking fast.

Then something godlike took hold of her. A spiritual moment she'd never forget. The beautiful sounds of a holy hymn skimmed over the glassy sea, casting a spell over everyone in the lifeboat.

No one spoke, but they listened. The hushed sound of their breathing filled the air, as if their icy breaths captured the musical notes drifting far out over the water.

Each one a silent prayer.

'Holy Mary, Mother of God,' she prayed with all her heart, repeating the words as if they were an act of contrition and would save their souls. Ava couldn't stop the oncoming range of emotions coming at her. The tense feeling was numbing but unshakable as an icy breeze scraped her cheeks. It was penetrating cold.

No one shivered in spite of it. They waited in fear, some sobbing, but all praying silently that as the ship passed over the threshold and into darkness, their loved ones would somehow survive.

Ava stopped rowing, not because her shoulders screamed and ached with pain, but because the realization of losing Buck hit her hard.

The liner getting lower and lower in the water. *Slowly... steadily*. One small explosion... then the lights went out, deck by deck. Then a louder explosion. Plumes of smoke rose into the sky. Horrible shrieking sounds like animals trapped with no way out hit her ears when the ship seemed to lift up of the water... and was she dreaming? It tilted up on its end and then cracked in two.

No... *no*. It couldn't be.

Before she could murmur holy words, the *Titanic* was gone.

So quiet... sinking into its watery grave.

But not the fleeing souls on board crushed or tossed into the sea. Their cries so painful to her heart, she couldn't breathe.

Her lips moved, but she couldn't get the words out and her body became limp. She stopped trying to be brave and let the tears flow.

For Buck, the countess, and Mr Brady.

All lost. She began to shake uncontrollably.

Better to have loved him than not, she thought, to lock in her heart the memory of his dark eyes and fancy words and her trembling with delight when he kissed her. His lordship putting his hands on her hair and smoothing it back and holding her in his strong arms. Her world would never again be a gray, flickering existence, for Captain Lord Buck Blackthorn had shown her how to be a woman.

If there was one thing she'd done right in the eyes of the Almighty, it was to give him the comfort of faith. He would need it if he were to survive. She didn't believe Buck would go down without a fight. She was betting on that.

For his sake. *And* hers.

Still, a heartrending sorrow had claimed her when she'd seen the grand ship *Titanic* lurch forward, holding steady but a few moments before the once elegant liner headed to the bottom of the sea.

'Buck, *Buck!*' she cried out now, the scene playing over and over again in her mind and ripping her heart apart, her voice lost in the dark night. Tears gathered in her eyes.

The warmth of his memory was all she had left.

* * *

Glassy icebergs entombed the lifeboats.

Ava tried to ignore the mountains of icebergs emerging through the darkness as daylight crept over the ice field. Impenetrable guardians, reminding her of their power to destroy everything she loved. Her stomach twisted at the sight of the bergs tinted a pale gray against a pinkish horizon. She fought back the pain. Fought hard, until all that was left was a nagging prayer reminding her she *still* wasn't safe.

She wasn't alone in her despair. Through her veil, she looked at the other passengers.

First cabin ladies mostly, and steerage women.

Babies, seamen.

All trying desperately to survive the night.

She pulled the chilly air into her lungs, held her breath, and then put her shoulder to the oar as they followed the green light of another boat. The night air stung her cheeks. Heart racing, she forced herself to breathe until it hurt.

Keep rowing, keep rowing.

Jesus Mary, she was so cold she couldn't stay warm. She gripped the oar all the harder, her sweat mixing with the ice covering the veil on her face. A brutal chill made her shudder, but she kept pace with the others. Each pull strained her whole body. Her arms and shoulders ached, but she didn't stop.

The sea will not take me. Not on your bloomin' life.

The blood pumped through her veins, knowing He'd smile to have her in His hands sooner, but Ava was no quitter. She'd last in spite of the fact they had no provisions, no water, not even a lantern.

A seaman lit a matchstick, but it flickered out. The sputtering little flame reminded Ava of her childhood and how her mother was always trimming the candlewicks to make them last longer.

The thought warmed her, seeing in her mind her sweet mum's face in the glow of the fire, the wick of the candle curling when it burned as she set down her cup of tea next to it. She wanted so, *begged* to see her mum's deep blue eyes twinkling as she told her daughters stories about the *gentle people*, the fairies, but the scene broke apart like cracked glass.

Ava let out a long, heartfelt groan. The bitter cold replaced the warmth in her heart and the nightmare started all over again. She wanted to stop, to rest... *to sleep.*

She stared deep into the freezing water. All she had to do was untie her lifebelt and slip over the side. The icy sea would do the rest.

It would all be over in a few minutes...

Are you a coward, Ava O'Reilly? Buck put his life on the line for you. You can't let him down.

She didn't stop rowing.

Ava shut herself off from feeling anything at all. It was the only way she could cope. A ship's officer in another boat called out for them to tie up with four other lifeboats, then take on board several men they plucked from the freezing water.

She could barely see in the dim light, but she didn't give up hoping one of them was Buck. Half-frozen, the men crumpled to their knees and hunched over in agony. She groaned deep in her throat.

His lordship wasn't among them.

A fierce anger gripped her. Would she ever know what happened to him?

She went back to rowing, her spirits sinking. Buck was dead, squeezing every hope out of her.

Would a broken heart make a lass give up and go about the devil's work? Sell her soul to see him again?

An impure thought, but she wasn't sorry she said it.

Ava went back and forth with her thoughts, wanting everything to be lovely again, when a cold burn chilled her ankles. She looked down. *Holy Mary*, the lifeboat was taking in water.

She helped the women bail out the water with their bare hands until they found the leak and stuffed it with a blanket.

Would it last long enough for the rescue ship to find them?

A faint murmuring erupted among the passengers as the dawn broke through the thick drift ice surrounding them. A few women started sobbing. Whispering and praying another ship had picked up their husbands. She said a quick Hail Mary it was true, then she said another prayer for the countess.

God rest her soul.

Mr Brady, too... and Buck... God, thinking about him was killing her soul. She drew in a sharp, gasping breath. She couldn't get the screaming out of her mind when the Titanic sank. All them people begging for another breath, another moment of life. Guilt that she survived clung to her like penance prayers never said. The crushing reality of having to face the truth if and when they were rescued weighed heavily on her mind.

And her heart.

Whatever happened, the Irish girl known as Ava O'Reilly was no more.

Every lady in the lifeboat believed her to be the Countess of Marbury. Ever since she'd gotten into the boat, she'd catch a curious eye watching her, whether she was rowing or helping a wounded seaman. Waiting to see what she'd do, how she'd act. Even in a crisis such as this, the feline curiosity to scratch away at her story with their sharp looks was there. Chip it apart word by word, if only as a way to forget for a little while and assuage their own overwhelming grief.

Ava kept her chin up, her shoulders straight, but the sheer scale of what she had to overcome to go from being a lady's maid to a lady seemed too much.

She reached into her coat pocket to warm her hand and found the countess's letter. Her wavy handwriting looping like a perfect curtsy urged her to carry on. *Could* she copy her signature? She could hear the countess telling her *nothing* was beyond her.

What if she failed in her deception? The way she spoke, her manners, her education were nothing like that of a lady. She was doomed before she began. She had been prepared to risk everything when it came to running from the law for something she *didn't* do, but taking on the life of another woman? That was different somehow.

Ava didn't feel so brave now.

What choice did she have? If she admitted to the port authorities she was a poor Irish girl and *not* the countess, her dreams would be shattered. Her word that she was innocent not believed. She'd be locked up and forgotten as surely as if she'd gone to the bottom of the sea.

Ava set about putting that behind her. She had one thing in her favor. From what Fiona told her, the countess rarely left Scotland and knew no one in America. That gave her a fighting chance. She was determined to make both Buck and the countess proud of her. Mr Brady, too. For *their* sakes, she'd carry on.

She took to her oar with spirit, determined to give it a go rather than let the devil have his way with her. Praying they wouldn't sink before help came, all the while thinking, *Why not pretend to be the countess to get me started in a new life, then be on my way?*

Is it possible?

It was then she saw the distress rocket light up the sky. *Glory to God, could it be—*

Yes. Her soul soared when later she saw the faint lights of a steamer headed their way, then heard a ship's whistle blasting through the dense fog.

The *Carpathia.*

She'd have her answer soon enough.

* * *

'Your name, miss?'

'Fiona.'

'Surname?'

'Winston-Hale,' Ava said, drumming her fingers nervously against her thigh, her black coat and red shawl brushed with sea spray. She removed her lifebelt and handed it to a steward. More than two hours had passed since she sighted the lights of the ship, then she was taken aboard the steamer through the open hatch, hoisted up in a boatswain's chair slung over the side.

Quiet and orderly. Everyone acting subdued and reverent, not quite believing what they'd been through.

'My good man,' bellowed the woman behind her, her patience wearing thin. 'Can't you see the countess is on the verge of mental collapse?'

'Countess?' asked the purser, impressed. He turned back to Ava, his curious eye taking note of the initials and crest embroidered on her shawl. 'Is that true?'

Ava's throat tightened. She *wanted* to answer, praying she had the audacity to go through with this charade. Knowing what she said would change her life forever.

Anything could happen if she answered. Anything at all.

Tell him, will you? Or you'll spend your days in the darkest pits of hell with not even a holy thought to comfort you.

'Yes, I'm the Countess of Marbury,' Ava said in a clear voice, surprising herself. Inexplicably, a sense of pride expanded in her chest, filling her up with a courage she didn't know she possessed.

Who was this prickly lass proclaiming without a flutter of her eyelids she was a titled lady?

'I'll speak to the captain about securing you a private cabin, your ladyship.'

He turned his tired eyes in her direction, expecting her to demand more. She didn't.

A steward brought her a warm blanket, hot coffee and brandy to fight the chill. She wasn't sure if the purser believed her. His gaze unnerved her because it brimmed with questions, yet his respect for her station demanded he refrain from continuing the conversation.

Can you believe it? The purser wanted to give *her* a private cabin? So fine it was, them treating her like a lady. Like filling her pockets from her mum's sugar basin to sweeten her toast.

It don't seem right, Ava thought, swallowing deeply. Offering her a cabin when so many others were sick with cold and bleeding, their fingers and toes numb to the warmest human touch.

She wandered off alone, knowing the man was still watching her. She was happy the first cabin ladies she shared a lifeboat with had never laid eyes on her before she got into the boat. 'Twas a blessing she kept mostly to the countess's cabin and whenever she wandered about the ship, she was careful to keep her head down. No second class ladies knew her either. She sent praises to up above the crewmen on the lifeboat had paid her no mind.

Though her heart was heavy, she couldn't help but smile under her veil. She could imagine his lifted brows when he saw her helping distribute blankets, then holding a baby in her arms while the child's mother tended to her little daughter. Next, she brought hot coffee to the young wireless operator who couldn't stand up because of his injured feet.

And why not? Blessed Virgin, she had to do something, *anything*, to make up for *her* being here and not the countess.

Thoughts of those last moments with her ladyship crept along the edges of her mind, taunting her. Why didn't she stop the countess from going back to her stateroom? Why didn't she move faster down those stairs after her? *Why, why?*

Ava couldn't shake off these questions, knowing she'd be spending long nights awake, wishing she had the power to make things different. It didn't matter her heart was crushed. It didn't matter she had no idea *how* she was going to keep pretending she was genteel and grand. She was bound to slip up.

What then?

She had to keep moving... keep her hands busy... Ava O'Reilly wasn't a lazy lass—

There you go, thinking of yourself as Ava. Your name is Fiona... your name is Fiona, she kept repeating to herself, though not one bone in her shivering body believed a bloody word of it.

She pulled the blanket closer around her. Somewhat warmed by the hot liquids, she paced up and down the deck. It didn't take away the grief now settling in her. A shiver traveled across her shoulders, then down to her toes scrunched in her wet boots. Her life took shape in the daylight. As the morning mist mingled with the remnants of that horrible night, she existed in a world of dull gray. No color. Just gray. As if the sorrow in her heart had sucked out the fire and passion that colored her world with his lordship and left it empty.

Painfully so.

For the next few minutes, Ava stood at the rail, looking out to sea. She couldn't move. Didn't really want to.

What if someone recognized her?

Don't go there. You made your choice. If you're caught, you can't fly off like an angel with the hand of God on their shoulder. You'll take what comes to you.

Ava forced her concentration on the sea again. She stayed at the rail with the rest of the women and watched each lifeboat pull up, praying she'd see Buck or Mr Brady. It was as if she wanted one more look. Wanted to say one more prayer.

'Your cabin is ready, Countess.'

Ava turned and saw the purser, waiting for her to answer him. How long had she been standing there? Long enough for another lifeboat to pull up alongside the ship, its passengers climbing up the rope ladders. Shaking and cold.

'Thank you, sir,' she muttered, then turned away, embarrassed. Too late she realized her mistake. She pursed her lips together. No titled lady addressed a member of the crew as 'sir.'

The sooner she disappeared down below, the better off she'd be.

The purser cleared his throat. 'A steward will show you the way, milady.'

Out of the corner of her eye, she could see him tip his cap, then he was off, bustling about with the swagger she'd seen him give the first cabin ladies. Chin up, chest out, making them *and* himself feel important.

Not so with the steerage women.

She watched him send them down to the open deck below to wait in the windy cold for blankets and coffee.

Dear God, Ava couldn't tear her gaze away, her eyes not believing what she was seeing. A sight so bloody wonderful it pierced her like a blessed arrow. There she saw the two Irish girls huddled together, their eyes ringed and tired, their faces pale.

Peggy and her sister Hannah.

Her heart swelled. Buck *had* saved them. God bless him, what a fine gentleman he was *and* a hero.

Then another thought hit her. One that enflamed her soul with a passionate longing she couldn't deny. Where was he? Had he climbed into the lifeboat with them?

Was he here on the *Carpathia*, looking for her?

She started down the small stairway to the deck below to ask them what happened to his lordship, then stopped, her heart catching in her throat.

Dear Lord, the girls knew her as Ava O'Reilly. If they discovered she was masquerading as the countess, her whole plan would dissipate faster than a puff of holy smoke.

Her excitement faded and all of a sudden she felt tired and very much alone. Not knowing what had happened to Buck haunted her.

So this was to be her unholy fate.

'*Countess!*'

She turned, her pulse racing. Had she been found out? She saw a steward moving quickly toward her, his mood excited.

'There's a gentleman come aboard asking for you,' he said.

'A *gentleman...* oh, no, can it be?' she cried out, not waiting to hear more but running along the open deck where the passengers had come up the ladders. She bit down on her lip, catching the veil in her teeth. She paid it no mind. A sudden smile spread over her face. The thought of seeing his lordship soothed her and sank into her heart, hugging her with a warmth she'd never thought to feel again.

'Buck... *Buck!*'

It wasn't Captain Lord Blackthorn she saw taking long strides toward her.

Instead a tall gentleman still wearing his lifebelt moved at a fast pace. A welcoming smile beaming on his face.

Her hand flew to her mouth. If all the saints themselves had whispered his name into her ear, she'd have not believed it.

Treyton Brady.

For a moment, she didn't know what to do.

Run, stay?

She had to face him, and her wearing the countess's coat and acting all fine and mighty. She pulled the blanket closer around her so it hid her face. He'd be angry with her and had every right to be. A lady's maid she was, and he knew it.

Her smile faded. Her game was over.

Jesus Mary, what was going to happen to her now?

A bitter disappointment overtook her, but it wasn't for herself. It was for *him*. He'd have to know what happened to the countess. And *she* had to tell him.

She died because she couldn't stop loving Buck, her heart broken. Her poetic soul searching for him in a deep pool of water until finally she let go. I'm telling you, Mr Brady, she loved him more than life itself.

But she wouldn't say that to him. Not now or ever. She'd never betray her ladyship's darkest secrets.

Secrets now her own.

Ava made the sign of the cross. What did it matter if someone saw her? She needed all the help she could get to bear up and do her duty.

'*Fiona!*' Trey called out, his arms extended to her. He looked so happy to see her she didn't pull away when he embraced her. He didn't know it was her with her red hair hidden under the countess's black cloche hat. She squeezed her eyes shut. She *hated* deceiving him. 'I thought I'd lost you.'

'Glory be, Mr Brady,' she said, keeping her head down, 'you're a beautiful sight to my poor eyes.'

'*Fiona?*' Trey asked, taken aback. He bent over her, his face puzzled.

'Don't be angry with me, sir. I've been praying that you and his lordship were saved.' Up until now Ava had kept her face covered by the blanket. When she let it drop, his eyes widened and he stared at her.

'*Ava... oh, my God...* I don't believe it.'

He grabbed her and looked hard into her face. She stared back at him, her lips quivering, her cheeks coloring.

'It's me, Mr Brady,' she whispered. 'Ava O'Reilly.'

'What the hell is going on here?' he whispered hotly in her ear. He looked around, then back to her. 'Where is Fiona?'

'She's... she's dead, Mr Brady.'

'*Jesus Christ...* it *can't* be true.'

'But it is. Don't give me away... *please...* I can't go back to Ireland... I *won't!*'

'Give you away?' He held her close to him, breathing hard, his whole body shaking with such emotion she swore he'd crush her. 'Oh, you poor, sweet girl, you're all I have left.'

'What unhappy words are you saying to me, Mr Brady?' Ava asked, shaking her head, struggling to come to terms with what he was telling her.

'Buck went down with the ship.'

Pacing her breathing, Ava tried hard to keep calm, holding onto Mr Brady's arm so tight she felt him flinch. She'd heard so many screams when the ship went down, so many dying souls, knowing Buck was among them was more agony than she could bear.

She started trembling all over, tears burning her eyes. She didn't try to wipe them away, but let them flow down her cheeks.

She *couldn't* lose control, not here. God wouldn't help her. He was too busy with all them other ladies sobbing and weeping. They had a better right than she did to receive Divine help. The *ship of widows*, they were calling the *Carpathia*. In the eyes of the Church she wasn't his wife, but Buck had called her his lady and that did her heart proud.

'No, *no*, it's not right, taking a fine man like his lordship,' she said, her mind working furiously to keep going, not to snap, the voices inside her crying and howling.

She inhaled sharply.

'You mean while *I'm* still here, Ava?' Trey dared to venture forth. In a fit of frustration, he took off his lifebelt and tossed it on the deck. He ignored her shocked expression and went on. 'We both know it should have been *me* down there and not Buck.'

'Oh, no, Mr Brady,' Ava said honestly. 'You and I are both sinners, but you're a good man. I cannot say the same about myself. I can never be as fine and grand as the countess.'

'You've got more than a pretty face, Ava. You've got a pure heart.' He gazed at her in concern. 'God help the man who doesn't see that in you.'

As cold as it was on deck, Ava made no move to go below. Neither did Trey. They'd both said what was on their minds and made their peace with each other. Now it was time to heal. They stood close together for several long minutes, wrapped up in their own thoughts.

Finally, Trey said, 'Tell me what happened to Fiona, Ava. I want to know.'

* * *

It was a morning of peculiar cold and it seemed right somehow to talk about Fiona here on deck where Ava could cast her eye out on the sea. Wreckage from the ship floated by. Deckchairs, pieces of wood. Cork. She drew in a deep, cleansing breath. She wanted to take her time, for what else did they have but time? Four days to reach New York.

Then what? It both scared her and excited her.

The words didn't come easy to her. They'd stood in silence for a while, each to their own thoughts, as if paying silent homage to the countess they'd sailed with for four days before coming to grips with her passing. The wind came up as it did on this cloudless morning, the salty air heavy with the smell of death and despair. Ava turned her face into the chilly breeze and let her eyes close shut. She thought hard about what she was going to say, overcome as she was by wounds that would take a long time to heal, if they ever did.

She could hear Mr Brady's quiet breathing next to her. He didn't press her. When she was ready, she opened her eyes.

And the words spilled out.

She recounted to him how the countess insisted on going back for her mother's earrings, how Ava begged her not to, then they were caught on the Grand Staircase with the water swirling up from several decks below. Mr Brady said nothing, leaning over the rail, his face slick with sweat, his eyes downcast.

'Before I could grab her,' Ava said, 'her ladyship slipped on the stair and fell to her death.'

She finished by explaining how the stewardess helped her carry the countess into an empty stateroom, and then locked the door, leaving her to her eternal rest.

She thought about that heartfelt moment but a few hours ago. Part of her still felt the guilt. The other part of her knew she'd done her best.

'I know it was wrong to pretend to be her, Mr Brady,' Ava admitted, 'but when the ship's officer thought I was her, I couldn't deny it or I'd be found out.'

'You did what you had to do, Ava. I can't blame you for that.' He smiled at her, his hand tipping her chin up so their eyes met. 'Strange, isn't it? We both lost someone important to us. Now we're alone. You no longer have a protector and I no longer have a countess to appease my mother.'

Ava nodded. 'We're two lost souls. The Almighty saved us for a reason, Mr Brady. We have to find out what that reason is.' Bold words, but what else could a lass do?

She waited for him to offer her a sign, a show of understanding that didn't need to be voiced between the two of them. He did. He acknowledged the look of longing in her eyes with a glance that told her he was hurting as much as she was.

Then he squeezed her hand and turned back to the sea.

'We'll push you through customs, Ava. The captain told me the usual regulations won't apply to the survivors.'

Ava let out a sigh of relief. 'A grand idea *that* is, Mr Brady, but what will happen when you don't come back with the countess?'

His eyes scrutinized her as if he were trying to figure out something. Then he smiled at her. 'I'll tell my mother Fiona changed her mind after her terrifying experience at sea and went back to Scotland. You'll never have to lay eyes on the woman. At least I can spare you that.'

They stood at the rail for a long time, Mr Brady with his arm around her and her praying to Our Lady for guidance when—

'*Look!*' someone cried out. 'Another lifeboat!'

Ava jumped out of her skin, her pulse racing so fast she couldn't stand it. Were her prayers answered?

'Buck... *Buck!*' she called out, all in a stew. She'd not give up hope of finding him.

Trey pulled her back away from the rail, so excited she was, as if she could fly over it without wings.

'Ava, *wait!*' Trey was shouting now. '*Buck didn't get into a lifeboat.*' He held onto her, but she wouldn't have it. She wrenched free.

'I'll not let my heart rot with wondering, Mr Brady. I have to find out for myself. *I have to know!*'

Ava dropped the blanket and raced along the deck. As before there was a great rush to the rail when a lifeboat showed up on the horizon, each passenger hoping to find their husband or father or brother.

She raised her hand to her breasts, but it trembled, as did her whole being. Mr Brady was close behind her as she ran full out to the other side of the ship, neither of them exchanging another word. She didn't know if she was feeling anger or relief that he'd tried to save her from suffering all over again the loss of his lordship.

It didn't matter.

She couldn't stop herself from joining the other women staring at the sea below. The lifeboat overfilled with passengers pulled up to the ship, the pulleys let over the side so they could climb aboard with the rope ladders or be hoisted up.

Ava was brazen, utterly brazen as she watched each one come up. No longer worrying about anyone recognizing her. She'd grieve as hard as any saint who'd lost their halo if that was how it had to be... but not if there was still hope Buck was alive.

She watched as cold, weary women in wet clothes were hoisted up... then an older man... a ship's officer... stokers and firemen... then a man semiconscious came up the rope ladder.

Ava tried to get through the crowd of women, but they blocked her way.

'Can you see who the man is?' she asked them, hoping.

'He's dressed like a gentleman,' a woman told her.

'Half out of his mind he is,' said another. 'Poor devil, he's not wearing a lifebelt.'

Ava turned away. Her chin down. She didn't want to look, telling herself it *couldn't* be Buck. He was wearing a lifebelt when last she saw him.

What good would it do to pain her sorry soul with false hope?

Her shoulders slumped, she pulled the shawl tighter around her. The morning had a frosty bite to it and the feel of despair was everywhere she looked.

She walked but a few steps when she heard a familiar voice calling out to her—

'Ava... *Ava!*'

A strangled cry it was, so filled with disbelief as it shot through her that her heart stopped.

She turned around, her mouth open.

Could it be *his lordship* calling her?

Would the saints send her weeping again or had the heavens rained with joy?

Tripping over her shawl, Ava pushed through the onlookers to where they'd laid the man down. She creaked her neck, looking hard, but she couldn't see his face clearly in the heavy mist. She pushed closer, then she saw something that made her heart almost cease to beat. His eyes, already wild and fierce, flared at her, widening in disbelief.

Her heart soared. Holy Father, it *was* his lordship. Alive. Not the swollen face of death staring at her, but the strong-jawed, handsome man she loved so much. Yes, he was ghostly pale and his sea-drenched body tested beyond human endurance, but he was here on deck. Come to her.

Looking upward, she blessed herself.

A miracle it was.

A bloody miracle.

'Ava, *Ava...*' he muttered again, and then reached out for her. He kept trying to get up but couldn't. Even in his weakened state, she could feel his strength and determination to reach her.

'*Buck!*' she called out, moving as fast as her feet would let her. She sucked in a breath when she saw him collapse on the deck, the steward wrapping him up in blankets, but not before she had the compelling urge to hang what anyone thought and sank to her knees beside him.

Her arms went around him and she pulled him close to her. She held his head tightly against her breasts and rocked him back and forth whispering, 'Buck... oh, my dearest Buck... you've come back to me. May all the saints be praised, I'll *never* leave you again.'

'*Ava*... my lady,' was all he said, his voice so low no one could hear him but her.

Then with a smile on his lips, so blue they were it pained her, he closed his eyes and his head drooped onto her chest.

She was so weary and sick of heart it took her a moment to realize he'd gone limp in her arms. She stared at him, not believing his face looked so colorless.

Oh, dear God, what darkest blasphemy was this?

Was he—

No, no! She tried to swallow, *couldn't*, her throat was so tight. She shook her head in denial. He was cold, *so cold*.

Tears streamed from her eyes, then dropped down her cheeks and onto his hair, melting the ice crystals nestled among the dark strands. Oh, if only she could warm his heart as easily.

She wanted to die.

The sight of him lying so still was so painful she couldn't stop the tears. Him leaving her she could accept, him angry with her she could live with. But taking him from her like this, so cruel it was, as if she was living in hell, and that she *wouldn't* accept.

She held him tighter, hugging him close to her, and all the while she screamed in her mind:

Oh... no... Holy Mary, Mother of God... no!

Bring him back to me, please.

30

Aboard the *Carpathia*
18 April 1912

He was gone. His cot empty. Blankets askew.

Ava gasped loudly when she returned to the ship's dining saloon with hot coffee. She tossed the blankets aside with abandon, her heart pumping wildly in her chest. Again, panic filled her as it had when Buck lost consciousness after they pulled him up on deck from the lifeboat, his body burning not with fever, but with cold. Filling him up and getting so deep inside him, he no longer had the strength to fight it.

So pale she had refused to leave his side. She'd checked his pulse with her cold, shaking fingers as many times as there were beads on her rosary.

Buck was in the last lifeboat brought aboard. He'd spoken her name, then pressed his hard, cold body against hers before he'd passed out.

She had made a spectacle out of herself *again*.

She still felt embarrassed. No one held it against her, she had been as distraught as every other woman on board. Wild-eyed and haggard, the women's sobbing didn't stop. Who could blame them? There was an edge to their despair that made the hairs stand up on the back of her neck. Nothing was more heartbreaking than when the *Carpathia* had made a huge circle around the area where the *Titanic* sank to look for more survivors.

Not even a ripple appeared on the sea to mark its grave.

Only when the ship blew her whistle and set course for New York had Ava let *her* tears flow. She would never get over losing the countess.

Ava wasn't alone in her grief.

A gale had come up that first night, making the seas stormy and tempers short. Ava had huddled in her blankets on the floor in the saloon near his lordship.

Though she had ached to feel his arms around her, they had to be careful, mindful that even on the rescue ship carrying the survivors of the *Titanic*, the rigid structure of the British upper class still prevailed. Whatever his feelings were for Ava, in the eyes of everyone on board, she was the Countess of Marbury and engaged to Trey. Only when no one was looking had she wrapped his arm around her while he was sleeping.

She wanted so much to stay by his side, hellbent on being with him wherever he went. Deep in her heart, she knew they had yet to speak about what would happen when they reached New York. She'd have to face that eventually, but until they docked, there was only the two of them. She had not shared her feelings with him. Nor had he with her. Which made her all the more nervous.

Especially when she found his blankets empty.

What was he about this evening? Running off like that with the *Carpathia* set to dock in New York Harbor in a few short hours.

Taking his exercise in this murky, foggy weather, was he?

Ava peered through the porthole, her face reflective. No other gentleman but Buck would have saved the Irish girls, nor pulled himself up the rope ladder after thrashing about in the cold, black sea.

The heavens had let go with buckets of rain for days, and if she didn't know better, she'd have believed the water falling from above were the tears of Himself grieving with the ladies on board. So distraught they were, their minds went blank and they kept to themselves.

Except one.

A pompous first cabin lady had made it her business to keep her eye on Ava. She'd lost no husband, she'd informed the captain, but she'd left a small fortune in jewels in the purser's safe and intended to make a claim.

She treated the sinking as a misadventure where she alone was a victim. She'd prance up and down the rows of sick passengers lying on blankets, stroking the matted fur of her small dog, boasting how she was helping collect funds for the *Titanic* survivors.

Ava ignored her and did her best to nurse Captain Lord Blackthorn back to health after his ordeal. She hadn't left his side, spending every waking moment with him in the makeshift emergency ward after refusing the private quarters offered to her.

She never tired of looking at him, his eyes closed, but his chest moving up and down in a steady rhythm, his pulse normal. His square jaw set in a determined line, his long angular nose that gave him a regal look along with his strong chin.

For three days, he had been all hers.

Until now.

'If you're looking for his lordship, Countess, he left in a hurry when a steward came to fetch him,' said the busybody. She pulled on the double strand of pearls around her neck, her diamond rings dulled by the lack of light in the over cramped saloon, but impressive nonetheless. 'Perhaps he's with Mr Brady, your *fiancé*.'

She emphasized the word in a disapproving tone, poking her nose around like a dog looking for a place to hide its bone. The woman was waiting for her to speak. Ava said nothing. She reminded herself the woman didn't know she was of the lower class and believed her to be an equal.

If there weren't enough unhappy souls aboard this ship, this woman claimed to make it so. She'd wasted no time spreading gossip among the first cabin ladies about Ava's behavior with Captain Lord Blackthorn. *Nasty* gossip. She was jealous of the countess with *two* men at her side, as if it were a stigma they survived.

Mr Brady confirmed her suspicions.

'Unfortunately, Ava, society women like her expect young ladies to behave in a proper manner and not allow their name to be mentioned openly with a gentleman of Buck's reputation,' Trey said, urging her to step out onto the deck where they could be alone. The saloon was filled with passengers lying about on beds made from blankets, while other survivors slept on couches in the lounge and steamer chairs on deck. 'Be careful. If she makes too big a fuss, it could spell trouble when we land in New York.'

'I understand that, Mr Brady, but his lordship needs me.' Ava stared off into the horizon. The rain had stopped and a cold wind had come up. It cut right through her.

'Call me Trey, not Mr Brady,' he said, smiling at her.

'That I can do,' she said, nodding. She pulled her blanket tighter around her. 'But it don't solve my problem.'

'No, but I did fix *one* thing for you.'

'And what is that?'

'I explained to the purser Ava is your middle name and you and Buck have been friends since childhood.'

'Impressed I am, Mr Brady... I mean Trey, with your glib tongue and fancy words.'

'Thank you, Countess,' he said, then set his mouth in a hard line. He had something on his mind. 'I don't see any way out of this mess, Ava, except for word to get around that you broke off our engagement.'

'I have a better idea, Trey,' said a deep male voice behind them.

Ava spun around. *Jesus*, it was his lordship, sneaking up on her like a disapproving archangel.

'Spying on me, are you?' Ava said, surprised.

'No, Ava, just thinking,' Buck said. 'About you. About us.'

Ava met his eyes. Darker and deeper than she'd ever seen them, a blackness that fixed on her but told her nothing. For a heartbeat she dared to believe he would say what she wanted to hear. About the two of them being together.

He didn't.

She let her breath go in a long sigh.

Instead, he turned to Trey, telling him they hadn't much time. The *Carpathia* was set to dock in New York tonight and they must have their plan in place by then. All the while acting like she wasn't standing there, shivering. It had suddenly gotten very cold.

'I'm certain my idea will work,' Buck continued. 'Everyone on this ship, including the first cabin ladies, believes Ava is the countess.'

Ava nodded. That was true. No one who had seen her locked up in steerage answered at roll call. Her heart saddened when she realized Mr Moody was among the victims, as well as the other seamen. The Irish girls were so grateful to be alive, their smiles told Ava they'd *never* give her away. Even the stewardess, Marta Sinclair, had addressed her as her ladyship when they met in passing.

'What are you suggesting, Buck?' Trey asked in a cautious tone.

'Nothing will bring Fiona back,' Buck said.

Was that a slight tremble she heard in his voice? She'd never forget the tears he had choked back when she'd told him the news. He hadn't let on how deeply the countess's death had hurt him. Instead he'd touched her cheek with his hand. It was icy cold. Then he'd gone off on his own to stare at the sea, his shoulders slumped, his fists clenched at his side.

She had made no move to interfere.

'I never should have left her,' Trey said, his look grim.

Buck grabbed him by the shoulder. 'Fiona wouldn't want you to keep blaming yourself, Trey. I'm certain she'd wish for you to go through with the marriage.'

Ava couldn't speak. What insanity was this?

'Are you crazy, old boy?' Trey said, astonished. 'With Ava? A lady's maid? We'll never get away with it.'

'What you mean is my speech and manners ain't – *aren't* that of a lady,' Ava interrupted, hands on her hips. She was shaking inside. There, she could speak proper when she *wanted* to. 'Is *that* what you're saying?'

Buck smiled, impressed with her efforts. 'You've got an ear for language, Ava, and I can teach you everything else you need to know to become a countess. I've traveled in the circle of aristocratic ladies and attended their dinners and balls. I know the tricks of their trade.'

Did he mean this mysterious Lady Pennington she'd heard the countess speak about? Ava wondered with dismay.

'I have no doubt I can turn you into a lady.' His lordship's eyes bored into hers. She didn't understand this fierce determination of his to marry her off.

'Why would you want to do that?' Ava refused to show him how disappointed she was.

'Because, Ava, I'm the second son of a duke. I have no lands, no fortune. Trey can offer you a life I never could.'

What blarney was this? Who cared about lands or fortunes? What about the two of *them?*

'It's true you're an aristocrat,' she stated boldly. 'I'll not hold *that* against you.'

Buck grinned, amused at her brashness. 'I'm also a gambler who lives by his wits, Ava, and where I go, *you* can't.'

'Oh, that's gibberish. Where is that?'

'The gentlemen's clubs where I ply my trade don't allow women to pass through their portals.'

'Mind you, I'll wait outside them fancy houses with a cuppa tea and a warm heart to soothe you.'

'It won't work, Ava. All my winnings were locked up in the purser's safe and what money I had on me was lost at sea. I'm back where I started. Penniless.'

'It don't matter to me, Buck, I... I... '

What was she going to say to the man, that she loved him? And look as foolish as a plucky pig with its arse stuck in a fence? She'd told him how she felt on the ship and he paid her no mind.

No, there was something else.

Something he wasn't telling her.

But what?

31

The telegram from Lady Pennington upset Buck more than he realized.

Damn the woman.

Her most recent ploy was an obvious trick to make certain he hadn't forgotten her, but stirring things up like she did was downright unconscionable. Leaking hints about their affair to the press who were hungry for *any* news of *Titanic* survivors was an ugly thing to do.

It started when the captain of the *Carpathia* sent a list of the first-class passengers who survived the tragedy to the *New York Times* on Tuesday. The London papers picked it up soon after.

That was when his troubles began.

What else did he expect from a woman who was as provocative as vintage champagne, taunting him as she pranced around in her red satin corset covered with French Chantilly lace? Only *he* knew her spine was forged with cold, blue steel.

Did the woman possess no morality? Over fifteen hundred lives were lost in the disaster and *she* could think of nothing else but using him to further her own personal interests.

He crumpled up the telegram and tossed it into the sea. His stature as a British peer dictated he be given his telegrams first before the other passengers. The others wouldn't receive theirs until the ship was steaming into New York Harbor.

He had received only one.

From Lady Irene Pennington.

She was beautiful, blonde and as spoiled as a Persian queen, and he had no intention of falling under her spell again. The lady had other plans. Plans to trap him and he didn't like it. He was so angry she made him forget he was a gentleman and somewhat civilized. That wouldn't stop him from telling her what he thought of her silly shenanigans and be done with her.

It wouldn't be that easy. She had her claws in him and they dug deep.

Buck had no choice but to play her game.

He was half filled with regret for taking advantage of Trey's invitation to sail with him on the *Titanic*. If he hadn't, things would have been different. The countess would still be alive. *Fiona*. So filled with fire under the surface, yet never having the chance to know the comfort of a husband's loving arms or the passion of his kiss.

The sincerity of her feelings toward him had embarrassed him, but he missed her understanding. How she always steered him in the right direction when he went off with his wild ways.

Now she was at peace, her resting place somewhere beyond the horizon. Fiona would always remain in his soul, forever young and charming. A true lady cherished for being that very thing a man dreamed of, but never believed he would find.

He held onto that thought as the rescue ship sped toward New York, held it tight in his heart when he suddenly realized his mood was changing and another woman claimed his attention.

Ah, yes. Then there was Ava. Bold and brash and the best thing that had ever happened to him.

And now he had to give her up.

Because of Irene.

Her ladyship had had the audacity to send Buck word she'd spoken with his father, the duke, about their affair. A servant had leaked the information to the scandal sheets for a few guineas, no doubt making His Grace livid. It didn't take long before the affair was part of a two-column spread in the *Times*.

Two columns because Buck was listed as a survivor of the *Titanic*. All London was buzzing about how he'd left on the ill-fated ship to escape the wrath of the lady's husband, who had so conveniently died a fortnight ago.

Leaving his entire estate to Lady Pennington.

Irene had the power to create an even *bigger* scandal if he didn't placate her wishes.

Whether or not that meant marriage, he didn't know.

What he *did* know was that she was on her way to New York on the next steamship to meet him.

Exactly what he'd feared. Buck would not rise to the bait. Instead, he must make preparations to keep the most important thing in his life safe. *Ava*. If Irene discovered his involvement with the Irish girl, she'd hire the best detectives to find out what they could about her. He deemed the woman could be trouble, full of cunning and duplicity and, although Irene didn't travel in the same circles as the countess, he couldn't take the chance of her discovering the truth.

If she did, Ava would be sent back to Ireland *and* to prison.

The only way he could keep her safe was to have Ava keep up her pretense as the Countess of Marbury.

And marry Trey.

What other choice did he have?

He had a difficult time accepting that. It punched him in the gut and left him senseless. The pain slashed through him as if an angry god had struck him down with a razor-sharp sword.

He looked at these two people who meant so much to him. His old friend, Trey. And Ava. They had been strangely silent, waiting for him to speak. He couldn't tell them the truth.

He looked away, trying to gather his thoughts. It seemed colder on deck than it had been all week, though the wind had died down and the coming darkness seemed almost comforting.

He made up his mind.

'You must go through with this marriage to the countess as planned, Trey,' Buck said, his tone firm. 'To make it more appealing, I have a proposition for you.'

Trey shot him a bewildered glance, then thought about it, as he knew he would. 'This better be good.'

'You always were a sporting man,' Buck said carefully. 'Would you care to make a bet that if I can pull this off, it would secure your future as well as Ava's?'

'What are you suggesting?' he asked warily.

'I bet you fifty thousand British pounds sterling I can pass Ava off as the Countess of Marbury.'

'What?' Trey's voice was incredulous. 'That's ridiculous.'

'It's the only answer to a dire situation. You'll get your inheritance by marrying the *countess* and Ava will be safe.'

'I thought Fiona was your friend,' Trey said with a sadness in his voice Buck never expected. As if the whole idea was disloyal to her memory.

'She was.' Buck tried to keep his voice from catching in his throat when he said, 'Yes, I know it sounds cold-hearted, and don't think I haven't thought long and hard before coming to this decision, but I know the countess would approve.'

He noticed Ava twisting her broken rosary between her fingers as if praying for redemption. Didn't she know if there was any sinner to be blamed for this whole damn mess, it was *him?*

The girl was guilty of loving him and nothing more.

He had to make it up to her and this was the only way he knew how. Whatever they'd had, like the grand ship *Titanic* herself, a silent lady of the seas, it was now but a memory. For her own safety it must remain that way.

Buck leaned closer to her and her scent spiked, sweet honey mixed with the salt of the sea, as if the heat of dancing the tango still clung to her as it did to him. He wanted to reach out and pull her into his arms and dance with her, their bodies pressing flesh against flesh.

He ached to dip her backward so her head touched the floor, her long, glorious red hair billowing out like silk.

Trey was not oblivious to the glances passing between them. 'Ava would get *more* than a finishing school education in your hands,' he said with a smirk. 'How do I know your so-called bet isn't simply a means to pick up where you left off on the ship?'

'I assure you, my interest in schooling Ava in the art of being a titled member of the Scottish peerage is strictly business,' Buck added. 'Young ladies of nobility are required only to learn the social graces and royal etiquette to secure a husband... or in Ava's case, to impress a mother-in-law.'

'What about *me?*' Ava cried out, her eyes so full of pain she couldn't stand it. 'Don't I have no say in the matter?'

'We're from two different worlds, Ava,' Buck said slowly. He chose his words carefully, letting his emotions and his spirit piece themselves back together. He hadn't spoken to Ava about what he'd planned to ask her when they reached New York. Now he never could. 'We're both rebels, but we knew from the beginning we could never cross that line of rigid class rules. I'm giving you the chance to do that now by marrying Trey.'

'But I don't love him.'

'Marriage isn't about love, Ava. It's a business proposition. Trey gets his countess, you get security and a position in society and I—'

'And what *do* you get, Captain Lord Blackthorn?' she shouted at him. 'A story to tell the gentlemen at your club about how you turned a pig's arse into a fine silk purse? No, the whole affair is to be kept a secret, so it's money you're after. And you, with all your fine talk about honesty and morals. I was just a game to you and now it's over.' She shook her head back and forth wildly. 'No, I'll not have anything to do with you *or* your silly bet.'

She was hurt and rightfully so. He wanted to soothe her, brush his lips across the back of her neck, hold her tight by the shoulders and nuzzle his face in her long hair. He didn't.

'Please, Ava, do what I say. It's for your own good.'

'No... *I won't!*'

And with that she was gone into the wind, racing down the deck as far away from him as she could get.

'You always did have a way with women, Buck,' Trey stated wryly.

'I'll convince her.' Buck didn't like it any more than Ava did, but what else could he do? He turned to his old friend. 'Then it's a bet?'

Trey smiled. 'This is one bet I'm going to *enjoy* losing.'

As the two men shook hands, Buck could see his old friend watching Ava running away from them, her hips swaying, Trey's eyes beaming. Whether he meant to or not, he'd just sent her into the lion's den. The lascivious smile on the American's face made him wonder if he'd made a fool's bet after all.

* * *

So she was worth fifty thousand pounds.

Ava couldn't bear to stay another moment and look into his lordship's handsome face after hearing his flippant remark. She found herself a place at the stern where she could think, staring out to sea over the rail until the first twinkling star opened its eyes and winked at her.

She barely noticed. She was at a loss for words. *Lord Jesus, can you believe this?* Bought and paid for she was, like a piece of silk come down from Belfast. Very *expensive* silk.

She'd be a fool not to go through with his insane plan.

Trey wasn't a bad sort. She'd come to respect him more these past few days.

Would it be so awful to be married to him? She didn't know.

What Ava *did* know was that his lordship wasn't telling her something. He was like a simmering kettle with hot steam blowing out of it, ready to boil over. She feared for him and, in spite of him betraying her, she'd not give up on him. The countess would want her to look out for his lordship and that she would.

She blessed herself. If that's what they wanted, then Ava O'Reilly was up to the challenge. She owed it to the countess to carry on her name and title and do it proud.

Why not? Trey had the money and influence. Buck had the polish of a gentleman.

And she?

She had the willingness to learn to be a lady.

Ava looked up at the darkening sky. Rain started coming down, but she smelled something else in the air. A foul, hot smell. She smiled. She knew that powerful stink that got into a body's lungs and stayed there. Smoke from tugs. They weren't far from the harbor.

A beckoning chill made her pull up the collar on the countess's coat, its thick black velvet hugging her neck. It warmed her, but her eyes felt tired, drawn, her heart heavy. The weeks ahead frightened her, being with his lordship day and night, teaching her how to be a lady, but not being able to feel his arms around her.

Dear Jesus, could He have given her a worse penance than that?

32

New York, Pier 54
18 April 1912

Glory be, Ava couldn't believe she'd done it.

Walked right past the immigration authorities with her nose up in the air and her heart in her throat.

She was in America.

She'd never forget the moment the *Carpathia* steamed past the Statue of Liberty, rain pouring down and lightning streaking through the sky overhead, making her tingle down to her toes. A grand feeling it was. And now she was *here*. Not once did they look at her and say she didn't belong.

What are you waiting for?

You were saved for a reason.

This is it.

Ava rubbed her eyes. She heard her mum's voice in her head, giving her courage. She reminisced about how the two women would sit down together in their cottage after Mum washed the dirty plates and Ava tended to the fire, brewing them each a cup of tea, then she'd read to her mother.

'You have a fine way of speaking, lass, when you read them words,' her mum would say, stirring the sugar in her tea with her forefinger. 'Makes me weep. You should be in a grand house.'

Her mum meant in service. She never dreamed Ava would be here in New York with everyone smiling and tipping their hats to her like she was a lady.

That was the *easy* part.

Now she had a new problem.

Mr Brady's mother.

According to the American, she'd waited for hours in the rain to meet her. Her manservant holding a huge black umbrella over her, though Mr Brady insisted the raindrops wouldn't dare touch her.

Thrown off guard, Ava stopped at the top of the covered gangway, losing her nerve. It if hadn't been for Buck taking her arm and whispering in her ear he wouldn't let her down before he left to chat with snoopy reporters, she'd have run the other way.

Jesus Mary, the woman was a sight to behold.

Tapping her foot as if it were a cane, Myra Benn-Brady waited for her down below on the pier. Taller than Ava expected, with a cinched-in waist begging to be let out, wrapped up in furs and attitude, she stood as straight as her pompous virtue. And then some.

She exuded the air of a woman who reveled in her perfumed lifestyle. Caught between the world of first cabin ladies in their fancy gowns and steerage women clutching their shabby shawls and peering out of floppy bonnets, Mrs Benn-Brady was more than a queen.

She was the supreme ruler.

The society woman possessed a cold elegance that made Ava shiver down to her toes.

The breath rushed out of her as the Irish girl sought to recover her nerve. She fluttered her eyes, then swayed her shoulders and raised her glove upward as if asking a gentleman to kiss her hand. Or light her cigarette.

After all, this *was* New York.

Gasping, heart pounding, she walked slowly down the gangway to meet her future mother-in-law.

Watch your back, girl, she's giving you the devil's eye. Saw you talking to Captain Lord Blackthorn she did, and him acting so protective toward you.

She'd never forget how Buck had looked at her when he made the bet with Trey, his eyes hurting as much as she was, worried and tired with a deep sadness she didn't understand. She'd been so *sure* he wanted her for himself, the way he'd leaned toward her as if he'd ached to hold her. Then his look had changed, his tongue tripping over words breaking her heart.

No, she was wrong.

It was obvious his lordship proposed this silly scheme to fill his own pockets. Was there an *ounce* of feeling for her in the man's soul? She doubted it. That hurt her more than anything.

Then the realization came to her she had no choice in the matter

Ava was urged on by the ever-present fear that had taken root in her chest. Fear that if she didn't succeed in making Mrs Benn-Brady believe she was the Countess of Marbury, she'd walk out of here with her hands tied behind her back.

You have it in you to fool them all, Ava O'Reilly.

Remember them streets of gold? They're right outside that door.

Waiting for you.

Ava felt like a loose button hanging by a thread. If she agreed to his lordship's plan, she'd be soothing his guilty feelings about what to do with her. She *could* get off this ship and make her own way in America. She wasn't afraid of hard work, but toiling in a factory for long hours and finding a decent place to lay her head down at night wouldn't be easy.

No, she had to go through with it.

More than twenty thousand people had shown up at Chelsea Piers, waiting breathlessly to get their first glimpse of the *Titanic* survivors. A sad lot they were. Her heart cried when a passenger on the rescue ship went around giving the ladies from the *Titanic* flannel from her night-dress for their babies, then soap and hairpins.

Hairpins. Oh, the sharp pain she'd felt in her chest, the memory still fresh when the countess gave her silver pins to pull up her hair. The sea wind blew in her face, urging Ava to smooth down her hair and fix the imaginary pins in place, as if the hand of the countess guided her.

She was willing to give up the man she loved for duty. And so must I.

Feeling dizzy, Ava slumped against the railing, her eyes taking in the crowd of reporters, photographers, relatives and friends. A special train with private cars also waited to whisk two wealthy first cabin ladies away from prying eyes as well as limousines for a lucky few.

For Ava, there was *no* way out.

She walked down the gangway, chin up.

'Delighted to meet you, Countess,' said Mrs Benn-Brady, her back stiff, her eyes curious. She didn't extend her hand or curtsy as Trey had suggested she might.

Instead she dismissed her servant, then smiled. As if everyone watched *her*.

Before Ava could utter a word, she ushered the girl into the enclosed pier and out of the rain. Away from the crowd of curious reporters, grabbing anyone they could to get a story.

'So grand it is to meet a fine lady like you,' Ava said, flustered. She took a step back. 'Mercy, I'm not doing this proper.'

Oh, no, the words had rushed out of her in a harsh whisper all *wrong*.

'I beg your pardon?' Mrs Benn-Brady straightened her bosom, making the diamond watch pinned to her collar bounce up and down. Her face tightened and she leaned forward, believing she'd heard incorrectly.

Ava started to make the sign of the cross, then stopped. Lord Jesus, this whole scene was fraying her nerves something awful. Now she'd done it. Sounding like a holy sainted sister prostrating herself.

'What the countess means, Mother,' Trey interrupted, racing to catch up to them, 'is that she's tired from her long journey from Scotland.'

'I see,' said Mrs Benn-Brady.

But she didn't.

Peering closer, Ava discerned that this arbiter of New York society would *not* forgive a misstep lightly. She was used to having her way. Armed with a considerable fortune, no one dared ignore her wishes. According to Mr Brady, his mother was so rich, she paid her gardener to replace the weeds in her garden with orchids.

'I must insist you stay at my residence on Fifth Avenue, Countess. After your dreadful ordeal, nothing else will do. There we can discuss the arrangements for the wedding.' Mrs Benn-Brady cleared her throat to make her point. '*Which* I have postponed.'

'Madam?' With a brief glance at Trey, then his mother, Ava wondered if she was done before she started.

Had the woman found out she was a fraud?

'The sinking of the *Titanic* is taking up *all* the best positioning in the newspapers,' the matron said with frustration. 'I pulled the announcement of your engagement until the fuss is over. I had no choice.'

Ava let go with a long shudder. Hearing the screams of the dying in her head, their pleas for help owning her soul.

No one gets away with treating the sinking of the ship like it's merely a bee in her bonnet.

Not even a society woman like her.

'What about the poor souls lost in the cold, freezing sea, madam?' she spewed. 'Don't *they* deserve to be remembered?'

She'd heard from Buck the press had ignored the steerage passengers with nary a name listed on any survivor list.

As if they never existed.

She fretted. By the holy saints, Mary Dolores must have heard she'd sailed on the *Titanic*. She wouldn't know if she was dead or alive. She'd write to her, but what was she going to tell her?

She was now the Countess of Marbury?

Not yet, girl. Look at Mrs Benn-Brady. Her curious eye moving over you like you're a pig in a poke.

She's a feisty one and not easily fooled. Keep your opinions to yourself or you'll be dragging your heels back to Ireland.

'I find your sentiments rather... *interesting*, Countess,' said the matron evasively. 'Have you spoken to any reporters yet?'

Trey came to her rescue and smoothed over his mother's ruffled feathers. 'The countess took her place in the same lifeboat as Mrs Astor and other first cabin ladies, Mother.' He mentioned the names of ladies well connected in high places. 'They were honored to have the Countess of Marbury take up an oar and help row their boat to the rescue ship.'

'Why didn't she say so?' said Mrs Benn-Brady, pleased Ava had made a good impression on the society ladies. She patted the girl's hand and the clusters of diamonds circling her wrists sparkled. 'Don't worry about a thing, my dear Countess, *I* will deal with the reporters. After you've recovered from your ordeal, we'll have a nice, friendly chat over tea. I want to hear all about Mrs Astor and the other ladies.'

Ava shivered. She knew she just wanted to hear the gossip about how the first cabin ladies sat on a hard, wooden bench with icy seawater swirling around their feet, their toes freezing in their pearl-beaded satin slippers.

'If you'd be so kind, madam, I need washing up to get the smell of the sea off my clothes,' Ava said, buttoning up the countess's long, black coat to hide her homespun clothes underneath.

Mrs Benn-Brady let out a deep sigh. 'In due time. I'm more concerned we understand each other.'

'Madam?'

'It's a matter of titles and diamond tiaras,' she said smugly. '*You* have the title, *I* have the diamond tiara.'

'Is that all you want from me?' Ava asked. 'A title?'

'My dear Countess, I may be rich and well connected, but my money can't buy entrée into the closed circle of New York heiresses married to English lords. Since I had the misfortune to have a son and not a daughter—' she sneered at Trey who, by the bored look on his face, was used to his mother's ranting '—you're my last hope to enter that circle.'

Ava sighed, then managed a weak smile. 'But I'm not English.'

'I also find your manner of speaking not quite what I expected,' Mrs Benn-Brady said with a critical eye.

'My governess was Irish.' Ava blurted out the first thing that came into her head and spun a tale about how she had no mother growing up and rarely saw her father, and the spunky Irish woman raised her.

'You'll have to do.' She waved her hands about as if she were hiring a housekeeper. 'Even if you are from Scotland. Cold, dastardly place from what I've heard.'

Mercy, she was beyond anything Ava had ever seen, even in the grand houses in Ireland.

No wonder Mr Brady – no, Trey, she *must* call him that – had no manners. Neither did his mother. She was bold, arrogant and if Ava was right, born with her foot in her mouth instead of a silver spoon. She understood the woman's need to better herself, but *not* at her expense.

She walked around Ava in a circle as if inspecting a prize filly.

'I hadn't anticipated you'd be so pretty. I expected a serious-minded young woman who wore thick lenses and read books.' She breathed into her face and Ava caught the whiff of a fine brandy. No doubt to warm up her cold heart, though she doubted that was possible.

'The countess is beautiful, Mother, and you damn well know it.' Trey put his arm around Ava's waist and squeezed it. She winced.

'You've outdone yourself, Trey.' She turned to Ava. 'However, before we finalize the financial arrangements of our contract, we have much to do. You don't look like a countess.'

What she means is you don't sound like a countess or walk like one. Careful, girl, or she'll see right through you.

'I lost everything when the ship went down,' Ava said, explaining. She'd not back down, not admit anything.

'You shall have a new wardrobe with morning and afternoon dresses, tea gowns, hats and gloves, jewels and fans, furs and ostrich plumes to dazzle the society crowd.' She smirked, then indicated with a wave of her hand the interview had ended.

'Is that all, Mother?' Trey asked, waiting to be dismissed.

Ava stared at him, puzzled. Was he always so reticent around his mother? No wonder he bounded about Europe like a schoolboy on holiday.

'Yes. Garrett will drive you home, then he'll return for me,' Mrs Benn-Brady said, as if Ava wasn't there. 'I have an engagement. I'm assisting with the Women's Relief Committee for the steerage passengers.'

'How generous of you, Mrs Benn-Brady,' Ava said, her cheeks coloring. Perhaps she'd misjudged the woman. She *was* kind, like the schoolgirls everyone was talking about who gave up candy and going to matinees to raise money for the survivors.

'Don't be ridiculous, Countess,' Mrs Benn-Brady answered quickly. 'Charity work gets my name in the newspapers.'

Ava tensed. It entered her mind the woman didn't have a charitable bone in her body. She'd get no sympathy from her if she was found out.

Without another word, Mrs Benn-Brady insisted Trey escort Ava to the waiting limousine, a shiny, black monstrosity with a running board, while *she* dealt with the press.

Though rain beat down hard on the umbrella the servant held over her head, Ava hesitated to get into the fancy motorcar, fearing she'd be swallowed up in its dark opulence. Surprisingly enough, when the chauffeur opened the door and she sat on the black velvet cushion, Ava sighed with relief.

You passed the first test, girl. But remember, each step is like a bead on your rosary. Only through prayer and persistence can you come full circle.

Sitting still in the motorcar, everything so black and quiet, a pungent smell made her sniff. Something she couldn't identify. Not leather. But heavy and spicy, like a garden overgrown with too many dandelions among the roses.

Crushed posies lay at her feet.

Like she'd be if she didn't pull this off.

Trey poked his head inside the limousine, then sat down. ‘You did it, Ava. You fooled my mother. Not an easy feat.’

‘For now. We have a lot of work to do if I’m to help you and Buck – I mean, his lordship – pull off this charade. Though for the likes of me, I must be as addled as a pig on its way to market to go through with this scheme.’

He flashed her a grin. ‘Why don’t we start your training now?’

Without warning, Trey leaned over and kissed her, a lip-stinging sweep of his mouth brushing hers, forcing her to part her lips. She barely had time to take a breath before a sudden breeze chilled her.

Someone had opened the passenger door.

‘There’s more to being a countess than knowing how to kiss a man, Ava,’ she heard a deep masculine voice say. ‘I see you no longer need my services.’

Buck. He’d seen Trey kiss her. Her heart cried out with new pain at the American’s audacity to grab an opportunity for an intimate moment at her expense.

‘She’s *my* fiancée, old man,’ Trey said, his tone possessive. ‘Not yours.’

‘As you wish, *old man*.’

Ava pushed away in time to see Buck slam the door and pull up his collar against the rain, then walk down the streets she had once thought were paved with gold. His stride was long, his mood angry. He didn’t look back.

She couldn’t stop the tears from forming. Her heart had been heavy since the scene on deck with his lordship. Now her spirits sank.

Why did Captain Lord Blackthorn break her heart so? *Why?* What right did he have to question her kissing another man?

It was *his* bloody idea for her to marry Trey.

It was all too much. What did he expect her to do? Live with the man like she was a holy sister?

Was he daft?

* * *

Women, Buck thought, paying no attention to the stares directed at him as he strode through the opulent hotel lobby of the Waldorf-Astoria. Hatless. His clothes wet, his eyes fierce.

They can soothe your ego, drain your bank account and then make you fall in love with them all over again.

Letting his guard down had left him open to many perils, but when saw his old friend kissing Ava, he came to grips with how much he loved her. *Really* loved her. And because of his own foolish actions, she was lost to him. *Again.* First on the ship and now in New York.

Damnation.

In his life he'd made a lot of mistakes, made love to many beautiful women, but he never left them until *they* ended the affair. Acted like a gentleman. Now, when he was down, he'd been kicked in the gut.

And it was his own fault.

'I believe you have a suite reserved for me,' Buck said to the hotel desk clerk. He tapped his fingers nervously on the desk, agitated.

'Your *name*, sir?' The bored clerk wiggled his nose at his appearance.

Buck couldn't blame him. His clothes were wrinkled, torn and smelled of more than the sea. The only reason the doorman didn't stop him when he pushed boldly through the revolving doors was because he'd arrived in a limousine sent by the hotel.

'Captain Lord Blackthorn.'

The clerk cleared his throat. '*The* Captain Lord Blackthorn... from the *Titanic*?'

Good God, had all New York heard about him?

'Yes,' Buck said.

Immediately, ladies and gentlemen in fur-trimmed overcoats edged closer upon hearing his name, eager to get a good look at him. He was the subject of heated whispers, hard looks and elegant sighs for the next several minutes.

Buck clenched his fists. He couldn't believe there was that much interest in him because he'd survived the sinking ship when so many gallant gentlemen had lost their lives. There was something else at play here, *but what?*

The desk clerk displayed an amused smile, then looked through his list of reservations.

Buck fought hard to control his emotions. 'I've had a long journey and I'd like to go to my room. Have you found the reservation?' he asked in a low voice.

'Ah, yes, here it is, your lordship. Lady Pennington's solicitor arranged for you to have our *deluxe* accommodations.' The desk clerk raised his voice for all to hear then added, 'The Waldorf looks forward to welcoming her ladyship when she arrives from London.'

Oohs and *aahs* from the ladies followed.

Buck winced. So Irene was behind his sudden fame. No doubt giving press interviews about their affair to the London scandal sheets. The New York newspapers, hungry for *any* story about the survivors, had picked them up.

Now he understood the hard-nosed stares.

'Your suite will be ready presently, your lordship,' said the desk clerk, ringing for the bellboy.

'I'll be in the bar,' Buck said, and then strode off before he was waylaid by curious ladies begging to hear about the sinking. Cripes, he wouldn't be in this mess if he hadn't caught Trey kissing Ava. He'd had no intention of accepting Irene's offer, but when he saw Ava's soft lips parted, her mouth bruised from another man's kiss, he was so angry he couldn't see straight.

So he'd bolted.

Only luck and a heavy downpour had led him to a curious policeman, who placed him in the waiting limousine when he identified himself as a *Titanic* survivor.

A vein throbbed in his forehead. Buck *swore* he'd pay back every pound to her ladyship out of his winnings. He *had* to win the bet.

For his sake *and* Ava's.

Getting rid of her accent wouldn't be easy, though he had an advantage since Fiona spoke with a winsome brogue. Still, he would have to instruct Ava in grammar, etiquette and the social graces without Mrs Benn-Brady finding out.

Buck ordered a brandy at the Waldorf café, a bar reserved for men only. Downing it in one swallow, he ordered a double, then made his plans.

First, there was the problem of Irene.

She had booked passage on a Cunard ship departing next week, which meant she would dock in New York in a fortnight. Once she arrived, she'd claim him as hers. To protect Ava, he'd not argue that.

Not much time, old man.

Buck stared at the empty shot glass, as if he could see the future. It was crystal clear. He had two weeks to turn Ava O'Reilly, a poor Irish girl from County Cork, into the Countess of Marbury.

Then he'd leave New York and never see her again.

God help him.

33

Fifth Avenue, New York
20 April 1912

'Who was that devilishly handsome gentleman I saw you conversing with on the gangway, Countess?' Mrs Benn-Brady asked over afternoon tea in the drawing room.

Tea with lemon, Ava noted, staring down into her cup. Not milk.

'Captain Lord Buck Blackthorn, madam,' she answered carefully. She avoided looking at Trey, though he watched her with interest. She wondered if he'd caught the warm feelings for his lordship in her voice, feelings so close to the surface they surprised her. 'I've known the gentleman since he came to stay at the hunting lodge belonging to his father, the duke, near my home at Dirksen Castle.'

Trey arched his brows, impressed with her knowledge of the countess. He raised his cup to her.

Lowering her eyes, she put the cup to her lips and finished her tea. No telling expression crossed her features to enlighten the woman what she'd said was a lie. Trey knew and that made her smile. A fine lie it was, too. The countess would be proud of her, reciting all that grand talk.

She would, wouldn't she?

Ava stiffened, not certain the countess would approve, even less certain she would succeed in her game. What if she failed? So far, the hand of an angel lay on her shoulder with Mrs Benn-Brady accepting her as the countess.

So far.

'You remember me speaking of Buck, Mother,' Trey answered quickly, smiling at Ava. After the kiss in the limousine, she was a bit wary of him. Once they'd arrived at his mother's Fifth Avenue residence, he acted the perfect gentleman. But for how long? 'We were at Cambridge together.'

'Ah, yes, the gentleman who acted as the go-between for your engagement to the countess.' She whispered a few words to her butler, Niles, who bowed, and then left. 'I must invite him to tea.'

Ava rattled her empty cup, her nerves shattered. Ever since she'd arrived at the stately mansion, she'd been in a dither trying to take it all in. Such a palace she'd never seen. The Benn-Brady residence sat squat on the corner, its drab appearance reminding her of an ancient cathedral. But if the outside was as plain as the church poor box, the inside reminded her of an enchanted fairy story.

She swore her feet barely touched the fancy mosaics made from shimmering marble as she glided down the long hallway with light streaming in through stained-glass windows edged with bronze. She waltzed through so many elaborate wrought iron and glass doors she didn't think she'd ever pass through the same one twice.

She slept until noon on a bed so soft Ava floated into her dreams, not like the cast iron bed she had slept on in the grand house in Ireland, with a mattress stuffed with straw.

Then the dreams had turned into a nightmare.

Those last, dreadful hours on the *Titanic* replayed over and over again in her mind. Raw emotion drove her to toss and turn, throwing off the fine linen sheets in spite of the chill from the rain. Seeing the countess in her mind, her face so pale and drawn in her last moments on the staircase. Then Ava was holding Buck close to her on the deck of the rescue ship, his heart nearly stopped beating…

Holy Mother of God, where did she go from here?

Hands shaking, her heart racing, Ava could barely stand still when Blanche, the French lady's maid, arrived with her morning tray of tea and toast and set about dressing her. Attaching her stockings to her corset, laced so tight she could scarcely breathe, a single petticoat eased over her hips, then a silky gown in a shade so green it put an emerald to shame. Two diamond clips held up her hair.

Ava was afraid to look in the mirror, but she did peek into a looking glass when Mrs Benn-Brady took her on a tour of the mansion. By the saints, was that her? Prim, genteel and unabashedly elegant. Couldn't be… but it was.

She was still prickling with goose bumps over her new look when they toured the library. Carved oak hugged the walls, but the decorator had outdone himself in the dining room with its black velvet wallpaper. According to her hostess, the electric lighting could be dimmed or brightened to showcase the colors of the ladies' gowns. Finally, they sat down in the drawing room, with gold threads and shiny crystals peeking out from the rose velvet brocade covering the walls.

Then afternoon tea with Trey and his mother, both listening intently while Ava told them all about the first cabin ladies in the lifeboat with her.

Nodding, Mrs Benn-Brady had her secretary write down the ladies' names to add to their list of wedding guests, then sent the girl off to type them up while Ava sat, stirring sugar into her tea and trying not to purse her lips when Mrs Benn-Brady insisted the footman drop another slice of lemon into her cup.

And still she waited.

But not one word from Buck.

Was he still angry with her for Trey's indiscretion? Did the man not know what she was going through? Ever since he'd left her, everything she did as the countess was a lesson in futility and frustration.

She'd die if Mrs Benn-Brady asked her one more question about the royals and being presented at court and what jewels the queen wore. Holy Mary, what did she know about that? Or weekends at a country estate? Where was his lordship? She'd never pull off this charade without him.

The afternoon took a different turn when Niles handed Mrs Benn-Brady a newspaper and her pince-nez. As the woman held up her spectacles and scanned the daily, Ava couldn't help but wonder if they ironed the newspapers here in New York to set the ink as they did back in Ireland.

'Ah, here it is, on page four,' Mrs Benn-Brady said with delight, and then turned to Ava. 'Your Captain Lord Blackthorn is quite notorious.'

Trey leaned over her shoulder and read the story, then slapped his knee, his laughter filling the high-ceilinged room. 'Leave it to Buck to create a scandal less than two days after the rescue ship docks.'

'What gibberish did the reporter write about his lordship?' Ava wanted to know, ready to defend him. 'He was a hero, saving the lives of steerage women and—'

'My dear Countess, such antics don't interest the society crowd,' Mrs Benn-Brady interrupted. She couldn't resist the opportunity to snub anything she considered beneath her. '*This* is what everyone is talking about.'

She showed Ava the double-page spread in the *New York Herald*. Her eyes widened and her jaw dropped. There he was, looking so handsome and fine, his lordship's picture published alongside other notables who had sailed on the *Titanic*.

Not Fiona's, though. Thank God, no known photos of the countess existed, since she'd been a recluse for years.

What gripped Ava more than anything was the accompanying story about his relationship with Lady Pennington.

'His lordship and that Pennington woman are all the gossip,' said the society matron with keen interest, then she continued reading the story and sipping her tea. 'It says here she's traveling to New York for a reunion with him.'

Ava fumed. The shame of the man. All along he was planning to return to that woman while he was spooning with her.

She turned her head so Mrs Benn-Brady didn't see her eyes brimming with tears.

Trey made the best of the situation. 'Buck does have a way with women, isn't that right, Countess?'

Ava nodded, and then said with the taste of grit on her tongue, 'He could charm a washerwoman out of her soapsuds.'

Mrs Benn-Brady nearly choked on her tea but recovered quickly. 'I've heard the British have peculiar habits, but *that,* my dear, is most enlightening.' She put down her cup on the small, round table edged with gold and turned to her son. 'We have much to do to prepare for the formal announcement of your engagement, Trey. The menu, place cards, floral displays—'

'I shall leave that in your capable hands, Mother. I have other business to attend to this afternoon,' Trey said, fidgeting with his collar. He'd come through the sinking of the ship without a scrape, but he was sweating now and no doubt anxious to escape his mother's never-ending tirades.

Ava wondered if he was back to his old ways and meeting a woman for a tryst.

You can't leave me here all alone, Ava's eyes pleaded with him.

He looked at her as if to say, *I told you she'd try to bully you.*

Mrs Benn-Brady had her own agenda. 'You will remain here until I finish, Trey. First, I want to make it clear we shall call the countess by her Christian name Fiona in private, but address her as your ladyship in front of guests,' she stated, pleased with her decision. Again, she spoke as if Ava wasn't in the room.

'The countess prefers to be addressed by her middle name, Mother,' Trey insisted, winking at Ava.

She winked back in a moment of playfulness. She was grateful to discover he was still her ally. Or was he just trying to get her into his bed?

'Oh, and what is that?' his mother asked, her tone advising him she was not pleased with any censure of her plans.

'Ava.'

'Hmm... I see the Scots have more peculiar habits.'

'Not as peculiar as lemon with your tea,' Ava said under her breath.

Watch your mouth, girl. It may seem that Mrs Benn-Brady accepts you, but the woman is as crafty as a banshee and just as powerful in her social world.

Ava shifted her weight on the plush red silk cushion and listened to her future mother-in-law explain her plans for the dinner party. *She* would select the menu and not her chef, who had a penchant for including too many brown sauces. And a quartet instead of an orchestra to give the soiree an intimate feeling.

The society lady was entertaining the idea of replacing her fine mahogany tabletop with plate glass when the butler returned with a silver platter holding a hastily scribbled note on a business card.

Mrs Benn-Brady looked at the card and smiled. 'Seems I won't have to invite Captain Lord Blackthorn to tea after all.'

'What do you mean, Mother?' Trey asked, then looked at Ava. She shrugged her shoulders, just as puzzled as he was.

'His lordship is here.'

34

The heat seething through Buck was unbearable.

Ava looked more beautiful to him than ever, poised on the edge of the antique chair like an enchanted princess holding court in a secret garden. Her green silk voile gown spread out around her like flower petals, her red hair shimmering with diamond clips that sparkled like dewdrops.

He'd spent the last hour walking up and down Fifth Avenue, thinking, *thinking*, trying to decide the best way to approach the situation. He hadn't much time to turn her into a countess.

And win his bet with Trey.

He wouldn't fail, he couldn't. He had half a mind to tell his old friend he didn't want the money, that it wasn't a fair wager. From his point of view, Ava's talents went beyond those of any 'dollar princess', as the newspapers termed the American heiresses seeking titled British husbands. She possessed a natural elegance that equaled her beauty. She had a quick mind and a wit, which he'd use to her advantage to impress Mrs Benn-Brady's social climbing friends.

An urgency to get started on his venture had driven him to arrive unannounced at the three-story residence on the famous avenue. Buck couldn't deny he was impressed. The house was square and broad with four tall columns, decorated in a pale gray limestone and ornamented with black and white marble.

Once inside, everywhere he looked he saw signs of a very wealthy woman. From the circular marble staircase to the lead-crystal chandeliers to the Persian rugs.

And gold ashtrays. Not thick-plated gold on silver, he noted, feeling its heaviness in his hand, but solid gold.

Seeing Ava in this opulent setting of satin brocade and art, surrounded by all that wealth had to offer made him even more certain she *could* pull off this charade. She took his breath away.

Turning her *into* the countess, however, could prove to be difficult.

Ava wouldn't even look at him.

She had given a loud gasp, her hand flying to her throat when the butler had introduced him. Afterward, she ignored him and sat as cold and rigid as a block of ice.

He grimaced. She was still angry with him for insulting her in the limousine. It was her own fault. Why did she have to let Trey kiss her?

It made no difference to Buck that *he'd* had every intention of taking her to his bed without the benefit of a wedding ceremony. That was different. That was before he realized how much she meant to him and then it was too late.

Still, he found her odd silence discomforting. That was so unlike Ava. Always ready with an opinion and colorful words that made him smile. Had he been wrong about her? Had her new position as a countess already gone to her head?

Was she as spoiled and manipulative as every other aristocratic female he'd met?

He wouldn't believe that. How blissful those four days on the *Titanic* with her had been. Wrapped up in each other's arms in an isolated world of satin and the tango, her unpredictable behavior amusing him, her beauty bewitching him.

His mouth tightened. Now her coldness toward him angered him.

That anger didn't go unnoticed by his hostess.

'I imagine you found it quite upsetting as a British subject to be called upon to testify at the U.S. Senate hearings,' said Mrs Benn-Brady, baiting him. She referred to the *Titanic* inquiry underway at the Waldorf-Astoria, with survivors giving testimony to a Senate subcommittee.

'I consider it my duty to testify, Mrs Benn-Brady,' Buck said, glancing at Ava. Did he see her soften toward him? 'I am most grateful to be alive. I'll do whatever I can to be of assistance in having maritime laws changed so this terrible tragedy never happens again.'

'Bravo, your lordship,' Mrs Benn-Brady shot back. 'I told Trey he must also do his duty, but I insisted to Senator Smith the countess not be called.'

Buck saw Ava let out a sigh of relief.

'The poor girl has been through enough already,' she continued. 'Besides, it's unseemly for a lady of her stature to speak about such things in front of a room of gawking politicians.'

Trey snickered and Buck couldn't resist a smile. He noticed Ava's expression didn't change. She looked as forlorn as ever.

'It does my heart good to know you told them what happened on that terrible night, your lordship,' Ava said, giving him a grateful look as she spoke. She struggled to say the words correctly. 'Especially for the passengers who can't be here to speak for themselves.'

Buck let out his breath. He could see the countess's death still weighed heavily upon her.

'Those who died will never be forgotten, Countess,' he said with fervor, looking at her saddened features.

She nodded.

'How long will you be staying in New York before you return to London, your lordship?' asked Mrs Benn-Brady, changing the subject. And the mood. He could see her scrutinizing him. She didn't trust him – and she was right. He'd win Ava back if he could.

But his hands were tied. Irene had seen to that with her capricious whim to fly to his side on the first ship sailing from Southampton.

'Long enough to complete my business here,' Buck said, leaning forward in his chair so he could look at Ava. He had so much more to say to her, but she wasn't ready to listen. She turned away from him. 'And to see my old friend married.'

Mrs Benn-Brady sipped her tea and munched on iced cakes. 'Get on with you, Trey,' she said, shooing him away. I want to hear all about his lordship's thrilling escapade on the overturned lifeboat.'

Buck looked at her, amused. She was as excited as a housemaid listening at the keyhole for gossip.

Trey winked at him, then left the trio to their tea.

'Yes. Don't keep us waiting, your lordship,' Ava said, challenging him with an edge in her voice that caught him off guard.

This was the Ava he knew. He beamed.

'You haven't told me what happened after you left... *us*... at the lifeboat,' she finished.

She means the countess, he thought.

Mrs Benn-Brady didn't blink an eye. She assumed Ava meant her son.

Buck could not let Ava despair. He noticed she was still shivering. Whether it was from the slight chill in the room or nerves he couldn't be sure. He wanted to hold her in his arms, feel her softness pressed against him, tell her he'd lost his heart to her. Yes, she hurt from losing Fiona, he wanted to tell her, but so did he. They would both heal with time.

Instead, he told his story.

'My pocket watch stopped at 2.20 a.m. when I jumped into the sea,' Buck began, snapping open his watch. The hands were still frozen, as if the winds of time refused to let go of that moment. 'The water was below freezing...'

For next several minutes, he recounted his amazing tale of survival, from the last moments on the *Titanic* as she went down, to grabbing onto the rope of the upside-down lifeboat and pulling himself aboard. He left out the details of saving the two Irish girls. He'd never be able to explain to the satisfaction of Mrs Benn-Brady why he'd risked his life to save steerage passengers.

'The captain of the *Carpathia* did a fine job rescuing the passengers fortunate enough to find a place in a lifeboat, Mrs Benn-Brady,' Buck finished, never taking his eyes off Ava, 'when so many lives were lost.'

'Most remarkable, your lordship.' The matron turned to Ava to ask her a question when Niles, her butler, a stalwart man with gray hair and hooded eyes, whispered something in her ear.

'A telephone call *now?*' she asked him. He nodded. 'Damn contraption is always interrupting me. I don't know why I let Trey talk me into having one installed. I never receive calls at this hour.'

'You are most fortunate to have a telephone, Mrs Benn-Brady,' Buck said in a convincing voice. 'If the *Titanic* wasn't equipped with a wireless room, we wouldn't be here now.'

A somber mood fell upon the room. The two survivors looked at each other. Buck knew what Ava was thinking.

There's one missing.

He answered her with his eyes. *We owe it to the countess to make this plan work.*

Mrs Benn-Brady, who had no idea what was going on, focused on her own agenda.

'Excellent point, your lordship. I shall relate that to the chairman of the Women's Relief Committee. It will make an interesting piece of conversation at our next meeting.' She grinned, eager to take credit for the idea. 'I'll take the call, Niles.' Then, with a curious backward glance at each of them, she left the drawing room.

Buck couldn't wait to talk to Ava alone, to tell her about his plans to win over Mrs Benn-Brady.

She had other ideas.

'I can't go through with this mad scheme, Buck. *I can't!*'

Ava dropped her shoulders and set her teacup down with a bang.

'Is this the girl who outran the constable to get aboard the *Titanic* so she could come to America?' Buck said, his tone angry. 'Who wouldn't give up even when they locked her up in steerage?'

'You don't understand, Buck. Trey's mother keeps asking me questions about my needlepoint skills and what tunes I can play on the piano. I can't play the bloomin' piano,' she said, frustrated. 'All day she follows me around, watching me. How I walk, sit. Hold my teacup. Every time I open my mouth—'

'And a beautiful one it is,' Buck said.

'Listen to your blarney, will you? Trying to sweet talk me into going through with your plan. It won't work. I know all about you and this Lady Pennington.' She paused, waiting for him to deny it. He didn't. 'That's why you made this ridiculous bet. To get rid of me so you could run off with that – that woman.'

'Irene has nothing to do with it, Ava,' Buck insisted. She didn't believe him. 'You'll never have a chance to make something of yourself with me. As Mrs Treyton Brady, you will.'

'I don't care. You lied to me and I'll not forgive you for that.'

'It's true Irene and I had an affair in London,' Buck admitted. 'That's over. I didn't ask her to come to New York.'

'And I didn't ask to take the countess's place,' Ava said, wringing her hands on the delicate silk. 'It's wrong, Buck, all wrong. I can't go through with it. I'm packing my things and out I go on the street where I'll take my chances. Goodbye.'

She fled down the hall and raced up the winding staircase to her bedroom before he could stop her.

Instead he was forced to cover up this unhappy episode on his own.

'Is the countess ill?' Mrs Benn-Brady asked Buck when she returned and found Ava gone, her tone suspicious.

'She's been through a traumatic experience, Mrs Benn-Brady,' he said, wondering how he was going to get Ava back. The last thing he needed was this woman grilling him. 'She's seen people go to their death. It's not easy on her.'

The woman nodded. 'That explains her strangeness, though at times I swear she's not the same girl Trey wrote me about in his letters.'

Buck narrowed his eyes. 'What makes you say that?'

'I can forgive her traveling alone without a chaperone, but when she arrived without a lady's maid,' she huffed and puffed, 'well, that is not done.'

'Her maid sprained her ankle and left the ship at Queenstown,' Buck said easily. That much was true.

'Oh?' she asked. 'Trey wired me her maid was intending to leave her employ after the ship docked.'

Buck attempted a smile. 'A simple mistake, madam. The girl who served as her lady's maid on board the *Titanic* was a stewardess.' He lowered his eyes and a sharp pain pierced his ribs for the lie he was about to tell. 'She didn't survive.'

'I see,' she mumbled, popping another iced cake into her mouth and eating it slowly, very slowly, while waiting for him for continue.

Did she suspect anything? How could she?

Buck bided his time. The woman was no fool. She'd see through Ava's charade if he didn't work fast. He had much to accomplish in two weeks.

'The countess spent only a season in London,' he said, 'but her lineage goes back a thousand years.'

'So the detectives I hired informed me.' She finished her cake, then wiped her fingers with care. 'Trey mentioned her reluctance to come to New York and gave me the indication the countess was a shy, reclusive young woman,' she said, her curiosity taking her voice up an octave. 'This girl reminds me of a wild creature challenging everything she sees. And that dyed red hair. Disgraceful.'

'I assure you, Mrs Benn-Brady,' Buck said with the confidence of a gentleman who remembered with delight burying his face in that red hair and smelling its fresh scent, 'it's her natural color.'

She eyed him sharply, and then picked up her fan and toyed with it. 'Trey said you've known the countess since she was a child.'

'Yes. Since she was in pigtails,' Buck answered in a firm tone that allowed no argument.

She fanned herself with the gray plumes. 'You are most polite in answering my questions about the countess, Captain Lord Blackthorn, but I know what you're thinking. That I have no claim to act like an imperial autocrat.'

'Madam?' Buck said, surprised by her admission.

'It's true. I was born Myra Benedict, dirt poor with my little sister to care for after my mother died because we had no money for the doctor. I worked as a seamstress in a hotel day and night after I turned fourteen, hunched over low gaslight until my eyes nearly gave out.'

She paused. Buck remained quiet, waiting. She wiped perspiration from her brow. He could see her face was wrinkled and spotted under the rice powder she lavished upon her skin.

'One night I worked 'til dawn fixing a gown for a guest,' she continued. 'The woman decided my sewing wasn't to her liking and ripped out every stitch I'd done.' She looked down at her hands, the skin papery and fine, her fingers long. 'I'm an excellent seamstress, Captain Lord Blackthorn, or the hotel would have never kept me on. This woman didn't respect what I did because she considered me beneath her. She wouldn't pay me until I'd done the work to her satisfaction. I swore then someday I'd get the respect I deserve.

'Around that time I met Mr Brady, a hotel guest who needed his shirts mended. He was good and kind. A frugal gentleman who believed a man shouldn't be judged by his clothes, but by what he'd done. For two years I sewed his shirts whenever he came into town, knowing little else about him.'

She waved the fan around, wisps of feathers flying about like dust on the wind.

Buck could see moisture in her eyes, which surprised him. Her hand trembled as she put down her fan and finished her tea before continuing her story.

'When Mr Brady asked for me at the hotel one afternoon, I was in my quarters tending to my sister who had contracted pneumonia. When he found me wiping her face with wet cloths, he insisted on getting help.

'My sister died and we buried her next to my mother.' She let out a deep sigh. 'He asked me to marry him and only then did I discover Mr Brady was the founder of a steel company in Pittsburgh.'

'That's an amazing story, Mrs Benn-Brady,' Buck said, her openness so very much the opposite of her behavior it startled him. Yet he couldn't help but feel a sense of camaraderie with the woman. As the second son of a duke, he understood her desire for respect. 'Trey never told me.'

'My son respects my wishes not to speak of my past, Captain Lord Blackthorn.' She smiled. 'However, I discovered not even a vast fortune like mine can buy me the respect I crave. I hoped if Trey stopped running around and married a real lady, a titled woman who could teach him how to be a gentleman, I would gain that respect. Yet the countess seems rough around the edges, owing to her seclusion in that drafty old castle, I imagine.' She rang the bell for the footman. Her next words were a bit more pointed.

'I'm worried, your lordship. It's very important to me the countess represents the Benn-Brady name in good stead when I announce their engagement.'

Buck paid no attention to the footman refilling his teacup. He couldn't sit another minute.

He started pacing up and down, thinking. What he felt after listening to the wealthy matron bare her soul was what he felt after downing too many highballs and drawing a bad hand of poker. He couldn't focus and would lose everything if he didn't get his game back on track.

He spied a copy of the *New York Herald* with its glaring *Titanic* headlines tossed onto the settee. A slow smile emerged over his lips. He'd appeal to the woman's hunger for publicity.

'Why not host a charity dinner party here at your home to benefit *Titanic* survivors?' Buck suggested. 'That way you can introduce the countess to society's elite and announce their engagement.'

'What a charming idea,' Mrs Benn-Brady said, pleased. 'We can't wait too long if we want to get good press coverage. The newspapers will tire of the story, as they always do.'

'Shall we say in two weeks?' Buck hadn't much time before Irene arrived and started poking her aristocratic nose into his business. Once the society matron's intimate circle gave Ava their seal of approval, her future was assured.

That was what he wanted, wasn't it?

Mrs Benn-Brady sat up straight and fiddled with the diamond bracelets on her wrists. 'That doesn't leave us much time to polish our Scottish jewel.'

'You take care of the dinner arrangements,' Buck said with confidence, 'and allow me to tutor the countess in whatever social graces she's lacking. As I'm certain you are aware, I am the son of a duke and well-schooled in the art of etiquette and manners.'

Then, using his charm as only an English gentleman could, he bowed and kissed her hand. He was pleased to see by the grin on her face she accepted his idea with enthusiasm. He let out a relieved breath. This was the first time he was ever grateful his father was a duke.

'What you mean, your lordship,' Mrs Benn-Brady said smugly, 'is having an old friend from the British aristocracy refine her style will ease her way up the New York social ladder.'

Buck smiled. 'Exactly, madam. I guarantee you the countess will be ready to meet your friends and do you proud as your future daughter-in-law.'

'Excellent. You shall be the guest of honor at the dinner party.'

'Me?' he said, surprised. 'I beg to defer, madam.'

'I won't take no for an answer, your lordship, not when all of New York is talking about your heroics on the *Titanic*... among other things.' Then, with a knowing smile, she added, 'Bring Lady Pennington with you. I'm sure that will prove most interesting.'

'It will be my pleasure,' Buck promised, then wondered if he'd lost his sanity for agreeing to bring Irene into the lion's den.

Or was it Ava who was the sacrificial lamb?

No doubt the society matron wanted to compare the two women side by side. Not to mention she'd be the envy of her friends to have a trio of titled aristocrats under her roof at the same time.

What the hell had he gotten himself into?

* * *

'You can't let the countess down,' Buck said, grabbing Ava by the arm. He had an idea he'd find her sneaking down the back stairs of the servants' quarters. From what she'd told him, she knew her way around a grand house.

Chin up, she glared at him. 'You mean I can't let *you* down, Captain Lord Blackthorn.'

'I'm not asking for myself, Ava. There's Trey to consider. And his mother.' He appealed to her sense of duty. 'Mrs Benn-Brady is depending on you.'

'On me? Hogwash. She doesn't need no... *anybody* to get what she wants.'

He grinned. 'And what about Ava O'Reilly? What does *she* want?'

She looked him straight in the eye. 'You know the answer to that.' The sincerity in her voice was so honest it took him time to recover.

There was a moment of dead silence between them. They were both in the grip of something they never expected to find aboard the *Titanic*. A fierce passion for each other that still burned.

He had no choice but to douse the flame.

'I'm warning you, Ava, if you run off and cause a scandal, you'll not only embarrass Trey's mother, but tarnish the proud name of the countess.'

To his relief, the dark, angry green of her eyes softened.

Ava laid her hand on his arm. 'I don't care about your bet... but I *do* care about the countess. Fiona was good to me and I'd be as vile as an unholy serpent if I sullied her name.'

'You won't regret it, Ava,' Buck said. He hadn't realized she was standing so close to him he could smell lemon on her breath. He touched his finger to her lips, tempting her to sigh. 'I'll see to it you're schooled in every drawing room trick known to a lady.'

Her dander went up. 'Will you? Don't you get no fancy ideas, your lordship. I almost sinned with you once and the Almighty looked the other way. He'll not do it again.' She rubbed her hands on her dress, her sweat staining the silk. 'I'll not lie with you or any man until I have His blessing. I'll not get that if I can't pass myself off as the countess.'

'Then I have your word, Ava?'

'Yes, but no looking at me like you want to dance the tango, are you agreeing to that?'

'I once offered you my protection, Ava. I now extend that offer to include my services as a gentleman. I shall guard your reputation with my life. No man will touch you until your wedding night. *I promise*.' His words came out different than he intended. Husky, almost angry.

She noticed it, too. Her eyes avoided his, but he could see her lower lip trembling.

'I accept your offer, your lordship,' she said in a clear voice. 'I will do all I can to be worthy of the name of the Countess of Marbury.'

Buck bowed slightly, and then escorted Ava back to the drawing room. Her head high, her walk regal, her step sure. Something had come over her. She'd changed, he noticed, watching her greet Mrs Benn-Brady with a confident gleam in her eye.

Why did he get the feeling he'd just won the bet?

35

2 May 1912

Captain Lord Buck Blackthorn was a devil of a taskmaster and Ava had the aching muscles to prove it.

The days following the sinking of the *Titanic* blurred into a series of gown and corset fittings, speech lessons and the proper way to hold her lace handkerchief.

Ava sat with her pinkie extended at a ninety-degree angle until it turned numb.

Her training consisted of a round of tasks morning, afternoon and night with his lordship making her enunciate her vowels over and over like an owl with insomnia.

When he insisted she dab the latest fashionable perfume reeking of lemon on her silk sachets, she balked, then said five Hail Marys while swearing under her breath she'd never add a slice of citrus to her tea again.

'Where is the etiquette book I gave you?' Buck asked on this early morning when Ava was still aching from working on her curtsy yesterday.

He referred to *The Blue Rose – An Etiquette Primer for Young Ladies* by Lady Arabella Brightmore.

'There on the table next to my tea *without* lemon.' She made a triumphant pout.

His brows arched, sorting out her statement with a devilish quirk. Did he linger too long on her mouth when she pursed her lips?

'Go to page sixty-seven, paragraph three. Entering a room like a lady.'

'We did that yesterday,' she argued.

'Did we?' He shot her an *I'm-not-convinced* look that made her insides rumble. 'Then we'll do it the correct way today or I shall—'

'You shall what, milord?' Ava dared him with a hip wiggle, sauntering close to him. *Too* close. He gulped. 'Spank me?'

He grinned so wide she wondered if he considered it.

'I agreed to remain a gentleman during our training, Ava.' Buck let out a heavy breath. 'Or I'd be tempted to grant your wish.'

Ooh... the audacity of the man set a fire under her. Her heart pounded. She was determined to show him her best, this constant need she had for his approval.

Even if in the end she'd marry another man.

She caught him peeking at her, an unhappy wrinkle creasing his brow and, for a moment she wondered if he was thinking the same thing.

'Shall we begin?' he said, breaking the spell. Once again they were teacher and pupil, the sensuality between them buried and that warm, pink feeling she had sparring with him turned into a cool shiver.

I shall miss our lessons, Buck... more than you'll ever know.

Ava set out to do her best, following the instructions in the book on how to enter a room. She stood in the doorway, careful to 'pause' and tilt her head to capture attention.

'Like this, your lordship?'

He took a moment to reflect. 'More like *this* when you're invited to a soiree.' He walked over to her and lifted her chin up more, his lips coming dangerously close to hers.

She sucked in a breath.

'If you come any closer, milord, I shall lose my self-confidence,' she whispered.

He grinned. 'A lady's self-confidence when she's out and about comes from *knowing* she's doing it right.'

'You mean like kissing?' She wanted so badly to kiss him.

A flicker of amusement crossed his face, but he didn't take the bait.

'I mean like knowing the popular artists of the Paris Salon,' he said, rattling off their names. Ava knew he wanted to kiss her, but he wouldn't admit it.

'I prefer van Gogh and Gauguin,' she said, remembering the flamboyant Impressionists from their lesson on French artists.

'You would.'

'Oh?' Ava was curious to know.

'Because they're rebels... and *don't* follow the rules.'

She put her hands on her hips, tilting her head just so. 'You know me too well.'

That evoked a loud grunt from his lordship. 'Yes, don't I?'

And with that, Buck ended the lesson.

* * *

By late morning, Ava had collapsed on the divan, tuckered out and ready for a nap. Walking up and down the marble staircase with the etiquette book balanced on her head made her wonder why anyone wanted to be a lady. After she perfected her posture, she learned the rules of making social calls, including turning down the upper left corner of her calling card to indicate she'd made a personal visit.

Which she hadn't.

And wouldn't until she finished her grueling education of how to act like a countess.

'You haven't shown me your curtsy today,' Buck said, wiping his brow. He looked as tired as she felt.

'Must I?' she pleaded.

'Yes.'

He paced up and down, rubbing the back of his neck. Ava wanted to rub it for him, to get close enough to breathe in his musky scent and let her head spin.

She didn't. Seeing him work so hard to help her made her heart swell. She went back to work on her lady skills.

Since Mrs Benn-Brady was obsessed with the royals, Ava had to master the 'court curtsy' and the rituals surrounding it, including wearing a white evening gown with a low neck and short sleeves. As for the curtsy itself – very deep with her head nearly touching the floor, then walking away from their majesties backward without tripping on her gown – Buck insisted it was all in her sense of timing.

What unnerved her more than anything was Mrs Benn-Brady sneaking around behind her with her skirts rustling and making comments about her red hair and threatening to make her wear a wig, while Trey went about his daily routine of clubs and handling his mother's business affairs. He poked his head into the drawing room at regular intervals during the day to check on her progress. He was as giddy as a little boy at Christmas waiting to unwrap his package.

Her.

All dolled up in silk and gossamer lace.

Gowns the flamboyant dressmaker had picked out when his lordship was busy elsewhere.

She looked more like a fancy gentleman's mistress, Buck said. Not a wife.

How would he know? He'd never had a wife, only a mistress. Or two. Ava didn't know *how* many.

She fretted as she stood for hours while he made the woman rip bows and spangles and rhinestones off her gown. That wasn't what had her tripping over her vowels this afternoon like a sinner pleading her case to the Almighty.

It was the matter of her underwear.

Her skin prickled with unsettling but delightful thoughts when the dressmaker showed her 'bewitching' silk French drawers. So beautiful and sensual. How lovely it would be wearing them with Buck watching her.

When the woman showed Buck the fabric, he shook his head and picked out the plain cotton ones instead with nary a pink ribbon.

'Chiffon peignoirs are all the rage in Paris, my dear Countess,' the dressmaker said with a charming smile. 'Perfect for your trousseau.'

'The countess will have *this* nightdress,' Buck said, indicating a high-necked nightgown with tiny petit-point flowers around the hem. His dark eyes brooded, as if he couldn't stand the thought of another man seeing her in dishabille.

Ava couldn't resist snapping back with a sassy remark. 'No doubt Lady Pennington will have a trunk filled with naughty garments when she arrives from London.'

'No doubt,' was all he said, then he gave her a wide, knowing smile to distract her from asking more questions.

Her ears were still burning and her face flushed under her pearl powder.

She wiped it all off.

Ava was as fired up as a band of angels battling the devil on holy ground. So he could have his mistress with her fancy underwear, but she had to wear cotton on her wedding night. Captain Lord Blackthorn may have talked her into this mad scheme, but she wasn't married yet.

The saints better hide their eyes because she was determined to show his lordship she could compete with this mysterious Lady Pennington.

Even wearing cotton underwear.

* * *

They skipped afternoon tea.

Ava's transformation into a lady picked up at a quickening pace when Buck announced they had two days left to complete her education. Mrs Benn-Brady had sent out the handwritten invitations to her charity dinner and she expected Ava to be ready for her debut.

The idea of meeting the society swells threw her into total disarray.

She stumbled in her practice sessions of learning to make conversation when she arrived at the opera, then how to leave during the second act.

Next, she couldn't find the list of her costume changes for the day and had to make a new one.

Then her hair came undone when she tripped and knocked over a dress form while overseeing her new gowns, their sleeves and bodices stuffed with tissue paper to keep their shape.

And she miscounted the rows of shoes lined up on her wardrobe shelves. Satin and suede pumps with buckles and seed pearls. Thirty-five pairs of shoes for one week's costumes.

Her head was spinning. How could a lass like her have the audacity to pull this off?

Only a ninny wouldn't be excited with such luxury and lace at her fingertips, but Ava was lonely. She didn't care how many pairs of shoes graced her shelves. Marriage was forever and she carried a secret love for his lordship in her heart not even the threat of the devil's fire settling under her arse could make her give up.

Ava could feel his eyes on her as she glided down the winding staircase with her etiquette book on her head, hand extended, his lordship telling her to keep her shoulders straight, when Niles the butler asked him if he wished to take a telephone call from a lady.

A very insistent lady.

Buck nodded, then told Ava to continue practicing her walk before leaving to take the call. But not before she caught a devilish look in his eye. As if he wanted to take her in his arms and kiss her.

Defiant, Ava dropped the book on the staircase. To say she was peeved put it mildly. She couldn't imagine a more annoying intrusion. She had no assurance he *would* have kissed her.

She just knew.

Now she understood why Mrs Benn-Brady hated telephones.

Mercy, has Lady Pennington arrived in New York already?

Knitting her brows, Ava sat down on the staircase, tucking her silken skirts under her, and flipped through the etiquette book. She needed help. There had to be a chapter on seduction. Could she find it before he came back?

Oh, the angels must be on her side, she thought giggling. She found exactly what she was looking for and read every word.

* * *

When his lordship returned, the loud rumble of a late day thunderstorm made its appearance on cue, throwing the large drawing room into a gray twilight with velvet blue undertones.

Perfect. Ava had one more trick up her sleeve. Literally.

The seductive art of unveiling by taking off her thirty-two button chamois gloves with the finesse of a lady and the speed of a caterpillar.

A teasing slowness that Lady Brightmore insisted would stir a husband's desire.

Oh, really? Ava wanted to find out.

She surprised his lordship with a supple, undulating walk down the staircase, then brushed past him without even a nod. She began unbuttoning her glove, one pearl bob at a time, and slid it down her arm. Slowly, *very* slowly.

It gave her goose bumps, but what about him?

Behind her she could hear his lordship let out a low moan. The sensual sound made her dig her nails into the silk sliding over her hips as she moved out of his reach. She shimmied with purpose as she glided over the marble floor, daring him to follow her.

And not take his eyes off her. Would he kiss her? *Finally?*

No. It didn't work. Buck remained a gentleman and gave her no more than a passing glance.

In the name of the Holy Ghost, the man was driving her crazy. Sure, she'd made him swear not to touch her. Sure, she knew He was waiting for her to slip up. But just once, before she covered her face with a white veil and kissed the white rosary with a prayer on her lips, did she want to see his lordship's eyes glimmer with desire for *her* and not this Lady Pennington.

Then she'd never ask for another thing. Never.

Are you sure, girl? It's a dangerous thing you're about, but I'll not stop you. You haven't learned jealousy is a heady perfume that dulls the mind and overwhelms the senses.

God help you. You'll have to find out for yourself.

'Your scheme won't work, Ava.'

'Why not?' she teased. She felt as nervous as if she were again that naïve girl on the ship.

'I have more important things to occupy my mind,' she heard him say, 'besides your schoolgirl tricks.'

Sweet Jesus, what was he about? And her with her knickers all tied up in a knot.

Rain stormed outside on the luxurious avenue, making the tall windows rattle like angry demons who wanted to get inside.

Ava dropped her glove on the thick Persian carpet, and then ran her hands down the silken smoothness covering her hips. Warmth surged between her legs. Her cheeks colored as deep as the pink roses sitting in a vase on the table.

She turned and risked a glance at him and her pulse raced. His right hand covered his face, but she could see him peeking through his fingers. A slow smile widened his lips. He *was* watching her, damn him.

A giggle rose in her throat.

'I have no idea what you're talking about, your lordship,' she answered in a flawless accent.

'Don't try to fool me, Ava,' he said with a terseness that pinged her ego. 'You want to know if I still find you as desirable as I did that first day on the *Titanic*.' He looked down at the scribbled note he was reading and without raising his head he said, 'The answer is no.'

She stood tall, muscles tensed, ready to strike back at him with all the words she'd tried so hard to forget these past two weeks.

'And why not?' she demanded. His lordship advanced toward her, his brows rising. She held her ground.

'Because you are my best friend's fiancée. Now continue walking as I showed you and no more tricks.'

His coy remarks set her to wondering what he *did* feel about her.

'Buck, I—'

He was past humoring her.

'If you're through tempting me, Ava, something has come up I must attend to right away.'

And with that, he left.

Pouting, Ava yanked off her other glove. By the impassioned look on his face, she had the idea that 'something' wore silk stockings and had a beauty mole where no lady would profess to having one.

36

'Ava is in danger,' Buck said, leaving his brandy untouched. Irritated, he shoved the glass across the oak table. 'It's all my fault for talking her into this mad charade.'

'What are you talking about, old man?' Trey asked, then signaled the waiter for another drink. The two men sat in comfortable red leather armchairs in the Waldorf café.

'That female reporter from the *New York Herald* rang me up about a rumor she heard regarding the Countess of Marbury,' Buck said, tapping his fingers on the table. 'I knew the woman was trouble when she raised her skirt to entice me to give her an interview.'

'Did it?'

'No. I gave her the exclusive rights to my *Titanic* story to keep her *away* from Ava. Now this.'

'It can't be that bad, Buck.' Trey leaned closer. 'Is it?'

Buck smirked. 'She doesn't believe Ava is a real countess, but an actress I hired in London to play the part.'

Trey turned white. 'Good God, if such an idea wasn't so awful, it might prove amusing.'

'We *can't* let her hurt Ava.'

'Agreed, Buck. There'll be hell to pay if my mother hears about this,' Trey said with an odd note in his voice, as if he'd been down this path before. 'She wants to control everything, including me.'

Which was why Buck had found him at the Waldorf instead of the 'stuffy old Union' as Trey called it. The high-ceilinged café paneled in a rich, dark oak provided its all-male clientele with a four-sided bar and a free buffet.

'She can't control the press, Trey,' Buck said.

'You don't know my mother. She invited a select group to her charity dinner but everyone who *didn't* get an invitation has their noses bent out of shape,' he said, laughing. 'All the newspapers are clamoring to cover the event.'

'We never counted on the press disputing Ava's title.'

'Where did this reporter come up with such an insane idea?' Trey wanted to know.

'She interviewed that woman who complained about losing her jewels when the *Titanic* went down,' Buck explained. 'She swore Ava acted strange on the *Carpathia*, as if she were hiding something.'

'Your reputation with women didn't help, Buck,' Trey said. Was that envy Buck heard in his voice? 'Ava never left your side on the rescue ship while you were unconscious.'

Buck couldn't deny once he'd found Ava again, he hadn't given a thought to what happened afterward. All he could think about was her. She was wearing the countess's black coat and when she gave him her sexy smile, he thought of nothing else *but* her.

She could do that to him, keep him off balance. What surprised him was her performance earlier when she swayed her hips and removed her glove with such sensuality he thought he'd been seduced by a sophisticated demimondaine.

Christ, what had he created?

The idea both worried and excited him, but he had no choice but to keep his hands off her. Still, he felt like a heel when all Ava wanted was for him to hold her in his arms and kiss her.

'The reporter smells a story,' Buck said. 'Whether or not it's true won't matter if it hits the newspapers.'

'Not to mention Mother would disinherit me.' Trey sucked in his breath.

'What about Ava?' Buck shot back, raising his voice. 'Or don't you care if they send her back to Ireland?'

'Pipe down, old man. Of course she matters to me, but I also care about my inheritance.' He finished his drink, then continued. 'I shouldn't have let you talk me into this, Buck. I'm not ready to settle down.'

Buck tried to control his temper. He stared at his old friend and saw a man haunted by the allure of money. It was the promise of a fortune that led him to follow a pointless life. That didn't excuse his behavior toward Ava.

'Explain yourself, Trey, and it better be good.'

'Fiona wouldn't complain if a man found the company of a pretty chorus girl desirable every now and then.' Trey sat back in the comfortable armchair. 'Ava's different. She doesn't understand a gentleman's indiscretions.'

Buck narrowed his eyes. 'You said you loved her.'

'I do... as much as I can love any woman.'

'I should knock your teeth down your throat.' Buck jumped up, ready to throw a punch at him until a waiter behind him cleared his throat. Loudly. He sat down. Nothing infuriated him more than letting Trey get away with his shenanigans with women.

'Calm down, Buck.' Trey smiled. 'It's obvious you're still in love with her.'

'I respect her,' he said, avoiding the question. 'That's more important.' He took a deep breath. 'I have an idea how we can save Ava's reputation *and* your inheritance, but I need your help.'

'What do you have in mind?' Trey was eager to be a part of any scheme that would enable him to continue his gadabout lifestyle.

'The reporter has only the word of a jealous woman that Ava is an actress. Why not discredit the rumor by showcasing her right here in the Waldorf?'

'Here?'

'Why not?' Buck said. 'Everyday, thousands of people stroll through Peacock Alley.'

The three-hundred-foot long corridor stretching along the Thirty-fourth Street side of the Waldorf was a showcase of wealth and glitter for the smart set. Ladies promenaded in their gowns and jewels, while eager shop girls gossiped and copied their fashion style.

Trey was shocked. 'You want to parade Ava in front of all New York? Are you crazy? She's not ready.'

Buck nodded. 'You wouldn't believe how much she's changed, Trey.'

Changed? Then why was she still trying to tease him?

It had warmed him to see her like that, but it also made him realize the sooner she took her place as Trey's wife, the better it would be for both of them. Peacock Alley was the perfect place to show the reporter how beautiful and accomplished Ava was as the countess, as well as give her the confidence she needed to face Mrs Benn-Brady's snooty society crowd Saturday night.

'If the public accepts Ava as the countess,' Buck continued, 'then the New York society snobs will have no choice but to accept her.'

'I'm not so sure, Buck. The shop girls ogling the ladies strutting up and down the corridor don't know a Vanderbilt from an Astor.'

'But the society crowd is well aware of Mrs Benn-Brady's fixation with marrying you off to an aristocrat. They know she'd never allow Ava to be seen in public before her debut if she wasn't *certain* she was the Countess of Marbury.'

'If my mother gets wind of this and finds out Ava is a housemaid, you're out fifty thousand pounds and I'll have to get a job.' He groaned.

'She won't, Trey.' Buck swallowed his drink in one gulp. 'I'd stake my life on it.'

* * *

Fiona 'Ava' Winston-Hale, sixth Countess of Marbury, strutted with an arch to her step along the marble amber corridor of the Waldorf-Astoria, much to the delight of the shop girls nearly fainting with envy. The haughty pout of her lips, the sweep of her long eyelashes and the rustle of her raspberry silk and velvet cloak lined with apple green satin would have them copying her walk for weeks to come.

And, Ava thought, if Buck had his way, her name would be in all the gossip columns in tomorrow morning's newspapers.

Holy Mary, was she really striding down the hotel hallway with his lordship and Trey like she was the Queen of Sheba?

She couldn't believe the throng of people walking up and down the passageway before dinner. Ladies resplendent in silks and taffetas chattering with gentlemen in top hats, clerks telephoning guests, bellboys calling out names through the corridors.

It was a thrilling spectacle she'd never forget.

Ava stood up straighter and her sable-trimmed hood fell to her shoulders, revealing her red hair pulled up into a fancy chignon. The crowd *oohed* and *aahed*. No feathers to mar its color, Buck had insisted. He wanted her to boldly proclaim who she was instead of hiding it.

Hide? Ava never felt more exposed. She could barely breathe. Her waist was pulled in, her breasts pushed out and her hips swathed in cherry red satin. Her clinging sheath dress undulated with color and her low V-neckline showed off her necklace of marquise diamonds shimmering under the blazing chandeliers overhead. An overskirt of frothy white Venise lace trailed behind her like melting snowflakes.

Inside she was shaking so badly that if she saw a mouse scamper in front of her, she'd happily swoon into a faint to end her misery.

Have you no backbone, girl?

Ava wanted to shut out her inner voice, that part of herself that kept her on her toes. She couldn't.

His lordship is counting on you to act like a grand lady.

Ah, but you're not listening to me any more. All them fancy clothes and pretty words coming out of your mouth can't make you a countess if you don't have the courage. Well, do you?

Ava took a deep breath and pulled up her long white gloves, nearly shaking loose the delicate orchid corsage fastened above her elbow.

Trey had bought it for her from Fleischman, New York's most exclusive florist.

Then she prayed with all her fingers crossed she *did* have the courage.

As Ava set a slower pace along the corridor, a burst of youthful enthusiasm from a young shop girl tested whatever courage she had.

'Look at her! So high and mighty,' said the girl. 'She don't even know we exist.'

Ava turned around sharply and locked gazes with a shop girl sitting on the edge of a sofa. Embarrassed, the girl gasped loudly, and then quickly covered her mouth with her hand.

She was right about one thing, Ava thought. She would not have seen her through the crowd of onlookers vying for position if the girl had not let her envy show in such a vocal manner. As it was, she walked toward her for a closer look.

She was clearly a factory girl, a seamstress perhaps. And about her age.

Why, the little—

'Pay no attention to her, Ava,' Buck said in a low voice, taking her by the elbow and urging her along.

She pulled away from him.

'After all I've been through, she can't talk to me like that,' Ava said, her ire up. 'By the saints, I'll—'

A gentle thought came to her then, along with a subtle fluttering of awareness as if someone had whispered in her ear.

The countess.

Fiona wouldn't walk down the corridor with her nose in the air. No, she would have the courage to share her wit and poetry with the people who adored her.

And those who didn't.

Like the shop girl.

What Ava did that night at the Waldorf had never been done before.

It was that moment which made her the talk of the town when she dared to step over the imaginary line followed by the delicate satin slippers of the society ladies and sat down next to the young woman in the battered floppy black hat and plain dark cotton dress.

The girl nearly choked.

A hush fell over the crowd of curious women, craning their necks to see better.

'These orchids will look lovely on you,' Ava said, removing the corsage from her arm. Then, before the shop girl could utter a word, she fastened it around her wrist.

'Oh, miss – I *couldn't!*' exclaimed the girl. 'Not after what I said.'

'It takes courage to speak your mind,' Ava said. 'Something I admire even when your harsh words are about me.'

'I didn't mean it. Honest. It's just that none of them other ladies ever notice us,' she murmured with a sigh. 'You're different. You're the finest lady I ever seen.'

Ava smiled and squeezed the girl's hand, and then rejoined her two escorts in white tie and tails, looking at each other with bemused expressions.

'Who is she?' the girl said in a hoarse whisper to the two young matrons standing next to her with their mouths open.

'The gentleman said she's the Countess of Marbury.'

'And a survivor of the *Titanic*,' her friend added.

'I should have known she was a real countess... and so brave,' Ava heard the girl say as she continued on her stroll down the famed hallway.

She peeked over her shoulder and saw the girl beaming with joy as the crowd hovering around her erupted into loud cheering when she showed off her orchid corsage with a proud wave of her hand.

Ava swallowed hard. She had a warm feeling inside that the countess would be proud of her and that brought a tear to her eye.

'You're the star of Peacock Alley tonight, Ava,' Buck whispered, acknowledging the smiles and waves from the giggling young women as they headed for the Palm Room.

'Buck's right,' Trey said proudly. 'After what you did for that girl, no woman can equal you.'

Not even Lady Pennington?

Ava couldn't forget the woman's shadow hung over her.

'I can never forget I was once like that shop girl,' she said, taking Trey's arm as the maître d' showed them to their table in the Palm Room. A bubbling fountain and flowering green palms made her believe she was in an enchanted garden, while overhead a high glazed dome of tinted glass gave the room a feeling of dining with the open sky above them.

'All that's changed, Ava,' Buck said. 'As the Countess of Marbury, this will be your life.' He indicated the stares in her direction from the excited hotel visitors chattering behind the plush velvet rope strung across the restaurant entrance to control who was allowed into the exclusive dining room.

Did his lordship sound wistful? Or was it her imagination?

Sinking gracefully down into the elegant chair as Buck had taught her, Ava was conscious of what he didn't say. Did he still care for her? Would she ever know?

All her attempts to tease him earlier had gone nowhere. When he'd returned late this afternoon and told her their lessons were finished, she'd been relieved. Then she'd nearly dropped her drawers when Buck had announced they were dining tonight at the Waldorf so New York could give their approval.

* * *

The evening accelerated, and with it, Ava's reputation as the beautiful and outspoken Countess of Marbury grew.

Buck was delighted when notable hotel guests and dignitaries stopped by their table, asking for an introduction to the beautiful countess. Others watched the goings-on from surrounding tables, gossiping, with their curious glances straying across the room as they peeked over the tops of their wineglasses, all whispers and smiles.

The exclusive restaurant catered to the opera crowd this time of night and full evening dress was mandatory – top hat, white tie and tails for gentlemen and gowns for ladies.

A crowd also gathered outside the Palm Room on the Fifth Avenue sidewalk, pulling up their collars to keep out the late-night drizzle as they pressed their noses against the plate glass windows to catch a glimpse of her.

By the time the waiter brought them coffee and cognac after an outstanding meal which included Smith Island oysters, breast of turkey stuffed with deviled sauce and mousse with blue raspberries, Buck was congratulating himself on a job well done.

He should have known his luck wouldn't last.

'Aren't you going to introduce *me* to the countess, Buck?'

A plume of elegant gray smoke with a familiar scent riding up his nostrils made him turn around.

Buck nearly choked on his cognac.

Lady Irene Pennington stood behind him like the Queen of Hearts, posing under the lights with her amber cigarette holder in her gloved hand.

And looking at Ava as if she intended to lop her head off.

37

'You're not what I expected, Countess,' Lady Irene Pennington said, blowing cigarette smoke in her direction. It curled under Ava's nose, making her cough.

'Sorry to disappoint you,' Ava said, her eyes moving over her ladyship's face. The blonde's finely arched brows and full red lips twisted into a jealous knot.

'Yes. From what Buck said,' Irene continued, puffing on her cigarette, 'I assumed you were the plain, quiet type.'

'Really? From what I read about you in the *New York Herald*,' Ava said, seizing her advantage by inflicting a taunting bite, 'you're *exactly* what I expected.'

'Oh?' Irene said, taking up the unspoken challenge. 'And what is that?'

'A woman who will do anything to get what she wants.' Ava shifted her gaze to Buck pulling on his high collar. He looked as out of place as a fox in a hen house when the feathers were flying.

'How do *you* know what I want?' asked Irene, refusing to look at his lordship.

'It's obvious, isn't it?' Ava asked. 'You couldn't wait to set sail on the next ship to stake your claim, even if it meant not mourning your late husband.'

Ava knew an aristocrat like Lady Irene Pennington should be veiled and wearing a high-neck black sateen dress with nothing more than a dull polished brooch out of respect for the recently departed Lord Pennington – not flaunting her splendid figure in a tight royal blue charmeuse gown. Her full-length satin sleeves were overlaid with black shadow lace and her low-cut bodice was embroidered with steel beads and gold threads. Over her shoulders she wore a black velvet wrap with the neck and sleeves trimmed with chinchilla fur.

Obviously her ladyship thought nothing of slinking along the edges of society, Ava thought, without regard to what she considered outdated rules.

Especially when it came to Captain Lord Buck Blackthorn.

Buck tried to keep the two women apart, but when Ava had her Irish dander up, there was no stopping her. She raised her chin and smiled in triumph. Never in her wildest imaginings did she think she'd ever have the opportunity to challenge an aristocratic lady as an equal.

It was a fight she wouldn't have missed for the world.

'I imagine you're used to breaking the rules, Lady Pennington,' Ava said, her curiosity daring her to keep going. She refused to melt like a rose candle under this woman's scrutiny. 'Or am I being too harsh?'

'Rules are made to be broken, my dear Countess. Which is why I crashed your little party. I couldn't wait to be introduced to you after what I heard from the bellboy.'

'I doubt if anything would shock you.'

'Perhaps, but speaking to a shop girl in a public hallway? A girl no better than a servant?' Irene said, crushing her cigarette into the crystal ashtray, then replacing it with a fresh one from her diamond silver case. 'How déclassé, dear Countess, even in America.'

'No more than a lady smoking in public,' Ava tossed back at her.

'Why, I wouldn't take that from anyone—'

'Except a countess?' Ava said without missing a beat. Neither guilt nor remorse trickled through her veins. The woman deserved to be put into her place. With each verbal attack, she was determined not to fall into her ladyship's well-laid trap.

'You must be tired from your voyage, Irene,' Buck interrupted, his patience coming to an end. 'Why don't I call on you in the morning when you're rested?'

Ava gave him a kick under the table, but he caught her ankle and squeezed it. The cad. He was ruining her game just when she was getting started.

Her ladyship had no idea what was going on and continued her attack on Ava.

'And leave the countess alone with two handsome gentlemen to entertain?' Irene said, eyes wide. 'I should say not, Buck – although I heard a rumor the countess is soon to become engaged to one of the wealthiest men in New York.'

She fluttered her darkened lashes at Trey, who responded as Ava knew he would. He leaned over to admire her décolletage, then offered to light her cigarette.

'You're overdoing it, Irene,' Buck warned her, though Ava didn't know if he was jealous or protecting her. How strange.

'Hold on, old boy,' Trey said, amused. 'Her ladyship is also *my* guest. A very *beautiful* guest.'

Irene smiled and blew smoke away from him. 'You have quite a charming fiancé, Countess. Too bad I didn't find him first.'

'That never stopped you before, Lady Pennington,' Ava said glibly. 'Why would it now?'

Where all that blarney came from, she'd never know, but she just couldn't sit there and let that woman think she was as simple as a country squirrel gathering nuts.

'You're treading on dangerous territory, Countess,' Irene said, directing her stare at Ava.

'No more than you,' Ava said, getting in the last word.

The Irish girl shivered from the chill in the air. Her ladyship's cool attitude slithered over her skin, the sharp, spicy odor of her perfume creating an intoxicating atmosphere that said she wasn't backing down.

She'd make a play for Trey if she could.

Ava smiled. Let her. All in all, she had done amazingly well holding her own as the Countess of Marbury, but she felt oddly depressed when Lady Pennington feigned a headache and asked Buck to escort her to her suite.

She sighed deeply. She may have won the battle, but she'd lost the man she loved.

* * *

'You acted insufferably tonight, Irene.'

'Don't be so bourgeois, Buck. I was merely amusing myself.'

'That's no excuse,' he said, irritated with her behavior.

He tossed his black silk top hat onto the Louis XV bronze armchair. The suite was luxurious to a fault, with ivory silk damask walls, thick Turkish carpeting and furniture covered in cut red velvet. Overhead a glass-beaded French chandelier cast a flattering light on her ladyship, but it didn't hide her scowl.

She didn't like being challenged by another woman. He had to admit, Ava held her own with the blonde beauty. He had the feeling it was due more to the Irish girl's innate strength than his training during the past two weeks.

'The countess went through a trying ordeal when the ship went down,' he said.

'You'd never know it, Buck. She's got quite a wit. And those *gorgeous* clothes. Venise lace and Russian sable,' she said with more than a trace of envy. 'Mr Brady is quite generous, isn't he?'

'Yes. But that's no concern of yours.'

'*Maybe...* maybe not.' She brushed by him, letting him get a whiff of her exotic scent and making him want to grab her and put her in her place. He didn't, then he wished he'd had when she said, 'I've heard American millionaires are fond of taking mistresses when it strikes them.'

'Don't try your tricks on Treyton Brady. He's in love with the countess,' Buck said, though it pained him to know that wasn't true. Trey could never love her the way *he* did, *damn him.*

'*No* man is immune if you catch him at the right moment.' She turned away from him, but not before he saw an impish smile light up her pretty face. 'Even you, Buck.'

What was she up to?

'Be careful, Irene. I have great respect for the countess. *Any* man would consider himself lucky to have her as his wife.'

Christ, he had to be careful or she'd suspect there was more to his relationship with Ava than he let on.

She lit her own cigarette, surprising him, then blew out the smoke. 'My, my, Buck, what bold words. I admit the countess *is* quite charming, though unsophisticated. I know life is dull in Scotland, but not *that* dull,' she said, eyeing him. 'Especially with *you* around to make it more exciting.'

Only a dead man would resist her charms when she dropped her fur-trimmed wrap and pulled him down on the settee. She knew how to play the game. She snuggled up close to him, whispering how much she'd missed him. He doubted that. Even lying, she was still beautiful, her breasts heaving up and down, her lips wet and luscious. Desire for him to make love to her consumed her.

What the hell had he gotten himself into?

Buck shifted his weight. He had the feeling it was going to be a long night. The woman with the golden-flecked eyes and light-colored hair was capable of sublime torture on a man to get what she wanted.

And she wanted something from *him*. But what?

'Take your mind out of the gutter, Irene. The Countess of Marbury needed my help to introduce her to a suitable match,' he said. 'I was more than happy to oblige.'

'You always were so direct, Buck. That's one thing I admire about you.' She ran her hand up and down his leg. Slowly. 'Among *other* things.'

'You haven't changed, Irene, have you?' God, she wasn't making it easy for him to resist her. Still, he had to play her game. For Ava's sake. 'Seducing every man who piques your interest.'

She didn't deny it.

'But *you've* changed, Buck,' she said. 'I see it in your eyes. You're in love. And it *isn't* with me.'

'You're jealous, Irene.'

He should have known she'd be up to her old tricks whenever a beautiful woman stole her spotlight.

She laughed off the idea. '*Me*, jealous? Of *her?* Hardly. Though for a moment I could have sworn you were in love with the countess. She has a certain *je ne sais quoi*, as if she's a different person from the one you described to me in London.'

'Then you think she's an imposter?' Buck ventured to ask. Her scent sparked, her eyes snapping with indignation that he would ask such a question. He'd let her have her way for too long, gone well beyond the line of a gentleman dealing with a woman who had once been his mistress.

He had to know where she stood.

'Of course not, Buck,' she said, smiling. 'Only a lady of noble blood with the regal bearing and impeccable manners of a countess would have the courage to challenge *me*.'

Buck smiled, relieved.

If Ava can fool Lady Pennington, she can fool anyone.

Irene pressed her breasts against him and brushed his lips with hers, a kiss as gentle as a summer breeze.

It had no effect on him.

What was wrong with him? Back in London, he'd be wondering what filmy lace underwear she was wearing beneath that tight dress.

Knock. Knock.

'What the bloody hell—' Buck said.

Irene laughed. 'It must be the bellboy. I'm having your things moved to my suite so you won't have to sneak down the hall.' She slid her hand underneath his jacket and toyed with the buttons on his trousers. 'Besides, it's cozier.'

'We'll see about that.'

While Irene pouted, Buck tipped the bellboy to return his things *back* to his rooms.

With the money Mrs Benn-Brady insisted he take for his expenses, he could pay for his own suite. He'd made a promise to keep Ava out of Irene's claws, but that didn't include allowing her ladyship to take over his life.

No woman controlled him.

With unanswered questions nagging him, Buck took his time assessing her, his eyes moving up and down her slender body, every curve accentuated by pure silk.

It all started to make sense.

'Enough of your games, Irene. Now tell me, what is the *real* reason you came to New York?'

* * *

Ava rushed through the lobby of the Waldorf. She was more unnerved by her encounter with Lady Pennington than she expected. Even allowing for the strain of the past few weeks, she couldn't come to grips with the effect the woman had had on her.

A trembling within her made her hands shake. Her head throbbed.

She bit down on her lip, fighting the temptation to cry.

Why in the name of heavens are you holding back, girl? Have a good cry. Then be done with it.

Cry? No, never.

You gave your word you'd go through with this marriage, but you'd best heal your heart first. Let him go, lass, or he will be the death of you.

The gilt clock in the main hallway chimed midnight.

All around her she heard corks popping, women laughing and the melodious strings of violins plucking out a lovely waltz. A sense of urgency hugged the air. This upper-class life with its finery and splendor was now *hers*, his lordship said.

Then he left. *With that woman.*

There was no escape.

Ava had known this day would come when Buck would rush back into the arms of Lady Pennington. Her carriage was as elegant as a haughty swan, her wit perilous to anyone she found threatening.

Ava hadn't expected to lose him so easily.

All night long she'd been imagining it was *Buck* she was engaged to, inhaling his masculine scent mixing with his black silk evening clothes, touching his forearm, feeling the contour of his hard muscle.

And now that dream had ended.

His job finished, he was gone from her life. When the story of her success hit the morning newspapers, she had no doubt Mrs Benn-Brady would announce her engagement to Trey at the charity dinner Saturday night.

What did it matter *when* she married Trey? Once she became the wife of the New York millionaire, Ava O'Reilly would be gone forever and she'd be safe.

Ava was trembling with frustration as she wound her way through the throng of people threading in and out of the tall columns of Sienna marble to get from one end of the hotel to the other.

With a deep sigh, she pushed through the revolving door leading to the street.

She hurried into the waiting limousine with Trey behind her. Ava insisted he order the car and take her home. She had to accept the inevitable. She would never be more than a passing fancy to his lordship. A way to pass the time aboard the luxurious liner, a frolic with a pretty maid. Perfect for a gentleman gambler.

No one could have foreseen the unbelievable series of events that had changed their lives.

All that mattered to Buck was winning his bet and making a lady out of her.

All that mattered to her was getting back to her room and sobbing her heart out. Then she'd be all right. She *had* to be.

'I found Lady Pennington quite charming,' Trey said with more than a hint of interest in his voice as the driver took off toward the Benn-Brady Fifth Avenue residence.

'If you call a serpent with blonde hair charming.'

She'd found the woman distant and fascinating, a creature who lured unsuspecting males into her web.

All except Buck. That's what made him so attractive to her. She hadn't given up until she'd finally snared him.

'Buck can take care of himself,' Trey said as if reading her thoughts. He waved to the crowd gathered on the sidewalk outside the hotel.

'He made that quite clear.' Ava pulled off her gloves, loosening a button, then two in her haste.

'I don't understand why he let that woman back in his life,' Trey said, taking her hand in his. 'Aboard the *Carpathia*, I *swore* he was in love with you.'

Ava looked at him directly. 'We were both wrong, weren't we?'

Tears filled her eyes, then before she could stop them, fell over her cheeks, streaking her powder and wetting her lips. She licked them dry, the salty taste lingering on her tongue. Trey sensed her disheartened spirit and withdrew his hand. He didn't try to kiss her.

Ava squeezed her eyes tight. She should be the happiest woman in the world. She'd proven to all New York she was the Countess of Marbury.

She *should* be, but she wasn't.

And it was all his lordship's fault.

38

3 May 1912

'I've been expecting you, Captain Lord Blackthorn,' Mrs Benn-Brady said, her voice as smooth as the mauve silk of her day gown and her curiosity as obvious as the large emerald-cut diamond ring squeezing her forefinger. She leaned forward in anticipation. 'Well, out with it.'

'You *know* why I'm here?' Buck said, surprised.

'It must be important, your lordship. You demanded to see me, pounding on the front door at the first sign of daylight.'

She bade him sit down in her private study while the housemaid opened the deep green taffeta drapes. A diffused light crept into the room with its teal velvet writing desk equipped with a telephone and Empire chairs covered with plum linen. Spring daffodils stood up tall in a red Chinese vase and embraced what little sunlight there was.

So much had changed since last night. Shortly after Buck had left Lady Pennington sulking in her expensive suite, he'd raced back to the Palm Room, but Ava had already left.

Frustrated, he took a taxi to the Fifth Avenue residence, then decided against barging in at that time of night. What he had to say would take some planning. After what Irene had told him, he couldn't go through with this insanity any longer.

He wanted Ava back.

Would it be so wrong? He would never have this opportunity again. What harm could come from fighting for her, from speaking his mind and using the faith she'd instilled in him to believe that *anything* was possible.

Buck had racked his brain all night, trying to figure out what to do. In the end, there was only one way out of this mess.

For that, he needed Mrs Benn-Brady's help.

'I've come about Ava—' he began.

'You're in love with the countess,' she said with a calmness he didn't feel.

Buck froze. And strangely, he didn't doubt for a moment she had known all along. 'When did you first suspect my feelings for her, Mrs Benn-Brady?'

'The night the *Carpathia* arrived. The docks were filled with anxious people grabbing each other, hoping to find a loved one, with excited reporters following them around like hungry cats.' She paused, observing him. 'It was obvious, the way you acted so protective toward her, while Trey... well, my son is a good man, but spoiled rotten. I've made many mistakes with him. It's time I fixed this one.'

Her sentiment toward him was unexpected. She'd struck him more as a woman who had perfected the art of ignoring what she didn't want to see and covering up her mistakes with convenient lies.

He tried to imagine Trey as a child drawing comfort from the motherly touch of this woman. Someone who loved him, who would heal his sorrows and patch up his bruises. Instead he saw Mrs Benn-Brady more as a woman who couldn't afford to show any weakness in front of anyone, even her son.

'If you knew how I felt about the countess,' Buck asked, 'why did you invite me into your home and encourage me to instruct her in the social graces?'

'At first I thought it would be amusing to see if *she* was in love with you. I must say, it's been fascinating, watching you two together, trying to deny what is so apparent to everyone, even Trey.'

'Did he—'

'No, he never said a word. He'll do as I ask to get his inheritance, nothing more. That saddens me, but I can't change it.' She withdrew a fresh yellow daffodil from the vase and inhaled its scent. 'Such a sweet fragrance, but its loveliness will fade if it's left to wither. It would be a pity if the same thing happened to the countess.'

'I don't follow you, madam.' Her words irritated him more than he cared to admit, though he was reluctant to tell her that.

'She's trapped by her feelings for you. She'll never love anyone else.' Her eyes were so bright when she looked at him, Buck didn't know whether it was a request or command when she said, 'Why didn't you marry the girl when you had the chance?'

'I have nothing to offer her,' Buck said honestly. 'Everything I had was lost when the ship sank.' He could still hear the screams of the passengers jumping into the cold, freezing sea, hear their pitiful cries for help, and he wondered again why *he'd* survived and others didn't.

Mrs Benn-Brady's eyes sharpened. 'A girl like that doesn't care about money. It's *you* she wants.'

Strange words that he never expected to hear from this society *grande dame*. He regarded her closer, the deep gray of her hair showing only at the temples, her finely penciled brows giving her face a queenly lift. She hid her humble past well.

'I shouldn't have come here. I have no right to jeopardize Ava's future with Trey,' Buck said with a determination in his voice that sounded more like a growl.

'And what kind of future is that? Fancy balls and nights at the opera? A husband who has no purpose in life? Silly women with nary a serious thought in their heads, all vying with each other to see who has the most elegant frock or the best cook?' Mrs Benn-Brady threw her arms up in the air. 'That's not a life for her. She's untamed and unspoiled and needs a fine man like you. Go to her and tell her how you feel.'

'What about the marriage contract she signed?' he asked, still suspicious of her intentions. Using the handwritten letter by the countess as a guide, Ava had executed her signature perfectly.

Mrs Benn-Brady smiled, the corners of her mouth crinkling. 'Tear it up. You have my blessing to pursue the countess, your lordship... *Buck*, if I may call you that. What are your plans?'

'I intend to stay in America, Mrs Benn-Brady. I've had a fine education and I have a good Army record. That will take me places.'

He'd never reveal to her that Ava couldn't return to Ireland and he'd made a bet to pass her off as the countess.

'What about Trey?' he asked.

'I have no doubt the dear boy will find himself another peeress.' She beckoned the footman to serve the tea with toast and sweet blueberry jelly. 'He can book passage on a ship to England after he recovers from his disappointment.'

Now it was Buck's turn to smile. 'He may not have to, Mrs Benn-Brady.'

'You mean Lady Pennington?' she said coyly, and then helped herself to a liberal spoonful of blueberry jelly on her toast.

'Yes,' he said, surprised. He left his tea untouched. 'How did you know?'

'I have my spies,' she said, consuming her breakfast quickly. She was eager to continue the conversation. 'I heard all about what happened last night in Peacock Alley and later at the Palm Room. Her ladyship has an impressive pedigree. Daughter of a baron, widow of a lord. I don't see why she would be interested in my son.'

Buck dropped his voice low so they wouldn't be overheard, and then spoke slowly. 'Her ladyship received a distressing telegram aboard ship from her late husband's solicitor. After all his lordship's debts were paid and his books audited, there was little left for his grieving widow.'

He went on to explain Lord Pennington had made the mistake of investing his fortune in a failed company abroad. No doubt the shock of losing everything had brought about his early demise.

'Shall we say the lioness is on the hunt again?' Buck said with a hint of the devil in his smile. It hadn't taken him long to figure out her scheme. Her eagerness to meet the countess and flirting with Trey. Then trying to seduce *him* to find out about his old friend's financial interests.

'Now that *is* a fascinating possibility. Lady Pennington strikes me as a woman who knows her primary duty in life is confined to looking beautiful and well-bred.' She twisted the large diamond ring on her forefinger nervously.

Mrs Benn-Brady thought a moment, then smiled to herself.

'My dinner guests are expecting a big announcement tomorrow night at the charity event for the *Titanic* survivors. I don't intend to disappoint them. I will introduce the countess as my esteemed guest then... well, you'll see.' She pushed away her breakfast tea and empty plate and walked over to the telephone on the desk. 'I knew this contraption was good for something. Leave everything to me.'

39

4 May 1912

The pink satin corset pinched her ribs so tight Ava couldn't breathe.

Blanche, her bouncy lady's maid, hadn't stopped chattering about Ava's small waist and lovely shoulders. *Perfect* to show off at tonight's party, she'd said, and then off she went to get her ladyship's gown – leaving Ava alone in her bedroom, pulling and tugging on the long lacings on her corset.

She was all in a tempest, wanting to pull out the pins in her hair and let it swirl around her shoulders like hell's fire. She should have fought harder for the man she loved, but time had run out for her. She'd give it all up to spend those restless nights again on the *Carpathia*, sleeping on the floor next to his lordship, listening to him breathe, then wrapping his arm around her when no one was looking.

There was no use crying for what she couldn't have. She had agreed to his lordship's plan and now she had to pay the price.

Ava opened the window and a hint of springtime found its way inside.

Now Fifth Avenue was her home.

She took a deep breath and smelled the violet and iris perfumes of the ladies strolling along the fashionable avenue below and heard the honking horns of motorcars. So unlike Queenstown with its cooked cabbages and salty smell of the sea.

No holy saint could change her back into Ava O'Reilly.

The voices in her head had been quiet since that night at the Waldorf. As if no one listened to her sorry self, praying for guidance.

Tonight she would be introduced to Mrs Benn-Brady's society friends as Trey's fiancée, the Countess of Marbury.

Sweet Jesus, what would Mary Dolores say?

All she knew was what Ava had written to her.

My dear sister Mary Dolores,
Don't worry if you don't see my name on the list of survivors. I'm safe in America. I have a job in a grand house in New York and I'll write to you soon. With lots of love, Ava.

It was all she dared tell her until she could send for her.

She laughed with glee. What a time they would have then with Mary Dolores not believing her sister was a grand lady *and* a countess.

It wasn't as simple with the countess's butler, Benson.

Ava lost her smile. Copying Fiona's handwriting, she'd penned him a letter and told him that the countess had gotten into a lifeboat and was saved. She could never tell him the truth.

She could never tell anyone.

Thinking about Fiona with her gentle ways and fierce love for his lordship, Ava vowed then to use her position as a society lady to help the *Titanic* survivors and collect money for the relief fund. Then something fine and holy would come of her grand pretense.

And so Ava, who'd never asked to be a countess, who'd never dreamed she'd ever wear silks and velvets, was determined to make it her mission to help those injured when the ship went down and who needed financial assistance.

That didn't mean her heart would ever heal. There was one man she'd never forget and would always love.

Captain Lord Buck Blackthorn.

When they'd walked through Peacock Alley and he'd leaned down to whisper in her ear, it had pulled her back to the night they'd clung to each other in his cabin. Each knowing it couldn't last in the class-divided world they lived in, but they couldn't resist grabbing onto a stolen dream.

Standing in her underwear, Ava let out a deep sigh and shivered with delight as those wonderful thoughts soothed her while she waited for Blanche to bring her gown.

When the door opened, it wasn't Blanche who barged in, but Mrs Benn-Brady, looking very smug. She was the epitome of elegance in her deep gold satin gown with a black chiffon overskirt and exquisite embroidery around the waist. Diamonds and white crystals gleamed through the veiling on her skirt as she walked.

'There's been a change of plans, Countess,' she said.

'I don't understand, Mrs Benn-Brady.'

'You're not to wear the blue dress tonight.'

What was she about?

The woman had made such a fuss over picking out what *she* considered the perfect gown for the dinner party. An empire blue satin draped dress with a pink chiffon overlay embroidered with delicate jet beads.

Why the change?

Standing in front of the French maid, partly cloaked by shadows, Mrs Benn-Brady stepped aside and her eyes flashed with brilliance when Blanche came forward, her arms filled with white satin and filmy netting.

Ava's jaw dropped. So beautiful a gown could only have been fashioned by nimble fairy fingers.

The maid held up a clinging white gown made from satin-faced organza, a richly beaded and embroidered satin that draped softly around the body with cap sleeves dripping with silver Bordeaux lace.

Ava let out a sigh of pure female pleasure when she ran her hand over the white satin ribbon trim and marveled at the yards and yards of ivory net covered with silk flowers and pearls that formed a long, elegant train.

A gown fit for a princess. And she was just a countess.

'Magnificent, isn't it?' said Mrs Benn-Brady. 'It lends extreme grace to a woman's figure and shows off her curves.'

She cast her a quick glance, making the girl blush.

'Why am I to wear this dress, madam?' Ava asked. 'A *white* dress.'

'Don't ask any questions, Countess, just do as I say.'

The bemused expression on her face left no doubt it was a command.

Ava knew something had changed and it had more to do with this dress than the woman was telling her. Could it have something to do with her obsession with the royals?

The Irish girl smiled back as she wiggled into the gown with Blanche helping her, but it was not a smile of submission. Ava guessed what was going on and her smile said so.

The society matron wished to show her off in a white *court* dress.

Glory be, would she be forced to make a grand curtsy in front of everyone?

There was no doubt in her mind Mrs Benn-Brady was excited about something as she chatted on about the exclusivity of her guest list and how excited she was that Fleischman's could fulfill her flower order on such short notice. All day long the fragrant bouquets arrived until the mansion was overflowing with vibrant blooms and fresh-smelling greenery.

As the maid finished buttoning up Ava's dress, they heard a knock on the door. It was Niles. He whispered something in Mrs Benn-Brady's ear.

'Tell him to wait. I won't be but a moment.'

Who could it be? Not Trey. She'd seen him leave for the Waldorf and his cronies.

Buck? He was the guest of honor tonight. Why would he arrive so early?

She had no time to think about it as Mrs Benn-Brady circled her, studying every seeded pearl on her gown. 'Perfect,' she said, 'but there's one thing missing.' She turned to Blanche. 'Hand me my Tossar tiara.'

'Oui, madame.' The maid snapped open a round mahogany box and Mrs Benn-Brady lifted the most exquisite tiara Ava could have imagined off a sea of black velvet. The elegant headpiece consisted of a diamond flower spray with seven large emeralds mounted atop the diamonds.

'Oh, it's beautiful!' she said, her voice barely a whisper. The society matron set the Victorian tiara on Ava's head as if she were performing a coronation.

'Emeralds contrast well with your hair, my dear Countess,' said Mrs Benn-Brady, finally giving her approval of Ava's red hair. She added that the tiara had originally been designed for a Russian princess, with jewels captured from an emissary of Napoleon during the Battle of Waterloo. It was later reset for a lady-in-waiting in Queen Victoria's court.

Ava didn't dare move her head. She had a great desire at that moment to cry for the pure joy of it. Never had she dreamed the likes of her would wear a crown.

'When I first met you,' the society matron continued, 'I said you had the title and I had the tiara. Now *you* shall have the tiara.'

'And *you* the title, Mrs Benn-Brady.'

She waved her hand. 'Not yet, Countess. Things don't always work out as planned, though I shall have the pleasure of impressing my guests tonight with an even *bigger* surprise.'

'Surprise?' Ava asked, curious.

'Yes, but it's a secret.' Laughing to herself, she left, but didn't close the door behind her, leaving it open slightly.

Surprise, was it? By the saints, what was going on?

Ava listened to each beat of her heart. The sound seemed to fill her ears, leaving no room for the words the maid was saying to her, fussing with her hair and setting the tiara in place. She wasn't listening.

Buck was there. Outside her bedroom, breathing hard, waiting. She had no doubt. Though she couldn't see him or catch even the slightest glimpse of his broad shoulders, his pure masculine scent lingered. She *knew* he was there. Waiting for her. But why?

To see her one last time before he collected on his bet, then vanished into the night with Lady Pennington?

'Shall I bring your white opera gloves, Countess?' Blanche asked, a twinkle in her eye. She nodded toward the door.

'That would be lovely, Blanche,' Ava said, smiling. The French girl understood. She scurried from the bedroom, but she left the door open wide enough so Ava could listen to the conversation in the hallway.

'Is everything ready for tonight, Mrs Benn-Brady?' she heard Buck say. Suddenly her pulse was beating rapidly.

The society matron chuckled. 'Yes, the countess doesn't suspect a thing.'

'Excellent. I wouldn't want to frighten her off.'

'Even *you* can't tame that wildness in her, Buck, though I have to admit I like that about her.' She rustled her silk skirts. 'I haven't had this much fun since Mr Brady and I woke up the local judge at three in the morning to marry us.'

Then their voices faded down the long hallway, both laughing.

What were his lordship and Mrs Benn-Brady planning? His words had penetrated deep in her soul when he'd said she might run away. No, never. This charity dinner was too important. For the *Titanic* survivors. For Buck. And for her.

It was Ava's way of paying homage to the countess.

Yet the moment she'd heard Buck's voice, something inside her had stirred. She felt sad she'd lost him, but strong. He hadn't merely changed her life. He'd changed *her*. She still had that wild streak, but he had turned her into a lady. Now it was her turn to do good with it.

She'd given him her word she'd go through with this marriage—

Wait... that was it! A wedding.

Here. Tonight.

At the Benn-Brady residence on Fifth Avenue. They'd made all the arrangements.

She was going to marry Trey in front of New York society.

Divine mercy, she was now in God's hands.

* * *

She was a beauty in white.

Buck stood very still, tugging on his high collar and loosening his white tie. His eyes fixed on Ava's pretty face. All night long he wrestled with how he'd feel when he saw her and now he had the feeling the ground had been swept from beneath him.

Standing at the top of the marble staircase under a bower of white roses, orchids and lilies, she was dressed like an angel, a halo of diamonds and emeralds setting off her upswept red hair.

Gorgeous, but unattainable.

To all but him. *If* his luck held.

Their eyes met and a quick flash of desire swept across her face. Her lips parted, but she didn't speak. Instead, she floated down the stairs with the distinguished grace and elegant air of a great lady.

Exactly as he'd taught her.

'I was right, Buck, you *are* in love with her.' Irene swished her train around her like a dragon's tail to get his attention. Dressed in a silver lamé gown that hugged her figure, the blonde waved about the red ostrich feather in her hair, causing the rubies at her throat and around her wrists to spark like fire. A long white ermine stole hung off one bare shoulder and trailed behind her.

'Does it bother you, Irene?' He didn't deny it.

'Surprisingly, no, Buck. Once I realized I had more debts than diamonds, I knew our relationship could never be more than an affair.' Smiling at him, she straightened his tie. 'I'll miss you terribly.' She gave him a look of longing, but it didn't last. Buck could see Trey smiling at her from across the room. 'Then again, we have our scruples, don't we?'

'Yes, we do, Irene,' Buck said with a sly smile. 'I must warn you, Trey is quite the ladies' man.'

'So I've heard.' Irene wiggled her shoulders and her ermine stole fell away, revealing her stunning figure. 'Not jealous, are you?'

'Should I be?'

She gave him a dazzling smile, inviting him to light her cigarette, he didn't, then she was off.

Buck looked around for Ava, but she was busily engaged with a dapper gentleman who couldn't take his eyes off her. *What man could?*

When she caught him staring at her, she turned away. No doubt she had seen Irene hovering around him with a possessive air.

Didn't the Irish girl know he was in love with *her?*

So was New York society.

He couldn't get near her. It was all Mrs Benn-Brady's doing. She knew how to play the game to her advantage. She'd introduced her aristocratic guests one at a time.

First, Lady Pennington.

Then it was his turn as her guest of honor. But she held the best for last.

The Countess of Marbury.

Buck had to admit the society matron had great organizing ability, brains and a flair for the dramatic. While another party was in full swing this evening at a Fifth Avenue palace with the archduke of an eastern European country as the main attraction, society's elite flocked instead to her soiree.

Not only to see him, but to show support for the *Titanic* survivors.

He felt privileged to make that happen. He knew the ladies would be divided into two arenas. Ladies who came to see if he lived up to his scandalous reputation and ladies who came to try to add to that reputation. Their claws had been out to get him since his name first appeared on the list of survivors.

They wanted to see who the next lady of his favor would be. They believed Lady Pennington couldn't compare to their New York debutantes.

A wry smile set his nerves on edge. The only woman he wanted was the one he couldn't have.

Ava.

Until now.

Before he could make his way over to her, several guests came up to him, asking about the fateful voyage. After answering their questions, he maneuvered his way over to where Ava was deep in conversation with several guests. He could see she was a spectacular success with everyone begging to be introduced to her. He tried to speak to her, but she was whisked off by a pair of ladies eager to be seen chatting with her as if they were old friends.

'The mayor has just arrived, your lordship,' Mrs Benn-Brady said, using his title in front of her guests to impress them. She was beside herself, showing off her trio of aristocrats. 'He asked to meet you.'

'Excellent,' Buck said. 'I want to thank him for coming and for his help in securing a special license.'

'The mayor tells me the relief fund has raised over a hundred thousand dollars so far,' Mrs Benn-Brady said. 'My spies tell me we'll *double* that amount before the night is over.'

He was pleasantly surprised. It heartened him to realize how giving these American millionaires with all their extravagance could be.

He said, 'This dinner party must be costing you twice that figure, Mrs Benn-Brady.'

She smiled wide. 'What's the use of having it if you can't flaunt it?'

A curious frown crossed Buck's brow. 'Did I notice a reporter from the *New York Times* among the crowd?'

'Why not? Publicity is the life blood of society,' she said, beaming. 'He's here to cover the wedding.'

Buck frowned, finding irony in the moment. 'I haven't asked Ava to marry me yet.'

'You'd better do it quickly, your lordship,' said Mrs Benn-Brady, regarding him with a touch of anxiety she made no effort to conceal. 'Dinner is about to be served.'

* * *

Ava's heart sank when she saw Buck with Lady Irene Pennington. How could he flaunt that woman?

It was a sin unto itself like no other. The woman was as brazen as the devil.

Her lips tightened.

Ava was hurt, but she'd not let him see it.

She ignored him, but his eyes followed her everywhere.

She let out a sigh of relief when she discovered she wasn't seated next to Buck at dinner. Why prolong her agony?

That didn't stop him from torturing her.

'Ava, I *must* speak to you.'

'Shouldn't you take your seat before your soup gets cold?' Ava lowered her head, as if signaling an end to the conversation.

'Listen to me, *Countess*,' Buck said, his frustrated tone giving away his underlying emotions. 'I've put up with your rebel ways long enough. I have something to say to you, and by *damn*, you're going to listen to me.'

The lady on her left choked on her asparagus tops as Buck leaned closer to her and whispered in her ear. The man on her left was speaking so loudly, Ava couldn't hear what his lordship said.

'I believe Lady Pennington needs someone to light her cigarette, your *lordship*,' she shot back.

'She can light it herself.'

Then, frustrated, he stomped off, leaving Ava to wonder what all the fuss was about.

Pride prevented her from going after him.

All the while Ava was thinking about how *her* life was like the pieces of her mother's rosary she kept hidden in her dresser.

Tangled and broken.

Warm memories that would always remind her who she was, along with the countess's letter, the folded-up menu from the first-class dining saloon aboard ship, her ladyship's red lace shawl—

And her third-class ticket for passage aboard the *Titanic*.

She kept her eyes lowered, her lashes wet and her heart heavy. Everyone had been so full of hope on that hushed morning when they boarded the ship at Queenstown.

And now so many of them were gone.

Beautiful souls taken too soon.

Oh, Lord, what a bloody fool she was. Thinking about herself, when she should be thinking about the countess and all the others who died that night.

An unholy chill made her quiver. Would that icy feeling ever go away?

As each course was presented, Ava peeked at Buck from out of the corner of her eye. He appeared nervous, his face sweating, but when he turned his head, she could see his proud profile. So noble, but there was something about his behavior that disturbed her. Something that moved her in a manner that had nothing to do with her bruised feminine ego. Something bigger than the both of them.

What was he trying to tell her?

After tea, fruit, and coffee had been served, Mrs Benn-Brady stood up from her place at the head of the long table and tapped her glass with a gold teaspoon. She thanked her guests for coming and for their generosity in helping the *Titanic* survivors, many of whom still found themselves housed in the city's shelter for the homeless.

'And now a word from our guest of honor, Captain Lord James Buck Blackthorn,' Mrs Benn-Brady said, clapping her hands. The others joined her in welcoming Buck as he rose from his seat.

He looked up and down the long table of dinner guests consisting of the charmed circle of New York society waiting to hear his story, each one hoping to catch his eye.

His gaze stopped on Ava.

She sat up straighter, her eyes glistening with tears as she listened to Buck speak about that fateful night. How the *Titanic* raced through ice-infested waters on what was an unusually calm sea, the blackness of the night with so many stars in the sky it was as if the heavens were trying to guide the liner through the danger.

But nothing could save the ship.

'For the next two and a half hours, every man, woman and child lived through the horrible reality that lay between the hope we had for rescue and the gnawing in our gut that said many would die,' Buck said. 'I'll never forget their faces. The young Marconi operator who worked the wireless until the power failed, the diligent ship's officers who stayed at their posts even when the ship foundered, the first cabin ladies who questioned why they had to get into the lifeboats while their husbands stayed behind.'

He inhaled a deep breath, then let it out slowly, wiping the perspiration from his face, his eyes burning like hot coals as the wrenching memories overtook him. The dinner guests held their breath.

No one moved.

'My heart broke when I saw an emigrant family with small children clinging to their mother's skirt make their way up on top only to discover all the lifeboats were gone,' Buck continued. 'I'll never forget the unmarried lady who gave up her seat in the lifeboat so her friend might live to see her children again. Or the elegant gentlemen standing bravely on deck when the liner went down, taking their place next to the faithful kneeling in prayer as a priest called on God to welcome all their souls.'

He paused, then said, 'My heart bleeds when I think about the unbelievable heroism of the ship's musicians who played until the end. Their courage serves as an inspiration to us all. I believe their music still echoes over the dark waters of the North Atlantic, reminding us that everyone who survived that harrowing night *must* tell their story. Mine is but one of many.'

Ava shivered, the clammy smell of ice visiting her again as she surrendered herself to her memories, but feeling strangely free, as if a great burden had been lifted from her soul. Buck spoke for every survivor, his deep voice rich with emotion, his words capturing every moment with such realism, a blur of images from that night rushed through her mind.

A sea like glass.

The bitter cold.

The women in the lifeboat whispering, 'She's gone' when the ship disappeared.

Buck was so brave, nearly drowning to save others. Swimming in the freezing water to find her, then struggling to hold her in his arms when he reached the *Carpathia* half-dead.

She couldn't help herself. She fell in love with him all over again.

'As a gentleman, my duty was to the ladies,' Buck said, 'but I'm no hero. I did what any man would do in *any* class. Get the women and children into the lifeboats, help a gentleman caught in the icy waters by giving him my lifebelt. And do my best to save the woman I love.'

Ava's heart skipped when he looked directly at her. What was he about? Saying such a thing in front of all these people?

He continued, 'I saw what needed to be done and God willing, I had the strength to do it. All I ask, ladies and gentlemen, is that *you* never forget the victims and the survivors of the *Titanic*. Thank you.' Applause.

Ava gathered her long white train over her arm and rushed to his side. Her lips trembled as she burst out with the words, 'You were wonderful, Buck. No one could have expressed the terror we faced better than you. The fear of death as well as the belief help would come, then knowing it wouldn't for so many... and finally, the unsettling peace that came with the dawn.'

She waited and saw him gazing down at her with an expression so reminiscent of how he looked that night when he kissed her, not knowing if he would ever see her again.

'Ava, my darling,' was all he said.

There was a moment of utter silence as they looked at each other. Buck was staring at her in an odd way, perspiration running down the sides of his handsome face. He waited for her to speak. She couldn't.

Darling, he'd called her. Had she heard right?

The loud murmur of the crowd broke the spell, sending Buck into action. Before a swell of people enveloped them, he pulled her aside. She looked over her shoulder and saw Mrs Benn-Brady again tapping her glass with her spoon, then making an announcement that the after-dinner entertainment would begin shortly and for everyone to take their seats in the drawing room.

That left Ava alone with his lordship.

'You won't get away from me this time, Ava,' he said, a deep huskiness coloring his voice. His eyes darkened into black pools, making it clear he would take no nonsense from her.

'Don't say a word, Buck,' she said, her pent-up feelings bringing her close to tears. 'I know what Mrs Benn-Brady is planning for her big surprise tonight.'

'You *do?*' he asked, not understanding. His expression changed to surprise. 'It was supposed to be a secret.'

'The mayor is going to marry Trey and me... *isn't he?*' she asked, her courage suddenly leaving her.

Look at him. Strong and handsome. How could she give him up?

She closed her eyes and a tremor slithered through her, such a delicious sensation it was. When she was brave enough to open her eyes, she saw that his gaze blazed at her as he fought to keep control. His jaw was clenched, as if he was holding back from taking her in his arms.

She had never seen him look so serious. There was an edge to how he moved, and then he grabbed her by the shoulders and stood there. Not speaking. Breathing hard.

'Not exactly...'

'Sweet saints, you're telling me the marriage is off?'

'Well...'

'Oh, Lord, I'm a fool. Mrs Benn-Brady found out I'm not the countess... and she wants to send me back to Ireland.' She lifted her head, stomped her foot. 'I'll not go. She can have her tiara and her grand ways. I'm staying here in America because... because...'

She fumbled for the words, wrinkling her white satin gown with her clenched fists.

Buck held her tight by the shoulders. His eyes pierced her heart when he said, 'Because why, Ava? Tell me.'

Ava puffed up her chest and all her pent-up emotion came gushing out of her. 'Because I love you with all my heart.'

'Oh, my darling, you're not going anywhere. You're going to marry *me*.' He held her tighter, his breath coming harder. His eyes searched hers as she blinked several times, believing she'd fainted and his proposal was but a lovely dream come to give her courage.

'*You?* Tonight?' Ava asked, her heart fluttering. She took a step back, her wits flying about her like goose feathers dancing on a breeze. Such beautiful words he'd said, but *no*, it couldn't be true.

A familiar ache in her heart swelled, her whole body trembling from the want of him.

Just one more moment with his lordship... the man I truly love... please.

Then when she thought she'd wake up and be thrown into despair—

'Yes, Ava. We're getting married... if you agree.' He held her close to his chest and she could hear his heart pounding. 'Oh, you crazy, wonderful girl, do you think I could ever let you go? You're my reason for living.'

Ava cried out with such joy, the tiara slipped off her head. 'Sweet Jesus, it must be angels I hear singing in my ears,' she said, feeling dizzy. 'I think I'm going to faint.'

* * *

'By the power invested in me by the state of New York, I now pronounce you man and wife.' With a twinkle in his eye, Mayor William J. Gaynor cleared his throat and turned to Buck. 'You may now kiss the bride, your lordship.'

'Thank you, Your Honor.' Without another word, he took Ava into his arms. He felt her trembling, her heart beating wildly, but no more wildly than his. Her kiss was filled with passion and he kissed her deeper, possessing his bride with a promise more binding than a kiss.

A promise he'd made on that starry night when the ship went down. That if he found her again, he'd never let her go.

It seemed impossible then, but she was here in his arms. He knew a vibrant joy and held a sincere belief in the future he never believed possible. Because of her. He'd never forget how the cream of New York society had watched him slide a plain gold band on Ava's finger, though he tensed when she stumbled over the part where she *promised to obey.*

He'd not have her any other way.

'It's more beautiful than any diamond,' she whispered to him after they broke the kiss, clasping the gold ring close to her heart.

'No more beautiful than you,' he said, then he kissed her again.

Tears filled the ladies' eyes, envy in the gentlemen's.

He couldn't wait to be alone with her.

But not before they held court seated on a splendid divan covered with plush red silk cushions and were placed on a raised platform where New York society could pay homage to them.

Buck was impressed with how Ava handled herself. She was more than a paragon of breeding, but a warm, generous lady. She never faltered in answering questions about the *Titanic*, though he knew her heart was breaking.

Fiona would have been so proud of her.

'This is a night *no one* will forget,' Mrs Benn-Brady whispered, smiling for the camera, then leading Buck and his bride to a quiet corner. A quartet began to play Brahms as a subtle diversion to encourage the guests to chat among themselves.

'What about Trey?' Ava asked, concerned.

She nodded toward her son and Lady Pennington wrapped up in champagne and in each other. 'I have a feeling there will be an official announcement of an engagement in the near future.'

Ava pulled the pins from her hair and removed the tiara. 'This belongs to you, Mrs Benn-Brady.'

'What am I going to do with it?' she said, pretending to be insulted. 'Keep it in a stuffy old box? It's yours, my dear Countess. Wear it proudly, knowing you made an old woman very happy.'

She smiled graciously, then went on her way, taking compliments from her lingering guests. He saw the society matron holding court as if she were the queen of the ball. She had everything she wanted.

Time to think of Ava.

'Let's sneak away from here,' Buck said. He loved her, and if he had to go through nearly drowning in the icy, cold water to be worthy of her, he'd do it again.

She belonged to him, and as long as he could tell her that for the rest of their lives, he'd be a happy man.

'Do we dare?' she asked. Her eyes told him she wanted him as much as he wanted her.

He pulled her close to him.

'Mrs Benn-Brady will never miss us,' Buck said. 'I'd bet on it.'

* * *

Waldorf Hotel
5 May 1912
1 a.m.

Ava settled into his lordship's arms as easily as if St Michael himself carried her through the gates of heaven. But it wasn't a foamy mist of clouds and good deeds that swirled around his feet as he carried her over the threshold, but plush white carpet.

And into the bridal suite at the Waldorf.

It didn't seem real. Her eye wandered everywhere, taking in the walls and ceiling decorated in white and gold, the Parisian furniture covered with blue brocade and gold fringe and the large marble fireplace with beveled Italian mirrors over the mantelpiece.

'A kiss for your husband, Ava,' Buck said, nuzzling his face in her hair. She grabbed him tighter around the neck.

'Is that *all* you want from me?' she said, looking squarely at him, teasing him.

'I want your undying love,' he said, his voice husky and deep, assuring her she was the only woman who mattered to him. Then in a playful manner he added, '*And* a romp between the sheets.'

His gaze traveled over to the canopied four-poster half-covered in shadows that deepened as golden lighting bounced off the white damask walls. He'd had his things moved to the luxurious bridal suite.

Ava knew he could well afford it. Trey had insisted on paying off the bet.

'A wedding present, old boy,' he said, and then he kissed the bride.

Finally they were alone.

Without a word, Buck laid her tiara on the round writing desk next to the gramophone, then turned her around and helped her out of her wedding garments except for her corset, chemise, stockings and slippers. Then he removed his shirt and tie. 'I want to make love to you every night.'

'Oh, do you?'

'Yes, but first...'

He flicked a switch on the gramophone and the strains of a sensuous tango filled the room. 'Shall we dance, Countess?'

She smiled, then kicked off her satin slippers. 'With pleasure, your lordship.'

Then Buck pulled her into his arms, his bare chest pressed against her breasts, sending her out of control. She didn't want to pull away, she *never* wanted to leave him.

The savory seduction of the tango and his tall, strong body pressing up against hers intensified an ache to have him make love to her, her heart drumming to the beat of each sensual dance step reaching down deep into her soul.

Just when Ava thought she could stand no more, he twirled her around and dipped her, his lips kissing her at last.

Then he took her with so much love, she couldn't stand it. She moaned and threw her head back, her body closing around him.

'I love you, Ava,' he said, holding onto her, tight and hard.

'I love you, too, my darling.'

And with a deepening pull to her heart, Ava knew the girl she was when she boarded the ship of dreams was gone. She was now a woman.

His woman.

And it was the grandest dream of all.

EPILOGUE

New York City
Spring, 1962

'Oh, Gram, that's the most beautiful story I've ever heard,' Elizabeth said, her eyes glowing with excitement. She sat still, her hands folded in her lap, the enchantment of all that was the *Titanic* overwhelming her.

Going back to that glorious time in her life hadn't been easy for Ava. There was an urgency in her to tell her granddaughter the truth. The girl needed to know and she prayed she'd understand the cold, hard facts that drove her to do what she had. The truth had lay hidden for far too long.

So she told her the story of Ava O'Reilly and the *Titanic*.

'It's not finished yet. There's Fiona to consider,' Ava said, her tone reverent as if the countess were sitting here with them in her New York penthouse. 'I have to make things right.'

'What do you mean?' Elizabeth asked, curious.

'I'm going to the press with my story.' Her tone was defiant, her heart racing with the thought of what that meant, of digging up the past that lay buried for so long. She could give the countess peace at last. She deserved no less.

'I'm so proud of you, Gram.'

Her granddaughter hugged her with a youthful enthusiasm that touched her with a flurry of emotions she hadn't expected. Warmth. Joy. And hope.

A fine girl she is, lass. Reminds you of yourself, doesn't she?

'It's the only way, Elizabeth,' Ava said, looking into the large mirror over the fireplace, expecting to see the girl she was. Instead she saw a face etched with the fine lines of a life lived, her green eyes full of secrets. No more.

'What's the only way, my love?'

Ava and Elizabeth turned to see Buck enter the room, his shoulders still broad, his hair flecked with gray, but his masculine presence as powerful as it was the night he had swum in the icy waters of the North Atlantic looking for her.

After all these years, Ava's heart still melted when she heard his deep voice and looked into his dark, brooding eyes. He was a fine husband and a man whose strength never wavered.

He would need that strength now.

After they repeated their marriage vows before a priest in a small church in Brooklyn, Ava and his lordship had gone west to San Francisco, a city rebuilt after the quake. There in the West they started a new life together, making a fortune in land speculation. They had lost nearly everything in the crash of 1929, but after World War II, Buck had become successful in land development and as a builder.

They had a daughter, who later died giving birth to her own child without revealing the name of the father. Ava and Buck came back to New York to raise their granddaughter, Elizabeth.

'Gram told me the truth about the countess,' said Elizabeth, awe sparking in her eyes. 'She must have been an amazing woman.'

'She was a poetic and gentle soul, a true lady,' Buck said, repeating his words from long ago. He held Ava in his arms and she snuggled her head against his chest.

'I'm going to take my story to the people of New York,' she said. 'Let them decide if what I did was wrong.'

'Are you sure this is what you want to do, Ava?' He held her by the shoulders, his eyes burning with questions. 'It happened so long ago. The world has changed since then.'

'People haven't forgotten the *Titanic* and they never will,' Ava said, her chest tight. She forced herself to keep her voice steady. 'That's why I must give up what is not mine. I owe it to the countess.'

'You've earned the title, Ava,' Buck insisted. 'No one can deny you that.'

Her eyes sparkled at the proud note in his voice. If she was a countess, it was because he had made her so. He had believed in her. He'd taught her the only charade played in life was to be untrue to yourself.

'Captain Buck is right,' said Elizabeth, using her pet name for her grandfather. 'You've worked hard, Gram, and made outstanding contributions to so many charities.'

It was true. Ava had done her best to make amends. Ever since the tragedy, she'd worked tirelessly for the *Titanic* victims and their families, setting up a trust fund with the monies she received from the sale of the countess's lands in Scotland. Over the years, she'd also raised money for the *Titanic* Trust and had orchestrated several charity events for the upcoming fiftieth anniversary of the sinking.

'I appreciate your concern,' Ava said, swallowing hard, 'but I've made up my mind.'

'I'll stand by you, Ava,' said his lordship.

'Me, too, Gram.'

'Thank you both.' She took their hands in hers. 'I'm going to call a press conference for tomorrow. The world will soon know the truth.'

* * *

'Ladies and gentlemen of the press, thank you for coming here today. You all know me as the Countess of Marbury and for my work with the *Titanic* survivors,' Ava began. 'I'm here to talk about another survivor.

An Irish girl named Ava O'Reilly, whose name never appeared on that list.'

Ava stood before the anxious group of reporters in a conference room in the Waldorf-Astoria Hotel. Not the original Waldorf where she'd made her famous walk down Peacock Alley fifty years ago, but the newer hotel built on a different spot.

She couldn't help but think of that night and the dinner in the Palm Room with Trey and Lady Pennington. Who would have thought that Trey would tire of his mother's meddling and Lady Pennington's shopping trips after they were married?

He'd secured a commission in the Army when the Great War broke out and was wounded in France in 1918 by a sniper while trying to save a fellow soldier. He was disabled, but to everyone's surprise, Lady Pennington had devoted herself to him. She had discovered a different side of herself when Mrs Benn-Brady convinced her to volunteer for the Red Cross and she had worked in a hospital with wounded veterans.

Mrs Benn-Brady was gone now, but they had remained close friends over the years with Ava making several appearances at her charity balls and dinners, always putting in a word for her *Titanic* Trust.

The woman had never suspected she wasn't the countess.

Ava smiled. She wondered what the famous society matron would have thought had she been here today. No doubt she would have loved the publicity.

'Ava O'Reilly was nineteen when she boarded the *Titanic* at Queenstown and escaped in lifeboat number four, yet no one ever saw her land in New York.' Ava paused, then said, 'That's because *I'm* that Irish girl. The real countess died that night aboard the ship before she sank into the cold North Atlantic.'

Excited murmurs erupted from the crowd of reporters, seasoned veterans, who, if Ava read their faces correctly, were stunned by the news.

She swallowed hard. She wished her sister, Mary Dolores, was here to see her. She had never let Ava forget she was a poor girl from Ireland, telling her not to 'act all fancy and grand'. Ava knew she was secretly proud of her.

She had brought her to San Francisco to live with her, but the big city wasn't for her. Mary Dolores had gone back to Ireland and married a fine lad with his own farm and had five children and eight grandchildren before she joined their parents in their final resting place.

Ava reached into the pocket of her navy-blue silk jacket and clasped the pieces of her mother's broken rosary. She'd kept the pieces to remind her of that night, knowing the pain would always be there, but she must go on. She'd touched so many lives since she'd boarded the grand ship *Titanic*. His lordship, the countess, Trey and his mother, the two Irish girls, Lady Pennington and all the survivors she'd helped over the years.

She gripped the broken rosary in her hand, her nails digging into her palm.

A tear for each rosary bead, she thought, her eyes burning, then she wiped the tears away. She'd already shed so many. She must face the truth.

'I'm not asking for forgiveness, but understanding. Imagine a young Irish girl so filled with hope and faith she risked everything to come to this great land, a place where no one was judged by the clothes they wore or how they spoke or their education, but by their willingness to work hard. Only by a twist of fate did I sail on the *Titanic* with a third-class ticket and find myself acting as a lady's maid to the lovely Countess of Marbury. A job I took to save my Irish arse from a wrongful charge of larceny.'

Laughter. Then flashbulbs popping, questions tossed at her. 'What did they say you stole, your ladyship, the royal jewels?'

'Or was it a man's heart?' called out another.

Ava smiled, then explained how the earl's daughter had accused her of stealing a diamond bracelet out of jealousy.

'I had no choice but to take the only path open to me and that was to board the *Titanic*.' She paused to take a sip of water. This was the hardest part of all. 'When the ship's officer mistook me for the countess and dropped me into a lifeboat, I had a decision to make. Risk being sent back to Ireland or go to America and start a new life as the Countess of Marbury.'

She looked over the crowd, every eye on her. 'I made my choice on the *Carpathia*. I vowed then I would never stop working to help the victims and survivors of the greatest maritime disaster up to that time. Whether or not I have succeeded in my mission is in your hands. Thank you, ladies and gentlemen, for listening to my story.'

ACKNOWLEDGMENTS

I am forever grateful to my editor, Nia Beynon, who embraced my feisty heroine and her story, and everyone at Team Boldwood for their dedication and hard work in bringing my book to publication.

ACKNOWLEDGMENTS

AUTHOR'S NOTE

The *Titanic* was called the 'ship of dreams.'

And a dream it was for her passengers who sailed on a calm, glassy sea. The dream shattered four days later when the ship hit the iceberg at 11:40 p.m. on 14 April 1912. Only 705 passengers and crew survived. 1,517 lives were lost. First and second class, steerage passengers and crew.

I wanted to relive the voyage through the eyes of three passengers from three different worlds. My characters are fiction, but what they experienced that night before the *Titanic* foundered is real.

A moment by moment account of those last few hours. From that first whistle blast when the ship leaves Queenstown to the foghorn sounding on the rescue ship *Carpathia*, my story is a tribute to those brave souls who lost their lives.

We will never forget what happened on that starry, starry night.

MORE FROM JINA BACARR

We hope you enjoyed reading *The Runaway Girl*. If you did, please leave a review.

If you'd like to gift a copy, this book is also available as an ebook, digital audio download and audiobook CD.

Sign up to Jina Bacarr's mailing list for news, competitions and updates on future books.

http://bit.ly/JinaBacarrNewsletter

Her Lost Love, another glorious historical romance from Jina Bacarr, is available to order now.

ABOUT THE AUTHOR

Jina Bacarr is a US-based historical romance author of over 10 previous books. She has been a screenwriter, journalist and news reporter, but now writes full-time and lives in LA. Jina's novels have been sold in 9 territories.

Visit Jina's website: https://jinabacarr.wordpress.com/

Follow Jina on social media:

facebook.com/JinaBacarr.author
twitter.com/JinaBacarr
instagram.com/jinabacarr
bookbub.com/authors/jina-bacarr

ABOUT BOLDWOOD BOOKS

Boldwood Books is a fiction publishing company seeking out the best stories from around the world.

Find out more at www.boldwoodbooks.com

Sign up to the Book and Tonic newsletter for news, offers and competitions from Boldwood Books!

http://www.bit.ly/bookandtonic

We'd love to hear from you, follow us on social media:

facebook.com/BookandTonic

twitter.com/BoldwoodBooks

instagram.com/BookandTonic